After a Dead Dog

AFTER A DEAD DOG

Colin Murray

CARROLL & GRAF PUBLISHERS
NEW YORK

Carroll & Graf Publishers
An imprint of Avalon Publishing Group, Inc.
245 W. 17th Street, 11th Floor
New York, NY 10011-5300
www.carrollandgraf.com

AVALON
publishing group incorporated

First published in the UK by Constable,
an imprint of Constable & Robinson Ltd 2007

First Carroll & Graf edition 2007

ISBN-13: 978-0-78671-961-7
ISBN-10: 0-7867-1961-3

Printed and bound in the EU

After whom is the king of Israel come out? after whom dost thou pursue? after a dead dog, after a flea.

I Samuel 24, 14

Prologue

Twelve years ago

Sometimes, it isn't necessary for stones to move or trees to speak.

I parked in the shadow of the stately Bentley that Peter, or possibly Margaret, had casually left out of the garage, untidily aligned with the front of the house. Even in the meagre yellow light thrown from the living-room window, the Nissan Micra looked tinny and graceless beside the grand and elegant old lady. I knew that my father would have said something like 'the man's the man for a' that' but I couldn't help feeling, as I so often felt when I turned up at the big house, awkward and gauche, out of my social depth.

The Micra wasn't exactly my pride and joy but it was my first car and, even though it was second-hand, over eight years old and had been around the world, or the equivalent, nearly three times, it did mean something to me. Seeing it dwarfed and outclassed made me aware of my own restricted horizons.

I stood next to the car for a moment or two, in order to gather myself for the ordeal ahead.

I tried to remember why I'd accepted the invitation. Carole had been, at best, half-hearted and offhand.

Things hadn't been quite the same between us since I'd dropped out of the postgraduate teacher training course that, in an uncharacteristic burst of enthusiasm, I'd signed on for. A mercifully brief mauling at the hands of thirty fifteen-year-old boys had graphically revealed the limited extent of the role that literature played in their lives and ruthlessly exposed my own inadequacies as an inspired and inspiring teacher.

I had returned home, aimless, feckless and apparently unemployable to a Carole who was contemplating her own bright future. She hadn't quite decided whether to take up the place at Columbia University that had been offered for the following year but it was looking increasingly likely that she would. Slowly and gloomily, I was beginning to suspect that her bright future probably wouldn't include me. Not that she'd said anything, and I acted as though nothing was wrong. But only because I didn't know what to do about it, not because I didn't care.

I reached back into the car, took out the flowers and the wine that I'd brought and shuffled towards the steps that led to the front door. I stopped and looked back towards the village, watching my breath drift in thin, ghostly feathers.

Of course, the reason for the hesitancy I detected in Carole's invitation probably had nothing to do with any real or imagined cooling in our relationship but was reflecting her reluctance to subject me to the strains and tensions of her family life.

It was common knowledge that her father and mother were not on the best of terms. Rumour had it that Peter's numerous affairs had caught up with him and that Margaret had finally had enough. Although I'd never gossiped about it, I could vouch that it was probably true. I'd certainly been present at more difficult family meals than most. And I'd seen Carole's taciturn younger brother become increasingly sullen and withdrawn over the previous year. Of course, he had entered a gangly and self-conscious adolescence but that only partially explained his perennial bad temper. Constantly squabbling parents probably accounted for a share too. I often wondered how Carole had survived intact, but then she had been away at college for most of the past three years.

All in all, I knew that dinner *chez* Crawford was unlikely to be a relaxed and pleasant occasion. But I'd accepted anyway. I suppose that I just wanted to see Carole, and I reasoned, if I reasoned at all, that my presence was more likely to offset any slight estrangement between us than my absence. How, when she was subject to the full force of my overwhelming personality, could she possibly have any doubts about out future together? Even if I could only afford a beaten-up, second-hand Micra. We wouldn't need that in New York.

It wasn't necessary to consult the I Ching, cast any runes or examine the gizzards of some unfortunate fowl to know that considerable quantities of alcohol would fuel the evening and that it was, therefore, a mistake to drive there. But what else could I do?

Dad had already been sitting by the fire, two chapters into *Our Mutual Friend* – again – when I'd asked him if there was any chance of a ride. He'd simply looked up from the book, pointed to the glass of whisky on the little table by his side, shaken his head and then resumed reading. Rory had gone out, presumably with the sweet-natured girl he was already planning to marry, but I wouldn't have held out much hope that he would have driven me anyway. Brotherly love didn't usually stretch that far. Although I was earning reasonable money labouring on a building site, the job would be coming to an end soon which meant that a taxi each way was an indulgence I couldn't afford. So, promising myself that I wouldn't drink, or, at least, not that much, it was in the little red Micra that I'd eventually swept into the long driveway.

I turned back and looked up at the dark, lowering house and shivered slightly from a sense of gloomy foreboding. One thing that I had learned in the time that I'd spent with the Crawfords was that wealthy people often stayed that way by the small economies they made: lights were turned off when you left a room and only exceptionally did the heating settings move from the minimum. I could almost hear Dad say that if he'd kept our house colder than a witch's tit for thirty years then he'd probably be able to afford a Bentley too. Except that Dad would never have used the word 'tit'. I smiled, shook off some of the gloom and foreboding I was feeling and bounded up the half-dozen steps to the house, bottle in one hand, flowers in the other, more or less on time for once.

Carole must have been standing behind the heavy, weather-scarred door, waiting for my knock, because it opened immediately. We stood and smiled at each other in the dim and dusty hall. Then she stepped forward, put her arms around my neck and brushed her lips against my cheek. I responded by pressing my lips firmly against hers. I tasted wine on her breath. She pulled away, then leaned in close again, her cheek against mine, her mouth against my ear.

'Best behaviour,' she whispered. 'It's worse than usual. Mum and Dad have been at each other's throats all afternoon. So, please, please, please talk a lot, tell some of those terrible stories of yours, laugh at Dad's jokes and praise Mum's cooking extravagantly. Otherwise someone is very likely to get a fork in the eye.'

'Just as long as it's not me for blathering on,' I whispered back.

'Don't be daft,' she said. 'It won't be you. For some inexplicable reason they seem to like you.' She stepped back to allow me to get across the threshold and looked at the flowers. 'For me?' she said, leaning back slightly, placing her hand above her left breast in a highly theatrical manner and opening her mouth a little in a soundless exclamation of mock pleasure.

I hesitated too long and so had to come clean.

'Sorry,' I said, 'they're for your mother.'

She jabbed me in the ribs and pointed at the wine, her mouth sternly pursed in mock anger.

'Well,' I said, 'it's really for your father . . .'

'The inexplicable suddenly becomes all too understandable. It's straightforward bribery and corruption,' she said, looking me up and down. 'Nothing for me?'

'An option on my person?' I offered.

She snorted dismissively, took my arm and steered me into the living room where a couple of lamps threw a gentle, yellow light and a small fire glowed pleasantly. I was relieved to see that the small table was set, which meant that we'd be dining there informally rather than trekking across to the cold, damp and dauntingly vast dining room.

Peter was standing in shadow, a slightly sinister presence, by the elegant walnut sideboard, decanting a bottle of wine. Two other opened bottles stood next to the decanter. He turned as we entered.

'Iain,' he said, holding up the bottle he was pouring from for my inspection. 'A rather nice *troisième cru* Margaux for later. Not too ostentatious and I think you'll like it. Scotch?'

'Just a very small one, Peter, thanks.'

'There is no such thing, Iain, as a very small Scotch.'

Carole took my bottle of inexpensive and definitely non-vintage Beaujolais and placed it on the sideboard. Peter didn't even glance at it.

He poured me a healthy measure of whisky, topped up his own tumbler, added a modest amount of water to both glasses, handed one to me and murmured, 'Cheers' just as Margaret entered the room.

If Peter was raffishly good-looking, with his untidy greying-blond hair, charmingly lopsided smile and surprisingly clear blue eyes, then Margaret was still, at forty-five or so, the cool society beauty. Although she had just come from the kitchen, she smelled of discreetly expensive perfume and her hand was cool as she took mine when I handed her the flowers.

'Oh, thank you, Iain,' she said. 'How kind. They're beautiful.' She held them up to her face and breathed in the fragrance. 'How lovely. I'll find a vase.' She was, as usual, making too much of my poor offering. She paused at the door. 'Peter,' she said, her voice as brittle and near cracking as a thin skin of ice, 'I wonder if you could perhaps find the time to light the candles. And would you be kind enough to pour me a drink. I'm about ready to serve.'

There was a grunt from Peter which she took to be assent and she left the room. I heard her call up the stairs to Martin that dinner was ready and he should come down.

And so it began.

Peter did light the candles in the three hollowed-out pumpkins that decorated the table, and he turned off one of the lamps.

The eerie, flickering light subtly changed the atmosphere in the darkened room, turning Carole and Peter into pale, gaunt-faced, spectral figures, and throwing strange and ghastly shadows across the ceiling. An arm raised to lift a glass became a huge and menacing mass; a head shaken in mild disagreement was transformed into a mountainous wave of denial that rolled grotesquely along a wall.

I nursed the glass of whisky, hoping that Peter wouldn't notice that I wasn't drinking it. But then Margaret appeared with a slab of pâté de foie gras and Peter, of course, like a stage magician producing a rabbit from a top hat, lifted a bottle of Sauternes from a cooler, flourished it and then pointedly waited until I had swallowed down the Scotch before pouring me a glass.

Martin slunk self-consciously into the room and slumped down into one of the chairs around the dining table. Peter glared at him.

'You might make some kind of effort to be here on time,' he said sharply.

'Leave him alone, Peter,' Margaret said.

'It's his turn to say grace and he's keeping us waiting,' Peter said without looking at her. He stared at the top of Martin's lowered head. 'Well,' he continued, 'would you be so kind as to allow us to eat?'

Martin mumbled something into his plate. It might have been a prayer of thanks. But it could just as easily have been a dirty joke.

Peter sighed irritably.

'Oh, do leave the boy alone,' Margaret snapped.

'He has to learn *some* social skills at some point in his life.'

'And you think that bullying him and embarrassing him in company is the way to teach him, do you?' Margaret said.

I gulped down some wine and glanced at Martin who was picking nervously at the skin on the back of his right hand. Carole, like me, was attempting to hide behind her glass.

'For God's sake, Margaret, I'm just trying to impart some rudiments of social behaviour.'

'Well, perhaps you could start by setting him an appropriate example.'

'What's that supposed to mean?'

'You know perfectly well what it means.'

'For Christ's sake, Margaret,' he said, 'give it a rest.'

Carole looked over the top of her glass at me and rolled her eyes, urging me to speak.

I coughed.

'This is excellent wine, Peter,' I said.

Peter turned towards me, paused for a moment, visibly relaxed and then, as I'd half-hoped he would, he started to talk about the left bank of the Garonne, south of Bordeaux, and Château d'Yquem, which I really would have to try sometime, and how young Sauternes is full of the perfume of fruit and flowers but quickly loses that characteristic and takes on a noble purity, ageing better even than the great red wines. It sounded to me like the dull recitation of an article in some worthy and authoritative wine book that he'd read, but it was preferable to the bitching. Margaret looked at him archly from time to time but he was oblivious. I wondered how many Brownie points Carole would be awarding me.

After carefully pouring out more wine, Peter was soon in full flow again, telling me of a Sauternes he had once sampled that was close to becoming '*centenaire*'. I was about to ask him to explain, in order to keep him talking,

13

when there was a knock at the front door. He looked irritably at Margaret.

'That'll be guisers,' she said.

'Oh, of course,' he said. 'Martin, go and answer the door.'

A petulant grimace momentarily animated Martin's features but they soon fell back into their natural sulk and he reluctantly rose to his feet, chair legs scraping across the carpet, and slouched out of the room.

He returned a few moments later followed by about a dozen assorted small witches, vampires, ghosts and skeletons, with one ballerina, or fairy, all in pink.

They shuffled around in the doorway, looking as uneasy and embarrassed as Martin, whispering and nudging each other, their thick, garish make-up and cheap costumes surprisingly effective in the dim and flickering light of the candles.

It was a strange, hallucinatory scene and I was momentarily unnerved as the milling crowd of small horrors filled the doorway. I looked at Carole to see if she felt it too. But she was smiling benignly, if a little vacantly, at the assembled tiny terrors.

Finally, one of the smaller skeletons stepped forward, gaunt face hollowed out by black and white face paint, and broke through the unease by piping out in a thin, shrill voice, 'Trick or treat?'

'Treat, of course,' said Margaret, standing up. She moved to the doorway and mingled with the children, adjusting a high-collared plastic cape or a tall, pointed hat and murmuring politely about all the work that must have gone into their costumes, effortlessly playing the semi-public figure. 'What lovely costumes,' she said. 'Do any of you have pieces to perform?'

Peter just sat and watched, making very little effort. I couldn't resist a smile as the thought that he would have been the one doing the mingling if the girls had been fifteen years older insinuated itself slanderously into my mind.

There was a little more whispering and then a couple of

the witches stepped forward and recited something I didn't recognize in that curious uninflected sing-song that children often adopt. They were followed by some bad jokes from a vampire and a ghost.

We duly applauded and groaned, then Margaret handed Martin a basket full of small chocolate bars and he self-consciously offered it to the children.

They surrounded him in a polite feeding frenzy and quickly emptied the basket as efficiently as deer stripping the leaves and bark from a young tree. Peter then nodded imperiously at Martin.

'Show our guests out, Martin,' he said.

There was a general chorus of 'thank you's and the little crowd shuffled through the door and out into the hall again. We heard them jump down the steps and squeal excitedly as they ran towards the road. I remembered doing it myself only a dozen or so years before.

Martin shut the front door and then reappeared in the living room. He risked one venomous, resentful glance at his father before settling at the table again. Peter didn't seem to notice.

We finished our pâté in silence and then Carole and Margaret carried the dirty plates into the kitchen. Peter poured what remained of the Sauternes into his glass and mine.

'No need to waste it,' he said. 'The lamb will be a few moments yet.'

I felt a stab of anxiety and resentment deep in my gut. Lamb meant that Peter would ask me, as eldest male guest, to carve. I wondered if, having watched me savage and ruin a roast chicken the last time I'd been there, he might show a little compassion, to the joint and the other diners as much as to me, but I rather doubted it. He didn't cut anyone much slack. I swallowed down the wine.

'I must introduce you to my wine merchant the next time he's here,' he said, swirling the wine around in his glass and staring at it. 'He usually comes over from Edinburgh in April with a few choice bottles to sample, in a

15

very successful attempt to part me from large quantities of money.' He laughed. 'Still, it's my one indulgence.'

If you didn't count the expensive holidays and, if rumour was to be believed, the young women.

Suddenly, he stopped staring into his glass and looked at Martin.

'It's time that you started to take an interest in wine, Martin,' he said. 'One day, the wine cellar will be yours. It's quite extensive and quite valuable. You'll have to know how to keep it and serve it.'

'I don't like wine,' Martin mumbled without looking up from his lap where he was still furiously picking at the skin on the back of his hand.

'You'll grow to love it,' Peter said.

'I won't,' Martin said.

'Of course you will. Won't he, Iain?'

'I really don't know,' I said. 'My dad has never got a taste for it. He's a whisky man. Not that he drinks that much. Unlike my grandfather.'

Peter abruptly got up from his chair and, carrying his glass, he went to the other end of the table and stood next to Martin, looming over him.

'Here,' he said, placing his glass in front of the boy. 'Take a sip of this. It is, as Iain, said, excellent.'

'I don't want it, Dad,' Martin said. 'I don't like it.'

'How do you know you don't like it if you won't try it?'

'I just know, OK?'

I didn't know whether to laugh hysterically or to squirm with embarrassment but, somehow, managed to avoid doing either. Peter, a little red-faced, veins standing out on his forehead, stood over his son, tense and angry, staring down at the top of his head. I wanted to intervene, to make a joke of it all, but I couldn't think of anything to say.

'Drink it,' Peter said sharply and, after resisting for a few more seconds, Martin reached out and picked up the glass. He raised it to his lips and took a little sip before banging it back down on the table.

'Good, isn't it?' Peter said.

'I don't like it,' Martin said. 'It's horrible.' There were tears in the corners of his eyes.

Peter snatched up the glass and strode angrily back to his seat. He shook his head and gulped down the rest of the wine.

'My son's a barbarian, Iain,' he said.

'Oh, I wouldn't say that,' I said.

'I would,' he said.

'I don't suppose that I would have liked wine at his age, if I'd been offered any,' I said emolliently. 'It's only recently that I've started to appreciate it. Thanks largely to you.' He inclined his head in regal acceptance of the compliment. 'When you don't know anything about it, it's difficult to know where to start. I still don't know enough to really appreciate it.'

'But you're open to the experience,' Peter said magnanimously. 'And that's all I ask. I just wish that Martin was too.'

'Well, I am now,' I said. 'But I'm not sure I would have been at Martin's age. He's still too young.'

Martin looked at me through narrowed eyes, resenting my reference to his age. I realized that the tears I'd noticed earlier were born of anger and frustration. We all lapsed into an uneasy silence until Margaret and Carole reappeared, carrying bowls of vegetables and a platter with a leg of lamb on it. The smell of garlic was wonderful but the edge was taken off my appetite by the sight of Peter taking the carving knife and the steel from the drawer of the sideboard.

'Iain,' he said, offering them to me, 'would you do the honours?'

'Actually, Peter,' I said lamely, 'I slipped in the woods this afternoon and sprained my wrist slightly. It's a bit painful when I put too much pressure on it.' I gently squeezed my right wrist and winced. It was a ridiculous and completely unconvincing performance and no one was taken in for a second. 'Can I pass?' I finished, aware of a whining tone in my voice.

17

He looked puzzled but then Carole rallied to my cause.

'Come on, Dad,' she said, 'let him off just this once.'

'Yes,' Margaret said sharply, placing the lamb in front of him, 'carve.'

'Is this some kind of conspiracy?' he said. 'I'm just trying to keep up standards and old traditions. Is that such a bad thing?'

'Oh, don't be such a snob and an old boor. Just get on with it and carve, will you?' Margaret said. The edge to her words was not modified by any hint of affection in her voice.

'Are you sure that you won't, Iain?' Peter said, offering me the knife again and looking at his wife with an unpleasantly dismissive expression on his face.

'I'd rather not,' I said. 'The wrist is quite painful.'

With a look on his face somewhere between indignation and bemusement, Peter stroked the blade forcefully along the steel a few times before neatly slicing a V-shaped chunk out of the meat. Then, delicately working his way along from the initial incision, he cut beautifully precise rounds from the joint, shaking his head as he arranged them around the carving dish.

'Stop showing off, Peter, and get on with it,' Margaret said. 'And pour me a glass of that ludicrously overpriced plonk.'

'You go too far, Margaret,' he said, waving the carving knife in her direction and pretending anger in order to disguise the real thing. 'There are some things a man cannot tolerate. Never have I served plonk at this table. Never.'

'Oh, go on, Dad,' Carole said, trying to sound as if she believed in his pretence at levity. 'I bet you have.'

'Perhaps the occasional bottle of inexpensive but well-chosen claret,' he said, 'but never plonk.'

'So where do all those empty Blue Nun and Mateus Rosé bottles come from then?' Carole said, smiling.

'Must be your mother's dark secret,' he said. 'I've always wondered what she did all day.'

'More like the empties from when you've been entertaining your cheap girlfriends,' Margaret said.

'I no more have cheap girlfriends than I serve cheap plonk,' he said.

'Well, at least you admit to girlfriends, even if you won't accept that they're cheap,' she said. 'That's a start on the path to a decent divorce settlement.'

Peter paused in a determined attempt to control himself.

'Don't be ridiculous, Margaret,' he eventually said in measured tones, putting down the carving knife and fork and reaching for the decanter. 'Don't worry, children. Your mother is joking. We are not getting a divorce. And I do not have girlfriends, cheap or otherwise.'

Margaret gave a discreet snort of derision, remarkably like the one Carole had given me earlier.

Peter looked thoughtful for a few seconds. 'What was it Tolstoy said about happy families, Iain?' he finally said.

'Oh,' I said, 'that they all resemble each other, or something like that.'

'I thought it was that they are all different.'

'No,' I said, 'that's the unhappy families, I think.'

'Oh, really,' he said, his forehead creased in thought, as though he was pondering some extraordinary revelation. He poured out the deep-red wine, staring hard into each glass as he did so. Finally, he looked up and said lightly, 'Still, what did Tolstoy know about families, happy or unhappy?'

And so it went awkwardly on and on.

Through the roast and more wine, and then through the cheese and still more wine, I found myself praying for another interruption from guisers, but there was no relief.

I attempted, as instructed beforehand, to tell little stories. I told the one about William Blake and his wife being discovered in the nude reading from *Paradise Lost*, which was about as risqué as I thought I should get. I even tried my impression of W.B. Yeats but, although Carole smiled encouragingly at me, no one seemed much interested and I steadily became gloomier and gloomier, and drunker.

Margaret's resentment towards Peter was a palpable, growing thing, which he watered and fertilized with his every comment and gesture. And he was clearly simmering with anger. Eventually, the pair of them fell into a grim silence.

Finally, mercifully, the meal reached an end. Carole shook her head at me when she saw her father reach for the brandy bottle. Then she, not very discreetly, pointed to me and to the dirty plates. I nodded my understanding and acceptance. She then stood up and announced that she was going to her room as there was a book she'd borrowed from me that I wanted back and she wasn't sure exactly where it was.

I took my cue, thanked Margaret for a lovely meal and insisted that she stay put while I cleared away the dishes.

I made a number of journeys to the kitchen, carrying plates, cutlery and glasses. The raised voices that I heard on my approach each time I returned to the living room lapsed into silence on the first three occasions when I entered with an apologetic grin on my face. The snatches of conversation that I did hear were worrying. The 'if you think that I'm going to stand for this any longer' and the 'just shut up about it or' did not suggest any imminent reconciliation between them.

Worse still, the last time I went in what I saw was an ugly stand-off. Peter was jabbing a finger at Margaret, who was standing her ground defiantly. 'I'm warning you,' he was saying, 'I'm not just going to sit back and take it. This is my business, my family home –'

Martin was lurking, pale-faced and grim, by the bookshelves, his head lowered, plucking compulsively at the back of his hand again.

Peter stopped speaking and they both froze when they became aware of my presence. He looked across and forced a smile.

'Ignore us, Iain,' he said. 'It's just a family disagreement. They always look worse than they are. It's more a problem of rampaging hormones than anything else.'

They glared at each other and, once again, I tried to think of something to say that would defuse the situation as I awkwardly collected the last of the crockery. But nothing offered itself. I cleared my throat and guiltily murmured that I was sorry to interrupt. Then I hurried back to the safety of the kitchen.

The argument flared up again as soon as I left.

Finally, I stood thankfully by the sink, in the peace and quiet of the kitchen, rinsing glasses and wondering when I might be sober enough to think about driving back. A quick inventory of my intake of alcohol, in as far as I could be certain of it, suggested that I might be able to leave a little after four in the morning. I looked at my pale face in the kitchen window and groaned aloud.

I had just taken a tea towel and started to dry and polish a whisky tumbler when I heard the shot. Even if the stones had moved and the trees spoken, I doubt that they would have prepared me for that.

Chapter One

We buried Margaret Crawford on a raw November morning.

The unforgiving slate-grey sky spat icy rain, and the brutal wind drove the stinging pellets into my face as I joined the other dark-clad mourners toiling up the steep mound that led to the uninviting, sombre kirk glowering down from the summit. The bitter gale tore at us across the old graveyard, forcing us to lower our heads and hold on to coat collars and hats as we stoically trudged along at the pace of the elderly and infirm.

Cheeks reddened and feet painfully chilled through the thin leather of my good black shoes, I finally reached the end of the gravel path and stepped to one side of the straggling knot of shuffling villagers huddling outside the church. I stood on the sodden grass verge and looked beyond the freshly dug grave, the earth heaped around it as raw as the day, over the little monuments and gravestones, past the slick black macadam of the road and the few white-painted houses, away towards the loch in the distance.

Angry, white-topped waves pursued each other relentlessly to the shore and spilled over on to the first green of the already saturated golf course, where they settled into sullen pools, the plastic bottles, empty drink cans, driftwood and other detritus they had picked up on their journey across the Atlantic bobbing peacefully on the now still surface. The few bare birches that fringed the water shuddered and twisted with every gust of wind that threatened to rip their roots from the soft salt bog they clutched at. Thin branches bent, swayed and broke as the remorseless storm battered away at them, contorting the fragile skeletal structures into ever more unlikely shapes, in a static parody of the medieval dance of death.

'And I would that my tongue could utter . . .' I murmured softly.

I stared out over the loch and consciously thought of Margaret. The constant roar of the wind and the flurries of icy rain seemed appropriate, very Tennysonian.

I hadn't seen her, apart from in passing, in more than a year. And that lunch party had not been a success. Except, perhaps, for her. My invitation had, I think, been less for my company and more to remind her son-in-law that he was not her daughter's first love. All of us, except again for her, had been embarrassed by her relentless pursuit of the theme. Such obvious machinations didn't show her in the best of lights.

I was suddenly aware of the smell of stale tobacco, wet wool and body odour not quite masked by cheap, sharp aftershave, and more than a hint of whisky, acutely aware of his presence before he spoke.

'Aye, aye,' he said. 'Rather him than me.'

'What's that, Danny?' I said, turning towards him.

He didn't reply, just stabbed a stubby, nicotine-stained finger towards the loch. I looked in the direction he'd pointed and eventually made out, way in the distance, a small craft, bucking and battling its way through the heavy swell.

'O well for the sailor lad,' I muttered under my breath. Danny didn't hear me.

'The price of fish, eh?' he said and, still staring, narrow-eyed, out at the tumultuous sea, lit a cigarette.

I nodded my agreement.

He had the large, blotched and pummelled head of an old-fashioned, bare-knuckle prize fighter balanced disconcertingly on the frail body of a fasting Hindu holy man. Even bulked out in sweater, Sunday jacket and greasy green waxed raincoat, he still looked, grey trousers flapping around his thin and unsteady shanks, as if a kindergarten tough, such as I'd been, could knock him over. Yet, for all his bashed features and his emaciated frame, there was a fragile dignity about him, and a refreshing humility. He cupped his hand awkwardly around the cigarette and sucked smoke greedily down deep into his lungs.

My grandfather, a man with a prodigious appetite for alcohol himself, and the prodigious nose and profusion of broken capillaries that went with it, always maintained that there were only two kinds of drunk: those that hurt other people, and those that hurt only themselves. He was wrong, of course. Drunks come in as many shapes as there are men who drink, and one type that my grandfather didn't mention – those that hurt other people *and* themselves – is, in my experience, over-represented. But his simple model certainly held good for himself and Danny McGovern. With his wide leather belt and hands scarred and hardened in the ring, on the streets and on the trawlers, Granddad would definitely have proudly placed himself among those who hurt other people. Danny, on the other hand, literally fell among those who hurt themselves. If there was an entry in *The Guinness Book of Records* for the number of times one human being had fallen over in bars and in the vicinity of bars, then Danny would be vying with Yeats' friend, the 'much falling' Lionel Johnson, for inclusion.

'See you later, Danny,' I said.

A quick glance behind me showed that most people had gone in and there were only a few latecomers hurrying into the church. It seemed like a good time to make my own entrance. I had no great desire to sit next to Danny for the duration of the service and it seemed unlikely that he'd extinguish a freshly lit cigarette in order to join me.

He nodded absentmindedly, still staring out at the white-flecked, steely sea, drawing smoke deep inside himself, as I crunched my way along the path to the great door.

The wind continued to buffet me even in the dark, chilly

vestibule as I joined the short line waiting, in a custom unique in my experience to the area, to be formally greeted by the chief mourners. There was a damp, unwholesome smell, as if a large, sick animal was lurking in one of the shadowed corners, waiting, perplexed and uncomprehending, to die. But it was probably just the miasma given off by the wet, shivering congregation uncomfortably perched on the thinly padded pews in the church itself.

Martin Crawford looked impossibly young in his dark suit and black tie, and a boyish lock of blond hair fell over his right eye to emphasize the point as he leaned forward to shake my hand and intone the mantra appropriate to the occasion, 'Thank you, it's good of you to come.' Then he looked up, saw through the tears in his eyes that it was me, just said, 'Iain,' and put his arms around me. I was surprised and, frankly, embarrassed at this unexpectedly physical show of friendship as we'd never been that intimate, but I held him for a few seconds and then whispered my condolences, extracted myself from his grasp and slowly edged my way towards his sister.

Carole, conscious perhaps of her husband to her left, offered no such intimacy. Formally, she held out her hand and I took it.

'Thank you for coming, Iain,' she said. 'It's good of you.'

Her hand was warm and dry.

'I'm really sorry about your mother, Carole,' I said. 'She was a wonderful lady and she'll be greatly missed.'

She raised her eyebrows slightly and gave me a wry look, and then she nodded.

'You will be joining us up at the house, after . . .' she said.

'Yes,' I said, 'I will be coming a little later.' And I reluctantly let go of her hand.

Duncan, her husband, immediately proffered his own huge paw and squeezed more powerfully than was really necessary when I reciprocated.

'Yes,' he said, 'do come. It wouldn't be right without you.' He smiled but there was something a little vulpine in it. Thanks partly to Margaret, he had no particular reason

25

to like me and he didn't, but he'd never shown me his teeth before. It fleetingly crossed my mind that he might well regard his mother-in-law's death as a liberating experience. Margaret had always been a forthright and unyielding lady, and the word was that she'd been more so with Duncan than with most. According to rumour, and I could partially confirm it, all had not been well between her and her son-in-law. There was talk of shouting matches in the boardroom and over Sunday lunch, although it hadn't come to that in my presence.

I nodded that I would definitely come to the house and backed away, through the double doors and into the bare, musty church.

The place was almost full, which wasn't really a surprise. Those of us who didn't actually work for the Crawfords, on the estate, in the fish-processing factory or in the Heritage Centre, depended on them, more or less, for their business or their patronage. Although some resented it, we all recognized that it was true and that paying our respects to Margaret Crawford was expected, an obligation. But it was one, for the most part, willingly fulfilled. Apart from the local fondness for a funeral, most of us had respected her, even grudgingly admired her; a few, like me, had been fond of her, even loved her a little, for all her faults.

I found a place on the end of a pew near the rear wall, next to Isobel Mackinnon, who ran the fruit and vegetable shop. She moved her ample body along a bit, to accommodate me.

'What a day,' she said, 'and no sign of it letting up at all.'

'Aye, Isa,' I said, 'it's brutal out there.'

'Och,' she said, 'you know I'll have to be changing my name. You make me sound like one of those government bank accounts.'

It was an old joke, one that Isobel had been cracking for far too many years, and it had been weak the first time I'd heard it, but I smiled anyway because Isobel was someone I had always smiled at, since I'd been a wean. Then the organ started to whine in that curiously off-key way that organs have and we both lapsed into an appropriate silence.

The coffin containing Margaret Crawford's earthly remains was balanced on a trestle in front of the pulpit and caught the eye immediately. The simple, light-oak casket gleamed a little too brightly, the brass fittings glittered a little too flashily, for the occasion and the gloomy building. Just as some had thought Margaret herself had gleamed and glittered a little too much for the dour grey village when she'd first married into the Crawfords. But that had all changed a dozen years back with the death of her husband. The flighty wee thing with the great legs, who the ageing wifeys remembered from twenty years before, was transformed into the redoubtable widow and the formidable head of the family.

Suddenly, everything started to happen. The organist, instead of just running her fingers aimlessly over the keyboard, launched into something that was almost recognizable as a tune and Carole, Duncan and Martin walked slowly and self-consciously the length of the aisle to join the rest of the relatives in the front pew. Then the minister swept flamboyantly into the church from behind a curtain and the congregation rose.

We dutifully sang 'Abide With Me', 'The Lord's My Shepherd' and the one with the line about forgiving our foolish ways. The irreverent thought that maybe the last was more appropriate to the wedding ceremony came unbidden. I suspected that it had been carefully chosen by Carole.

We stood up and sat down at the minister's word, listened silently to his prayers and surprisingly respectfully while he spoke anodynely of a Margaret Crawford only he had known. Well, I doubt that I was the only one present who didn't recognize the humble Christian whose faith was iron clad or the calm, gentle soul whose simple presence brought such comfort to so many. I imagine that more than a few others, besides myself, her son, daughter

27

and son-in-law, reflected ruefully on the number of occasions we'd been on the receiving end of her caustic tongue and had quickly fled to find safe harbour at the first sign of one of her frequent and sudden emotional squalls. I was more than a little surprised that no member of the family had wanted to deliver the oration. I could only think that the circumstances of her death had led them to think it inappropriate.

We finished with what I felt sure must have been Margaret's least favourite hymn and Carole's second little joke, 'All Things Bright and Beautiful'. But the minister sang lustily in a clear, thin tenor, while I thought of Margaret and the last incredulous line of Blake's 'Tyger, Tyger'.

The sharp, warm smell of wet wool from tweed overcoats and sensible skirts and dark trousers floated by as the bearers, including Duncan and Martin, carried the polished coffin outside and the other chief mourners plodded slowly behind. Most of the women were sniffling into handkerchiefs but Carole, although pale and drawn, was dry-eyed and held herself commendably erect, staring beyond the coffin, into the distance.

It suddenly crossed my mind that no one had thought to ask me to act as a bearer. I tried to shrug off the brief flash of anger and hurt as I waited to squeeze myself into the aisle and join the shuffling exodus, but somehow I couldn't. It rankled.

I stood at the back of the huge rolling maul that had formed around the grave. The howling wind ripped the minister's words from his lips and the freezing rain hammered down harder than ever. A thin stream of fresh red water flowed slowly down from the solid mound of mud waiting to refill the grave and trickled over my decent black shoes.

The dense thicket of people standing between me and the rest of the service steamed a little in the chilly air, shuffled and murmured a ragged amen.

I didn't see Margaret Crawford lowered into the ground, but I bowed my head and said my own farewell.

The Crawfords' house was a large, graceless nineteenth-century pile, built by some long-forgotten Glasgow merchant to holiday in and play the genial laird. It had the dour look of something that had endured but had paid a price. The place was draughty and damp even in June and a dreich November afternoon, with the light fading fast, did it no favours. A broken drainpipe directed a noisy stream of water from the gutter on to one saturated wall, and the greyish render was blotched and scabrous. An untidy pile of slates of differing sizes leaned against an old wheelbarrow filled with rubble, and ugly tufts of yellowish grass thrust up through the gravel driveway. It was unlovely and unloved.

But I could remember a time when Margaret had done her best to fill it with warmth and good cheer. That had been a hard row to hoe, and she had ultimately been unsuccessful. Latterly, she had given up the struggle and succumbed to the inevitable. The house was not somewhere to play happy families.

I had parked my elderly Rover 620 behind a new, silver, left-hand drive Mercedes C class with Dutch plates on the sodden grass verge just inside the front gate about fifty yards from the house. I wondered who it belonged to as I scrunched my way through the driving rain to the front steps and the musty hall beyond the open front door. I hadn't seen it around before and it did rather stand out among the battered Volvos and the superannuated Ford Mondeos. It had to be a distant, wealthy relation.

I stood in the quiet, damp hall, dripping on to the wooden floor, looking up the wide staircase, listening to the muted hum of conversation carrying from the family's big, comfortable living room to my right. Margaret's room. It was the room where I'd first seen her and it was the room where I had last seen her. I tried to think of an occasion when I'd been there and she hadn't. Apart from a couple when I'd been alone with Carole for a few snatched moments, I couldn't.

I heard a door close up the stairs on the first floor and the heavy sound of big men pounding along the corridor. Duncan Ferguson hove into view, as I somehow knew he would, flanked by two men I didn't recognize. He paused on the top step and gazed benevolently down at me.

'Iain,' he boomed. 'Delighted you could make it. And I know that Martin will be thrilled that you've come.' He paused. 'And Carole too, of course.'

I wondered at this sudden intense friendship with Martin that I seemed to have acquired. In reality, I scarcely knew him. He'd been a gawky, inept, monosyllabic, resentful adolescent when I'd been seeing Carole. He'd hardly registered on my social radar. But I'd been even more self-obsessed and egocentric then than now.

I nodded to Duncan and smiled, and he plodded down the steep staircase, followed by the two men who exchanged an enigmatic glance behind his back. Duncan held a crystal glass of golden whisky in his right hand, which he waved expansively, and his face was flushed.

'Iain Lewis,' he said, when he was standing directly in front of me, 'meet two new business associates of mine: Patrick Donnelly and Colm Kelly.'

They stepped forward and offered hands, which I took in turn.

A journalist acquaintance had once asked me to accompany him to a pub to meet a well-known ex-criminal. The man was something of a celebrity, having been involved in a series of high-profile and very violent armed robberies in London and Manchester some years before. He had served his time and been completely rehabilitated, taking a degree in sociology and marrying his solicitor. We met up in a big, old Victorian pub in south London just after opening time. The man was unquestionably intelligent but he was far too wary and humourless for my taste. At one stage, he excused himself for a minute and had a quiet word with another man who was sitting at the bar. As he returned to the seat opposite me, the other man scuttled off, leaving behind a full pint. I must have inadvertently looked the question at him. 'He owes me money,' the man said quietly by way of explanation, and he couldn't help breaking into a brief, unpleasant smile, as if acknowledging that his reputation was menace enough.

I was reminded of the incident as soon as I saw them. They didn't have the prison pallor, but they were hewed from the same rock. They were genuine hard men. The beautiful Italian suits and silk shirts were draped over squat, powerful bodies, and the English shoes, although expensive and elegant, were tough enough to inflict real damage, if a situation were to arise.

'So, Patrick,' I said to the older of the two as we all strolled towards the wake, 'what business is that, then?'

He looked at me and his mouth twitched into a slight smile. I took in the immaculately cut silver hair and the recent tan and I knew that the ownership of the silver Merc was no longer a mystery.

'Fish,' he said simply and dismissively and walked away. His voice was very quiet but it was an ugly sound, working-class Dublin, and he used it like a blunt instrument, to intimidate.

'Ah,' I said, nodding sagely, 'of course.'

'Everything piscine, from the serene majesty of the mighty salmon to the plump sardine on the counter of a Spanish bar, fascinates Mr Donnelly,' the younger man, Colm, said in an equally unattractive accent, sweeping past me. He pronounced it sour-deen. 'He is much taken at the moment with the humble mackerel and its possibilities. An underrated fish, don't you think?' As soon as he spoke, I revised my opinion of the relationship between the two. Donnelly may have been rude and dismissive, but Kelly was laughing at him as well as at me. He had no doubt who was in control here. The Merc was probably his. He was the one who pulled the trigger, not Donnelly. I decided to keep my distance.

He gave me a brief sideways glance and then dismissed me from his mind as he followed Patrick Donnelly into the living room. His broad shoulders and back, impeccably tailored in dark grey, lightweight wool, and topped by a large head adorned with thick, wavy, auburn hair, seemed to fill the wide doorway for a moment. I stood silently on the threshold as the three of them ambled confidently through the crowded room, Duncan accepting whispered words of condolence with a regal inclination of his head and a pat on the shoulder with the sweaty palm of his large, soft, pink hand. He was the reincarnation of the Glasgow merchant who had built the house, playing the paternal and benevolent clan chief, the laird, for the benefit of his two guests. It certainly wouldn't cut the mustard with anyone else.

Martin saw me in the doorway, broke away from the knot of factory workers he was talking to and joined me. He looked at me a little slyly but then he watched the stately progress of his brother-in-law through narrowed eyes.

'Our new business associates!' he said. 'What did Duncan tell you about them?'

'That they're two Irish businessmen with extensive interests in fish,' I said and smiled.

He returned my smile with a knowing look.

'They're a bit more than that,' he said. 'What do you make of them?'

I shrugged.

'I don't know,' I said, trying to sound non-committal, 'I've hardly had a chance to make anything of them.'

'They're going to pump a lot of money into the company,' he said.

'Really?' I said. 'Well, that has to be good news.'

'All the same,' he said wryly, 'they always remind me a little bit of gangsters.'

'I guess that's because gangsters dress like, and pretend to be, businessmen these days. They started it after the flamboyance of Al Capone got him jailed. On the other hand, lots of businessmen talk tough, apeing gangsters, and have no taste. It's a lifestyle thing: sharp suits, SUVs, expensive cocaine habits, executive toys, Alma-Tadema paintings, the automatic weapons in the cupboard under the stairs . . .'

Martin looked across to the bar where his brother-in-law was pouring drinks.

'Mum never liked Duncan, you know,' he said wistfully. I noticed a tiny blue vein trembling under his left eye.

'Nor do I,' I said. 'Probably for the same reason.'

'Probably for some of the same reasons,' he said. 'Certainly Mum wasn't happy about Carole's choice of husband, but she had some of her own reasons as well. But he's not such a bad bloke.' He pursed his lips and took me by the arm. 'Come and get something to drink and eat,' he said and ushered me into the crowded room.

There was a framed photograph of Margaret, draped in black silk, on the mantelpiece. Apart from that, the room was much as I remembered it.

Martin steered me over to the long table where Duncan was holding court and serving drinks. His two new business associates were standing next to him, sipping decorously from tumblers of heavily watered Scotch.

'What are you drinking, Iain?' he asked.

'Just a tonic water thanks, Duncan,' I said, adding when he looked up at me in frank disbelief, 'I'm driving. And I have some work to do tonight.'

He nodded and moved ponderously around the table. There was something so studied and deliberate about his movements that he had to be very drunk.

'I'll have another small whisky while you're there, Duncan,' Martin said, proffering his glass.

Duncan and Martin were joking with their Irish guests, using the word 'fish' as though it were a code for something else. Martin whispered something in Colm Kelly's ear and Kelly gave me another quick glance, then grinned at Duncan and nodded slightly. It was faintly disconcerting and I turned back to the room, to look for Carole, but I couldn't see her.

I found my gaze drawn to the picture of Margaret above the fire. It was a formal portrait taken when she was much younger. I was surprised at how like Carole she looked. I started to feel very sorry for myself but, fortunately, Duncan chose that moment to thrust my drink into my hand.

I took a sip and then excused myself and made my way towards the other end of the room where a table was heaped with food. I sniffed at my drink again and knew that I wasn't mistaken. There was a very large slug of gin lurking with malevolent intent in its clear depths. I left the glass on a small side table next to one of Margaret's Tiffany lamps and filled a plate with poached salmon and potato salad.

I moved away from the table and stood by the big bay window, looking out at the dreary scene. The light was now completely gone and the dismal afternoon was turning into a bleak November night.

I was forced to make small talk with an old wifey who claimed to have known me when I was a wee bairn. I pretended to remember her while I stuffed my face with forkfuls of the Crawfords' delicious salmon and home-made mayonnaise. Mercifully, she didn't mention my mother and I was able to remain pleasant. I even managed to be polite to the minister when he showed up.

However, I found my gaze constantly drawn back to Duncan and the big Irishman, Kelly. They were talking together and occasionally looking across at me and laughing. As I watched them, one of the older guys who worked in the Crawfords' fish-processing factory stepped back and jogged Kelly's drinking arm, splashing whisky over his shirt. The man turned to apologize but Kelly reached out, grabbed the man's tie, pulled him viciously towards him and threw the rest of the drink in his face. Then he turned and stalked out of the room, leaving a shocked and bewildered man behind. Few people in the room seemed to have noticed.

Then Carole appeared at my side.

'Duncan noticed that you weren't drinking and sent me over with this,' she said, offering me a large tumbler, obviously unaware of the little scene behind her. I decided not to draw her attention to it.

Apart from briefly at the church, which didn't really count, I hadn't seen her since the dreadful lunch party and I took the opportunity to look at her.

She was still neat and trim, and still had the ability to make my heart flutter, even though our affair had been over for more than a dozen years. There were a few faint lines around her eyes and mouth, and her hair, still the colour of old gold, was cut shorter than I remembered it, but it suited her.

'That was thoughtful of him,' I said, eyeing the glass suspiciously.

I took it from her and raised it to Duncan who was watching us from the other side of the room. I was sure that, like the first, it contained a lethal shot of gin. When he turned away, I put the glass down on the window sill. If we continued like this for another hour, there wouldn't be a surface in the room that wasn't playing host to an untouched glass of gin and tonic. Carole didn't appear to notice that I had set the glass aside.

'How are you, Iain?' she said.

'Och, things are fine with me, Carole,' I said. 'But, far more importantly, how are you? If there's anything I can do, anything at all, you know you only have to ask. I was very fond of your mother.'

'I know, Iain, and thanks for your letter. It was kind of you to write. Believe it or not, it was a comfort. I would have called, but there wasn't anything you could do, and we were tied up with inquests and solicitors and the police. To tell the truth it's been a bit of a nightmare. Almost as bad as last time, with Dad. You remember what it was like.'

35

I nodded but said nothing and Carole looked down at her feet. Her father's death had detonated an intense grief and anger in her that had savaged and changed her every relationship – particularly ours. She'd gone away for a while, when everything had settled down, first to America, then to France, and had never come back. Not to me, anyway. There was nothing I could say that wouldn't hint at recrimination.

She looked up shyly, giving me what I'd always teasingly referred to as her Princess Diana look.

'How's the writing?' she said.

'Do you want the long answer or the short answer?' I said, looking for somewhere to put my empty plate. It joined the glass of gin, precariously balanced on the window sill.

'I'll take the abbreviated version for now, given the circumstances,' she said and gestured helplessly at the crowded room. 'I'll have to take a rain check on the longer answer.'

'It's fine,' I said. 'The bills get paid. Just.'

'That's it?' she said.

'That's it for the short version,' I said.

'Well, that's good,' she said and smiled warmly. 'Give me a call next week and you can take me out to dinner and give me the long answer.'

I raised my eyebrows.

'Only if you want to, of course,' she said archly.

'Actually, I'd like to take you out to dinner very much, Carole,' I said. 'I just wasn't sure that Duncan would share my enthusiasm for the idea.'

Her eyes narrowed a little.

'Don't be so silly. This is nothing to do with Duncan,' she said evenly. 'If he even notices that we're out together – which I rather doubt – he knows perfectly well that we're just two old friends catching up. I don't check up on him and he doesn't check up on me, Iain. We go our own ways.'

I wasn't sure what to read into the change in her mood

and manner, and her words sounded carefully rehearsed, a little too studied, but I decided to take them at face value. She had, after all, just buried her mother. And I'd never been in an unhappy marriage. I didn't know how those who were stuck in them behaved.

'OK,' I said, 'I'll call Monday.'

'Great,' she said, and managed another little smile. 'I could do with cheering up and you could always manage to do that.' She smiled again and drifted away.

'Except for the once,' I muttered to her retreating back, 'when it really mattered.' I watched her slowly walk away and felt again a great sense of loss building in me. Suddenly, I just wanted to leave.

I wandered aimlessly around the room, making my goodbyes, collecting a couple more glasses of something close to neat gin sent to me by Duncan, and eventually sought out Martin and Duncan to offer my condolences again. They both shook my hand warmly, and they both expressed the wish that I shouldn't be a stranger. But they kept looking at each other knowingly and I had the uneasy feeling that they were sharing a joke at my expense. As I plunged out into the murky evening, I shrugged it off as shared knowledge of the spiked drinks. Kelly and Donnelly were nowhere to be seen. I wasn't sorry.

The wind had died down and the rain had slackened off to a fine mist. It was pleasantly cool and refreshing against my face and I stood for a couple of minutes just staring at the gloom that surrounded the old house. The dull yellow light that leaked from the windows was insignificant in the darkness that was creeping up on it.

Suddenly, I remembered the night of Peter's death and the flashing lights of the ambulance and the police vehicles, the sudden dull roar of the gun that had preceded everything, Margaret's deep, visceral cry, the strange wheezing of the wound.

The Mercedes had gone, confirming its ownership and leaving me a convenient space to turn, and soon I was through the gate and heading out on the six-mile drive to home, brooding about Carole and the Crawfords.

There wasn't much traffic about but I took it very easy through the village. There was an unreal quality about the night. The drizzle damped down any sound and I felt as if I was driving through a dream.

A car came charging up behind me some minutes after I left the village and I expected it to overtake at the first opportunity. Instead, it settled in at a comfortable distance and then followed me on to the single-track road that led to my isolated little house.

I pulled into the first passing place to allow it to glide on past into the night but it didn't. It just pulled in ahead of me, and I knew why immediately. The yellow and red stripes and the Strathclyde Police sign were an obvious clue.

Sergeant Angus Darling and I have a history. As a boy he'd been a sly and vicious bully and we'd often fought and, though he was much bigger than me, he hadn't always come off best. I was a nasty little tough and I'd been trained. I'd even broken his nose once and it still had a slight kink in it to remind us both. As a man he wasn't much better than the bully he'd been as a kid. He affected a bluff, plain man approach but he enjoyed the uniform and the little brief authority it gave him much too much for anyone's comfort.

He opened the car door, heaved himself out and lumbered slowly towards me, his bulk wrapped in his luminous yellow jacket. I lowered the window.

'Hello, Iain,' he said. 'Not a very nice night.'

That seemed uncontroversial.

'No,' I agreed.

'Been at the wake?' He was looking up at the night sky, chewing gum.

'That's right, Sergeant,' I said. 'You were missed.'

'I'll pop in at the house later,' he said. 'When I'm off

duty.' He paused and delicately sniffed at the air. 'Been drinking, have you?'

'No,' I said, 'I haven't.'

He ran two fingers along his crooked nose.

'Then you won't mind blowing into this, then,' he said, producing a breathalyser from behind his back, bending down to my level and staring at me with a smug smile on his face. I could smell the mint from his gum.

I shrugged.

'You know the form, Iain: just blow into this until I tell you to stop.'

Unfortunately, he was right and I did know the form. I took the proffered tube from him and blew long and hard into it. I got some small pleasure from watching the irritating smile slowly fade.

'That's odd,' he said, looking with obvious dismay at the display. He paused. 'Blow into it again.'

I took it from him and obliged.

He looked at the display again and shook his head.

'Keep going,' he said.

'If I blow into this any longer, I'll pass out,' I said.

He shook his head again.

'I think you'd better come in and give a blood sample,' he said. 'This isn't working: it isn't registering anything.'

'It's working. It isn't registering anything because I haven't been drinking anything,' I said. 'You've been misinformed.'

He bridled and started to bluster.

'I haven't been informed about anything,' he said. 'I started to follow you when I noticed that you were driving erratically.'

'Sure,' I said, thinking that I'd be having words with someone in due course.

There was a long pause while he weighed up the pleasure that inconveniencing me for an hour or two would give him against the bollocking the doctor would give him for calling him away from his tea on a fool's errand.

'OK, Iain, I'll take your word for it this time,' he finally said, 'but I'll not give you any more warnings about drinking and driving. On your way.'

To be fair to him, the doctor has a very sharp tongue. And I have a very bad track record.

'Thank you,' I said, 'you're too kind.' And I pulled out around him and drove on, feeling a dangerous combination of self-righteousness and indignant anger.

I watched Darling in the rear-view mirror, a large, faintly devilish figure in the red glow of my tail-lights.

It just couldn't be coincidence that he'd stopped me after Duncan had spiked my drinks. He must have been called. Unfortunately, Duncan wasn't the only person vindictive enough to shop me. However, since he was the only one who knew for sure that my drinks had gin in them, he was still favourite. Thank God the stupid sod had used gin and not vodka.

I was so preoccupied with Duncan Ferguson and his unholy alliance with Angus Darling that I only subconsciously registered the large car parked at the entrance to one of the forestry roads. It wasn't until I turned into my own rutted driveway and realized that the gate that kept the sheep out was open that I remembered the car. It was an expensive saloon: a Mercedes, I was almost certain. I stopped the car just inside the gate and got out to close it. It was then that I realized my house was haemorrhaging light from every orifice. Every window and every door emitted a gentle, golden glow that made long, shapeless and frightening shadows out of every shrub and tree. The house was lit up like an early Christmas decoration. Since I never leave lights on when I'm not there and, as far as I'm aware, the cat hasn't yet mastered the ability to manipulate electric switches, the probability was that I'd been burgled, and recently.

I wasn't sure what to do and so I just stood there watching the house. I thought about going back to see if I could catch up with Sergeant Darling but, as a plan, it never got beyond the thought stage because, in the event, I didn't have to do anything. Either the noise of the engine or the light from the headlamps had alerted the intruder, and a burly figure I was sure I recognized from earlier emerged from the back door and lumbered across the neighbouring field, doing, I fervently hoped, serious damage to an expensive Italian suit and handmade English shoes.

I cautiously drove the rest of the way along the drive and parked in front of the house. I sat in the car for a moment or two, watching the windows mist up, listening to the tick of cooling metal, wondering what Colm Kelly, if it really had been him, had been doing in my home. It made no sense. No one else emerged from the house as I sat there and eventually I decided I'd better venture in.

I stood at the open doorway for a moment, listening.

In the distance I heard a car start, overrev and kick up gravel savagely as it roared on to the road. There was a sharp squeal as the brakes kicked in too sharply and a soft thump, then the whine of a car reversing too fast followed by the gentle purr of a powerful engine accelerating away.

Chapter Two

I used to be a poet. Most people think I still am, but the truth is that I haven't written a poem in two years and I haven't written one worth the name in five. However, the two slim volumes I have had published are still in print, largely because of the insanely high print run – in the region of two and a half thousand, it was widely rumoured – that a wildly optimistic editor insisted on, and each of them sells a few dozen copies a year and earns enough in royalties to keep the cat sleek and fat for a month or two.

I survive because, five years ago, at about the same time as I stopped writing decent poetry, my agent convinced me that I should try my hand at writing a sitcom because she was convinced that I could do it. Surprisingly, she was right. With a pile of joke books on the floor and a publicity photograph of the washed-up soap star (much less glamorous in person and much more likeable and intelligent than I would have believed possible from the carefully posed and rather bland picture) who was looking for a vehicle to revive her career pinned to my cork board, I sweated out thirteen episodes of *My Kingdom for a Horse* in thirteen months. The riding stable setting permitted a certain earthy humour that proved to be popular and the digital and satellite revolution keeps what my agent calls the residuals trickling in. Since then I've written a few pilots which haven't come to anything but have been paid for and I am called upon to write for ongoing series when the regular writers are ill, on holiday, without inspiration or just can't be bothered because they're working on something else that pays better.

All of which means that, although I'm by no means a successful screenplay writer (or even close), I'm not a starving poet and I do possess some of the consumer gewgaws that would help to support a serious heroin addiction for a few days. But I hadn't got the impression that Kelly – if it had been him I'd seen lumbering through the field – was short of a quid or two and would be even vaguely interested in walking off with them. He looked like someone who acquired state of the art equipment and, if he was a crook, he'd long since graduated from breaking and entering.

Anyway, none of my possessions seemed to have been taken: the wide-screen television still stared blankly out at me; the green display lights on the video still blinked on and off, begging me to reset them after the last power cut; and my camera and pocket tape-recorder still lay on the table where I'd left them. Even my one real indulgence, the frighteningly expensive CD player, continued to gather dust undisturbed.

I stood in the living room for a few minutes and then went slowly and nervously from room to room, edgily checking them out: first to the kitchen, then creaking up the stairs to the bedroom, guest room and bathroom. The lights were on everywhere but nothing seemed to have been disturbed. I touched nothing, not even a light switch, and stared morosely around, trying to make sense of a burglar who took nothing. Sure, he'd been disturbed, but all the same . . . There was something eerily wrong about it.

I ran down the stairs to what had been the dining room when my father had been alive but which was now my study. Warily, I peered in. The overhead light was on but, again, nothing appeared to have been touched. Even the piles of books, magazines and typescripts were exactly as I'd left them. I went in, sat down at my desk and picked up the phone to call the police but, as I did so, I kicked something at the back of the well. I bent over and looked down. It was a briefcase, tucked neatly away against the modesty board – a new and expensive black briefcase.

And it wasn't mine.

Trembling slightly, I replaced the phone on its cradle and then knelt down and stared at the shiny leather that gleamed dully even in the dark space under the desk. My mouth was very dry but I could taste something metallic.

I thought of bombs in bags and suddenly realized that I was frightened and that the metallic taste was fear.

I don't often react hysterically, but I did then, standing up and lurching from the room before I even thought about it. I raced through the living room, away from all that harsh light and out into the gentle moist embrace of the dark evening. I shivered in the cold air and looked up at the black sky, then into the old half-derelict dairy where I sometimes park the car. The heavy punchbag that is suspended from one of the roof beams there was swinging slightly in the light breeze. It looked like the elongated torso of a hanging man.

Impulsively, I wrenched open the car door, climbed in and drove erratically and too fast along the hundred yards or so of my bumpy driveway, stones spurting out from under the wheels, turned on to the road and, tyres squealing shrilly, accelerated away.

I switched the headlights on to full beam and concentrated on the narrow strip of tarmac ahead, which was just as well as I hadn't gone more than seven hundred yards when I saw a large motionless lump slumped half across the road. It was obvious that I couldn't pull around it without risking ending up in the ditch and going over it wasn't an option, so I slowed and pulled into a passing place, turning on my hazard lights. I was parked in the same spot as the car that I'd passed earlier.

I climbed out of the car and went to investigate the lump in the road, although I already had a good idea of just what it was.

My breath blossomed in the cold, damp air and drifted

slowly away, clearly visible in the light from my head-lamps. The hazards blinking on and off lent an eerie, garish glow to the scene as I knelt down beside the bleed-ing deer. It feebly moved its legs at my approach, strug-gling to get up, but there was no strength in them and it lay quietly, its moist, bright eyes glittering in the strange, yellowish light, its breath coming in slow, ragged gasps.

I was still by its side, paralysed, wondering what to do when I heard another vehicle approach. The driver parked behind my car and climbed out.

I stood up and, with some relief, recognized the new-comer. It couldn't have been anyone better able to deal with the situation. It was the local Forestry Commission ranger.

'What's up, Iain?' he said. 'Hit a deer?'

'No,' I said. 'I just saw it here, Derek.'

He nodded but he couldn't resist a glance at my car as he passed it, looking for damage. Then he sank down next to the injured creature. He ran his hands gently and, to my unpractised eye, expertly over the animal's side and then stood up.

'She's taken a hell of a thump,' he said. 'There's no way she's going to live. Best put her out of her pain.'

He marched briskly back to the Land Rover, rummaged around in the back for a couple of minutes and then returned, a blade glinting in his hand.

'Haven't got the rifle with me,' he said and then grinned. 'Hope you're not too squeamish.'

I shrugged haplessly.

'Hold her for me. I'm going to have to cut her throat.'

I reached down and placed my hands either side of the animal's head and then turned away. She gave a surpris-ingly human gasp, spasmed and kicked her legs feebly and tried to twist her head away when the knife blade sank in but I held her steady. Derek stepped back briskly and swore under his breath as the black blood pumped out. After a few seconds her head was dead weight.

'You can let her go now,' Derek said. 'We'll just let her

bleed for a few minutes and then you can help me carry her to the Land Rover. I'll drop by with some venison burgers sometime. Unless you want a haunch?'

'No, burgers will be fine,' I said listlessly.

We both stood in silence for a minute or two, staring off into the night.

'You at the funeral?' he said suddenly.

'Aye,' I said.

He nodded. 'They give her a good send-off?'

'Fair,' I said.

He smacked his lips and nodded again.

'Good,' he finally said. 'She was OK. Always decent to me. Well, nearly always.'

'Aye,' I said, 'and to me. Nearly always.'

He rubbed his jaw, and then stroked his chin. The rasp of his thumb against his thick stubble was surprisingly loud in the quiet of the evening. I was aware of him studying me.

'You all right, Iain?' he suddenly asked.

'Me?' I said. 'I'm fine. Why?'

'Only you don't seem yourself,' he said.

'I'm OK,' I said and then, because that sounded ungracious even to me, I added, 'But maybe the funeral took more out of me than I thought.'

He shrugged and we lapsed into silence again as I watched the dark blood puddle around the deer's head and, following the camber of the road, stream off towards the grass verge and the ditch beyond.

'I'll get an old blanket to wrap her in,' Derek said after a few minutes and immediately marched off to his vehicle.

We rolled the deer on to the smelly old blanket and then half-dragged and half-carried her the twenty-five yards to the Land Rover and tossed her into the back. Derek climbed in, gave me a thumbs up, executed a quick and expert three-point turn and headed off back to his house and game larder.

I watched his tail-lights disappear into the distance and then got back into my car. I turned off the hazards and dipped my headlights. Everything seemed strangely unreal. I just sat and waited for more than three-quarters of an hour.

A couple of cars passed me but nothing else happened. No dull boom rattled teeth and perforated eardrums, no lethal shards of flying glass threatened to shred flesh, no intense orange flame lit up the night sky, no pall of acrid smoke hung over my house.

I felt as if I was in a dream, with no control over what was going on. I knew that I should call the police, tell them what had happened, but I was too lethargic to move. If the briefcase did contain a bomb, it would have to be dealt with. And if it didn't, it would have to be explained. But I couldn't raise the energy to move.

I just let my mind follow whatever tortuous trail it would and, as so often lately when I allowed it that luxury, I thought of Carole and of the first time I'd met her. It was also the first time that I met Margaret Crawford.

I was eighteen and it had been my last summer before going to university. I'd been earning a little money as a beater, striding out from the woodland, through the yellow-flowering ragwort, the elegant rosebay willow herb, the blooming heather, delicate purple and white flowers like tiny beads, the rampant bracken higher than my shoulder, past the rugged broom and the towering rhododendron bushes, in a line with all the other beaters, under the watchful eye of the ghillies, shouting and whistling, frightening the poor, stupid birds out of the undergrowth towards the guns.

Unfortunately, one of the guns hadn't been quite as careful as he might have been and I found myself up at the house with a few pellets of shot in my right leg, being ministered to in the kitchen by one of the ghillies armed with a pair of tweezers, some cotton wool and surgical spirit.

Margaret had supplied the cotton wool and the surgical spirit and Carole had supplied the tweezers and they both stayed around to see them employed. They always joked that the first time they'd seen me it had been with my trews around my ankles. They were more amused than I was but, in the event, a few slugs of birdshot in my thigh was a small price to pay for the introduction, and the invitation to take tea at the house that followed. It could hardly be described as love at first sight, and I'm still not sure if I was more taken with Carole, her mother or the thrill of mixing for the first time with the local aristocracy, but I found myself going up to the house on a regular basis on one excuse or another as that long ripe summer turned into a damp autumn. My father, unreconstructed socialist that he was, wryly tugged an imaginary forelock and offered some acerbic observation about the traditional sub-servience of the rural Scot every time I left the house, but I was impervious to his sarcasm and embarrassingly unembarrassable about my fascination.

Another car roared past me in a blaze of blinding light and brought me back abruptly to my present predicament.

I thought again of the briefcase and I just couldn't conceive of it containing a bomb. The idea was suddenly ludicrous. What was I thinking? Sure, Duncan didn't like me but he was hardly going to blow me up for having had an affair with his wife before she'd even met him. That would be taking retrospective jealousy a little too far.

All the same, the briefcase presumably contained something and the prospect of explaining a briefcase full of anything to Sergeant Darling was not appealing. Nor, when I thought about it, was finding a suitable reason for the long delay in reporting the alleged break-in. Darling, after all, knew, more or less to the minute, when I'd arrived home. There'd be the little matter of more than an hour to account for. And Sergeant Darling had a suspicious mind where I was concerned.

Having sicklied o'er the noble hue of resolution with the pale cast of thought for far too long, I roused myself, turned the car around in a much less expert three-point turn than Derek had executed and drove slowly and carefully back to the house. I passed through the open gate, turned off the engine, hauled myself out of the car, closed the gate and stood silently by the car, listening to the sounds of water all around me, trickling along the ruts in the driveway, gurgling in the drainage ditch behind me, dripping from the shadowy, gnarled hawthorn hedge, rushing across the stones in the burn below.

The cloud had thinned and a sliver of moon, liverish-yellow and hazy in the chilly, damp air, was visible low in the sky. There were no stars out yet.

Finding the torch that I always kept in the driver's door bin, I left the car where it was and stumbled my way down to the house, splashing into some of the larger puddles and muddying the bottoms of my dark suit trousers. In the storm porch by the back door, I found some tough gardening gloves and pulled them on. I paused briefly and took a deep breath to compose myself and then strode purposefully into the study.

Clearly, opening the briefcase was the wrong thing to do. I knew it at the time and I'd decided that I wouldn't force the lock. If the case was locked, it would stay that way and I would hand it in to the police.

I reached down into the well of the desk, gripped the handle firmly and pulled. There was definitely something substantial in it – a house brick or two, perhaps – and I half-dragged it into the centre of the room. I walked around it a couple of times but there was nothing to be learned by looking. It was just a black leather briefcase with gold-coloured metal fittings, solid and elegant.

I knelt down next to it and examined the clasps. Each had a combination lock next to it and the numbers were all set at zero. I breathed in deeply, placed a thumb against each clasp and pushed. The mechanism worked soundlessly and slid smoothly at my touch; the clasps sprang open with a satisfying clunk. I opened my eyes and lifted the lid.

The gun was lying on top of two large packages, both of which were carefully wrapped in white butcher's paper. It was a big blue-black Colt .45 automatic, a weapon long

49

favoured by the United States Army. I recognized it immediately, not because I'm a gun nut but because it's one of the very few guns I had seen before. I lifted it out. It felt substantial in my gloved hand.

I set the gun down on the floor, picked up the first, very large, package and unfolded the paper that was wrapped around it to be greeted by the unfamiliar sight of English fifty-pound notes. There were a lot of them, maybe three or four hundred. There could have been more but I didn't bother to count them, just wrapped them up again and replaced them in the case.

I had a feeling that I already knew what the second package contained and I was nearly right. I've been offered enough class A drugs in my time to recognize cocaine, but I'd been expecting heroin.

I sat on the floor and just stared at the contents of the case for a few minutes, wondering what to do.

Alfred Hitchcock once responded – or, if he didn't, he should have – to a question about his plots that his characters didn't go to the police because that would be boring. My reasoning was a little more complicated (as, indeed, are Hitchcock's plots). I was imagining Detective Sergeant MacPlod's raised eyebrow and his pithy summing up: 'So, Mr Lewis, what you're saying is that a man broke into your house, took nothing and left a briefcase containing twenty thousand pounds in cash, a weapon known to have been used in three gangland murders and cocaine with a street value of X million pounds. [Here MacPlod would spirit a figure out of the air to fatten his end-of-year clear-up statistics.] Interesting sort of villain you get out this way.'

And then I would have to concede that he had a point. I was not sure that I would have believed me either. Especially given that eight years before I had been admonished and fined for possession of a microscopic amount of cannabis resin. It was the sort of thing that country policemen tended to remember, embellish and hold against you.

I picked up the gun and placed it back in the case, on top

of the other two packages, and firmly closed the lid. Then I went to the phone, picked up the handset and listened to the steady buzz of the dialling tone. It wasn't quite like holding a conch to your ear and hearing the gentle murmur of the sea, but it had a similarly soothing effect.

I punched in the number from memory and waited for the dull burrr that would tell me I was connected. After a few rings BT's answering service cut in and asked me to leave a message. I broke the connection without obliging and looked at my watch. What was I thinking? It was after six on a Friday evening. He'd be on his way to the pub, or he'd already be ensconced on his stool at the bar, white froth on his ragged mouser, his huge, soft mitt wrapped around his first – or possibly second – pint of Guinness. And he'd likely be there all night. Dougie Henderson was a man of habit.

I tucked the handset snugly back on to its cradle, wandered into the kitchen, found a tin of catfood in the cupboard and yanked it open. The smell caught at the back of my throat as I forked it into the cat's dish and I nearly gagged. No wonder the poor animal's breath stank. I left his dish by the catflap at the back door.

It was eight forty-five when I parked outside the Botanic Gardens in Queen Margaret Drive opposite the BBC. I walked along the wide, quiet street towards the rushing traffic of the Great Western Road. It was almost nine when I stepped out of the damp and misty November night into the warm fug of the Argyll Arms just off the Byres Road.

Dougie had never ventured too far from the stamping ground of his uni days. He had bought a big, handsome flat a mere five-minute walk from University Avenue when the paper made him what he liked to call its chief crime reporter (a title I'm reliably informed doesn't, in fact, exist). He reasoned that almost all of his creature comforts could be catered for within a half-mile radius. Chinese and Indian restaurants, a decent bookshop, a library, a cinema, a taxi rank, the Ubiquitous Chip and, of course, the Argyll Arms were all to hand. Although I'd never asked him about it, as far as I knew sex had never figured prominently, if at all, in Dougie's priorities.

I didn't see him immediately through the crowd of boisterous mid-evening drinkers, and I made my way slowly through the mêlée to the bar, my eyes adjusting to the sudden light, my ears to the raucous noise. And there he was, surrounded by four or five other large men, pint in hand, holding forth at the other end of the long, slender, drink-splashed bar.

The solitary barman nodded that he'd seen me as he scurried between the till and the beer pumps, coping coolly with the shouted orders and the notes thrust at him. Eventually, he made his way over.

'Ardbeg,' I said. 'A large one. And a pint of Guinness for Onan the Barbarian down there. And whatever you're having.'

'Thanks. I'll just take a half of heavy, Iain,' he said as he deftly pulled and poured drinks. 'And we still don't stock Islay whisky.'

'Macallan, then,' I said. 'And you should.'

'There's nae call for it,' he said, without looking up. 'Except from you and we've not seen you in a while. How are you? You been away?'

'Fine thanks, Gus,' I said, and suddenly realized that I was telling the truth. I'd felt better ever since entering the bar. 'I've not been away. Too busy. I just haven't been near the wicked city for a few months.'

I handed him a ten-pound note and watched the swirling Guinness settle in the glass as he made change.

The Argyll Arms isn't one of the vast Victorian drinking barns, full of solitary men muttering angrily into their beer. It's what the French might call *intime*, which usually translates as small and sweaty. Dougie drinks there because he'd frequented the place when he'd been at uni, and the students who flitted through reminded him poignantly of passing time and that he'd been young once. The bright young things and the slightly tarnished and not so young things, like Dougie and myself, were packed in and all in animated conversation. Peels and hoots of loud and unforced laughter came at me from all sides.

Gus walked to the other end of the bar, said something to Dougie and pushed the glass of Guinness across the bar towards him, tilting his head slightly in my direction. Dougie, characteristically, looked first at the Guinness and then at me. I raised my glass to him and smiled. He rose to his feet, murmured something to his companions and, the crowd of drinkers sliding around him like water around a fish, he lumbered towards me. Even though he'd probably been drinking for some hours, he still managed to look alert and smart. His expensive dark-blue silk tie was still carefully fastened in a neat half-Windsor knot and the collar of his powder-blue, buttondown-collar Jermyn Street shirt was still immaculately buttoned. His moustache, of course, was coated in foam from his drink.

'Iain Lewis, as I live and breathe,' he boomed at me and I could smell the sour beer on his breath. 'How's my favourite poofter poet?'

'Not so bad, Dougie,' I said. 'And less of the poet, if you don't mind. You'll be giving me a bad reputation.'

He looked me up and down and a puzzled look creased his face.

'What's with the whistle?' he said.

'Oh,' I said, looking down at my dark, damp and creased suit, 'funeral.'

'Anyone I know?' he asked.

'Margaret Crawford.'

'Aye,' he said, 'of course.'

The awkward silence that normally ensued whenever I mentioned the Crawfords in his presence was filled by him drinking deeply from his pint. He never knew what to say to me about Carole and so usually elected to say nothing.

'Do you know why she –' he started but I cut him off.

'No, I don't, Dougie, and I haven't asked.'

He nodded. 'And the family? How are they? Carole . . . and Martin, is it?'

He was looking over my shoulder when he spoke, as if distracted by something. I supposed he was just embarrassed by mentioning Carole by name for the first time in years.

'They're coping,' I said.

He nodded again, then looked at me with a broad smile. 'So, what brings you out on such a dreich night?'

'I need a bed for the night. And some advice,' I said.

'Well now,' he said, 'the bed's free but the advice'll cost you. You can take me to my favourite curry house. I take it that it's a matter of some urgency and delicacy that forces you on a two-hour drive on a drizzling November night without having ascertained that I am not otherwise engaged.'

'I took a wild guess on your whereabouts, Dougie,' I said. 'And you're right. It is a matter of some urgency.'

'Right,' he said. 'Drink up and we'll be on our way.'

He took a huge swallow of his beer, plonked the glass on the bar and then belched mightily. I finished my whisky and waited while Dougie wandered back to his companions, retrieved his overcoat and said his loud farewells. Then he was back at my side, ushering me out into the chill air.

We walked in silence amid the bustle of Byres Road. I was carefully rehearsing what I was going to tell him and how. Dougie was probably simply anticipating the meal. For a man who is systematically ruining his digestive system and his taste buds with vast quantities of beer, he is remarkably discerning and knowledgeable about food, and very appreciative of it. He likes to savour a meal in advance, thinking through the various options available to him. It enables him, he maintains, to choose wisely and too well. The echo, a faintly remembered, if scarcely understood, phrase from Shakespeare, is typical of Dougie – they pepper his crime and court reports – but it doesn't make it any easier to understand what he means.

54

I looked up at the big man.

'It's good to see you, Dougie,' I said.

'And it's good to see you too, Iain,' he said. 'It's been too long. It's always too long. You should come back to the city. You're vegetating out there. You need a wee bit of excitement back in your life.'

I laughed.

'I can't afford Glasgow prices these days,' I said. 'And I rather think I've got all the excitement I can handle in my life just at the moment.'

'Oh, aye,' he said. 'I suppose the local farmer's finally found out about you and his prize ewe, has he?'

'Something like that,' I said.

The curry house he flamboyantly showed me into was elegant and stylish, with no flock wallpaper in sight. It was light and airy and each table was covered with a crisp, white tablecloth and on each there was a small vase with a single red rose. The restaurant was, though, nearly empty, with only a middle-aged couple sat at a corner table. It seemed likely that the Friday night clientele usually arrived after last orders, a fact confirmed when the maître d' greeted Dougie.

'You are early tonight, Mr Henderson,' he said and beamed. 'Of course that means that there is much room for you.' And he led us to a table set for six.

'We shall have to eat heroically,' I said after he'd gone, staring at the vast expanse of table that stretched before us.

'Oh, I intend to,' Dougie said.

We ordered and I started to tell Dougie about my strange afternoon and evening when the Kingfisher lagers and the pappadums arrived. Dougie is a surprisingly good listener and my tale didn't take very long. I'd finished by the time we were ordering our second lagers and the waiter was taking away the remains of our chicken and prawn hors d'oeuvres.

'So,' I said, 'what do I do?'

'Dump the gun in the ocean, offload the C to the highest bidder, and spend the money,' he said.

'What?' I said.

He leaned back in his chair and let out a snort of laughter.

'You probably should go to the police,' he said. 'Trouble is, it would have been difficult to explain earlier this evening. Now it's close to bloody impossible. Suspicious bastards, the police. Give 'em a pilchard and they smell a rat.' He paused. 'You can't blame 'em, really, given that the toe-rags they spend their lives dealing with lie on principle. And then their lawyers lie for them in court.' He paused again. 'I could have a word with one of my contacts on the force, if you like. Sort of vouch for you.'

I sat quietly, thinking how unreal it all seemed.

'He's a good bloke. Very discreet, very intelligent. He won't jump to conclusions.'

I still didn't say anything.

'Iain, what did you think I'd advise? Do you think I've got some kind of magic wand that makes money, guns, class A drugs and murderously dangerous criminals disappear? I haven't. But I do have some friends in the police. I rather assumed that was why you came to speak to me.'

'Sorry, Dougie, I was miles away,' I said. 'Yeah, please, speak to your contact. I'd be grateful. I just don't know what to do in the meantime.'

'You sure it was one of the Irishmen?' he said.

'No,' I said, 'I'm not sure. How could I be? But it certainly looked like him, in the dark and from a distance.'

He shrugged. 'There are some very hard men shipping industrial quantities of all kinds of shit into Dublin. I hope you haven't come across one of them. They are not nice people.'

'I didn't think they were,' I said.

'Mainly they just kill their own: those who try to rip them off, encroach on their territory. But they kill them pretty horribly. They have, however, taken out the odd journalist who was proving to be a bit of a pain. They don't often touch civilians, though. So, how do you know them?'

It was my turn to shrug. 'Like I said, I just met them

56

today. Barely even said hello. They were at Margaret Crawford's wake with Duncan Ferguson. He said that they were business associates, interested in his fish. For all I know, that's exactly what they are and they have nothing to do with the break-in and the briefcase. But if it wasn't them, I don't have a clue who it could have been. But, anyway, even if they are Irish drug dealers, why would they leave something like that in my house? Are they setting me up, or what?'

Dougie shook his head in a non-committal way.

'And the husband,' he said. 'You sure he was spiking your drinks?'

'Oh, yes,' I said, 'I'm sure about that. And that Angus Darling had been tipped off that I was driving after drinking.'

Dougie looked up at the ceiling.

'Where's the briefcase now?' he asked.

'In my septic tank,' I said.

He looked across at me, leaned back in his chair and roared with laughter.

'That'll really cheer Alistair up,' he said, still laughing. 'Literally up to his armpits in your shit. I'll tell him to take along your Sergeant Darling, to do the hands-on stuff.'

'It was the only place I could think of,' I said defensively, 'and it's wrapped in three dustbin liners. What else could I have done? Bring it with me?'

'Heaven forfend,' he said.

We lapsed into silence for a few moments.

'So, what do I do, Dougie?' I finally said.

'Pay the bill, come back to my place for a few drams, give me the names of your new Irish acquaintances, talk to Ali Macfarlane, go home and await developments.'

'The first one sounds OK and the second is even attractive. The third doesn't present a problem, though I suppose it may, depending on what you do with the information. But I don't care particularly for the other two, especially the last,' I said.

57

'Och, it'll be fine,' he said. 'Ali's a very good man. You'll like him a lot. And home is where the heart is.'

As it turned out, Dougie was unable to contact Alistair Macfarlane the following morning as he'd intended – Macfarlane's mobile phone was switched off, his answerphone switched on and he was not at his desk – and so I drove the hundred and ten miles home not knowing whether I liked him or not, or, indeed, anything about him. Except that he could be very elusive when he chose to be. What Dougie was able to tell me, after only half an hour spent at his laptop, was that Patrick Donnelly was, indeed, a fish merchant with an office in Dun Laoghaire. Colm Kelly, on the other hand, appeared to have no business interest in fish at all. But he was, as they say, known to the police and not because he was a freemason.

The weather had changed completely overnight and the sun, low in the winter sky, glinted brightly on the steely waters of Loch Lomond and brushed the steep, wooded braes with light, shadowing the deep hollows on the hillside.

November has never been my favourite month – 'No fruits, no flowers, no leaves, no birds, November!' Although it's not always quite as bad as Thomas Hood would have it, the bare trees, the heavy rain, the sodden fields, the dead and rotting vegetation and the muted colours do conspire to give the landscape a barren, bedraggled appearance out of keeping with its natural grace and majesty. But the bright sun helped.

A single small hawk circled above the empty road as I swept around the rubbish-strewn shores of Loch Long and past the rugged slopes of the Arrochar Alps. I couldn't hear its thin, eerie cry.

Although I tried to put it from my mind, I was very apprehensive about returning home and about what and who I might find there. The fact that the only other living thing I could see was a hungry predator was not a comfort.

It was a relief to discover, when I was through the mountain pass and had caught up with and overtaken a sluggish, yellow-painted Argyll and Bute Council lorry just before the Dunoon turn-off, that there were other people on the road. I discovered a little nugget of optimism deep within me. Everything was going to be fine. Dougie would locate Alistair Macfarlane and explain my problem. Macfarlane would be in touch and together we would sort it all out. There would, of course, be a little awkwardness, a little difficulty, a number of interviews with the police, but it would all work itself out. After all, it wasn't as if I'd actually done anything wrong.

The first dark clouds scudded across the sun and muddied the light as I swooped around a bend and saw Loch Fyne. By the time that Inveraray thrust itself prettily into the loch, a light rain was falling steadily, a mist was gathering and a deep gloom had insinuated itself into the afternoon.

I stopped for petrol and bought bread, milk and a newspaper at a service station just outside Lochgilphead. As I wandered back to the car, I saw and heard Martin Crawford's distinctive old green E-type Jaguar rumble into the forecourt. As always, it rattled and groaned as if some important component was about to expire noisily and messily but, somehow, he kept it on the road.

Instead of returning to my car, I strolled over to greet him.

'Martin,' I said as he climbed out of the low-slung seat, 'how's it going?'

'Not so bad, Iain,' he said. 'The will's being read on Monday and I guess we can start to get on with our lives after that.' He paused, sighed and brushed his blond hair away from his eyes. He looked pale and tired. 'It's not going to be easy, though.' The vein under his left eye still throbbed and he was developing a noticeable tic.

'No,' I said, 'I guess not.' He removed his petrol cap and inserted the nozzle of the pump into his tank. 'What's with the two Irishmen who were at the wake? They still around?'

He looked up and gave me a narrow-eyed, suspicious glance.

'Patrick and Colm?' he said. 'Well, Patrick's left. Gone back to Dublin.' He carefully avoided my eye. 'Colm's still around. Something came up. He's had to stay for a day or so.' He paused and concentrated on pumping petrol. 'Donnelly's looking to ship a container of our shellfish a week into Dublin.'

'Isn't that a bit like sending coals to Newcastle?' I said.

He gave that suspicious, narrow-eyed look again. 'What do you mean?'

'Dublin Bay prawns are a fairly well-known food item,' I said and shrugged.

'Oh, aye,' he said. 'But we can undercut the local producers and supply better quality fish.' He finished filling the car, making sure that the last drips from the nozzle went into his tank, and then replaced the nozzle in its cradle. 'The margin's terrific.'

'What about Kelly?' I said. 'What's he got in mind?'

He didn't reply immediately and looked down at his feet.

'He's always looking for investment opportunities,' he finally said, still staring down, 'and he reckons we offer him a good one.'

'Really?' I said. 'Congratulations. Did your mother know about all of this?'

'She knew what was happening,' he said warily.

We stood there, looking at each other morosely. I was thinking of my mother and I assumed that he was thinking of his.

Suddenly, he looked up, gave me a perfunctory wave and strode off to pay for the ocean of petrol he had just pumped into the Jag. I looked at the sleek machine for a moment, shook my head and went back to my sedate Rover, feeling just a bit middle-aged.

I'd never really known Martin, just as I'd never really known, or liked, his father. Peter, in spite of the apparent interest he had shown in me, had always been Margaret's supercilious husband, and Martin had always only been

Carole's kid brother. I guess I was more interested in the female side of the family at the time.

The rain was still a fine misty drizzle when I arrived home and the windscreen wipers thumped across the glass intermittently. I hadn't noted any suspicious vehicles on the road and my gate was closed but I still paused after opening it and looked around carefully before proceeding.

The light was fading fast and the house looked a little spooky in the gathering gloom, the windows dark and blank against the grey walls, and I shivered, hearing my mother's voice at almost the same time murmuring, 'Someone's walking over your grave.'

I climbed back into the car and drove through the gate. I paused again to close it and then continued down the driveway and parked outside my back door, realizing that I'd forgotten to check the mailbox.

The cat had emptied his dish, or something very like a cat had, and the answerphone was blinking away in the darkness. Apart from that, there was no sign of life, or mischief, in the place.

I turned on lights all over the ground floor, switched on the radio in the kitchen in time to hear Geoffrey Smith intone his theatrical 'hello' at the start of *Jazz Record Requests* and busied myself making coffee. The delicate sound of Miles Davis playing 'Summertime' filled the room and dispelled most of my disquiet but my hand still shook slightly as I poured from the cafetière to the cup.

I found myself thinking about Martin, wondering what made him tick, what had turned him into an accountant, what demons tormented him, if he had been part of Duncan's plan.

Fats Waller started to rip through 'Ain't Misbehaving' as I listened to my phone messages. There were two. The first was from Dougie. He hadn't tracked down Alistair Macfarlane but he'd keep trying. The second was from Carole. She sounded upset and asked if I could ring.

The number had changed a little since I had first used it but I still had it by heart. My heart sank when Duncan picked up on the fourth ring.

61

'Duncan,' I said, 'it's Iain. Iain Lewis.'

'Iain,' he said and his voice was thick with alcohol, 'how are you? Come on over and have a drink.'

'Possibly later, Duncan,' I said, 'as long as you promise not to turn me in to the blue meanies.'

'The blue meanies?' he said. 'Oh, yes. I heard that you had a wee bit of trouble last night.'

'It was nothing serious,' I said. 'What did you hear?'

'Got it straight from the horse's mouth. Angus Darling.'

'I think you mean the horse's arse,' I said.

'He dropped by,' he said, ignoring me. 'To pay his respects. Said he'd just pulled you over for drunk driving.'

'And what did you say?'

'I said I wasn't surprised after what you'd put away here but that I hoped he'd be lenient, considering that Margaret was like a mother to you.'

'That was kind of you,' I said. 'But I wasn't drunk so there was no problem and he let me go anyway.'

There was a long, thoughtful pause. I could almost hear the synapses in his brain popping.

'Anyway,' I said, 'is Carole there? She called while I was out and asked me to ring back.'

'No,' he said, 'no, she isn't here. Don't know where she's gone, to tell the truth. You'll be over later for a drink, is that it?'

'No,' I said, 'just tell Carole I called.'

'If I see her,' he said. 'See you later, then.'

'Maybe, Duncan. Bye.'

I broke the connection, took a sip of coffee and heard the mellow tone of Gerry Mulligan's baritone sax coming from the kitchen. It was, clearly, a vintage night on Radio 3. Then the phone rang, shrilly urgent, disturbing the moment, nearly causing me to spill my coffee.

It was – Who could have thought that my shrivell'd heart could have recovered greennesse? – Carole.

Chapter Three

The bar was bright, crowded, hot and very loud. A warm fug hung in the air and the hundred or so mid-evening drinkers were pink-cheeked with the heat and the drink, and the sheen of sweat on their foreheads and pates gleamed and reflected the yellowish light. The sound of thirty or forty raucous conversations, the occasional shriek of laughter and the loud shouted greetings hit me hard after the quiet of the night-time street as I entered, stood by the door and looked around. There were some blond heads, a few more authentic than others, bent over drinks or tilted back, laughing open-mouthed, but Carole's wasn't among them.

A huge log fire roared in the grate at the far end of the room, singeing the buttocks of the pool players as they bent suggestively over the table.

I started to manoeuvre myself through the crush, twisting and turning, dipping to avoid brushing against drinking arms, until I found myself at the bar, standing next to Danny McGovern. There was always a little space around Danny. It may have been to accommodate his aura, but it could just as easily have been that the odour he gave off was slightly stronger than most of us like to cope with.

'Aye, aye, I was just thinking about you,' he said, staring across the bar at the lines of sleek, dark bottles that stood stolidly on shelves at the backs of the bar staff. One hundred and fourteen different malts waiting patiently for next summer and the extravagant curiosity of tourists.

'Why was that, Danny?' I said, trying to catch the eye of a barman.

'An interesting thing about that boat,' he said.

'What boat would that be, Danny?' I said, leaning across the bar and waving a ten-pound note in an apparently hopeless attempt to attract attention.

'Why, that boat we saw yesterday,' he said.

'Oh, *that* boat,' I said, humouring him. I hadn't the faintest idea what he was talking about.

'Aye,' he said. 'Well, it pulled in way down the coast. By the Old Mariner's Grave.'

'Did it now?' I said.

The barman came over, looking harassed.

'Evening, Iain,' he said, 'what can I get you?'

'A half of Guinness for Danny,' I said, 'and I'll just take an orange juice and tonic water.'

'Is that fresh orange, Iain?'

'Aye,' I said. 'Fresh out of the bottle.'

'And a glass of white wine,' a soft voice whispered in my ear.

'And a glass of dry white wine,' I called to the barman's departing back before turning to face Carole. 'Hi,' I said.

'Hi yourself,' she said.

'Well, it was strange,' said Danny.

'What was?' I said.

'Well, I don't believe that that boat was fishing at all,' he said.

'Oh, aye. Well, I'll catch you later, Danny,' I said as the barman came back with the drinks for me and Carole. I handed him the note and said, 'Don't forget Danny's Guinness.'

'It's coming, Iain,' he said. 'It just has to be enticed from the barrel with honeyed words, is all.'

I smiled amiably at him and slid the change into the pocket of my jeans where it felt heavy and bulky, picked up the drinks and guided Carole away from the bar, towards a table with two vacant seats, close to the fire.

We sat and I just looked at her for a few seconds, while

she peered over my shoulder at the crowd and the pool players. She was wearing an ivory-coloured silk shirt, jeans, black boots and a black leather jacket, and she was glowing as if she'd come straight from the shower. She was smelling of apples.

'You're looking good, Carole,' I finally said.

She looked at me and smiled.

'Thank you,' she said. 'And you're not looking too bad yourself.'

'I wish.'

'No, really. You are,' she said and then she stared wistfully down at her drink.

'I could do with losing a few pounds,' I said.

She shook her head. But I wasn't sure if she was dismissing my comment as an irrelevance or denying it.

'So,' I said, 'what's the story? Why the sudden burning desire to meet up?'

'Do I need an excuse to have a drink with an old friend?'

'You haven't found the need in the last dozen years,' I said. 'If your mother hadn't invited me over for lunch, I wouldn't have seen you since you got back.'

She laughed.

'Oh, I've had the need, Iain,' she said. 'I just didn't have the courage.'

'Duncan's not that frightening, surely?' I said.

'I didn't need the courage to face up to Duncan,' she said.

I must have looked puzzled.

'It was you, you clown. I didn't have the balls to face you.'

I must have looked even more puzzled.

'I didn't think *I* was that frightening either,' I said.

She picked up her glass and sipped at her wine. She finished drinking and just stared into the glass.

'You're right,' she said. 'You're not at all frightening. I just didn't know what to say to you, how to explain what happened. I'm not even sure I know what happened to me when Dad died. We never talked about it, did we?'

'We didn't have much of a chance,' I said. 'You went into purdah after the death, and you went away after the funeral.'

'Well, I want to talk about it now. And about Mum. I don't understand any of it, Iain. And I desperately want to.'

She paused and sipped delicately at her wine, waiting for me to say something. I gulped down some orange and tonic water too quickly and spluttered for a few seconds.

'I'm sorry, Carole,' I finally managed to say, 'I know that the death of your father was deeply upsetting for you and that, for whatever reasons, you couldn't turn to me at the time. I was hurt by that but now I think I maybe understand. I was too young, too callow, too unstable, to be the emotional rock that you needed. You somehow knew that.' I paused and shook my head. 'The only thing that's changed is that I'm not so young any more. I'm just as callow, just as unstable. I still substitute quotes from poets for thought, and hide behind them. You complained about it once. Remember? But I'll help in any way I can. If I can . . .'

She looked at me, a small smile on her lips and a little brightness in her eyes. 'Got any, now?'

'What?' I said.

'Apposite quotes.'

I shrugged helplessly but she tilted her head on one side and waited.

'Well, I guess Philip Larkin's most famous opening line – the one from "This be the Verse" – might fit the bill. Unless, of course, you subscribe to Adrian Mitchell's theory that a disaffected linotype operator changed the entire meaning with a malicious misprint and that Larkin intended to write, "They tuck you up, your mum and dad."'

She laughed.

'Well, mine did both. Tucked me up and fucked me up. Pretty comprehensively.' She smiled sadly, reached across

66

and put her hand on mine. 'But I'm very sorry that you got hurt because of it.'

'I guess that's all behind us,' I said.

She shrugged.

'Maybe,' she said. 'I'm not so sure. The past just sneaks up on you and bites your bum when you least expect it.' She shook her head slowly and her short hair haloed around her. 'I don't think Mum ever got over Dad's death. Any more than I have. Somehow, I always thought that she was carrying a bigger burden about it than was warranted.'

'I don't think you ever do get over it,' I said. 'But what do you mean?'

'I don't know exactly,' she said. 'It's just that she was always oddly evasive about the events of that night.'

'I wouldn't have thought there was anything odd about that,' I said. 'She was intimately involved in a suicide, she felt a deep guilt about it. She saw it happen and couldn't stop it. I was there and I don't talk about it either.'

The conversation had taken a decidedly morose turn and we both looked miserably around the bright, cheerful bar, full of loud people. I knew quite a number of them and was vaguely aware of the financial or marital problems that some of them were experiencing. I read the crime and court reports in the local newspaper and recognized two guys who'd been admonished and fined by the sheriff only the week before. All of them seemed to be able to put their personal difficulties and tragedies behind them. I wondered if Carole and I could. Carole seemed to want something from me and I couldn't quite work out what it was. I didn't know if I dared hope, but it was no secret that hers was not a happy marriage.

'Talk to me about it,' she suddenly said. 'Tell me what you remember from that night.'

'You were at the hearing, Carole. You heard what the procurator fiscal had to say. That's all there was to it,' I said.

'I remember,' she said. 'But I never heard you talk about it.'

'I was a witness,' I said.

'I know, but I wasn't really listening then. I know what the procurator said but it didn't seem to have anything to do with Dad, or Mum, or me or Martin.' She paused. 'It was a funny sort of suicide. Shooting yourself in front of your wife and fourteen-year-old son is not usual. And there was no note. It was a strange, impulsive gesture for a man in his late forties.'

'He was always an impulsive man, Carole,' I said.

'I know that,' she said. 'It's just that I've always been sure that there was something not right about the verdict. Mum was always so guilty if the subject came up. And Martin is always so innocently unaware, so fresh-faced about it and just as evasive as Mum, at the same time.' She looked puzzled at the paradox.

'He had a difficult couple of years, Carole,' I said. 'The psychiatrists, psychologists and all. It wouldn't be too surprising if he had excised it from his memory.'

'I know,' she said a little more sharply than was justified. 'I may have been away but I was in touch with my family.'

'Of course,' I said. 'I didn't mean . . .'

'Dear Iain,' she said. 'I know you didn't mean anything. I'm sorry.' And again she reached across the table and placed her cool, pale hand on mine. The woman at the next table glanced our way and noted the act of intimacy with pursed lips and raised eyebrows. I smiled weakly at her and she turned away. 'Tell me what you remember,' Carole continued, still resting her hand on mine. 'About that night.'

I sighed, took a deep breath and began.

'It was Hallowe'en, and the usual carnival of midget witches, pirates, fairies, ghouls and ghosties paraded along the driveway to the house. The guisers could hardly leave out the big house. They didn't know that your mother and father were only talking to exchange barbed comments. They'd been bitching at each other all through dinner, the same as always. We'd all drunk too much, the same as always.'

'It's funny,' she said. 'I don't remember the bitching.'

'Really? As I recall, the atmosphere at dinner was only tolerable when the children interrupted to show off their costumes and to pick up their treats. Anyway, your mother told me later that your father's philandering was the cause of the trouble between them and that she had presented him with an ultimatum that morning. She said that she hadn't realized how miserably unhappy she made him, or how desperate he had made her. Anyway, that ghastly evening meal finally came to an end. You went off to your room to do something or other and I, at your urging but grateful for the chance to get away from them, volunteered to wash up. I cleared the table and left your father and mother drinking in the living room. I heard the occasional raised voice and I think they were really letting rip at each other.

'Unfortunately, Martin was still in the room. I remember him looking even more withdrawn than usual whenever I went back there to collect the dishes and things. Anyway, I was in the kitchen when I heard the shot. I ran back to the living room as fast as I could and I found your mother kneeling by your father. He was sitting up on the sofa, coughing blood, with an ugly wound in his chest which was bleeding freely. Martin was standing behind your mother in shock, I think. The gun was next to your father on the sofa. You came in almost immediately after me.'

'Yes, and I still remember the look Mum gave you – her don't-you-dare-say-a-word look – and she sent me out to phone for an ambulance and the police,' she said. 'Was that so you could get your story straight?'

'I don't know what you mean, Carole,' I said, looking guiltily at the woman at the next table who seemed fascinated by our conversation. 'We were just trying to stop the bleeding, that's all. And I really know no more than that.'

'There's something else,' she said, tightening her grip on my hand. 'There has to be.'

'Not as far as I know, Carole,' I said. 'Anyway, it was a long time ago. It mustn't dominate anyone's life any longer. It can't be allowed to be that important.'

'How important is it allowed to be?' she said, a sharp ugly edge to her voice. 'You don't think the possibility that my mother killed my father is important?'

The eyes of the woman at the next table opened even wider than before. Carole was speaking a little louder than earlier and I wondered if anyone else had heard her.

I realized that I was genuinely shocked that Carole could have contemplated such a possibility.

'I don't think that's an obvious conclusion to draw, Carole. And I'm sure that she didn't,' I said very clearly. I smiled as reassuringly as I could at the woman, who I still couldn't quite place, and she looked quickly away, obviously thinking that I was leering at her.

Carole took her hand away from mine, finished her wine and started to twirl the glass, holding the stem between her middle finger and her thumb. Her mouth was set in a thin, hard line but she seemed to have calmed down.

'I always suspected she did,' she said. 'Always.' She paused. 'That was why I went away, initially. That was probably why I married Duncan. If he hadn't been such a useless wanker I would never have come back. Do you know why we came back?'

I shook my head.

'Because he went spectacularly broke and needed a job, that's why. The family rallied round. I hated coming back, throwing myself on Mum's mercy. She loved that. You can imagine.'

'Maybe you misjudged her,' I said. 'Maybe she was just happy to have her much loved daughter back home.'

She shook her head firmly.

I wanted desperately to leave the subject but I just couldn't.

70

'Do you,' I said tentatively, 'have any idea why she did what she did?'

'Washed down an overdose of barbiturates with whisky and cut her wrists?' she said savagely.

I nodded.

'No,' she said curtly but more calmly.

I didn't know what to say and swallowed down the rest of my orange juice.

'Another drink?' I said.

'No,' she said.

'Come on, then. I'll drive you back.'

She nodded but made no attempt to rise. She sighed heavily and leaned forward, her eyes moist.

'I meant what I said earlier. About lacking the courage to face you. I should never have walked away from you, and I should definitely never have married Duncan.'

I was suddenly acutely aware of the heat from the fire, the smell of beer and fried food, the clinks of glasses and the torrent of conversation that flowed around us. I wanted to reach out and take her hand, but I knew that news of such an unseemly display of public intimacy would reach the house, and Duncan, before she did. It had already been noted that she'd held my hand but I thought we might get away with it if I didn't reciprocate.

'Nothing to say?' she said.

'Twelve years is a long time,' I said. 'You'll have to give me a day or two to compose a suitable response to that. The cat and I have reached an accommodation over the years. I wouldn't want to do anything to upset him.'

She leaned back in her chair and laughed. 'Iain, I'm not proposing a change of domestic arrangements. I'm just trying to apologize.'

'Of course,' I said. 'I know. It was just a joke. Come on, let's go before Duncan *does* think that you've left him.'

She rose elegantly from her chair, put her hand on my shoulder, bent down and brushed her lips against my cheek.

71

'Darling Iain,' she said and I felt the heat from the fire suffuse my cheeks as I blushed uncomfortably.

So much, I thought, for my earlier discretion and restraint. It would only be a matter of minutes before the entire village was convinced that something wasn't right up at the house and that I was a part of it.

I stumbled after her towards the door, imagining all the eyes in the bar on me. All, that is, except for Danny McGovern's. I saw him as I stood up, still perched on the same stool at the far end of the counter, still staring through his dark beer, like some blind, ancient, Highland seer, at something a very long way away.

In May 1911, Archie MacIntosh, an old and, by all accounts, slightly mad shepherd, followed his dogs down on to a wild, isolated beach about ten miles from where I live. He was looking for a wandering ewe and her lamb. Whether he recovered his sheep or not isn't recorded – I like to think that he did – but he did find the almost complete skeleton of a man. It was missing only one hand and a foot. After a necessarily perfunctory police investigation (the early-twentieth-century equivalent of Angus Darling puffing on his pipe and ascertaining that there were no obvious suspects in the vicinity) and an inconclusive inquest, the remains were placed in a ramshackle coffin and, in this area of seafaring folk, given a dignified, if brief, ceremony and buried where they were found. A simple cross, inscribed with the words 'God Knows', marked the spot. Over the years, a number of crosses have replaced that original but they have all carried the same simple, if ambiguous, legend. Today's is a handsome, wheel-headed affair that resembles a Celtic cross.

The beach was a favourite haunt of my father. He loved to brood about life and the sea and he took me there often when I was a boy. He would sit on a rock, smoke a cigarette and gaze out on the islands of the Inner Hebrides while I marauded along the shore, my little brother plodding morosely along behind me, skimming stones across the sometimes placid water or investigating the debris blown on to the beach by the big Atlantic storms. There were rarely more than a couple of people there and usually it was deserted apart from us. The orange-billed oyster-catchers scuttled along, rummaging in the sand, undisturbed, except when I rampaged past.

On a cold, overcast Sunday morning in November there would be no one else around and the beach would be a good place to think. I guess that Danny McGovern mentioning it had put the notion of going there into my mind. After all, I had a lot to think about. I couldn't help but believe that Carole was back in my life and that needed careful consideration. There was also the little matter of the briefcase. I had no great desire to hang around the house.

The cat had left a dead fieldmouse in the kitchen, presumably to show his gratitude that I continued to remember to feed him, and I padded out into the unkempt garden in bare feet to dispose of it.

The ragged grass was moist, yielding and cold to the touch. I shivered and looked down. My feet resembled dead things, pale and blue-veined. A chill wind carried the thin cry of a hawk and the hint of rain. I knelt and dug a shallow grave in the muddy earth with a small trowel and covered the pathetic little body.

I straightened up and turned at the sound of a powerful engine labouring up the hill and nervously watched the road, but, to my great relief, it turned out to be a big white Crawford's truck and it swept on by. Quite what it was doing that early on a Sunday morning barrelling along past my house I couldn't imagine, but that was something for Duncan and Martin to take up with the driver and nothing to do with me.

I went inside the house and stood with my back to the storage heater in the kitchen for two or three minutes, soaking up the warmth. Then I made coffee and toast, switched on the radio went into the office and called Dougie.

'Hi, big yin, how's it going?'

'Iain? Jesus Christ on a bicycle, do you know what time it is?'

'Aye,' I said, 'it's eight twenty-five. I didn't wake you, did I?'

'Of course you bloody woke me,' he said.

'I'm sorry, Dougie, but I was just wondering if you'd made contact with your policeman yet.'

'No, I haven't,' he said. 'When I do, you'll be the first to know. His girlfriend says he's off climbing somewhere. He should be back tonight.'

'OK, Dougie.'

'And, Iain, I love you dearly, but not before midday on a Sunday. I don't even love my sainted mother before midday on a Sunday.'

'I didn't even know you had a mother, Dougie, let alone loved her.'

'Ha bloody ha. I'll call the night,' he said and hung up.

I went back to the kitchen, my coffee and toast and the end of what I thought had to be the suite of *The Italian Straw Hat*. Whatever it was, the music definitely did not match my mood and I turned the radio off.

I poured the last of the coffee from the cafetière into my mug and carried it back to my office. I sat down at my desk in front of the computer, clicked on the email shortcut and went online briefly. Three messages: a very bad joke about a feminist conference forwarded by a poetry professor in Texas, a flyer from a mail-order wine merchant and an invitation from my brother to join him, his wife, three children, assorted in-laws and colleagues from his small computer company for Christmas lunch. Well, it's the thought that counts, I guess, and with Christmas only a month away and flights to New Zealand full, I knew what fervent hopes that thought came with. I toyed with the idea of ruining his next few days by accepting but I couldn't be bothered and politely declined, pleading a very busy schedule and asking for a rain check. I even remembered to ask after the kids and begged him to send some recent photographs. I deleted the bad joke without so much as chuckling over it, wondering yet again why a man I'd never met felt that he knew me well enough to send me this stuff on a regular basis. I couldn't afford any wine and so I deleted the flyer from the wine merchant without even opening it.

After that, I stopped stalling, snatched up the telephone again and did what I'd known I was going to do eventually. Luck was with me and Carole answered.

'It's Iain,' I said. 'Hi.'

'Hi yourself,' she said.

'I didn't need a couple of days, after all,' I said.

'I'm sorry, Iain, I'm not with you,' she said. 'It must be too early for me or something.'

'Last night,' I said, 'I said I'd need a couple of days to come up with a response to you saying that you made a mistake in leaving me. But I didn't need a couple of days, just a sleepless night, staring at the shadows on my ceiling.'

'I didn't mean you to have a sleepless night,' she said.

'That was because of the chat with the cat,' I said. 'And I've got a few things on my mind at the moment. Not that you weren't a big part of it.' Stop babbling, Lewis, and get to the point. 'Anyway, I was thinking of taking a walk on the beach by the Old Mariner's Grave. Fancy coming? We can talk some more.'

'Duncan seems to have possibly the worst hangover in recorded history, or just the worst one since the last one he had, and I can't see him emerging from his pit before this evening. In any case, he never gets up much before Monday on a Sunday, even when he hasn't been drinking all day Saturday. So, why not? I'll pick you up in an hour.'

'Great,' I said. 'I'll see you then.'

I shaved, showered, dressed and was waiting at my gate, armed only with a thermos flask full of fresh coffee, more than fifteen minutes before she arrived. There was still a cold wind but the cloud had lifted a little and the threat of rain had receded. A large robin hopped around inquisitively on one of the bare hawthorn trees and a plump pheasant, its neck luminescent red and green in the dull, grey morning, scurried inelegantly into the undergrowth on the other side of the road when I pretended to step towards him. I hoped that I hadn't driven him into the murderous clutches of the marauding band of robber mink who lived there.

As I waited, I reflected on what I'd told Carole about the bleak and bloody night that had changed our lives, the night her father had died. And I thought about her suspicions about her mother.

I didn't believe it and I couldn't see how Carole could even think it. I'd been to see Margaret some months after the funeral. The weather was February cruel and, unusually for this part of the west coast, which is just kissed by the Gulf Stream, there was a thick layer of snow on the driveway. I crunched my way through it and knocked on the door.

Margaret herself opened it and looked very happy to see me. She ushered me into the living room where a log fire roared in the hearth. The house was eerily empty. Carole was off on the other west coast, out in California, and Martin was staying somewhere expensive, being treated for trauma or whatever. It was understood in the village that he was a troubled youth.

Margaret sat calmly on the sofa where Peter had slowly bled to death and asked if I wanted anything to drink. She looked poised and rather beautiful but, callow as I was, I could see that she was lonely. I declined the drink but we talked for an hour or two about nothing very much. My visits became a regular thing. She would give me a little news of Carole, although I think she sensed that it was wrong to encourage any hope that Carole would return to me, and I would talk about my literary aspirations and even, embarrassingly, read her some of my early poems. She was always scrupulously polite and pleasant about them, however bad they were.

We only once talked about that dreadful night and that

was when she confided in me that she had decided a week or so before that either Peter stopped his habitual womanizing or the marriage was over, and she had told him so. In fact, she had been to see her lawyer and had started divorce proceedings. She had been hoping to shock Peter into changing his ways but he had reacted very badly when she'd told him and had started drinking. She said that what disturbed her most was that Martin had witnessed everything: the backbiting and, especially, the final row when I'd been in the kitchen. No one knew that Peter even possessed an unlicensed Colt .45 automatic, let alone kept it in the house. When he took it from its hiding place in the living room, starting flourishing it about and ranting on and on about how she'd never loved him, she'd thought he was going to kill her. She reiterated to me her belief that he had never intended to commit suicide and maintained that the gun had gone off accidentally. Peter, she said, was far too fond of the pleasures of the flesh – particularly other women's flesh, she said bitterly – to end it all. Although, she admitted, if he was going to do it, he was selfish enough to do it in a way that would produce maximum pain for his family.

I had never questioned what she told me.

As Carole's black VW Golf came up the road, I wondered if she'd ever be able to finally accept that the father she idolized had been a shallow, deceitful, drunken serial adulterer. I rather doubted it.

The twenty-minute drive to the beach passed pleasantly enough in amiable banter. I pointed out some of my favourite caravans and told her of my, entirely facetious, plan to produce a photographic essay entitled *The Caravans of Argyll*: ninety-six pages of wistful, brooding long shots of wrecked caravans wedged between huge rocks, sinking into the mud of sodden fields, perched precariously on the tops of hills, stranded like driftwood at the high-tide mark of beaches, slowly being reduced to rubble by the winter gales.

As the islands came into view, I regaled her with the tale

of the pirate Paul Jones intercepting the Tarbert packet bound for Islay and relieving the Duke of Argyll, newly returned from the Indies, of a very substantial purse.

It suddenly struck me that it was a story I must have told her before and that I was behaving like an eighteen-year-old, trying to impress a girl on a first date, and talking far too much. I shut up.

Carole didn't say very much, not even that she'd heard most of my jokes and nearly all of my stories before. At least, I reflected, the *Caravans of Argyll* idea was relatively recent. She smiled a little at my jokes, even if she had heard them before, but mainly she just concentrated on her driving, looking thoughtful, changing gears fluently and negotiating every bend with a practised ease. She'd always been a good driver.

She was wearing the same black leather jacket and faded jeans as the night before but, in a concession to the weather and terrain, she had replaced the silk blouse with a thick, hand-knitted, dark-blue sweater, and the elegant high-heeled boots with a pair of sturdy walking boots.

She pulled off the road, and the Golf bumped over the sparse grass and rutted earth that served as a parking lot for the few people who found their way to the Old Mariner's Grave, and then we stopped abruptly. Carole hauled on the handbrake and switched off the engine. In the ensuing silence, she stared intently through the windscreen at the heavy, rolling sea and the distant, rugged, cloud-shrouded peaks of Jura, much as my father had done. The small car jounced a little as great gusts of wind swaggered across the beach and buffeted it.

I felt vaguely uneasy as I pushed open the door against the wind and clambered out. The beach was deserted and there didn't appear to be any real reason for unease, but I found it difficult to shake off the feeling as I walked around the car to open the door for Carole. She buttoned her coat and slipped her arm into mine as we strolled along the sand.

We stopped by the grave, still marked by the cross and

edged by big quartz stones, long since worn smooth and round by the sea, to pay our respects and then we strolled on down towards the sea.

'What was it you wanted to say to me, Iain?' Carole asked, not looking at me, her head bowed against the wind.

'Well,' I said, 'I guess the only way to say this is to come right out with it: I have never stopped loving you.' I paused but she said nothing and still didn't look up. 'It's not that I haven't tried. For a while I was really angry, with you and with the world in general. And I was badly hurt. It was that we never talked. You just went away, you know? Just walked away. When I heard you'd married Duncan, I even thought that maybe I was over it, and then you came back and I realized that I wasn't, would never be.' I paused again and shook my head. 'Och, I'm babbling. I'm sorry.'

She stopped walking but she still looked down at the sand. The wind whipped her words away from her and I had to strain to hear.

'Don't be sorry,' she said. 'It's very sweet of you. For what it's worth, I don't think that I ever stopped loving you either. But you were so much a part of what happened that I just couldn't seem to come back to you. I know I ran away and I know that it was hard on you, but it was hard on me too. Marrying Duncan was a bad mistake. I should never have done it. But,' and now she did look up and straight at me, her clear blue eyes disarmingly frank, 'I can't just walk back into your life. That would be another mistake. I am going to leave Duncan but not to drift into another relationship. I'll need a lot of time out of this one before I'm ready for another.' She shook her head. 'It wouldn't be fair on you. Or me.'

There didn't seem to be anything further to say, so I said nothing, just nodded and gave her a weak smile.

We continued walking slowly down to the sea. This time she didn't link arms. I missed the soft weight of her brushing against me.

There were bad-tempered herring gulls stomping along

the foreshore, leaving hieroglyphs in the damp, dark sand. I turned back to face inland and then I understood what had made me uneasy when I'd first left the car.

About five years before, an old, green and white, beaten-up caravan had suddenly appeared, dumped about five hundred yards from the grave itself, out in the open, vulnerable and exposed, away from the protection of any of the large striated rock formations that framed this particular stretch of beach. It was a fine example of Argyll Caravan and had stood up well to the battering of the elements. Door panels and windowpanes had been torn out and had long since disappeared, paint had blistered and peeled, but it had still been recognizably a caravan.

And now it wasn't there. There was just a small pile of rubble to show where it had been.

'*Où sont les attraits touristiques d'antan?*' I said.

'What?' Carole said.

'The caravan that used to be here,' I said. 'It's gone.'

She looked around without interest. 'The council probably disposed of it.'

'Of all the possible explanations for its disappearance, for plausibility that idea has to rank somewhere behind the Starship *Enterprise* having beamed it aboard.'

'There it is,' she said. 'Way over there, by the rocks.'

She pointed off to the left and I squinted in that direction. She was right. There was something caravan-shaped wedged in the gap between two large rocks at the further end of the beach. It was difficult to see how it had got there other than by human intervention. It would have had to have been some wave to pick it up from above the high-water mark and carry it sideways for over a hundred yards.

'That's very odd,' I said and wandered away from her, towards it.

As I got closer I could see that it had been dragged there very recently. Two deep furrows had been gouged through the pebbles, shells, seaweed, driftwood and general debris that littered the sand, showing its path. I followed the trail.

My feeling of uneasiness – an unpleasant roiling in my stomach – returned as I approached the caravan. It looked as if this was some monumentally incompetent attempt to hide the thing. In fact, it had done the opposite and drawn attention to it.

I turned to look back at Carole. She was still strolling casually by the sea, stooping occasionally to pick up a shell or an interestingly shaped stone, a tiny, black figure against the grey infinity of the sea. I almost went back to join her but, instead, I plodded reluctantly on.

The sharp smell of stale urine caught at the back of my throat as I peered into the empty doorway, and I gagged.

He hadn't cut an attractive figure in life, with his large, lumpy head, scrawny body and thin, graceless limbs, but, in death, he was very unappealing. His pale face was coloured by heavy bruising that hadn't been there the night before and his open eyes were bulging and blood-shot. His mouth was wide open and full of some hard, whitish-grey substance. Those graceless limbs had been bent at grotesque angles by his death throes. It was clear that his hadn't been a peaceful or a natural death.

I stood staring at him for a few minutes, unable to drag myself away. The image scratched itself savagely on my memory; the impossibly twisted limbs, the unnaturally bloated mouth, the thin trickles of blood that had run from his nose and ears, black against his chalk-white skin.

I started to heave again and managed to get well away from the caravan before throwing up the coffee and toast I'd consumed earlier, in a thin, dark acidic stream. I leaned over and spat out what remained, to clear my mouth of the taste. Then I closed my eyes, tried to compose myself, thought of what had to be done and then I ran back to Carole.

I was breathing heavily by the time I arrived and she looked at me, concern all over her face.

81

'Where's the nearest phone, Carole?' I finally managed to gasp out.

'In my bag,' she said. 'In the car. Why?'

'We need the police,' I said. 'There's a body in the caravan. Danny McGovern's.'

'Danny?' she said. 'How did Danny get here?'

'How did Danny get anywhere?' I said. 'Hitched a ride, walked. I don't know. Let's get to that phone.'

'Are you sure he's dead?' she asked. 'Maybe I should take a look.'

'I'm sure he's dead,' I said, 'and he really isn't a pretty sight. I don't think you should go anywhere near him.'

'Shouldn't we just check? To make sure there's nothing we can do.'

'There's no need, Carole, honestly,' I said. 'He's dead.'

The police took nearly an hour to arrive and the ambulance sixty-five minutes. If Danny hadn't been dead when I saw him, he most certainly was by the time the authorities arrived.

I wouldn't let Carole anywhere near the caravan while we waited. We just sat in the car and drank coffee from the thermos and maintained a grim, tight-lipped silence.

I took Angus Darling and a fresh-faced young constable, whose name I didn't catch, to the caravan. The two of them peered into the gloom for a few minutes.

'Sweet Jesus,' Darling said, when he emerged. 'Do you know what that stuff in his mouth is? It looks like that polystyrene wall-cavity filler. Jesus! Someone must have pumped it into him and, as it expanded in his lungs, he suffocated. What a dreadful way to die! Ugly.'

I felt sick again. And, by the look of him, the fresh-faced young constable felt no better.

I concentrated hard on not throwing up and I started to talk in clichés.

'But who'd want to kill Danny?' I said.

'Some kids out of their brains on something?' Darling said.

'Around here?' I said.

'Iain, where have you been? We've had two stabbings this year, one of them fatal. What do you think that was all about?' Darling glared at me as if I were a recalcitrant schoolboy and he an irascible, strap-wielding Jesuit teacher.

'I don't know,' I said. 'The local newshounds aren't always quite as illuminating as they might be in their reports.'

'Drugs,' Darling said. 'Dealer falls out with customer, customer ends up dead. Customer's mate takes revenge. Dealer ends up with fifteen stitches in a stomach wound. It's small time, but it's no less vicious for that. Even around here.'

Darling went to his car and radioed in for reinforcements, then he started talking idly to the paramedics.

It was another two hours before Carole and I were allowed to go.

We were cursorily interviewed by a gum-chewing, and apparently very bored, detective inspector and his sidekick, twice. But mostly we just sat in the car, hanging around, watching as bright yellow tape was draped around the caravan, the detective inspector's sidekick smoked a lot of cigarettes, the Scene of Crime Officers donned their space-age suits and entered the scene of the crime, and a small crowd of onlookers gathered. I had no idea where they'd come from.

The detective inspector said very little but Angus Darling more than made up for his taciturn colleague by talking non-stop. I assumed he was nervous. I was just deeply and blackly depressed.

Eventually, we were allowed to leave and we drove back to my house in silence. Carole stopped the car by my gate. Neither of us moved or spoke for a few minutes, then Carole cleared her throat and put her hand on my shoulder.

'Would you like me to come in and stay with you for a while?' she asked.

'What about Duncan?' I said.

She shrugged. 'What about Duncan?'

'Nothing,' I said, thinking of Colm Kelly and the inventive things he might do to me. 'And, yes, I'd love you to come in.'

I climbed awkwardly out of the car and opened the gate. Carole drove through and waited for me to get back in before driving down to the house.

She stopped the car behind my Rover and switched off the engine. Then she released her seat belt, turned towards me, put her arms around my neck and laid her head on my shoulder.

'Poor Danny,' she said and started to cry.

Chapter Four

I slumped disconsolately in my battered old green armchair, half-listening to the muted sounds that Carole was making, clattering and banging around in the kitchen as she prepared cheese toasties and tea, which was all that my not very extensive larder and fridge would run to in the way of a very late lunch.

Not that either of us admitted to being hungry, but breakfast was a long time ago and eating seemed like a sensible, normal thing to do. And Carole needed to occupy herself with something, needed to be busy.

I just wanted to slump and brood.

Danny's death had shocked, disturbed and depressed us both. At least Carole hadn't seen that contorted body, the horribly distorted face.

I'd only ever seen four dead people in my life, and half of those had died violently, which seemed like an implausibly high percentage. After all, I was a civilian living in a time of relative peace and I didn't work in the emergency services, and I did try to keep myself to myself. On the other hand, I was very conscious that I was lucky to have reached what was once, and not so very long ago, considered to be the midpoint of my life and to have only encountered death at first hand four times.

By the time he was my age, my grandfather had seen maybe a dozen men drown, one of them a brother, and had fought in the North Africa campaign. He himself had died suddenly but relatively quietly in the pub when a massive stroke laid him low. The legend was that he'd got up off the floor to finish his pint before agreeing to dance away with the Grim Reaper. I was seventeen at the time and his peaceful body, lying in the crimson-lined coffin, was the first that I encountered.

My father had been sent to Malaya during the 'Emergency' when he was called up for National Service. Like so many gentle men of his and earlier generations who had lived through and seen terrible things, he never spoke of his time there. But I'd made a point when I was a boy of reading about the events and I had some idea of what he'd witnessed.

I thought of his thin, ravaged body after two years spent fighting lung cancer. I remembered the haunted, hunted, uncomprehending look in his eyes, which were huge in his emaciated face, the day before he died. I'd just received copies of my second volume of verse and I'd taken one with me to the hospice to show him the dedication: 'To John William Lewis, the better man'.

It had been Margaret who had gently pointed out to me that making my mother the dedicatee of my first book might not have been the most sensitive thing I'd ever done, and my brother had confirmed that my father had been very hurt. I'd hoped, I think, when I'd written 'To my mother, Eileen Lewis, wherever she may be' that, somehow, she'd see it and make contact. She hadn't.

I'd tried to make it up to my father with that second dedication but, by the time copies were available, he'd long since given up speaking, aware that the secondary tumour pressing on the speech centre in his brain was turning his thoughts to gibberish, and the desperate look in his eyes, so large in that thin, sunken face, whenever he was addressed, suggested that he was hearing only gibberish as well. So, he'd never known that I was sorry to have hurt him. Or that I really meant that dedication.

His death may have been natural, but it was far from peaceful.

I may be wrong, and I certainly don't imagine that either my father or my grandfather ever became inured to the sight and experience, but I can't help thinking that I am less equipped to cope with death than they were. Danny's was certainly giving me trouble.

I didn't buy Angus Darling's speculations about Danny's murder. His drug-fuelled gang warfare sounded to me more like an old grudge, in the long, allegedly honourable, and decidedly bloody, Highland tradition of interfamily squabbles and revenge for assumed slights. The rich and fertile glens of Scottish history would be barren without them.

The families involved in Darling's brutal and tragic crimes had a long history of feuding and fights. The boy who'd died and the lad who'd been stabbed later may well, for all I knew, both have been users but if drugs were involved I suspected that they were the occasion rather than the reason for the stabbings.

Whenever there's a break-in or a fight, or some criminal damage, the old wifeys always put it down to drugs. And sometimes, of course, they're right – although the drugs aren't usually heavy duty. But Angus Darling had fallen into the same trap as the old wifeys and had either failed to recognize, or didn't give enough weight to, the fact that bad blood had existed between the families for at least two generations to my certain knowledge.

Anyway, I didn't see local lads killing Danny, and certainly not in such a calculated and cruel way. Everyone knew him and everyone, even the would-be tearaways, looked out for him. I guess that Darling's point was that whoever had done it was so strung out that they would have butchered their own granny if she'd happened along at the wrong moment. But pumping cavity-wall filler into Granny's lungs seemed to me a wee bit exotic and imaginative for the rural west coast and, as far as I was aware, Quentin Tarantino hadn't yet shown the way. Not enough blood, I suppose.

It was possible that there were some petty thieves on whizz up from Glasgow in November. But they'd have to be very optimistic, or very stupid even for Neds. Tourists left their cars at ferry terminuses unprotected and full of cameras, mobile phones, expensive camping equipment and other juicy and irresistible consumer durables in the summer, not when the gales blew up the lochs and it was dark by four o'clock in the afternoon.

There was something missing from Darling's easy judgement, which had rolled off his tongue with the glib facility of long-held prejudice. Unfortunately, I had more than an inkling of just what that was. My own involvement did not make me feel very comfortable; in fact, I was sick to my stomach. I wasn't sure just how the briefcase in my septic tank featured, but I knew intuitively that it did. Which meant that the shock and anger I felt at Danny's death was seasoned by more than a pinch of guilt. I'd told the phlegmatic detective what Danny had said to me in the bar, but I hadn't told him about the briefcase and my own troubles – not with Angus Darling within hailing distance. And I couldn't help but wonder if Danny would still be alive had I told the police about the briefcase and the break-in on Friday evening, as soon as it had happened.

I tried to dismiss the thought, but it wasn't easy and I was still brooding on it when Carole called to me from the kitchen. I reluctantly levered myself out of the chair and stumbled off to join her.

The kitchen table was set for two and Carole was already sitting down. She gave me a sad little smile and indicated the chair opposite her. I tried to smile back and lowered myself into it awkwardly. It suddenly occurred to me that I was turning into something of a recluse. I hadn't sat down with someone at that table in more than a month, and that had only been to offer a cup of tea to the engineer replacing the element in my oven. Worse, I hadn't shared a bed with anyone in more than three months.

I sipped my tea and cut queasily into the sandwich, watching cheese flow like anaemic molten lava on to my plate. Somehow, Carole homed in unerringly on one aspect of my thoughts.

'How come you never married, Iain?' she asked.

'I think you know the answer to that,' I said morosely.

'Not really,' she said, 'I don't buy the you-never-got-over-me line.'

I shrugged extravagantly, trying to assume a flippancy I didn't feel.

'No, it wasn't that,' I said. 'I don't really know. The question just never arose.' I pushed the uneaten sandwich, still oozing pallid cheese, away from me. 'Just never met the right girl, I guess. But hope springs eternal. I haven't given up yet, not entirely.'

'None of those doe-eyed bohemian poetry groupies, smelling of patchouli oil and joss sticks, dressed by Monsoon, were up for it?' she said, smiling mischievously and nibbling at a corner of her sandwich.

'Well, maybe I did meet one or two,' I said.

'So? What happened?'

'Nothing much. I just wasn't right for them, I suppose.' This wasn't a conversation I wanted to have.

'I don't believe that,' she said. 'I bet you've broken a few hearts.'

I shook my head and took refuge in drinking tea.

'Come on, Iain,' she said. 'You're a very attractive man. And a famous poet.'

'Not at all famous,' I said, shaking my head again, more vigorously this time. 'And my matinée idol days are way in the past. Nor am I rich, and I know that I'm more than a wee bit dull.' I paused and stared down into my cup. 'And I no longer write poetry.'

She looked up.

'You've given it up?' she said.

'More like it's given me up,' I said.

'That's a shame,' she said. 'I really enjoyed both books. None of the poems you showed me when we were going out prepared me for the emotional power of them. To be honest, I thought you were a bit of a poseur in the old days.'

I let her comments about my juvenilia pass without comment. I agreed with her about them, and me. The truth was I *had* been a poseur when I was younger – still was, come to that.

'I didn't know that you'd ever read the books,' I said.

'Of course I did,' she said. 'How could you possibly think that I wouldn't?'

I shrugged. 'You never sent me any fan mail.'

'No, I didn't. I thought about it and decided it was best not to. Let sleeping dogs lie and all that.' She looked thoughtful before continuing. 'No, that isn't true. I did think about it but I havered. I wish now that I hadn't.' She paused and looked down at the remnants of the sandwich on her plate. 'Some of the poems were about me, weren't they?'

Only most of them, I thought.

'Yeah, I guess they were,' I said.

'I thought so,' she said. 'I was touched. They were . . . charming.'

'Yeah, that's probably the word,' I said, feeling decidedly miffed that that was how she saw them.

'And profoundly sad.'

'I think I prefer "poignant" there,' I said, a little testily.

She missed, or chose to ignore, any edge in my words and followed her own line of thought. 'They all seemed to me to be about loss.'

'Well, that's one way of looking at them,' I said.

I've always hated readings and workshops because, inevitably, they lead to discussions about meaning and recurrent themes, and people seek explanations. I'm not very comfortable with that. I feel like I'm appearing under false pretences. I've said what I want to say in the way that I want to say it in the poem. I really have no more to add. I don't mind talking about other people's work – well, perhaps I draw the line at Poetry in Motion's, working on the premise that if you can't say something nice, it's better to keep your mouth shut – but I have nothing to say about my own. I must be a great disappointment at such gatherings, listening and nodding as politely as I am able.

90

'How come you stopped writing?' she said. 'If you really have.'

'I guess I just stopped losing things,' I said. The implication, even if I knew it to be near the mark, that I hadn't stopped posing rankled more than a little.

'No, really,' she said, again ignoring any acerbity in my answer, and certainly refusing to be put off by my obvious reluctance to discuss the matter.

I sighed.

'The images still come from time to time. Not as often and, somehow, they don't seem as original. But they do come.' I paused. 'But I find it very hard to put them into the right words. I never found it easy to balance a line of verse or to sustain and explore a thought but I used to be able, eventually, to resolve the problems, after a fashion. Now, I find it impossible. I guess I've just lost it. *C'est assez simple.*'

She nodded and picked up the last fragment of her sandwich and bit into it. A string of cheese squelched out of one corner and her tongue flicked out, delicate and serpentine, to catch it.

'Where did you get this horrible cheese?' she said.

'Service station,' I said. 'It was all they had.'

'You should go to the delicatessen counter in the supermarket. Give them some business. Convince them that there are customers for their more exotic wares. Even way out here in the sticks. You know the old line – use it or lose it.'

'Use it and still lose it, more like,' I said, peering at my own untouched sandwich. 'But you're right. I really should shop with more discrimination. Would you like some more tea?'

She nodded and I left the table to busy myself with the kettle and the pot.

We took our cups into the living room and I put Ravel's String Quartet on the CD player and sat back in my old armchair to listen.

91

Carole perched on the arm of the chair and leaned against me.

It was well after three and the light was fading rapidly. In the increasing gloom, the green lights on the display of the CD player flashed as brilliantly as the music. I didn't want to move to turn on a lamp and spoil the moment.

An image of Danny McGovern's scrawny body, a whitish blue under harsh, clinical lighting, waiting for the pathologist's scalpel and cleaver, lurked menacingly in the back of my mind. But I was feeling the warmth and soft weight of Carole's breast pressing against my shoulder, and the light touch of her arm draped across my back.

Now get you to my lady's chamber, and tell her, let her paint an inch thick, to this favour must she come; make her laugh at that.

I turned slightly to look up at her and, as I did so, she lowered her face towards mine and our lips met gently, tentatively. Neither of us pulled away.

Carole slid from the arm of the chair, her lips never leaving mine, and nestled firmly against me.

The kiss became increasingly urgent and her tongue forced its way between my lips and into my mouth. Her hand was on my chest, my hand on her breast, our breathing became a little ragged and our hearts started beating faster.

The dramatic, elegant pizzicato of Ravel's second movement faded slowly into the background.

When the phone rang, Carole was dozing on her back, snoring lightly, occasionally twitching and sighing. I was looking at her naked body in the golden light of the bedside lamp. Her breasts were fuller, heavier, than I remembered and her dark-blond pubic hair was more luxuriant but, apart from that, her thirty-three-year-old body wasn't all that different from her twenty-one-year-old body. The legs were still pale, slim and muscular and the belly still firm.

I wondered what she must make of me: twelve years older, maybe ten pounds heavier and carrying most of that around the middle, hair thicker on the body and thinner on the top of the head.

The heavy musk of sex and sweat was all around me, almost overpowering.

Our lovemaking had been less joyous, more fierce, than I recalled it. There had even been just a hint of desperation as we clung to each other fiercely. But perhaps that had just been us grasping at the opportunity to share some raw emotion other than inchoate grief, in my case tinged with a little guilt and fear, to put Danny's death aside, however briefly. But it had certainly been vigorous and ardent.

I gently brushed Carole's hair with my fingertips and wondered if, this time, she'd stay, not quite knowing whether I wanted her to or not. A sense of loss that hovered on the wrong side of self-pity fluttered inside me. I lay back down and thought of Carole, eyes half-closed, moving rhythmically above me, tossing her head and muttering to herself.

She stirred at the sound of the phone and rolled over.

'You going to answer that?' she said, squinting into the light.

'I guess so,' I said but lingered a while to gaze at her before heaving myself up and padding off to take the call.

I was hoping that it was Dougie with some news to relay about his policeman friend. But it wasn't.

'What have you done with my wife?' Duncan said before I had a chance to announce myself. 'She left me a note saying she was out walking with you. So, where is she now?' He sounded peevish and tired. 'It's dark, Iain. It's been dark for quite some time.' He forced a humourless laugh. 'I hope you haven't been indulging in the old horizontal jogging.'

Feeling very cool and remarkably guiltless, I completely ignored his last remark.

'She's here, Duncan,' I said. 'We came back to grab a bite to eat. Do you want a word with her?'

He grunted something unintelligible which I took to be a 'yes' and, at that moment, Carole came into my study, still naked. She pointed at the phone and then at herself. I nodded and handed the receiver to her.

'Duncan, has Iain told you the dreadful news? About Danny. Danny McGovern. We found his body. At the beach near Iain's, where the Old Mariner is buried. Danny's been murdered. The police kept us for ages and then we came back here . . . Yes, it was awful . . . Sorry, we just forgot about the time, you know how it is.' She smiled at me and raised her eyebrows. 'No, don't worry, I'm fine and I'm on my way now. See you soon.'

She replaced the receiver on the cradle, put her arms around my neck and kissed me. Then she pulled back.

'One more for the road?' she said with a mischievous smile and reached down, cupped my testicles and gently squeezed. 'No? Oh, well, some other time perhaps . . .'

She went into the living room and I followed. She wandered around, gathering her clothes together from the various corners of the room where they had been cast in the early throes of passion.

'I'm missing a sock,' she said as the phone rang again.

I raced off to the study.

'Dougie?' I said as I picked up.

'Would that be Bernard?' someone with a strong Irish accent said.

'No,' I said, 'sorry there's no one by the name of Bernard here.'

'Oh, I'm sorry to have disturbed you,' he said.

'No problem,' I said and the phone went dead.

Carole was still naked when I rejoined her in the living room but she was brandishing a sock in each hand.

'Found it,' she said. 'Who was that?'

'Wrong number,' I said and then something clicked. It could just be coincidence that the caller had an Irish accent, but suddenly I didn't think so.

Carole looked across at me and smiled.

'Don't you want a shower?' I said. 'You know to . . .'

'What could be more suspicious than coming back from a hearty walk in the country smelling of soap and shampoo?' she said. 'I'll have one when I get in. Far less suspicious.'

'Oh,' I said lamely, thinking that she must have done this sort of thing before.

She bustled about, pulling on pants, fastening her bra, talking over her shoulder.

'I promised myself I wasn't going to do that with you, you know,' she said. 'It isn't that I don't want to and it isn't that it wasn't most enjoyable. It was. And just what I needed. But, like I told you before, I'm really not looking for another relationship at the moment. One is more than enough.'

'I was in a restaurant just outside Dublin once,' I said. 'Before we sat down, the owner said that, although he could serve wine, he didn't have a liquor licence so gins and tonic were off the menu. Well, at the end of the meal, after the usual eye-opening Dublin floorshow – in this case a married couple slugging it out over the soup – the owner came up again and asked if we'd like anything else. I was genuinely puzzled and muttered something about thinking that he'd said he didn't have a liquor licence. "Sure," he said, flourishing a bottle, "and the Hennessy's isn't liquor."'

She laughed.

'Meaning?' she said.

'Sure,' I said in a cod Irish accent, 'and a little sex on a Sunday afternoon doesn't count as a relationship.'

'No,' she said thoughtfully, 'I suppose that's true. But it could turn into a bad habit, and a bad habit can all too easily turn into a bad relationship.'

I shrugged. 'Maybe this time we should allow things to run their natural course.'

'Maybe we should,' she said as she finished tying her bootlaces. 'Call me.'

I nodded.

I walked her to the back door and, in the storm porch,

we kissed again. It was a long, yearning kiss, full of promise. Then she was gone.

I watched the red glow of the rear lights of her car moving away from me, bouncing up the uneven drive until I could see them no more, and listened as she accelerated away along the road.

My father's melancholy, smoke-roughened voice resonated in my head. 'You can't go back, Iain. Even if you get the chance, you probably shouldn't.'

But it was cold standing naked in the storm porch and, anyway, I had no time to brood. If I was right about the last phone call, there were things to be done.

I went back into the warmth of my study, picked up the phone and thumped Dougie's number in. The BT answer service kicked in after a few rings.

'Big yin, where are you? Where's the cavalry when you need it? Things have been happening here. Danny McGovern's been murdered. And I had a strange call. It sounded like someone might be checking to see if I was in. I think I'm not going to be, just in case I get a visit. Can you get your man in touch soon, before it's too late? I've got a very bad feeling about all this.'

I hung up and wondered if I had time for a shower but decided against it. Then I briefly wondered if I was overreacting to a wrong number, thought of Danny McGovern's body and decided that, even if I was, it was understandable and that I'd rather be guilty of that and behaving a little foolishly than wait around hoping that I was wrong.

I dressed very quickly, then I threw a few essentials into a rucksack – a sleeping bag, warm socks, binoculars, a torch, compass, spare shirt and trews. I rinsed out the thermos flask and filled it with boiling water and four spoonfuls of instant coffee, put that in the rucksack together with two wrinkled apples that I found loitering in the fruit bowl and a packet of biscuits, struggled into my heaviest boots and fleece-lined anorak, left some food down for the cat and headed for the hills. Well, hill.

About three-quarters of a mile behind my house, across rough, broom-strewn and boggy sheep pasture, is a green and craggy protuberance that rises about five hundred feet above the land below. There are a couple of smaller grass-covered rocks around it but it is something of a geological oddity and it rises dramatically out of flat meadow. The climb is a stiff one but it's well worth it. The view on a fine day over the brilliant blue of the loch towards the distant islands of the Inner Hebrides, often wreathed in mist or cloud, is enchanting, and commanding.

Which is why, in about AD 600, the local warlord built a dun there. It's not really a castle, more a fortified farm, somewhere all the locals and their animals could gather when invaders were spotted coming up the loch.

It's a ruin now, just a jumble of stones, but enough of it remains to show just what an effort went into building it and how defensible it had been. It must have been quite impressive. Those dry-stane walls still standing are about six feet thick and there's a 'secret' entrance, a low, narrow tunnel running through one of the walls, that's well hidden by bracken and other dense undergrowth.

The place is traditionally known as the hill of the fair (though white is a plausible translation) boar, probably after the banner of the tribe that once lived there, and there are, of course, many stories and legends surrounding it, involving giant stags, ferocious wolves, faithful hounds, handsome and headstrong Irish heroes, beautiful princesses and ruthless and vengeful kings. The truth is probably more prosaic, a quiet farming community taking sensible precautions against the brutal seafaring invaders from Scandinavia who marauded up and down the coast.

A neolithic burial chamber nearby is known locally as the giant's grave and a smaller, neighbouring bronze age grave marked with a curious pyramidical stone is, somewhat anachronistically, said to be where the giant's dog is interred. The rich, fertile land of the peninsula has always, it seems, been heavily populated.

Now the hill is inhabited only by myth, the occasional rabbit, the unusually well-informed tourist, a lone piper called Hamish, who goes there once a week in the summer to practise, and me. Whenever I feel the need to work on my stamina and don't fancy slogging away on road work, I run up to the top of the dun. It's exhilarating exercise over difficult terrain and I usually manage it six or seven times a month, when it's not too wet.

It was a clear, cold night and the stars were already splashed extravagantly across the dark sky. A sliver of pale moon, as thin as a blade, hung low in front of me as I nervously trudged across the muddy field, torch illuminating the few yards directly in front of my feet, breath drifting away in delicate, white wisps.

The air was damp and still, the ground soft and yielding. I looked up at the stars, their light blurred by the moisture in the atmosphere, and felt myself disappear into the night. It was probably only the warm afterglow of strenuous and satisfying sex, but I felt exhilarated and vital for a brief moment. It was good to be doing something physical and challenging, rather than waiting around for something to happen. I almost, although not completely, forgot why I was doing it.

Walking through the darkness was like pitting myself against another element, a resistant, physical barrier that had to be fought through. I imagined teeth-shattering and flesh-splitting collisions lurking just ahead, and elaborate, quasi-sentient root networks that would snake out to ensnare a foot. I avoided hitting major obstacles, like trees, with my head, only because there aren't any, but I did stumble and trip a lot.

After the initial exuberance of hitting the night air, I soon settled into a steady trudge, grateful for the extra physical effort required just to walk. Concentrating on avoiding spraining or breaking an ankle meant that I worried less about what I was leaving behind. It also meant that I had no time to think about Carole – although vivid images of her naked body flashed continually, achingly clearly, across my mind.

This wasn't the first time I'd spent a night on the hill, though it was the first time that I'd decided to do so. I'd slept there once before when I was a boy of twelve but then it just happened. It was only a matter of days after my mother had left us and I was a confused, angry and distraught lad.

My father, unsurprisingly, had been distracted and distant, nursing his own wounds and desperately making arrangements to cope with two boys on his own. He was so preoccupied with practical considerations and his own suddenly bleak and circumscribed future that he couldn't find the time or the right words to reassure my brother and me. Then, of course, I didn't see it that way: he didn't care about us or that Mum had gone.

It was only later that I learned just how deeply he'd been affected. For a few months he'd intermittently kept a journal, recording his thoughts and feelings, documenting his love and loss in a raw, emotional and unpolished prose of surprising power. It was one of the very few personal effects I found after he died.

In all it amounted to less than twenty pages in an exercise book; just some fragments really, a few observations on his personal circumstances, his emotional state and that of his sons. All of the entries were carefully dated and neatly written with very few amendments and none of them was longer than a few paragraphs and the shortest was an uncompleted sentence. But they were all deeply affecting.

He wrote of his feelings of desolation and incomprehension, and he wrote that he couldn't bring himself to talk to us, the boys, about it because of his fear of breaking down completely in front of us and because he didn't know how to explain it to us, anyway. He didn't understand it himself. She had just gone, with no explanation and no warning, although he castigated himself for being a fool for not seeing it coming, though he never explained why. He was acutely aware of my and Rory's fragility and the need to keep some stability in our lives and he didn't dare risk showing weakness. And so he never spoke of her.

To be fair to Dad, Rory, my brother, did apparently take the disappearance in his stride, shrugging it off in what I saw as his usual, bovine fashion. It wasn't true. He simply retreated into his shell. His schoolwork suffered for years. Dad probably expected me to respond in much the same way. Rory and I looked a lot alike, and Dad had never differentiated between us much. Or he didn't seem to, and he certainly never played favourites. His journal, however, suggested otherwise and showed that he worried deeply about us both, recognizing all too clearly my rash and impulsive nature and Rory's deep need for security.

Rory wept silently when, after the funeral, I showed him what Dad had written, and we held each other in an awkward display of fraternal affection for the one and only time.

It wasn't that we didn't get on – we rubbed along easily enough – it was just that we were never close, never shared enthusiasms or childhood conspiracies. I know now that, as the elder, it was up to me to show the way but I never made an effort to understand him or interest myself in him and he simply reciprocated. I was just his big brother, prickly, stand-offish, difficult, academically successful and sporty: all the things that he wasn't and never aspired to be. I'm sorry for it all now and often wonder what he might have achieved if I hadn't been around, or if I'd ever encouraged him in anything. He says he's happy in New Zealand, that he has a nice life, that he loves his wife and adores his three young kids, and enjoys running his little software-troubleshooting company.

Sometimes he surprises me by some remark about Dad, which shows that he was closer to him than I was, knew more about him. And I can't help it: I feel a deep resentment of my little brother, and bitter regret at the callow, shallow, self-obsessed and thoughtless adolescent and young man that I'd been.

As I plunged into the darkness, my torch only mitigating it slightly, fearing that at any step I might fall off the edge of the planet, I thought of that strange night twenty-three years before.

I spent a cold, wet and lonely fourteen hours on the dun and, because it was summer, I'd been bitten to distraction by the midges. I arrived back in the morning, bone weary, chilled and scratching incessantly at dozens of inflamed lumps on my arms and neck.

But I'd seen things on the hill, strange, fleeting, elusive images. I guess I was dozing, but dark shapes had flitted about all night and I'd heard a continual susurrus of whispering voices. I thought that the people of the hill were talking to me.

It was a significant experience for me, a kind of epiphany: frustrating, ungraspable, disquieting but intellectually engaging.

My father said nothing about my disappearance but I heard him phone the police to say that I'd reappeared and I seemed all right, and there was nothing to worry about. Then he turned a tired gaze on me that told me that the last thing he needed just then was a troubled son but that he'd learn to live with it. He cooked me bacon and eggs and told Rory to leave me alone while I ate. Then he sat and watched me as I wolfed down the food, sipping a cup of tea and smoking a cigarette. When I'd finished, he suggested that I go to bed for the morning and I did.

I can't explain why, but when I got up I knew that I could face life without Mum and, later that afternoon, I wrote my first poem.

It is important to me now that I shared that at least with my father. At a time of deep personal turmoil, we both found a refuge in the power of words.

The strange whispering I'd heard on the hill had probably only been the sound of running water, and the dark shapes flitting about were almost certainly bats, owls and other night birds. But the dun had seemed to me a frightening, mystical, magical place. It still does.

After about eight minutes of careful walking, I was halfway to the path that leads to the top of the hill and I heard the unmistakable sound of a car arriving at my house.

I switched off the tell-tale torch and immediately turned to look back.

Headlights on full beam were cutting a broad tunnel of light through the night, flicking up and down as the car bounced across ruts and through puddles. I was way off to the right and the house was between me and the car, so there was no chance of them catching me in the beam.

I hoped that they'd hit a deep hole at speed and burst their exhaust or rupture the oil sump. But the gratifying scrape of tearing metal didn't screech through the nighttime air.

The driver killed the engine but not the lights and the silence was palpable. I could hear my heart beating in my chest and the air whistling in my lungs, then the doors of the car slammed almost simultaneously, the muffled sound carrying through the still night. I heard the faint thump of a fist on my storm door and the low bass rumble of a scrappy conversation. I remained where I was, waiting for them either to go into the house or to leave. I didn't want to risk using the torch until there was little or no chance of them spotting me. The thought that Colm Kelly had come for his property was unavoidable. And, I was forced to admit, scary.

I hadn't locked any doors and so the way was open to them to enter whenever they wanted. But, apparently, it didn't occur to them to check.

One of them hit the door again and called my name loudly enough for me to hear it clearly, the other one stepped out on to the driveway. I even heard the peculiar squelchy crunch of his steps on the muddy gravel as he walked around the side of the house.

I stood completely still. I was well over seven hundred yards away and I knew that they couldn't see me in the dark. I could only see the one who had walked to my side of the house as a small and shapeless shadow, bathed in the faint, yellow glow that shone through my kitchen window. I'd forgotten to turn off all the lights as well.

For all that I was invisible to them, I was as afraid of discovery as I'd been as a small child, blankets pulled over my head, when I'd heard the creaking boards outside my bedroom door that announced the approach of the bogey man. My breath came in harsh, shallow gulps, my heart was beating hard and fast, and cold sweat broke out and prickled my scalp.

I suddenly realized that I was having a mild panic attack, the sort that I usually associated with confinement in an enclosed space, like an unbearably crowded London tube train stalled in a tunnel. It was a strange and terrifying feeling. I knew that I was losing control, certain that soon I wasn't going to be able to breathe at all. And I didn't know why.

The darkness closed in on me, pressed against my face, blocking my mouth and nose, suffocating me. I was struggling desperately for air. Danny McGovern's tortured, straining face, screaming soundlessly in death, flashed across my mind.

The image sobered me: Danny, after all, had been helpless. I was far from that. I consciously tried to relax, but that awful velvet darkness still crowded in on me.

I hunkered down, lowered my head, closed my eyes and concentrated on breathing deeply for a few moments. My racing heart gradually slowed and my breathing returned to something approaching normal.

I opened my eyes and looked back at my house.

It was visible in that deep, tangible, suffocating darkness because of the little light that spilled out from a couple of windows. The car headlights had been turned off. The house existed only as three small points of light. Without them, there would have been no indication that thick, solid stone walls that had been standing for a hundred and ninety years or so rose there. The blackness made everything but itself insubstantial. I looked up at the vast sky and the cold, dead, useless light of the Milky Way. The massive indifference of the universe was too immense to contemplate.

There was no sign of either of the intruders and I couldn't hear them. But I hadn't heard them drive away and so I knew they were inside the house, waiting for me, the lid already removed from a large tub of polystyrene cavity-wall filler.

I turned and trudged towards the hill. After stumbling and stuttering along for maybe forty or fifty yards, tripping over branches, stones, ruts, even clumps of grass, and stepping in piles of sheep droppings the size of small cairns, I felt I had to use the torch. I tried to shield the light from the house by holding the rucksack directly behind it, but I still felt as visible as the George Square Christmas illuminations. If one of them glanced casually out of the kitchen window they'd only see a weak point of light bobbing about on the hillside but I couldn't help worrying that, if luck wasn't with me, it was highly likely that they'd jump to the right conclusion.

I was a little out of breath but, as far as I could tell, undetected and unpursued, by the time I plodded up the final, almost perpendicular, sixty-yard stretch to the very top of the hill and the fort. I clambered across the thick wall and crouched down on the wet grass behind it, relieved and, relatively, safe.

After a few minutes, I turned and peered over the wall. I could still see the light leaking from the house but there was no indication that anyone was following me. The only sounds came from an apparently asthmatic and insomniac sheep rummaging around close by. I glanced down at the illuminated face of my watch. It was only six forty-five. I realized that I was in for another long night on the hill.

The 'secret' entrance smelled of decaying vegetation, warm earth and generations of animal droppings. Oddly, as I squeezed into it, there was no recurrence of my earlier panic nor any hint that claustrophobia would set in. I unrolled my sleeping bag, took off my boots and snuggled into it. I drank a little of the bitter instant coffee, ate a couple of the biscuits and wondered what to do.

I wished that my relations with the local police were better but I really didn't like or trust Darling, and he certainly didn't like me. Anyway, what could he possibly have done? I wasn't Salman Rushdie. I hardly warranted twenty-four-hour protection because someone had dialled a wrong number. 'Ah, but there is the little matter of the money, drugs and gun hidden in my septic tank, Sergeant!'

About the only conclusion I came to was that I was pinning a great deal on Dougie and the understanding nature of his tame but elusive policeman. I felt useless, anxious, restless. I wanted to hit something.

I slept fitfully through the night, waking often, my head full of vivid, fractured dreams. Carole, naked, in a huge, empty pub, coyly holding out a black briefcase to me; Dougie and Darling, sweat popping out on their grimacing faces, Indian arm wrestling in front of a baying, snarling crowd; me, lying helpless on a hospital trolley in a morgue, trying unsuccessfully to explain to the attendant, who was something of an obdurate jobsworth, that I wasn't really dead; Margaret Crawford, dressed in black, her face veiled, standing apart from the mourners, at her own funeral. It wasn't a fun night.

At four fifteen, I wriggled out of the sweaty, clinging embrace of the sleeping bag, found my boots and anorak and went out to empty my bladder in the darkness. A

105

gentle, rinsing rain brushed against my face, and I shivered in the sudden, sharp cold as the thin stream of urine arced and steamed towards the ground.

There were still two lights issuing from my house and I wondered what the two waiting men were doing. There was a cold anger building in me at the thought of them sitting in my chairs, drinking my whisky, pissing in my toilet and rummaging through my things. They wouldn't find any dirty magazines hidden in any closets and there wasn't any pornography on my computer, though I supposed that they could find it easily enough if they wanted to.

Then it suddenly occurred to me that I was guilty of typecasting and the men could have been opera buffs who had spent the night listening to Callas singing Tosca. Or they could have been avid consumers of modern poetry and had passed the time reading Seamus Heaney's translation of *Beowulf* or poems by Paul Muldoon out loud to each other. Opera-loving, poetry-reading villains appealed to me. Maybe there was a comedy drama in the idea.

I yawned and went back to my tunnel. The light from the torch was getting weaker so I turned it off and sat in complete darkness. I finished the biscuits and the coffee, which was still just about warm, and thought about Samuel Beckett's Murphy and his well-balanced lunch – tuppence for a cup of tea (which he, by a combination of histrionics and ingratiation, contrived to turn into nearly two cups) and tuppence for a packet of assorted biscuits. For some reason the main theme from Coltrane's 'Blue Train' resounded in my head. Outside, the rain brushed and rustled against the grass and the dead bracken, and the cool breeze whispered eerily through the gaps in the stone walls.

I dozed off again and the legends of the hill murmured to me. A huge, barefoot Irish warrior paced out the length of a dead boar, scratching his foot against the sharp spines that bristled at the creature's back. The cuckolded husband of the hero's lover coldly watched as the hero

106

died in agony from the poison that had been painted on the boar's spines.

When I woke, I munched both of the disappointing apples, tossed the cores out to biodegrade and stuffed the sleeping bag into my rucksack.

It would start to get light in another two hours or so and I could use the remaining hours of darkness to my advantage. I wasn't sure how yet but there had to be a way. After all, I knew the layout of the house and garden. And I knew where there was a gun. Not that I had a clue how to use it.

I was fed up with not doing anything and I was in a foul mood. I was tired and my head was aching. I resented being forced to spend a night on the hill. I resented the presence of unwelcome strangers in my house. I resented not being able to jump into a hot shower. And I particularly resented not even having any lukewarm instant coffee to drink for breakfast. The cold anger inside me wasn't about to dissipate.

I slumped down to wait until an hour or so before dawn and brooded on Carole and what had happened only, I suddenly realized, fourteen hours before.

It didn't seem possible that she'd come back into my life. It also seemed likely, given what she'd said, that she hadn't. I wasn't even sure it was what I wanted. I'd spent so long adjusting to life without her, defining myself in terms of her absence, mining a rich vein of self-absorption, that I was hesitant about considering any alternative. I thought back to the savage two-year bender that had followed the realization that I'd lost her and winced at the hazy memory of the mess I'd been. I promised myself that I wouldn't go through that again, whatever happened. But I'd probably seek out Dougie for a night or two of beer and curry in the big bad city if things didn't work out.

I thought of the athleticism of the sex the previous afternoon, the infinite promise of her maturing body, and a big, shit-eating, self-satisfied grin spread across my face.

But not even that memory could take the edge off the

quiet fury that I felt against the two men in my house. Kelly was big, confident and, I had no doubt, nasty but it was becoming apparent I'd have to face him sooner or later. Now seemed as good a time as any. My grim mood lightened briefly with the slow approach of what promised to be a bleak, grey dawn but my anger was still a palpable thing, straining inside me, waiting to be unleashed.

I ducked out of the fetid little tunnel into the cold, moist morning, hoisted the rucksack on to my back, clambered over the wet wall and started purposefully down the hill in the semi-darkness.

Chapter Five

My paternal grandfather had been a notoriously angry and pugnacious man, especially when he'd been drinking, which was much of the time. And he had a longish police record for affray, breach of the peace, resisting arrest and even assault, which reflected his nature. He was a compact and dapper little man, a strutting and swaggering bantam cock, but years of labouring on the boats, lugging boxes of fish and ice from the deck to the quay, and on building sites, trotting up ladders with hodfuls of bricks, had swelled the muscles in his forearms to the size of Popeye's after a can or three of spinach.

By the time I was of an age to remember him, he was in his mid-fifties and he had still been strong, of a murderous disposition and completely fearless. He always wore the sleeves of his shirt rolled up above his elbows to exhibit those fearsome forearms, and his large, scarred hands sported a number of broken and rearranged knuckles when he formed a fist. From his hammer-toed feet to the blue, knotted veins that pulsed and twitched at his scarred temples there was nothing remotely gentle or forgiving about him. He was hard and unyielding through and through, quick to anger and a great bearer of grudges. But he always liked me.

When I was nine, he decided, against my father's wishes, to teach me to box. Characteristically, my father didn't stand up to him but let me decide whether I wished to learn or not and I, uncertain of what was expected of me, elected to take the lessons.

109

It turned out that my grandfather had been a very useful lightweight in his time in the army, and had even fought for the regimental championship, losing, if he was to be believed, in an epic bout of unprecedented brutality. What he taught me, however, and this supports his story, was not the noble art, or even some canny ringcraft, but rather how to punch my weight, and how to launch a ferocious assault on a potential assailant.

What he passed on were the essentials of survival in a street brawl, not the skills of the ring. But I didn't know that at the time. I think he must have seen in me something that he hadn't seen in his own sons who, apart from my father, had moved far away as soon as possible. He must have caught the glint of the same diamond-hard rage against the world that he lived with. And if it wasn't there, he certainly intended to impart it.

I was a quick study, with fast hands and nimble feet, and, for a few years, until my mother left, I was a terror in the ring and, as Angus Darling had cause to remember, in the playground, and the old man was quite proud of me. He couldn't understand why I gave up and he never forgave me, refusing even to be civil to me for the last year or two of his life.

It was partly as a sop to him and partly to make a statement about still being working class that I joined a sweaty gym in my first year at uni.

I still remember what the old fellow taught me and, when I decide that I lead too sedentary a life, I have months when I work out with weights a couple of times a week, run a daily five miles and hammer the heavy bag that hangs in my barn-like garage. On more than half a dozen occasions, when glass has been breaking in pubs and drunken men, faces shining with sweat and arms whirling, have come at me, I've had good reason to be grateful for my grandfather's lessons in controlled savagery.

As I walked down the hill that dark morning, I was nursing a cold and unreasoning anger that I knew could well end in me inflicting real damage on someone, given the opportunity.

I crept quietly around the house, giving the noisy gravel a wide berth, and ducked inside the high, doorless edifice that, although known as the old dairy, now functioned as an occasional garage, when I could be bothered, or remembered, to park the car there.

There was a black, left-hand-drive Audi, the rain beading on its immaculate, waxed surface, parked carelessly behind my mud-splattered Rover. A painfully thin young man with the lean face of a rodent and a pronounced overbite rested against it, a cigarette cupped in his hand. He was wearing a rumpled dark suit and a tired, irritable look. (Question: What's the difference between a hedgehog and an Audi? Answer: The hedgehog has the pricks on the outside.) I wondered again just how it was that people like him had come into my life. It made no sense.

Dirty grey cloud was smeared across the sky, and the rain, although light, was now persistent, adding to the young man's irritation and discomfort. Argyll rain is, the locals are fond of saying, very wet. I took the rucksack from my back and lowered it quietly to the ground. Then I crouched in the darkness of my garage and just watched him.

A memory of Danny McGovern's tortured, desperate face, stark and vivid, came and overwhelmed me with raw anger. I didn't know if this was the man responsible for force-feeding Danny building materials, but I believed him capable of it.

He threw the half-smoked cigarette down and ground it out viciously with the heel of his black shoe.

'Come on, Liam,' he shouted towards the house. 'I'll not fuckin' wait for the little fucker any longer. I'll fuckin' kill him when I see him.'

A bear of little brain and limited patience and vocabulary then. Not to be underestimated for all that. But he'd told me that Colm Kelly wasn't there, which was a relief.

I clenched my fists to control and concentrate the power that rippled along my trembling arms.

Another man appeared at my storm door. He was well built and, with his auburn hair and ruddy complexion, he could have been Colm Kelly's younger brother.

'We wait,' he said, so quietly that I could only just make out the words, 'as long as it takes. As we agreed. He has to come back sometime.' I wasn't sure but I thought that maybe he had made the phone call the previous evening.

'Ah, come on, Liam, we've wasted the entire fuckin' weekend,' the man whined.

'I know, Dermot, and I'm as unhappy about it as yourself. But it can't be helped. Things are screwed up and we have to put at least part of it right. You know that.'

'But I had plans,' the one called Dermot practically snarled. 'I was on a promise.' He shook his head in regret and frustration. I wondered about the sanity of any girl who could promise him anything. 'And we were supposed to be heading back to Amsterdam by now.' He kicked at the ground. 'What was Colm thinking of, leaving the goods here? We could have brought them in. Customs didn't even sniff our armpits! We could have brought anything in.'

'But you can never be sure of that,' Liam said, very reasonably. 'You know that better than most of us. It pays to be careful.'

Dermot turned away and Liam shrugged and went back into the house.

So, I concluded, they were here for the duration. I couldn't simply wait them out. I realized that that suited me just fine.

Dermot, the thin-faced ratty one, moved slowly away from the car to follow his partner back inside and, as he did so, I barrelled out of the garage, low to the ground, like a sprinter leaving the blocks, covering the ten yards that lay between us very fast.

He heard me coming and turned slightly just before I slammed into him, knocking him completely off balance.

He managed a plaintive, 'What the –' before my momentum plastered him against the side of the house. I planted my left hand firmly in his back, so that he had no chance to recover or turn, and I punched him hard in the right kidney, twice. He gave a sigh as the air whooshed out of him and he started to slide towards the ground. On the way, I hit him once above the right ear, for Danny, and his head cracked against the thick stone of the wall. He slumped over, inert, the wool and silk mix of his rumpled dark suit turning darker as it soaked up the rain and the mud.

I stood over him for a second or two, breathing heavily, my right fist cocked, waiting for him to stir. He twitched a little but he was unconscious. I quickly ran my hands over his body for any sign of a weapon, but he was unarmed. He moved slightly and started to moan, softly but loud enough for my purposes. I stood in a fighting stance by the right side of the door.

Within seconds, I heard the other man muttering and coming through the storm porch.

'What's up, Dermot? Missing your anger counsellor?' he said quietly as he came out of the door.

As soon as his head appeared, I threw a left hook and a right jab. Both connected sweetly and he sat down heavily, blood trickling from his mouth, a dazed and confused expression on his face.

He lolled over and looked up but his eyes were unfocused and he was decidedly out of it. I was ready to hit him again if he came up fighting but, sometimes, it takes remarkably little to knock the stuffing out of someone.

He shook his head and put his hand to his face, then scrambled away from me a little before reaching into his pocket and pulling out a handkerchief which he held to his mouth.

'So,' I said, 'you've been waiting for me all night. I can't help but wonder why.'

He shook his head again and looked away, still confused. I took a step towards him, reached down, grabbed the lapel of his coat and held my right fist in front of his face. I felt ugly.

'Do you want me to hit you again?' I said. 'Because I will.'

He held up a hand in front of his face.

'No,' he said. I could see blood washing over his front teeth. 'No, there's no need for that. It's just that we thought – were told – that something was left here for us. But we were obviously mistaken. This must be the wrong place.'

'What?' I said. 'What were you told was left here for you?'

'Just a package. Nothing at all, really. My mistake,' he said.

'Nothing's been left here,' I said.

'Like I said, there's clearly been a misunderstanding,' he said, dabbing at his mouth with the blood-soaked handkerchief. 'An honest mistake. There's absolutely no need for further violence, I assure you.'

'Isn't there?' I said. 'But you're right about one thing. You've made a mistake. Nothing was left here for you. Now, I suggest you get off my property. I'll be calling the police in two minutes.'

As I stepped away from him to allow him to stand up warily, I realized I wasn't bluffing about the police. They could hardly admit that they'd come to collect the briefcase, but if it could be connected to them, I was more or less off the hook.

The one called Liam made his way to his groaning companion, helped him to his feet and half-carried him to the car. The little rat-faced thug gave me a venomous sideways look as he stood hunched over, leaning on his friend, clutching at his back. Suddenly, his body convulsed and he started to retch violently. Liam stepped away from him, cursing softly. Then Dermot straightened up.

'You're a fuckin' dead man, you!' he shouted at me. 'You're dead.'

I shrugged.

'As far as I can see,' I said, 'you're the one with the

deathly pallor and the contusions. And, I'm not sorry to say, you're the one who'll be pissing pure Burgundy for a day or two. If I were you I wouldn't push my luck.'

'I'll be back,' he snarled. 'I'll be back and I'll cut your fuckin' cock off, if I can fuckin' find it.'

I shook my head and took a purposeful stride towards him. 'I'm here now, if you want to give it a try.'

'Fuck!' he said.

'Shut up!' the other man barked at him. Then he wrenched open the passenger door and, putting his hand on Dermot's head like the police always do, he half-pushed him into the seat. He held up his hands to me, palms out, in a gesture of surrender. 'It's OK,' he said. 'He doesn't mean it. He'll calm down. There's no need to hit anyone.' Then he walked around the front of the car to the driver's door, dabbed at his mouth with the blood-sodden handkerchief, gave me a sad look and shook his head before sliding in behind the wheel.

I stepped smartly inside the storm porch, just in case he decided to use the car as a lethal weapon, and listened to the crashing of protesting gears and the strain of the engine as he pumped the gas pedal and the car gave a high-pitched shriek and squealed off in reverse.

I waited in the storm porch, trembling slightly as the adrenaline continued to pump through my body. After about fifteen minutes I decided that they weren't coming back immediately, that they felt they'd taken enough lumps for one morning. But I knew for sure they'd be back sometime.

I stood in the shower for more than ten minutes, letting the hot water wash the sharp, metallic smell of violence and fear from my body. If I could only have washed the vivid memory of it away as well.

It had only taken a few brief, savage seconds, as it always did, but I knew that I'd have to live with the mild depression and remorse for days.

The water poured over me and the steam billowed as I soaped myself neurotically and scrubbed at my back with

115

the loofah. Reluctantly, I turned off the shower and stepped out of the bath. I thought about shaving but decided that it would be an hour or two before I could bear to look myself in the face.

I wrapped myself in towels and padded to the warmth of the kitchen.

My night-time visitors had used up all my instant coffee, finished the milk and ransacked the kitchen cupboards, presumably looking for sugar, but, apart from that, the house seemed remarkably unmolested.

My coffee beans were still in the freezer, untouched. I boiled water, ground beans, and washed the cafetière, still conscious of the slight tremble in my bruised hands. If I drank enough coffee, I could pretend it was a caffeine buzz.

It was half past eight, I was halfway through my second pot of coffee and the radio was telling me to expect delays on the M8 into Glasgow when the cat shouldered his way into the kitchen through the flap in the door, bringing a cold, fresh blast from the great wilderness outside with him. He rubbed his back against my legs and started to make a noise like an old Lancaster bomber rumbling in to land, which I interpreted as an expression of pleasure at seeing me.

I was feeling surprisingly relaxed about things. I thought I could justify the pre-emptive strike on my two night-time visitors. Somehow, I doubted that a pleasant, reasoned approach would have cut much mustard with them and I was pretty sure that I'd been less rough with them than they would have been with me. My only misgivings were that they hadn't gone away for good and I didn't know what I'd do when they returned, probably with Kelly. I don't make a habit of battering people, but on the few occasions in the past when I have had to defend myself I've always felt stricken and depressed about it. I was basking in the pleasure of handing out a relatively guilt-free beating.

I stroked the cat for a few minutes and then left him curled up on the chair I'd just vacated and went to my study to attempt some work. I'd barely even begun looking at the last page I'd written way back on the previous Thursday when the phone rang.

It was Carole and she sounded a little furtive, as though she was trying not to be overheard, and a little brittle, as though she expected to be. It was five past nine and I deduced from that and her manner that she was in the office.

'Hi,' she said.

'Hi,' I said, 'how are you?'

'Fine,' she said and then paused for a second. 'Listen, we have to talk. About that business the other day?'

'Oh,' I said archly, 'and what "business" exactly would that be?'

'You ken fine well what I'm talking about. Can you make lunch sometime? Today?'

'Sure,' I said. 'Where and when?'

'I thought your place about twelve thirty.'

A sudden vision of the little rat-faced thug, Dermot, turning up, wielding a pickaxe handle, bent on revenge, flashed into my mind.

'My place might not be such a good idea,' I said.

'Why not?'

'It's a bit of a mess at the moment,' I said. 'How about your place? I'll organize lunch.'

'Your place didn't seem particularly disreputable yesterday,' she said. 'But I suppose it'll be OK to meet up at home. Duncan and Martin are lunching with our accountants. I'll ring the cleaner and tell her to leave a key in the flowerpot by the front door.'

'Fine,' I said. 'It's a date.'

'No, it isn't,' she said a little more sharply than was really called for. 'Hold on.' There was a pause and I heard a muffled conversation. Then she said, 'Got to go. See you later.' And she hung up.

I turned back to my computer screen and the phone rang again. A polite man from BT asked me if I'd like to buy a mobile phone from them and I declined for what felt like the fiftieth time but wondered, for the first time, if I might actually need one.

It was ten to ten when the next call came and I was, of course, in the loo. Now, there's an argument for mobile phones that isn't often invoked. As I zipped up and dashed back to my office to pick up the phone, I knew it would be the usual Monday morning double-glazing call. But it wasn't. It was Dougie.

'So, wee man, where were you last night?' he said.

'Och,' I said, 'I was away with the fairies.'

'You're always that,' he said. 'But I got your message and rang back about half eleven and there was nae answer. I was worried about you. Your call sounded as if you were already halfway down the bottle.'

'Alcohol was not involved,' I said. 'I got a call. It claimed to be a wrong number but I had the distinct impression that I was being checked out. You know, someone was calling to make sure I was out. Only this time they were calling to make sure that I was in.'

'That makes a lot of sense,' he said.

'No, it doesn't,' I said. 'But, anyway, it put sufficient wind up me that I left the house and slept rough. And I was right. Two Irish guys turned up and spent the night waiting for me.'

'The ones you met at Margaret Crawford's wake?'

'No, two different ones.'

'Are you collecting them, or something?'

'Do you want to hear what happened or not?'

'Of course I do. So, what happened?'

'Nothing much. I had a word with them and they left this morning.'

'Oh, say it ain't so, Joe. You didn't tangle with them, did you? Oh, Jesus, you did. I can hear it in your voice.'

'Just a little bit, Dougie. They were reluctant to leave and I had to persuade them.'

'Och, Iain. Why is it always the wee fellows that cause the trouble?'

'I'm just minding my business here, Dougie. They shouldn't have come,' I said, a little defensively. 'I'm hurt that you should think I'm a troublemaker.'

'Aye, well, listen. I spoke to Ali Macfarlane just now. He's tied up in court this morning and maybe for the next couple of days. He can't get out of it. He'll give you a ring later in the week. He says you should talk to the locals. I told him that you didn't want to, that they regarded you with completely justified suspicion . . .'

'Thanks a bundle,' I said.

'What are friends for? Anyway, I told him you're not a villain, not even close, just an unrespectable and disrespectful citizen. But what's this about the murder? I checked it out after your message. Just down the coast from you?'

'That's right,' I said. 'Danny McGovern, a harmless alkie. I found the body.'

'You did?'

'Yeah.'

'That's great. I'm on my way. I'll get the midday bus. Can you pick me up?'

Dougie doesn't drive.

'Sure.'

'I hope the drinking arm's in working order. I'll be on expenses. A piece, I think, on rural crime. You can be my local researcher. And, Iain?'

'Aye?'

'Try not to get into any more trouble before I get there. I need you to chauffeur me around.'

'Aye,' I said as he cut the connection.

I looked at the handset for a moment before replacing it.

Dougie can smell a story. He's a journalist of the old school who follows his nose. Inside the big man in his expensive suits and shirts is a little newshound in a greasy

119

trilby hat and a shabby, belted trenchcoat who doorstops people and insinuates his way into their secrets by making them feel important and by buying them far too many drinks. He's a throwback to the 1960s, more at home licking a stubby pencil than booting up a Toshiba note-book. I knew he was after my story, such as it was, but I was glad he was coming for all that.

It was clear to me that I wasn't going to be able to settle to do any work and so I decided to cut my losses and take the morning off. In any case I had to pick up some food for lunch and for breakfast, if Dougie was coming to stay.

I drove into the small village that we laughingly refer to as 'town' and parked on the harbourside. The tide was in and greyish water, oily rainbows playing on its still sur-face, was lapping at the harbour wall. It was cold and the slight breeze that came off the sea, although barely ruffling the water, had a keen edge to it and carried the promise of more rain. Some fishermen were emptying the bilges on a couple of trawlers and the heavy, sickening smell of diesel wafted across.

I walked swiftly to the Co-op and filled a basket with eggs, butter, bread, cheese, fruit, orange juice, bacon, salad, coffee and a bottle of dry white wine: *omelettes aux fines herbes* and a green salad for lunch; bacon and eggs for breakfast for Dougie.

Duncan was waiting for me when I left.

Large and graceless, blocking the exit, he was com-pletely indifferent to the problems he was causing the tutting pensioners, with their litres of milk, white loaves, packets of Benson & Hedges and half bottles of Famous Grouse whisky, struggling to get past him. The collar of his black overcoat was turned up, his shoulders were hunched and his hands were deep in his pockets. He looked pale and tired. There were dark, purplish pouches under his bloodshot eyes and patches of dark stubble on his neck and at the corners of his mouth which he'd missed when shaving. He looked seedy and easily ten years older than he was. I found myself wondering, not for the first time, what on earth Carole had ever seen in him.

'Iain,' he said when I appeared at his side, unable to get past him. He waved an arm airily in the direction of the water. 'I had a meeting in the bank and saw you arrive. Have you time for a coffee or something? We need to talk.'

'Sure,' I said. Then I held out my bags. 'I'll just dump these in the car. I'll meet you in the bar at the hotel. And it really is just coffee for me.'

I walked slowly back to the car, deposited the bags in the boot and then walked even more slowly to the hotel. This was a conversation I was not looking forward to. What could I possibly say to him? 'Yes, sure, it's true. Your wife and I spent yesterday afternoon in bed together. No, I don't know if there's going to be a repeat performance. Your guess is as good as mine.' It did not have the makings of a relaxed coffee morning.

He was sitting by the cheerless, smoking fire, staring morosely into a glass of brandy when I entered.

'Hair of the dog,' he said, lifting the glass and smiling weakly. 'I'm afraid I rather tied one on yesterday.'

I nodded unsympathetically and sat down opposite him as he sniffed at the brandy and then took a swig.

'Coffee's on its way,' he said.

'Great,' I said. 'Good meeting?'

He looked puzzled.

'The bank,' I said.

'Oh,' he said. 'Not bad, really. A lot better than they've been of late.' He paused. 'That was a nasty business yesterday,' he continued. 'About Danny. Carole was very upset.' He was tense and distracted, not fully engaged with what he was saying. His right leg was bouncing up and down apparently uncontrollably and his jaw was working backwards and forwards. He was clearly no keener on saying what he had to than I was on hearing it.

'Aye, she would be,' I said. 'But at least she didn't see the body.'

We lapsed into an uneasy silence, then Duncan looked at

me mournfully and licked his dry and cracked lips. Abruptly, he sat upright as though he'd made a decision. His leg was still bouncing and his jaw was still working away.

'Iain, I'm not sure how to say this. It's difficult for me,' he said.

I nodded.

'Well,' I said, 'it's probably better to say it straight out. Whatever it is.'

He licked his lips again.

'I guess you're right.' He sat back, took a deep breath and looked up at the dingy ceiling. 'I've got myself into a situation. And you're part of it.'

'Oh aye,' I said.

He looked straight at me.

'Iain, I'm going to level with you. Some friends of mine are not very happy with you,' he began. 'They're not happy at all.'

So this wasn't about Carole after all. I tried to look puzzled rather than relieved but I don't think I succeeded.

Fortunately, there was a rattle of crockery to cover the moment as Fiona Blair carried my coffee tray through from the kitchen. She was a stocky, sweet-natured woman and she smiled at me warmly while Duncan sat and stared at her impatiently, willing her to get on with serving and go.

'How are you, Iain?' Fiona said solicitously. 'It must have been terrible for you, finding Danny like that.' She looked across at Duncan meaningfully. 'You and Mrs Ferguson.'

'Aye, Fiona,' I said. 'It was.'

'What an awful thing,' she said and shook her head sadly. 'The poor wee soul never hurt a fly.' Then she made a conscious effort to brighten up. 'You still doing the writing?'

'Yes,' I said. 'But I'm still hoping to find a proper job. How are Derek and the boys?'

'Och, they're all fine, but the boys are getting that excited about Christmas already. The list of things they want! Well, you wouldn't believe it. Computers and games consoles and mountain bikes and I don't know what. Not like in our day, eh?'

I risked a sly glance at Duncan, who was sighing in exasperation.

'Aye, a mouldy orange, a stale and foul-tasting chocolate cigar and a jigsaw of some ice-skating vicar, but only if you were lucky and your parents were rich,' I said. 'Come on, Fiona. I can remember fine the lists we all put together.'

'True enough,' she said. 'But we didn't expect to get the half of it. This generation does.' She looked across at Duncan, saw his pursed lips and got the message. 'Well, I'd better be leaving you to your business. Enjoy your coffee. If you want anything else, just give me a yell. I'll be in the kitchen.'

I watched her walk away.

'I was at school with her,' I said to Duncan completely unnecessarily, just to irritate him further.

He leaned forward. 'Iain, this isn't funny. Or easy. These friends of mine who are unhappy with you are not, I'm afraid to say, very nice people. They are not civilized like you and me and they are not patient. They've asked me to explain things to you.'

I poured coffee and gave him my best wide-eyed innocent look.

'Go on,' I said.

'Something – a package – was left at your house. By mistake,' he said.

'Oh? What was in it?' I said and sipped at my coffee. I was rather enjoying myself. Duncan was not a very menacing figure.

'I don't know what was in it,' he snapped. 'It was just a package.'

I pretended to ponder the matter.

'I don't think so,' I said. 'No one left a package at my house. I would have noticed. But it's funny that you should say that because I found two fellows at my house this morning and they said much the same thing. That they were looking for a package that had been left there. Eventually, they agreed that there must be some kind of mistake. But they took some convincing, I can tell you. We had quite a little argument about it.'

'I heard,' he said, 'and, believe me, my friends are not at all happy about that either.'

'You have some very strange friends, Duncan,' I said.

'Needs must . . .' he said.

He rubbed his tired eyes with the heel of his right hand.

'The problem was, is, that the company had a downturn in its finances and we needed an injection of cash. But, like all injections of cash, this one came with some strings attached.' He shook his head wearily. 'Just give it to them, Iain,' he said. 'It'll be easier that way.'

I drank some coffee and then looked straight at him.

'Just so I'm clear about all this, Duncan,' I said, 'would I be right in thinking that it has something to do with you spiking my drinks on Friday at Margaret's wake and then tipping off Sergeant Darling that I was on my way home and that I'd been drinking? I just want to be clear about it.'

He sighed and looked away. As he did so, the weariness left his face for a brief moment and I saw something mean and ugly deep in his rheumy eyes and in the vicious set of his mouth. When he looked back, he was attempting a smile but there was a glassy look in his eye as he stared anywhere but at me.

'I'm sorry, Iain,' he said, 'but I don't know what you're talking about. As far as I'm aware no one spiked anyone's drinks at Margaret's wake.'

He looked away again, towards the kitchen.

'Round he cast his baleful eye,' I said under my breath.

I was still enjoying myself but I'd decided that it was time to quit while I was still ahead and leave. I was just finishing my coffee when he leaned forward again. He was starting to look a little flushed, and there was sweat glistening on his forehead.

'Iain, I don't want to involve Carole in this conversation. But if you force me to I will.' He was struggling to control

124

himself but, as he grew angrier, his voice was growing louder. By the end of the sentence he was almost shouting.

'Calm down, Duncan, calm down,' I said. 'If we can't discuss this rationally, I don't see any point in discussing it at all. I also don't see how Carole's involved. Except as a director of the company, of course.'

He made a real effort to control his temper and he sat back before continuing.

'Carole isn't part of it. She doesn't work on that side of the company. But I think you know what I'm talking about. I'm not blind or, whatever you and Carole think, stupid. I've got eyes. I can see that my wife's been having an affair with you ever since we came to this god-forsaken place.'

I must have stared at him in open-mouthed amazement for a moment or two. So that's what he thought. I didn't want to lie to him and say that it just wasn't true. But it wasn't. The affair had only started the day before.

'You're mistaken there, Duncan,' I finally muttered.

'Right,' he said, 'so, all those weekend-long "shopping trips" to Glasgow weren't spent with you.'

The blank and uncomprehending look that I gave him was authentic enough to stop him from plunging on. It ought to have been. It wasn't faked.

'No, Duncan,' I said, aware that my cheeks were reddening. 'Carole and I have never spent a weekend in Glasgow.'

'Yeah,' he said, 'and all those furtive phone calls. I suppose they weren't to you.'

'Until after her mother's funeral, Carole hadn't called me since she came back.'

He laughed dismissively and took a quick gulp of brandy. Then he looked at me for a few seconds without speaking. I felt like it must seem as if I was protesting too much. And I suppose I was. If I'd been genuinely innocent, as I had been until the day before, I would have ignored him, laughed off his accusations. As it was, I was guilty enough to think that he deserved an answer of some kind.

He smiled thinly and leaned back in his chair.

'Do you know, I've never liked you,' he said. 'I disliked you even before I met you.' He put on a strained falsetto. '"To think, I could have married Iain Lewis and instead I chose you. He's a famous poet, you know."'

'Quite apart from the fact that's the worst impersonation of Carole I've ever heard, I just don't think she'd ever speak about me like that,' I said.

'Maybe they weren't her exact words,' he said, 'but you don't know the half of it. Iain Lewis this and Iain Lewis that. You ruined my marriage before we'd even had the bloody honeymoon.'

'Come on, Duncan. How can that possibly be true?' I said. 'I hadn't seen Carole in over ten years before you came here and I hadn't so much as got a postcard from her. I didn't even know she was married until the local paper carried the announcement. If your marriage is in difficulties, it isn't down to me.'

'No?' he said. 'You don't think so. If she wasn't bad enough, going on about your shitty little rhymes, when we came here, there was her mother, always ramming you and your virtues down my throat. Looking down her nose at me. Half the bloody family's in love with you. Did you know that?'

'Duncan,' I said, 'when anyone starts talking about my virtues my eyes glaze over. I don't have any and I really don't know what you're talking about. I haven't been having an affair with Carole since she returned here.' Which was a politician's lie, of course, true as far as it went. 'And your friends are mistaken in believing that they mistakenly left a package at my house.'

'God,' he said, the exasperation evident in his tone, 'half of me really hopes that you carry on like this, refusing to give up the package. Because, if you do, they'll kill you. And I think I'd like to see that.'

'I'm sorry you feel that way, Duncan,' I said, deciding to stand on what little dignity I could muster, 'and I'm sorry I can't oblige your friends. But I can't give back what I don't have. As for them killing me . . . Well, the pathetic specimens they sent around this morning didn't look up to the job.' I lifted my coffee cup, drained it and carefully placed it on the saucer. Then I stood up. 'I rather think that we have nothing else to say to each other and I'd better be about my business.'

I gave him as hard a look as I could manage across the table, narrowing my eyes and setting my mouth in a thin line. But it didn't intimidate him at all. His expression suddenly changed and he started to smile as some kind of realization came to him.

I turned and walked away but, as I did so, he called to me, just a hint of incredulity in his voice: 'Good God! It really wasn't you, was it? You didn't know.'

I carried on walking across the bar. I was almost at the door when he yelled again. This time his voice was touched by anger and desperation.

'Iain! Give it back to them. Give it back to them and I'll turn a blind eye to you and Carole. Or whoever it is. At least you know how I feel now. She's been shagging someone else behind both our backs.'

I almost went back and pointed out the illogicality of what he'd said. If he accepted, as he appeared to, that I hadn't been having an affair with Carole, then she couldn't have been doing anything behind my back. Not that that meant the fact of her having an affair with someone else didn't unsettle me. I was ashamed to recognize that it unquestionably did.

But I didn't pause or turn. I didn't dare. Tempting as it was to use him as a punchbag, it would probably get me arrested and in bad odour with Carole and most of the village. In any case, I had no stomach for a second fight that morning. Anyway, it was difficult to feel anger, or any other deep emotion, at a man whose life resembled a slow-motion car wreck. This was not a Greek tragedy. I just carried on and walked out of the bar, his words lashing at my back.

Chapter Six

The rain had started to fall steadily as I emerged from the hotel on to the damp and chilly pavement outside.

I tried to dismiss what Duncan had said. He was clearly upset and under pressure from his 'business associates', by which I understood Colm Kelly, and his marriage was falling apart. He wanted to put some of the pressure he was feeling on me, and he would certainly want to express his anger. If he could sow discord between Carole and the person he regarded as her lover then so much the better. And it was working. The thought that Carole had been having an affair had already started to gnaw away at me. Beware, my lord, of jealousy. Tis the green-eyed monster that mocks the meat it feeds on.

And being told that made Othello's life so much easier.

I crossed the road and walked briskly to the little row of payphones that sat precariously on the edge of the harbour and punched in the impossibly long number to her mobile phone that Carole had given me. A blandly pleasant recording told me that the Vodaphone I was calling could possibly have been switched off and encouraged me to call again later.

I tried again with the same result which, I suddenly realized, was just as well as I didn't have any idea what to say to her. I decided that I might as well meet her at the house as originally planned. I walked back to the car in something of a daze. I kept telling myself that it was nothing to do with me if Carole had had a lover since her return. But, ludicrously, I couldn't help feeling betrayed.

The cold rain was still falling when I arrived, just before midday. Martin Crawford's Jag was parked carelessly by the steps leading to the front door, its engine still running.

I parked as far from the Jag as was possible – Martin was well known in the village for taking wing mirrors with him if anyone was unwise enough to put their car within clipping distance – and gathered up my plastic bags of shopping from the boot. Then I climbed up the steps. The key was, as promised, in a large earthenware flowerpot on the top step. But I didn't need it. The door was open.

I stepped cautiously into the hall, the sound of my footsteps echoing in the silent house.

'Martin?' I called out.

'Iain?' His disembodied voice came from the big living room, the room that his mother always received in, the one that she had most stamped her personality on, the one where we had all met on Friday afternoon after the funeral.

'Yes.'

'I'm in here.'

I opened the door and walked in. I didn't see him at first. My eyes were drawn to the mantelpiece where Margaret's portrait, edged in black, still stood.

'What are you doing here?' Martin said.

I turned and saw him, standing just in front of the spot that his father had shot himself. He was looking faintly distracted, staring towards the window.

'Oh,' I said. 'Well, Carole wanted a quiet lunch, after yesterday, you know. So, I've stopped by to put it together.'

'Of course,' he said absently, 'it must have been very disturbing.' Suddenly, he turned towards me and smiled. 'Don't worry, I'll be on my way in a moment. I just dropped by to pick up some figures I left here. I'm not spying on my big sister.'

'Nothing to spy on. It's just going to be a little light conversation. And there are omelettes and salad. I've got enough, if you want to stay. And there's a bottle of the Co-op's finest Orvieto.'

'An almost irresistible offer,' he said. 'But I'm lunching with our accountants. That's why I had to come back for the figures. So, it'll have to be some other time.'

'OK,' I said, 'some other time.'

He brushed his hand through his blond hair, turned away from me, walked over to the window and stared out over the drab driveway at the bare rowan and birch trees that dripped icy rain from their emaciated branches, towards the distant hills and the slate-grey sky. But I thought he was seeing something else.

When he spoke, it was so quietly that I had to strain to hear.

'You know, I picked up the figures from my study and just stepped in here. I saw the picture of Mum on the mantelpiece. I miss her, Iain.'

'That's understandable,' I said.

'Yeah,' he said. It came out as a deep sigh. 'Then, for some reason, I remembered Dad. All those years ago and that awful night. I recall it all so clearly, Iain.'

'It's not the kind of thing you forget easily,' I said warily. This was not a conversation I wanted to prolong. There was something odd about his demeanour which was disturbing.

'I was only fourteen,' he said.

'Not an easy thing to see at any age,' I said.

'You know, for years I thought it was all my fault that Dad was dead. I went from trick cyclist to trick cyclist like I was sleepwalking. They all went through the same ritual. Why did I think it was my fault? Because I killed him, I would answer. Why did I think that? Because I had.' He shook his head.

There was a long silence and I started to feel even more uncomfortable than before. I coughed quietly but he didn't stop staring out of the window, into the past. Eventually, I had to ask.

'Why *did* you think that?' I said.

He didn't reply immediately and I thought that maybe he hadn't heard me. I was about to repeat the question when he started to talk in a dull monotone.

'I have a strong memory of doing it, of shooting him. I remember him shouting at Mum and I remember her slapping him and him slapping her back. And I remember going to the bookcase where he kept it and grabbing the gun. I remember walking up to him, shoving it against his chest and squeezing the trigger. I remember the deafening noise, the bone-shaking recoil, the cartridge case pinging to the floor at my feet, and I remember Mum prising the gun from my hands. I remember all that vividly. And yet everyone told me it didn't happen.'

'It didn't, Martin,' I said. 'You didn't shoot your father. It was suicide. Your mother said so. She saw it happen.'

'Yes,' he said. 'She did. I often wondered what she really saw.'

'It was the procurator fiscal's verdict as well.' I said. 'No one had any reason to doubt it.'

'No,' he said. 'Except me.' Slowly, he turned back into the room but he wasn't looking at me. 'But the trick cyclists finally wore me down and convinced me it was a strange case of false memory. I'd seen my father kill himself. It was a traumatic event. It was bound to have a profound effect on me. In my case it came out in these false memories. Then, hey, I was cured.' He paused. 'Now Mum kills herself and I'm back where I started. I'm reliving the whole thing again. Wondering if I didn't do it.'

His face was pale and, although he was a good-looking man, bland. The clear blue eyes were perhaps a little bright, glittering unnaturally, although that might have been a trick of the light, but, that apart, the only suggestion of writhing inner serpents was the tiny, trembling vein tugging repeatedly at his left eye.

'Only now it's different. I'm convinced that I killed both of them. I can see myself forcing the pills into her mouth, making her swallow them.'

'You didn't kill your mother, Martin,' I said.

131

He turned a bright smile on me. 'No, of course I didn't. I know that and I don't need the expensive hours of therapy again. But I just can't escape that memory, that image. It's as if I did it. I don't understand.'

'We all have our demons,' I said.

He laughed. 'Don't we just. Listen, I'd appreciate it if you didn't tell Carole about this conversation.'

'What conversation?' I said.

He looked puzzled for a moment, then he laughed again and leaned forward, reaching out and putting his long, thin hand on my shoulder.

'Good man,' he said, pummelling my upper arm. 'Good man.'

Then he strode from the room.

I heard his feet thump across the wooden floor of the hall and then slap down the wet steps. His car door banged dully and the Jag roared away, spitting gravel. I stood for a while, momentarily regretting that my involvement with the Crawford family was not still in the past, then I walked slowly to the big, old kitchen to pre-pare the meal and brood. Mostly brood. I'm only a modest cook but I am a world-class brooder.

I dumped my purchases on the scarred pine table, put the bottle of lukewarm Orvieto, which really was the best the Co-op had to offer, in the freezer to cool quickly, and then scoured the place for utensils. I wondered briefly why I was staying. My two encounters with the family so far that day hadn't done anything for my peace of mind. I didn't imagine that lunch with Carole was going to be anything other than a strained affair, as I studiously avoided asking her about my chat with Duncan. I knew that I had no reason to feel betrayed, or jealous, but it was, nevertheless, with a bleak and empty heart that I awaited her arrival. Anyway, I had a feeling that whatever she wanted to say to me I wasn't going to want to hear.

I wasn't sure what to make of the conversation with Martin. It had been unreal and slightly spooky, like watch-ing a movie starring Christopher Walken. The quiet, eerie voice and the slightly glassy, unfocused eyes had all been a bit too theatrical to be for real, although he had definitely been wound up tighter than the traditional coiled spring.

But there was more than a hint of the farcical about his performance, as well. Suspects were being offered and offering themselves for a murder that had never happened. First, Carole had told me that she thought her mother had done it, and now Martin not only 'remembered' shooting his father, he had convincing 'memories' of force-feeding pills to his mother as well. What a family! Never settle for a tragedy when you can easily make it so much worse. Maybe Aeschylus could have done something with them.

I didn't know how worried to be about Martin but I certainly had no intention of keeping my promise not to disclose the conversation to Carole. I couldn't even begin to think why he'd spoken to me about it anyway, if he didn't intend it to get back to someone. It wasn't necessary to have spent years studying the works of Sigmund Fraud to conclude that, in spite of his protestation about not needing therapy, he recognized that that was exactly what he did need, but that he wanted someone else to be responsible for taking him, kicking and squealing, off to the funny farm.

I'd tell Carole what he'd said and leave it up to her and Duncan to make a decision about what should be done. Whatever happened, I made a mental note not to get into any car which he was driving in the immediate future. He had the look and the sound of someone who might well find the impulse to drive into the headlights coming towards him too strong to resist.

The encounter with Duncan was far more personally worrying. Quite apart from his revelations about his feelings about me, which were not too much of a surprise, and the unwelcome news that he thought Carole had been having an affair for the last eighteen months or so, there was the matter of his unhappy friends.

All the clichés came to mind: the rock and the hard place; the devil and the deep blue sea; damned if I did, damned if I didn't. I'd made a bad call when I hadn't reported the briefcase to the police straight away on Friday evening. And I was stuck with it. I couldn't very well call it in now, not without some very difficult explanations, and I couldn't just hand it back to the bad guys. I had to have the stuff when Dougie's man came calling. If I simply handed it over to them, I'd also be handing over the only bargaining position I had, weak though it was.

But I still couldn't fathom why they'd used my house as a poste restante anyway. It didn't make any sense. They didn't know me or even where I lived. The only possible explanation was that Duncan, or someone very like him, and every bit as vindictive, had set it up. He'd just showed that he thought he had good reason to dislike me enough. But that didn't make much sense either. Not really.

And lurking behind my every thought, and throwing long and terrifying shadows, was Danny McGovern's horrible death.

I was washing gritty salad under the cold water tap and turning events over in my mind when I heard the car arrive. She was a few minutes early.

I still wasn't sure what I was going to say to her about my conversation with Duncan, but I was glad she was here. We could at least start to talk about things. I dried my cold hands on kitchen roll and ambled slowly towards the hall to meet her.

As I left the kitchen and stepped into the corridor, I heard the bare boards creak under a wary tread. I stopped by the dark alcove that housed the downstairs cloakroom. Whoever it was stopped moving too and, for a moment, all I could hear was the pounding of the blood in my ears and the constant drip of water from the leaky cistern behind me. Then the floor creaked again, as if someone was shifting weight from one foot to the other.

I waited for a cheery greeting and when none came, I decided to err on the side of caution and slipped quietly into the cloakroom, leaving the door half open and ducking down behind it. I reckoned I'd remain undiscovered unless someone urgently needed a piss.

I stared at the heavy, dark door with its swirls and whorls of dense grain, like gigantic fingerprints, as the two men – I was suddenly sure there were two of them and they were men – started to prowl around, looking, I assumed, for me.

I couldn't recollect if I had heard Martin shut the front door or not and suddenly it seemed important, but I didn't know why.

One of the men started to climb the stairs – I heard the soft sound of his feet on the thin carpet getting steadily higher – and the other crept past me on the way to the kitchen. He paused just outside the cloakroom and I imagined him peering in. I tensed, waiting for the door to be pushed in, but he moved on. Then I heard the sound of another car arriving, glanced at my watch and realized that, this time, it had to be Carole.

I didn't really think about it. I had decided by now that, somehow, Liam and the rat-faced Dermot, my visitors from the previous night, had found out where I was and had come for me. I knew that I didn't want Carole in the same house as them and I stood up and peered around the door. I saw nothing and seized my chance. I ran into the hall at full pelt, skidded through the open front door and leapt down the steps. I fancied I could hear them behind me but I didn't risk a look back.

Carole was still in the Golf, behind a black Audi that I recognized, and I wrenched open the passenger door and slid in.

'Don't argue,' I said. 'Just drive. I'll explain later.'

She was about to remonstrate with me when the thin little thug called Dermot appeared at the front door. She said nothing, just shook her head at me, smoothly found gear, turned the car around in a beautifully described and economical arc and drove down the driveway, moving swiftly up the gears.

I looked back and saw the two of them standing forlornly by their car and I couldn't resist giving a little wave.

Dermot bent, picked up a stone and hurled it after us. It fell a long way short and hopelessly wide. He'd obviously never swooped on a cricket ball and thrown it in from the deep. I smiled with some satisfaction as he clutched at what I hoped was a real stab of pain in his back.

Carole was composed and controlled as she drove swiftly along the narrow, winding road that followed the loch around to the harbour, past the other, slightly less grand, detached villas where the professionals – the bank manager, the headmaster and the doctor – had all lived when I was a boy. Now, they all seemed to have been divided up into apartments for holiday lets when the yachtsmen came to town. The good, solid professionals who had replaced the fearsome figures of my youth were all incomers from Glasgow who inhabited large new houses outwith the village.

Carole's lips were pressed tightly together in concentration but she occasionally glanced across at me through narrowed, appraising eyes. I knew that she would worry at me remorselessly for answers, when she no longer had to focus on her driving. But that seemed fair enough, in the circumstances. Part of me wished I had answers to give her and part of me didn't really care, thinking resentfully that she owed me some kind of explanation as well.

There was very little traffic about to impede our progress and she negotiated the occasional selfishly parked car that jutted out into our path like a natural hazard with an easy, fluid grace when we reached the shops and the small houses where the ordinary people who I'd grown up with lived and worked.

The steady, awkward flick of the windscreen wipers, like the absurdly attenuated antennae of some giant alien mantis, was oddly hypnotic as they swept the water away and smeared rainbows across the glass. I sat uncomfortably hunched around, the seat belt pressing painfully into my shoulder, looking out for signs of pursuit.

Carole suddenly indicated and turned left off the harbour road. She pulled up opposite the part-time police station, in front of a line of other cars, with a gap between us and the nearest vehicle behind us. Then she turned towards me and broke her stony silence.

'Well,' she said sternly.

I peered through the rear window again, just in time to see a black Audi speed past the turn-off, driving along the harbour road, heading down the peninsula, in the general direction of my house.

'I don't know why you've stopped here,' I said as I shifted to a more comfortable position in the seat. 'It's Monday.'

'So what?' she said.

'The *polizei* are only here on Tuesday and Thursday mornings.'

'I know that,' she said, 'but I thought it was just possible that the men in the black hats, and black saloon, don't. Anyway, it seemed like a nice, comforting sort of place to park. Now, are you going to tell me what's going on? For instance, why those men were in my house, and why we've just run away from them.'

I felt very weary, and it wasn't just because of a night spent sleeping rough. There was a dull ache behind my eyes and a throbbing in my temples. All I wanted to do was go home, sleep for eight hours and wake refreshed and problem-free. I sighed and closed my eyes.

When I opened them, the sky was still grey; a steady, cold drizzle still dripped remorselessly down; behind me, the chilly water of the loch still lapped at the harbour wall; my bank account was still overdrawn by seven hundred and eighty pounds; a black briefcase wrapped in dustbin liners still lurked at the bottom of my septic tank like a venomous spider; Danny McGovern was still dead; and Carole was still glaring at me, tight-lipped and waiting for answers.

'Come on, talk to me,' she said.

There was an intensity about her gaze that was mildly unnerving. It was the determined stare of a primary schoolteacher seeking out the miscreant and turning the bowels of the entire class to water in the process.

'I don't know that I can explain,' I said weakly, knowing that, for all my bone-weariness, I was going to have to try.

'Well, I'd better call the police,' she said, reaching into her bag for her mobile phone.

I closed my eyes again briefly, then put my hand on her arm.

'You could,' I said. 'In fact, you probably should. But you might want to wait until you've spoken to your husband or your brother. It's more than possible that one of them invited those guys into the house.'

'What?'

I looked at her pale, puzzled, angry face and started, haltingly, to describe what had happened to me since Friday evening. I tried to keep it as neutral as I could and not stack the cards against Duncan too much. But the spiked drinks and the conversation that I'd just had with him were pretty damning. I mentioned that Martin had been in the house when I'd arrived and told of her of the strange conversation I'd had with him, and my worries. I then said that the Irishmen had turned up not long after he'd left. The implications of that were, I thought, glaringly obvious. Carole, however, was not just unimpressed: she was downright incredulous.

'I don't believe it,' she said.

'I can show you the briefcase and I imagine that Sergeant Darling will confirm stopping me on Friday evening. You know that Duncan pressed at least one drink on me. You brought it over. I assure you it contained gin. Those two Irish guys are carrying bruises from this morning's encounter.' I paused and shrugged. 'Other than that, it's speculation and I can't prove a thing.'

It had been something of a relief to tell her just about everything, but her frank disbelief rather undermined the feeling. The only subject I'd been reticent about had been Duncan's statement that she'd been having an affair. I'd told her that he had accused me of being involved with her since her return and left it at that. If I'm honest, it wasn't to spare her any embarrassment – it was so I didn't appear to be a sullen, resentful, irrational, jealous prick.

I knew that I had no right to feel betrayed or angry, but I felt both. Unfortunately, reason never entered into matters involving jealousy, retroactive or otherwise. I knew that it wasn't me she'd been unfaithful to. But it felt like it. It had slowly dawned on me in the last hour or so that, deep down in my murky and surprisingly reactionary subconscious, I had always thought of it that way, ever since I heard that she had married Duncan.

In the event, I needn't have bothered as she came straight out and admitted to the affair.

'Oh, God,' she said. 'I'm sorry about that. Duncan must have added up two and two and, as usual, come up with five and one eighth.'

'If his maths is that bad, he probably shouldn't be in charge of a company,' I said.

'You're not wrong about that,' she said, 'but it's not his maths that's at fault. It's his whole approach to life.' She swallowed hard and looked out of the side window. 'The truth is that I *was* having an affair. Until about a month ago. Then it stopped. Duncan must have guessed and assumed that it was you.' She paused and then she turned towards me. 'It wasn't a grand passion or anything,' she said.

I looked at her forlornly, wondering how many others there had been, recognizing, not for the first time, how ill-equipped I was to deal with her and her entire, dysfunctional family. It was the casual way she assumed that I'd take any revelation in my stride that threw me. It always had.

I wanted to get out of the car and just walk away. I could see myself doing it, striding self-dramatically down the street towards the harbour, impervious to her pleas. Then the camera would pull back and the credits would scroll down the screen.

'I was unhappy, Iain,' she said bleakly. 'I've been unhappy for a very long time.'

And I knew I couldn't do it.

I stared grimly through the windscreen, the headache swelling behind my eyes. Kids, their red and blue sweat-shirts visible under unbuttoned and bulky anoraks and waterproofs, were wandering down the hill from the school to the chipshop for their lunch. I recalled doing that twenty years before.

Carole nudged me gently in the ribs.

'Nothing to say, Iain?' she said quietly. 'No clever, appo-site quotation lurking in that ragbag of a mind of yours?'

I thought gloomily of my age and predicament.

'*Nel mezzo del cammin di nostro vita / mi ritrovai per una selva oscura, / che la diritta via era smarrita,*' I murmured.

'OK, smartarse,' she said, shaking her head, 'so you did a year's Italian. You know I don't know what that means.'

'Everyone knows that,' I said. 'It's the opening three lines of Dante's *Inferno.*'

'Is it?' she said. 'Well, I'm here to tell you that everyone doesn't know what it means. I don't, for a start.'

'At thirty-five, I found myself in a dark wood, having strayed from the straight and narrow.'

She snorted and started to laugh.

'But I'm not thirty-five yet,' she said.

'No, but I am. And I'm the one in the dark wood,' I said. 'A very dark wood. Full of knotty, knarry, bareyne trees olde.'

'Enough quotes already. If that one was a quote. That was always one of the more irritating aspects of your conversation,' she said, leaning across and kissing me gently on the cheek, 'as you pointed out yesterday.'

The soft touch of her lips and the delicate perfume that filled my nostrils intoxicated me and my childish, sullen anger at her dissipated. I put my hand to the place that she'd kissed.

At the same time, I realized that there might be a way to buy myself a little much-needed time and my mood brightened considerably.

'Call the police,' I said. 'Tell them about some intruders up at the house. They're driving a black Audi and heading south down the peninsula. I can identify them and I'm happy to make a statement.'

'Why bother?' she said. 'All they have to do is get Duncan or Martin, I suppose, to vouch for them.'

'Ah, but will they? I don't know for sure that either Duncan or Martin sent them. They may know nothing about it. In any case, even if one of them does know all about it and is prepared to give them a clean bill of health, it'll get the thugs out of my hair for a few hours while they have to explain things. Which is all to the good. Who knows? The police may be able to keep them on something. They are looking for Danny's murderers, after all.'

'You don't seriously think they're anything to do with that, do you? That Duncan, or Martin, is implicated in a murder, however remotely?'

I spread my hands and shook my head.

'I honestly don't know,' I said. 'But I'd just like these guys to have something other than me to worry about for a while. It's not impossible that they're involved. If they are, it certainly won't hurt to point the police in the right direction, will it?'

'What about Duncan?' she said. 'And Martin?'

'I'm guessing that these guys won't involve Duncan or Martin,' I said.

'Just guessing?' she said.

I nodded. 'Just guessing. But they don't seem like the type to me to say anything to the police. Unless they really have to.'

'Oh, God,' she said. 'Mum was right. They really are criminals.'

'Please ring the police, Carole.'

She looked at me helplessly and I felt myself melt. 'But

what about Duncan? Martin? The business? Suppose they do talk to the police about *them*?'

'If they're not involved, they've nothing to worry about, have they? If they are . . .' I shrugged in my best Gallic manner.

'I can't do it,' she said.

'OK, then I will. I really have to,' I said.

I held my hand out for the phone.

Carole fell silent and her mouth set in that thin, determined line again.

A movement in the rear-view mirror caught my eye and I glanced at it. A black Audi was drawing up behind us.

'Carole,' I said, 'they're right behind us. I'm getting out of the car. Keep your eye on what happens and be ready to drive away. Fast. Don't worry about me. Look after yourself and call the police if you think it's right.' I glanced at my watch. 'All being well, I'll be in the hotel bar in twenty minutes.'

'Iain,' she said, 'don't do anything stupid. Give them what they want.'

'I don't think I can, Carole,' I said. 'That wouldn't be the end of it.'

I wasn't really sure what to do, but I knew I didn't want to be trapped in the car when Liam and Dermot got out of theirs. And I certainly didn't want Carole there if violence was about to erupt.

I hauled myself out of the Golf just as both the doors on the Audi opened like wings unfolding. I quickly moved away from the car and Carole. There was a narrow alleyway between two houses just behind me, wide enough for one person to enter. If the worst came to the worst, I could take refuge there and they'd have to come at me one at a time. I figured that would give me all the edge I needed. Unless they were armed.

They ambled warily along the pavement towards me, with none of the swagger that I imagined they usually employed, and stopped maybe three yards away, well out of punching range.

My mouth was very dry, my legs weak and my stomach was roiling alarmingly. I felt rather as I had always felt just before a bout when I was anticipating a beating in the ring. I felt the cold sweat break out on my scalp and I breathed little whoops of air through my mouth a couple of times and then breathed in slowly through my nose. I rolled my head to loosen my neck and forced my reluctant legs to pound the pavement a little. I let my hands dangle in front of me, fists half formed.

The auburn-haired one called Liam put his hand up to his jaw and looked at me ruefully. He had a slight swelling just under his mouth and a livid bruise on his right cheek. He glanced nervously over at the police station, which looked, I thought, obviously unlit and empty. However, I was grateful that this meeting was taking place in the open, and I was particularly grateful that Carole had been inspired to park somewhere that would at least give the pair of them pause to think before resorting to coercion and violence.

Liam touched the bruise on his cheek, inclined his head on one side and smiled a sweet, sad, little smile.

'Mr Lewis, Iain,' he said, 'there are no hard feelings about this morning, even though you pack quite a punch. Even Dermot here is prepared to live and let live. And he is, as you rightly prophesied, passing more than a little blood when he takes a leak.'

I glanced at Dermot. The look of pure venom that he wore didn't suggest that he intended to let me off that lightly.

'Your reaction to our presence this morning, although a little precipitate, was certainly understandable. We really don't want any more trouble, Mr Lewis, Iain,' Liam continued. 'However, we are reliably informed that a package – a briefcase, in fact – was put in your house on Friday. We want it. It isn't where it was left, which suggests to me that you must have moved it.'

He spoke quickly and his look kept drifting away from me over to the police station.

I said nothing and he took another step towards me. The rodent-faced Dermot, shuffling along next to him, was not moving easily. His tongue flicked out and moistened his lips. I tensed, my fists clenching, and readied myself for an attack.

'Come on, Iain,' Liam said, holding his hands out in front of him in a gesture designed to show that he meant me no harm. 'Be reasonable. I'm asking nicely. Just tell us where it is and that'll be that. No unpleasant repercussions. Definitely no hard feelings.'

I coughed nervously.

'I don't have it,' I said quietly.

'Then, where is it?' he said. He glanced meaningfully at Dermot who moved away from him, further to my left, presumably to widen the angle of attack. His hand slipped furtively into his coat pocket and tightened on something there.

A group of four kids, all about twelve or thirteen, came up behind them, on their way back to school, and eyed us suspiciously as they went past, stepping out into the road to do so. I waited until they were more than twenty yards away before speaking.

'The police have it,' I said.

Liam shook his head sadly.

'No, no, no,' he said. 'I don't buy that. Which means that I'm forced to conclude that you've looked inside the case and you are planning to rip us off. I have to tell you, Iain, that's a very dangerous route to take.' He paused to allow the implications of his words to sink in, to add some menace. Not that he had to. I understood perfectly well what he was saying and so, judging by the evil little smile that slowly spread across his face, did Dermot.

Liam looked pale and tense and his hands were trembling slightly. Over his shoulder, I saw a police patrol car prowl slowly along the harbour road.

Suddenly, Carole opened the car door, got out and strode determinedly towards us.

'Leave him alone,' she said, 'or I'm going to the police.'

Liam didn't even look at her.

'Stay out of this,' he said, 'and you won't get hurt.'

I held up a warning hand to her and she stopped well back from us. Then I narrowed my eyes and looked as menacing as I could.

'If you or your creature takes so much as one step towards her, I promise you you're both going to be in traction for a very long time,' I said quietly.

'There's no need for *anyone* to get hurt,' he said. 'Just tell us where the briefcase is.'

'Tell him, Iain,' Carole said.

'Yeah, tell him, Iain,' Dermot mimicked.

'I don't have it,' I said sullenly.

'For God's sake, Iain,' Carole said. 'It's in the septic tank, behind his garage.'

'That's the big, dilapidated building, right?' Liam said.

'That's right,' she said.

'Fine, that's cool,' he said. 'Now all we have to do is collect it. Iain, Mr Lewis, perhaps you'll be kind enough to jump in the car and we can go and take a look.' Rain was beading in his thick, auburn hair.

'I don't think so,' I said.

'Just get in the car,' he said. 'Nothing's going to happen to you. If she's just told us the truth, that is.'

'Why is it that I don't believe you?' I said. 'Could it be because I don't think that you can vouch for your trained weasel over there?'

'Well, of course,' he said, 'if you will go around gratuitously insulting people, you may have to take the consequences.' He looked across at Dermot and a thin smile tugged at his lips, which caused him to wince. Another little knot of children was struggling up the hill towards the school and Liam glanced nervously over at the drab, rain-stained concrete of the police station. This time it was a longer look, as if he were getting a little suspicious about the closed door and the lack of activity. At least he was aware that we were attracting more attention than he was comfortable with. I decided to play that for all it was worth.

'I'm not getting in the car,' I said.

145

Liam looked puzzled for a moment, as if unsure what to do. He glanced over at the police station where, miraculously, an outside security light at the rear of the building suddenly responded to a cat or a bird and switched itself on. That seemed to make up Liam's mind.

'OK,' he said decisively, 'but it had better be there.' He leaned forward and, his temper visibly fraying, barked out, 'If it's not, I will let Dermot off his leash. I am tired of this shithole. And I am very tired of you.'

He stared at me for a few more seconds and then stomped off back to the Audi. Dermot glared viciously at me, then limped awkwardly to the car, favouring the right side of his body. Seconds later, they were gone.

Carole came over to my side and put her arm on my shoulder. She looked pale and worried.

'I'm sorry,' she said. 'But I thought they were going to attack you. I didn't want them to hurt you. I had to tell them.'

'It's OK, Carole,' I said. 'I was about to tell them myself anyway.' I paused because that wasn't true and wondered what would have happened if she hadn't. 'Call the police. Tell them most of what's happened. Tell them you came across some intruders at the house. Describe the vehicle and say it's headed south.'

I reckoned that, with a patrol car in the immediate vicinity, the police would pick them up in about ten minutes, instead of the more usual forty-five minutes to sometime never.

Neither of us wanted to return to the house immediately, so we took refuge and ate lunch in the safety of the crowded hotel bar, almost oblivious to the knowing nods in our direction and the answering raised eyebrows. The old wifeys would have a little extra sparkle in their gossip over the next few days. I found that I really didn't care.

Carole picked at her salad and smoked salmon and sipped decorously at a glass of water. I hadn't eaten properly for quite a while and, in spite of some worries that the police would probably miss Dermot and Liam, tore hungrily into a rare fillet steak. As I wasn't planning to drive anywhere for a few hours, I washed it down with a half bottle of Merlot, thinking guiltily of the Orvieto turning to ice in Carole's freezer.

Apart from a few desultory remarks, we ate in silence. Carole was preoccupied with her thoughts. I was too preoccupied with food, and concerns of my own, to either speak or try to discover the cause of Carole's unease. Anyway, I thought that her husband's business partners, as described by me, and the recent confrontation with two of their 'associates' gave her good reason to be both worried and thoughtful.

Although I hadn't intended to tell Liam and Dermot where the briefcase was, I wasn't unduly worried that Carole had. I was hoping that the police would pick them up before they got to it. It wouldn't be the end of the world if they didn't, but I would have an uncomfortable time answering some difficult questions if they were discovered with it and mentioned where they'd got it.

When I pushed my plate away, emptied the last of the wine into my glass and sat back with a satisfied sigh, Carole spoke.

'About the affair,' she said, staring over my shoulder and out of the window at the grey, lugubrious loch and the greyer mountains in the distance. 'It wasn't really an affair. Just a few meetings – not all that many, really – between two lonely and unhappy people. Although it did last for quite some time.'

'You don't have to explain anything to me, Carole,' I said. 'It's none of my business.'

'Well, it is in a way,' she said.

'No, Carole, it isn't. Who you chose to sleep with in the past is really nothing to do with me. And I don't want to know. Really, I don't. You may feel that you owe Duncan an explanation, but you don't owe me one.'

In truth, I was more than a little curious about Carole's affair. I had a raging desire to know who it was, but I thought it best to pretend to a maturity that I could lay little claim to. I didn't want to feed the ravening beast that padded silently around, captive, in my id.

'I'll skip the explanation-to-the-husband thing, if you don't mind,' she said. 'He's an unpleasant oaf at the best of times, these days.' She looked out of the window again. 'He wasn't always, you know. He was something of a romantic when I met him. And he didn't drink anything like as much. I think we've been very bad for each other. I bring out the oaf in him, and he brings out the petty bitch in me. We were so wrapped up in each other in the early years, we had no time or patience with anyone or anything else. All our scorn and petulance was reserved for others. Now, we seem to have turned on each other. Sometimes, I think that maybe I'm not a very nice person.'

I had a strange, brief glimpse of another life, another bar, another time where Carole was talking about me that way.

'Och,' I said, broadening the accent to imitate my grandfather, 'the only thing wrong with you is that you didn't get enough good skelpings when you were a wean.'

'And you think you're man enough to put that right now, do you?' she said, a definite hint of challenge in her voice. But at least she was smiling.

'Not me,' I said. 'My grandfather perhaps. I'm unapologetically new man. And, as for your marriage, I'm strictly neutral, an innocent bystander.'

'Not you. You've never been that,' she said. 'And you're certainly not that now.'

'No, maybe not,' I said.

A sudden darkness clouded her eyes.

'Should I be really worried about Martin?' she said.

'Worried enough to have him looked at by an expert,' I said.

'Oh, God,' she said, 'I thought he'd taken Mum's death surprisingly well. I mean, he was in grief and all that, but he wasn't in bits or anything. I hope it's not all going to start again. I was away last time . . .' Her voice trailed off. 'Mum hinted that all wasn't well. She never did tell me much about it, though. Didn't she speak to you about him?'

'Sure she did. And I went to see him a few times. In the hospital. He was a troubled boy,' I said, 'and he looked to me earlier like a troubled man. He spooked me anyway.'

She nodded.

'I'll try,' she said, 'but I don't think it's going to be easy. The only thing he really seems to have taken from his earlier experiences is a strong antipathy to mental health professionals.' She looked up at me with her shy Princess Di look. 'I could probably do with a little help.'

I glanced away, pretending to contemplate my watch, and decided to cut the conversation off before it went anywhere. I didn't want to take on any responsibility at all for Martin. He really had spooked me.

'What do you remember about that night, Carole?' I said. 'The night your father died.'

'Why?' she said. 'You were there. You saw more than I did.'

'I guess so,' I said, 'but we've never talked about it. We never got the chance. And what you said the other night and what Martin said earlier got me thinking. You don't have to be an expert in the field, or a trained psychiatrist, to see it as an odd sort of suicide.'

'That's what I've always felt,' she said. 'But what do I know?' She leaned forward and her blue eyes clouded again. 'What do I remember? I honestly don't know. It's a jumble. I remember the stifling heat in the hospital corridor where we waited. I remember, before it happened, going up to my room to find the copy of *Fighting Terms* that you wanted back. I remember looking at a poem and then I think I remember the sound of the shot. I must have heard something, otherwise I wouldn't have come running back down to the living room. Mum was kneeling down by Dad who was lying on the sofa. You were leaning over him, pressing something to his chest. Mum told me to call the police and an ambulance. In that order. And I did. Then it was all waiting for tired doctors and interviews with sombre policemen.' She paused. 'When it comes down to it, I don't really remember very much. Just what you described the other day.'

149

'Did you know your father kept a handgun in the house?'

She shook her head.

'No, not at the time,' she said. 'That all came out afterwards. How he'd won it in a game of poker with one of the American officers down at the base. It was unlicensed and he kept it hidden.'

'Did Martin know about it? Or where it was hidden?' I said.

'I don't know,' she said. 'I was much more likely to know about something like that than he was. Though he was a sneaky little thing, always mooching around, rummaging in drawers. So, I suppose he might have come across it. Why?'

'Just something he said earlier about going to the bookcase and getting the gun. It's probably not important, probably not what happened. Just one of his false memories.'

'He said that he went to the bookcase and got the gun?'

'That's right,' I said. 'Well, what he said was that he *remembered* going to the bookcase. Which isn't necessarily the same thing.' I looked at my watch. 'I'll pay and then we'd better get back to the house,' I said. 'Didn't MacPlod say to expect him for two thirty?'

She nodded, still looking pensive, but she said nothing. Then she stood up, worried herself into her coat, gathered up her bag and went to wait for me by the door.

I paid the bill quickly and joined her. She slipped her arm into mine as we walked down the steps to the pavement and slowly started to retrace our steps to the car.

The cold, dreary rain blew in across the harbour and soaked us in seconds. Two large and cold-eyed seagulls squabbled raucously over a crust of bread, and a wagtail bobbed along in front of us. The few passers-by, round-eyed and curious, looked up from under umbrellas, glanced pointedly and subjected us to a few more knowing nods. I felt like an adolescent again – proud and a little reckless, vulnerable and guilty.

Chapter Seven

It was time to mislead the police again. A rough count indicated that this would probably be the third charge of obstructing them in their enquiries they would be able to level against me. I was tempted to keep it to two and tell the complete truth when they arrived at the house.

I was entering further into a deeper, darker and more labyrinthine legal maze with every passing day. The hidden briefcase was weighing heavily on my mind. I had no way of knowing whether Liam and Dermot had been picked up and, if they had, whether they had retrieved the briefcase first. The fact that I had hidden it wouldn't look at all good in court. I might even find myself charged as a major drugs trafficker. I wondered if I could depend at all on Dougie's tame policeman. It was a ticklish situation and I wasn't sure how to resolve it. Making a clean breast of it certainly had its attractions as a way of proceeding.

The two policemen who showed up both looked very young and tired and I didn't want to make their lives more difficult than they already were. Somehow, I couldn't see that attempting to explain my convoluted thinking on Friday night was going to make anything easier for anyone. I didn't think they'd understand that breaking Angus Darling's nose in primary school was not the best way to ensure a fair hearing from him in later life.

There was a sweet-faced, soft-spoken, blond detective constable with a heavy head cold, and an even younger, uniformed officer with huge feet, who blushed when Carole smiled at him and asked if he'd like anything to drink. He finally managed to stammer out something that sounded like 'tea' and Carole worked on that assumption.

The detective constable, who had confidently asked for coffee, white, with three sugars, apologized for their delayed response to the call but explained that everyone was tied up with 'the murder'.

I nodded understandingly from the chaise longue where Carole and I had first furtively, and briefly, made out whenever her mother had left us alone, looking at the window that Martin had stared out of so unnervingly earlier. The little patch of sky that I could see was an ominous dark grey and raindrops pattered gently against the pane of glass and rolled, like clear beads, erratically down to the sill.

The uniformed man mumbled something incomprehensible and left the room, presumably to look around, while the other took my statement.

Although the apparent innocence of the officers, and my self-destructive urge to seek absolution, had almost tempted me to tell the truth, I had few qualms about embroidering my story, adding two hefty pickaxe handles to justify my flight. I described Liam and Dermot in loving detail, mentioning that they both looked as if they'd been in a fight. Encouragingly, whenever I hesitated for the sake of verisimilitude, the officer prompted me more than a little, leading me to believe that he had certainly seen the two men I was describing.

Carole brought in tea and coffee and then gave her admirably succinct statement. After that, the man with the cold relaxed and passed on the welcome, if not entirely unexpected, news that they had already picked up two men matching the descriptions that I had given and they were languishing unhappily in custody.

'No pickaxe handles on them, though,' he sniffed sadly. 'And no sign of forced entry here, either,' when the other one had whispered in his ear.

I offered the observation that they may have had time to dump the weapons and explained again that when I'd

152

arrived the front door had been open and I wasn't absolutely sure that Martin had shut it when he'd left.

They both nodded in a world-weary way, as though this was the crucial detail that was bound to determine the sheriff's not proven verdict, and then the one with the cold asked me, apparently casually, if I'd seen the car before.

I shook my head and he leaned forward in his chair and started prompting me again.

'Like yesterday,' he said, 'when you were on your way to the beach.'

And I'd been thinking that he hadn't made the connection. But it would be difficult for a police officer working in the area, even a very young one not born here, not to recognize Carole's name.

I looked at Carole and said that it was possible but I didn't remember it. Carole said nothing. I managed a puzzled look.

'Well, you never know, sir,' he said, knowingly. 'Strangers in the area, with a predisposition towards violence. A murder . . .'

'I see,' I said, trying to make it appear that it hadn't occurred to me and succeeding only in sounding disingenuous. 'And you think that might not be a coincidence.'

'Well, like I say, sir, you never know. The two incidents could be related.'

'What are they saying?' I asked as casually as I could. 'The two men you picked up?'

'Nothing at all,' he said. 'Except that they haven't done anything and they want a solicitor. Not a local one.' He blew noisily into his handkerchief and carefully inspected the contents. 'Not the usual response of your upright and blameless citizen.' He paused, still apparently transfixed by the mucus in his handkerchief. 'If there is such a thing.'

I couldn't escape the unsettling feeling that the last remark had been aimed at me.

He definitely had the look of a man who, given minimal encouragement, would cheerfully stay chatting, in the warm, blowing his nose loudly and drinking coffee all

153

afternoon. But his partner, having risked a scalded throat by gulping down his tea in one long swallow as soon as it was poured, was looking wretchedly uncomfortable, pulling at his collar as if it restricted his breathing and beating a constant tattoo on the wooden floor with his size fifteen feet. The detective took the hint, finished his coffee, reluctantly pulled his black, quilted anorak on over his stiff, green, tweed jacket and walked purposefully to the door.

'We'll be in touch,' he said, 'and, if you recall anything else, please let me know. Especially if you find those pickaxe handles lying around.'

I ignored the touch of scepticism in his final remark and cheerfully agreed that if anything came to mind, I'd call him. Then I realized that if he had given his name I couldn't recall it. Maybe Carole would remember.

He turned towards me on the steps as I was showing him out and he sneezed.

'By the way, sir,' he said, hauling his huge handkerchief out of his pocket again and rubbing it against his reddening nose, 'DI Stewart would like you to drop by and see him again tomorrow morning. Just to go over a few things. He asked if you'd give him a call.'

I nodded my acknowledgement and watched as he climbed into the unmarked blue car, and drove slowly off. Stewart was the name of the bored-looking detective who'd turned up at the beach and who was, presumably, in charge of the investigation into Danny's murder.

Carole was in the kitchen, washing cups at the sink, when I returned. I slipped my arms around her waist and kissed her neck, breathing in her warmth and freshness. She leaned back against me, her eyes closed.

'Do you think that he thought it was odd? You being here?' she said.

'Maybe,' I said. 'He didn't seem unduly perplexed. He probably leapt to the right conclusion. Perhaps, behind that innocent, angelic appearance, he's a hardened, world-weary thief-taker who's seen it all, and is completely unshockable.'

I held her a little tighter.

'I ought to get back to work,' she said. 'Board meeting at four thirty.'

'It's only three fifteen,' I said.

'Things to do before the meeting.'

'OK,' I said, stepping away from her.

'No need to stop that quite yet,' she said.

I mover closer again and slid my hand over the faint curve of her belly.

'What do you think this is all about?' she said.

'What, the world, life and the meaning of the universe?' I said.

Her elbow jabbed me painfully under the ribs.

'No,' she said.

'Well, there's cocaine in the briefcase. So, drugs is a possibility,' I said.

'It can't be drugs,' she said. 'Duncan wouldn't have any truck with drugs.'

'Well, that's my best guess, for what it's worth. And Dougie's.'

'You've told Dougie about all this then?' she said.

'Yes,' I said. 'I had to tell someone. By the way, he's coming up this afternoon.'

She turned around to face me.

'Dougie?' she said. 'Coming here?'

'Aye, I'm meeting him off the bus.'

She busied herself with the washing-up and I noticed that she looked a little flushed.

'How long's he staying?' she said. 'And where?'

'He'll only be here a day or two, I expect. And he's staying with me.'

'That'll be right,' she said. 'It'll give you the chance to drink yourselves stupid.'

Carole had never approved of big Dougie. There was about her attitude towards him, although she'd never admit it of course, something of the tight-lipped Protestant distaste and mistrust of Catholics endemic to the west coast. Although I think she also believed, erroneously, that he led me astray. Her feelings also meant that, half the time, I had never been sure that she entirely approved of me, and I was of impeccable working-class, bigoted, Proddy stock. I even had an aunt, on my mother's side, who spent her vacations in Northern Ireland in order to hear Ian Paisley preach, or rant, as my father had it. Dad used to tell her, drily, that she should save her money and leave her windows open. She'd hear him easily enough, if the wind was in the right direction.

'I suppose it's always possible that we may have the odd dram,' I said. 'But he's working. Going to write about Danny's murder. And about rural crime in general, I think. That's what he said, anyway.'

There was a short silence broken only by Carole banging cups forcefully on to the draining board. Finally, she turned away from the sink.

'Well, I'd better be about my business. Give Dougie my best, when you pick him up,' she said, ripping some paper towels from a roll and vigorously drying her hands.

'Do you mind if I stay a little longer?' I asked.

'Not at all,' she said. 'Kettle there, coffee pot there, filters and coffee in the cupboard over there. Just be sure to close the door when you do leave.'

'I'll be the model house guest,' I said. 'I promise not to take too much of the family silver and I won't tread mud into the living-room carpet or pee in the sink.'

She gave me a tight little smile as I helped her into her coat, then she pecked me lightly on the cheek, broke away abruptly and strode briskly towards the hall when I tried to turn the contact into a lingering clinch.

I briefly wondered what I'd done to deserve the sudden icy shoulder but decided not to worry about it too much. I'd probably never discover what it was and, anyway, chances were it was more about Dougie than it was about me. I heard the distant clunk of her slamming the car door and then the sound of the Golf driving away and I wandered over to the sink to fill the kettle, full of strange and troubling thoughts.

I had no doubt at all that the two Irishmen, Liam and Dermot, had been looking for me when they crept into the house. And I didn't see how Duncan Ferguson could have known that I was coming up to the house. Martin Crawford, on the other hand, had known exactly where I was. The coincidence of the two thugs turning up ten minutes after Martin had left was too great to ignore. It could have been just coincidence but I was disinclined to think so.

I poured boiling water on to the coffee in the filter, watched it froth and steam, heard it drip into the pot, and sniffed the warm aroma. I poured more water and then remembered the bottle of Orvieto and took it from the freezer. The frosted surface of the glass stuck to my hand for a second or two as I tried to put it down on the big pine table, and a fleeting, treacherous, insidious thought crossed my mind. Carole had known where I would be at twelve twenty. Suspicion, I realized, could easily become a habit. I dismissed Carole from the equation. She wouldn't have turned up in time to drive me to some form of safety if she'd been involved, would she? No, as far as I was concerned, Martin was definitely in the frame for this one.

The coffee finished filtering and I poured myself a cup. I carried it through to the living room and sat again on the chaise longue, facing the window. The light was already fading and the room felt cold.

I remembered again that this was the room where Peter Crawford had shot himself and I shivered. I was sitting close to where it had happened.

I took my coffee to the kitchen, warming my hands on the mug and staring out of the window at the bare trees and the damp, yellowing grass. If I leaned forward, over the sink, and looked up, I could just see the ivy-covered ruins of Robert the Bruce's castle, high on the hill, overlooking the village and commanding the loch. I wondered idly if any of that once-great edifice had been used in the construction of the Crawfords' house.

I hadn't been up there in years. The truth was that there wasn't much of the castle left to see, just a few ivy-covered walls surrounded by fencing and warning notices, but it was a great spot to sit and think.

The first time I remembered climbing up the steep, uneven steps and narrow, dirt path was with my mother in the May of the year I started school. My brother, Rory, had been just a toddler and it had taken an eternity to reach the castle. He had to be coaxed, cajoled, bribed, waited for and, mostly, carried. Then, when we had finally arrived, we had sat in the hot sun, drunk Irn Bru that tasted like warm, liquid bubble gum, eaten cheese and tomato sandwiches and watched the tiny fishing boats far below us land their catches.

My mother had worn a yellow cotton dress with blue flowers printed on it and had told me about the Bruce, while Rory rolled in the long, fragrant grass behind us. She didn't mention mimsy stuff, like the cave and the spider. Instead, she told me the real stories – the murder of the Red Comyn, Bannockburn and Berwick. I didn't understand much of it, but the names were evocative of a rough, heroic age and captured my imagination completely, and it didn't seem as if it was all that long, although it must have been a year or two, before I was reading everything I could find on that ruthless, driven and canny man.

There had been other people there that day, I remembered; other mothers with their young children, friends of my mother, I think. But all I could recall was sitting, enchanted, beside her as she told tales of intrigue, bravery and dirty dealing. I searched in my memory for her face and her voice. But they weren't there. The skirt of a yellow dress with blue flowers printed on it fluttered in a slight breeze, a work- and sun-reddened hand reached out to help me to my feet, and a hank of thick, brown hair fell forward over her pale forehead. And that was all.

A sudden, sharp, grating noise outside, like a slate slithering down the roof, drew me abruptly back to the present. I tensed and stood completely still, waiting for something else to happen. Nothing did, but I couldn't relax.

I stepped away from the sink and the sound of my

footfall echoed in the big, old kitchen. Suddenly, the house felt achingly empty: empty of Carole and empty of my long-gone mother.

Dougie wouldn't arrive for an hour and it would only take me fifteen minutes to wash up and get to the bus stop. But I could waste half an hour or a little more among the books in the gift shop and then just sit in the car. I found that I didn't want to stay in the Crawfords' house any longer.

Dougie was, inevitably, the last person off the coach. He ambled slowly down the steps, his laptop dangling precariously from his loose grasp, and he beamed cheerfully at me before rejoining the five passengers retrieving their bags from the enormous underbelly of the bus.

He looked out of place, in his well-cut suit, silk tie, dark woollen overcoat and polished shoes, among the greasy anoraks, baggy jeans, scruffy trainers and shopping bags, but he was completely at his ease, bantering with the driver and an elderly lady as he helped her gather up her luggage and pointed out his own in the depths of the hold.

The rain had stopped half an hour before but the bus headlamps gleamed on the still-wet tarmac, like twin moons casting one beam on the dark, dense surface of some alien lake. The cloud had disappeared and the temperature was dropping rapidly. Little white puffs issued from everyone's mouth, like speech bubbles in a cartoon. The engine growled out a powerful note, low and rumbling, and the sleek, yellow-and-blue coach throbbed and vibrated to it. The glass of the bus shelter that I was leaning against was pocked by brown-edged cigarette burns and one pane had been kicked out altogether. The smell of decaying fish wafted over from the Crawfords' jerry-built processing plant in the adjacent, grandly named industrial estate.

Dougie broke away from the rapidly dispersing maul

that had formed around the side of the bus and handed me his soft-leather overnight bag.

He looked around with a sweet smile on his face, sniffed the air and peered into the shelter.

'This bus stop hath a pleasant seat,' he said.

'No it doesn't,' I said, taking his bag and strolling towards the car. 'It's painfully narrow and extremely uncomfortable.'

He laughed and followed me.

'So,' he said, as I fumbled to open the boot and then dropped his bag in, 'how are you? Apart, of course, from the piles aggravated by the cold, damp, unyielding moulded-plastic bench that have clearly done nothing for your disposition.'

'Och, I've had better days, Dougie,' I said. 'But I'm glad to see you.'

Then he stood by the car, staring up at the sky, apparently lost in thought.

'What's up?' I said.

'Just wondering what to eat tonight. What do you think?' he said. 'Fish or meat?'

'It's Monday,' I said.

'So?' he said.

'No fishermen out yesterday, so no fresh fish today,' I said. 'Only, as the bard said, connect.'

'Which bard was that, I wonder?' he said. 'All right, lamb, beef or venison, then?'

'Whatever you fancy.'

He shook his head sadly. 'I don't suppose that, by some miracle, an Indian of impeccable taste, refinement and limitless Kingfisher lager has opened since I was last here?'

'No, Dougie,' I said, unlocking the car, 'there's still no curry house.'

'Thought not,' he said gloomily, sliding into the car and then adjusting the passenger seat to accommodate his long legs. He sat back and fastened the seat belt. 'Very well, Carruthers, we shall just have to accept the primitive conditions of the natives, adjust as best we can and slum it in some three-star restaurant.' He banged on the dashboard. 'To the hotel, James.'

'Hotel?' I said. 'I thought you'd be staying with me.'

'Och, the secretary booked me a room and I'd better use it. You know how it is. Receipts for everything when you're on expenses. Why don't you stay there as well?'

'Because I don't have an expense account and I can't see Herr Taxman accepting a night in the local hotel as a legitimate business expense.' Then it dawned on me. 'You're scared, aren't you? You don't want to stay at my place until everything's sorted, do you?'

He chewed at his moustache for a few seconds.

'Not scared, exactly,' he finally said. 'More cautious, really. And I'd advise you to take the same precautions. Your man Kelly is heavy-duty. I looked into him a little. I'm serious. Check into the hotel the night.'

'I'll be all right,' I said.

'I'll pay,' he said, 'if you're broke.'

'Nah, it'll be all right,' I said and started the engine.

We drove the short distance to the hotel in an amiable silence. I didn't know what Dougie was thinking about – it could have been anything from the correct glass to serve tomato juice in to why Quentin Tarantino thought he could act – but I was pondering his last remarks. It was tempting to check into the hotel for a couple of nights but I was feeling too bloody-minded to say so. I promised myself that if he suggested it again, I'd agree.

He didn't and I waited in the bar, nursing a cup of coffee, while he checked in and deposited his belongings in his room.

The bar was much warmer and more comfortable than it had been in the morning, and much less crowded than at lunchtime. The fire was blasting out heat, and the smell of ammonia and bleach from the morning had been over-written by spilt beer and fried food from lunch.

'You'll be taking up residence soon,' Fiona had said when she had brought my coffee. 'Who are you meeting this time? Martin Crawford? Everyone thinks the family must be offering you a job. Or selling you the company. Which is it?'

I'd smiled and declined to answer. Then, when Dougie had appeared a little later in his charcoal-grey suit, still clutching his laptop, 'Your banker, is he?' she asked as I stood at the bar and ordered him some tea. 'Or your stockbroker?'

I smiled again and shook my head. Gossip was a strong currency.

Dougie and I sat huddled over our tea and coffee while I told him what had happened in the past day.

'They won't be happy about being arrested,' he said quietly when I had finished describing the confrontation in the street and its aftermath. 'These are paid-up members of the Irish Drugs Marketing Board. Hard men. Very rich, very hard men. It's not a good idea to piss them off, and you seem to have done that pretty comprehensively.' He sat back and drank his tea, looking thoughtful. 'But I suppose there are other things going on, other possibilities besides drugs. Drugs is favourite, though. I remember a couple of murders a few years back in a nice little seaside resort called Scheveningen, just outside The Hague. Some Irish drug traffickers found in a burnt-out flat. Thing is, the authorities found some weird stuff in one of the charred corpses. It was cavity-wall filler: in his lungs and his gut. Your man, Kelly, was implicated. Nothing proved, of course.' He licked his mouser. 'What a guddle! Why don't you stay here the night? We can make an evening of it. Eat, drink and be relatively merry. And you won't have to worry about driving back.'

I didn't even have to think about it.

'OK,' I said, 'you've convinced me. I'll stay.'

He smiled and glanced meaningfully at his watch.

'I'll get the pints in,' he said.

'You have one,' I said. 'I'll just pop home, pick up a clean shirt and a toothbrush, feed the cat and check my messages.'

'You sure?'

'Yeah, it'll be fine. The two thugs are safely banged up. Anyway, I can still look after myself, remember?'

'My hero,' he said solemnly, rising to his feet. 'How's Carole, by the way? You have seen her?'

I stood up. 'Aye, I've seen her. At the funeral and all. She's not so bad, considering.'

'That's good,' he said, nodding thoughtfully.

I left him at the bar, talking to Fiona while his Guinness flowed, slow as black honey, into the glass.

It was turning into a clear, cold night as I stepped from the bright entrance of the hotel. A small colourful poster placed strategically next to the bar menu reminded me that this was the week that the Mid Argyll Musical Society was performing *Me and My Girl*, 'the happiest show in town', and I hadn't bought a ticket yet. A council gritting-lorry rumbled slowly past, its 'spreading' light flashing, rock salt spraying out in a fine, reddish cloud all around it.

The village was dark and hushed, and there was a haze around the moon, hanging like a thin, lopsided smile. A few stars had already appeared, tiny pinpricks in the thick, black sky. I gazed up for a few seconds, trying, unsuccessfully, to convince myself that my problems were not so very great in the wider scheme of things, before walking to the car.

I drove slowly through the night, encountering very little traffic, listening to a tape of Django Reinhardt and Stephane Grappelly with The Quintet of the Hot Club of France. They had launched into their gentle romping version of 'Sweet Georgia Brown' when the headlights paralysed a small group of deer standing in a field near my house, their eyes glittering eerily, like tiny fragments of broken glass. As the music loped to its jovial conclusion and someone – I liked to think it was Django – grunted his satisfaction, I parked the car at the entrance to my driveway and jumped out.

The heavy white gate swung open easily and I looped the noose of rope that hung from its top bar over the waiting stake. The rich, mellow sound of Reinhardt and

163

Grappelly playing 'Belleville' was suddenly oddly grating in the cold, silent night and I turned off the tape when I climbed back into the car and drove down to the house.

I threw a change of clothes, a book and some toiletries into a small bag, opened a tin of catfood and emptied it into the cat's dish. There were no messages on my answerphone and only two emails sitting in my inbox when I checked. Neither of them looked as if they were worth opening and I deleted them unread. In less than ten minutes I was ready and threw my bag into the boot of the car.

Then the thought of the briefcase started nagging at me and, instead of just driving off as I knew I should, I decided to see if it was still where I'd left it. I went back into the kitchen, grabbed a torch and a pair of old rubber gloves and then trudged carefully across the muddy field behind the garage. The ground was rapidly hardening and there would be a sharp frost before morning.

I stopped at the septic tank, put the torch on the ground, pulled on the rubber gloves, dragged the heavy wooden lid to one side and recoiled from the warm fetid smell. When I peered in, it was immediately obvious that the length of string that I had attached to the package and carefully tied to the lid was no longer in place and nowhere to be seen. I held my breath and plunged one hand into the mess and rummaged around half-heartedly, but I knew that I wouldn't find it. The briefcase had been collected. At that moment, my torch flickered and went out.

I stepped back, sighed and stripped off the rubber gloves, dropping them by the side of the tank. Then I wrestled the lid back into place. Well, if the two Irish thugs had retrieved the briefcase before being picked up by the police, then they really did have a lot of explaining to do. No wonder they weren't planning on saying anything without their solicitor.

As I turned back to the house, there was a sound from the garage. I stopped and slowly twisted around. Three weak pools of light, the colour of pale Italian wine, were steadily making their way towards me. And in each pool was a pair of highly polished black shoes. I bent to retrieve my own torch from the ground but it eluded my groping hand. I stood up and turned to face the three men who were advancing towards me.

Christopher Marlowe stabbed through the eye in an altercation about the reckoning in an inn in Deptford: Pier Paolo Pasolini's head crushed under the wheels of a car in a car park in Rome when he tried to pick up the wrong boy: Iain Lewis scared to death next to his septic tank. Just as squalid and seedy certainly, but without the right ring to it somehow. Not that I was under any illusions that my death would be remembered as a tragic waste.

The pools of light halted some yards away and I squinted into them, trying to make out who was lurking behind them. Then one of the beams shone straight into my face, dazzling me, and a rough, urban voice that I recognized sent a chill through me.

'I take it from your reaction, Mr Lewis, that you are as surprised as we are that the briefcase isn't where you left it. Either that or you were just checking that it had been collected, as arranged.'

I said nothing but reflected that these boys learned quickly and must have left their car in the passing place beyond my house and walked down through the field so that I wouldn't be alerted to their presence before they wanted me to be.

'Which is it, Mr Lewis?' Colm Kelly urged a response.

'I imagine,' I said, 'that your brother collected it sometime earlier this afternoon.'

'I assume that you're referring to poor Liam. Unfortunately, he was detained by the police on some trumped-up charge before he could act on the information he was given and retrieve our property,' he said smoothly. 'Now, do you know where it is or not?'

'If your brother doesn't have it, then no,' I said.

165

'Liam is not my brother,' he said, 'and nor does he have the package.'

I shook my head wearily.

'Why did you have to leave the damn thing here in the first place?' I said.

'Someone's little joke,' he said.

'Ha bloody ha,' I said.

'I must confess that I was uncertain about the comedic potential myself,' he said. 'But it seemed amusing to go along with it at the time and indulge him. We needed a poste restante. It doesn't seem at all funny now, though, I agree.' He paused and whispered to his two companions.

I peered into the gloom and tried to make out who they were. It seemed as if Dermot and Liam had said enough to the police to talk their way out of custody.

As they spread out to take me from either side, Colm Kelly continued. 'Now, unfortunately, I need to be certain that you don't know the whereabouts of the briefcase and so we are going to inflict a certain amount of pain on you. I'll be honest: this does not bother me in the least. You have caused a great deal of trouble.'

'Hold on,' I said, holding my hands up placatingly, 'none of this is my fault. I didn't ask to be used as a mailbox.'

'That is certainly true, Mr Lewis,' he said, 'but it is also largely irrelevant.'

I decided that the real threat would come in the thin, dark shape of the weasel-faced Dermot who was approaching from my right and I turned to face him. He was holding the torch in his left hand and he swung a big, roundhouse right at me. He was off balance and clearly didn't know how to punch anyway. I stepped inside his swing and took his fist on my left shoulder, jabbing him sharply with a straight right to the chin at the same time. He rocked back on his heels and looked as if he was about to fall. I danced away from him immediately and backed into Liam, who had come around behind me. I hammered my heel into his shin and then sank my elbow into his stomach. He fell back, muttering curses under his breath.

Then they both rallied and closed in on me again. Much more warily this time.

Dermot feinted with his right and I fell for it, leaned back and was grabbed from behind by Liam and held tightly. Dermot came at me with an even uglier expression on his face and I kicked out at him but I only managed a glancing blow to his knee before he landed a couple of serious blows to my ribs and stomach. I fell to my knees, retching a little and gasping for breath, reflecting that even someone who can't punch can hurt you.

'Pick him up,' Colm said.

I was dragged roughly to my feet, held up with my arms pinioned to my sides by Liam's surprisingly large, meaty hands. Dermot grabbed my right arm and hit me in the ribs. Colm Kelly came towards us. He took his hand from his overcoat pocket. In the light from his torch I could see that he was holding an open flick-knife, the blade glinting.

'I have the distinct impression that you haven't been taking us seriously,' he said. 'Well, I intend to change that.'

He pressed the blade against my shirt front and carefully cut off every button. He slipped the knife under my shirt then held it flat against my bare chest.

'What do you want?' I said.

'You know what we want, Mr Lewis,' he said, turning the knife and suddenly running the edge about three inches across the right side of my stomach. I didn't realize at first that he'd cut me but then the cold night air hit the wound and I looked down in pain and surprise and saw the blood running in a ragged line down towards my jeans.

I gagged, Kelly stepped back and nodded at Dermot who pummelled me for maybe ten seconds. Then Liam dropped me to the cold, hardening ground and Dermot aimed a desultory kick at my head but missed and struck my shoulder. I vomited painfully and then just lay, catching my breath in little ragged gulps as that was marginally less agonizing than breathing normally. I felt like I'd been at the bottom of a collapsed scrum and walked on by seventeen-stone forwards.

The rutted ground was cool against my face and damp was seeping into my bruised and bloodied body. No one spoke and the only sound was the heavy breathing of Dermot and Liam as they recovered from the effort of holding and beating me. I tried to curl up into a pathetic foetal ball, waiting for the kicking that I thought would shortly follow.

After a couple of minutes, Colm Kelly turned the beam of his torch on me.

'Now,' he said, 'tell me who has the briefcase.'

I raised myself up a little and attempted to stare beyond the light.

'As I told you before we were so rudely interrupted, I don't know,' I finally managed to gasp, sounding even to my ears like a stiff-upper-lipped refugee from a fifties POW movie. 'And you can dance a hornpipe on my liver after you've cut it out and I still won't know.'

'I just might do that,' Kelly said. Then there was a long, long pause before he eventually said, 'OK, you've got twenty-four hours to find it. We'll be back this time tomorrow.'

And then suddenly it was brutally dark again, and I was alone.

After I hauled myself to my feet and lumbered wearily back into the house, I examined the knife cut. It wasn't too serious and I held a tea towel to it while I phoned Dougie on his mobile and told him I'd been delayed and I'd be a little late for dinner. He said that'd be all right and he'd make the booking for eight thirty. Then he asked if everything was OK and I said it was and we both hung up.

I tried to persuade myself that I hadn't told Dougie about the minor mauling I'd just received to stop him from worrying, but I knew that it was because I didn't want to admit to him that he'd been right about me not returning home and I'd been wrong about maintaining that I could look after myself.

I limped off to the bathroom to examine my wounds further and was relieved to discover that there was nothing too extensive. The cut was quite painful but it had more or less stopped bleeding and, apart from that, I hadn't been roughed up much at all. I had at least been right about Dermot's inability to punch properly. And he hadn't had all that much time to work on giving me a decent pummelling. I ran a bath.

As I lay in the hot water, soaking my not too badly bruised body, I ruminated on the future. A little dab of witch hazel and a large Band-aid and I'd be OK this time, but I knew I wouldn't escape so lightly the following day. Broken limbs and ruptured organs were very much in the offing – and that was assuming I found the damned briefcase. It wasn't where I'd left it and Colm didn't have it. If the police had it, I had little doubt that they would have mentioned it to me. Which meant that someone else had taken it.

There's a particular kind of petty villain who snivels and whinges when sober that the world never gave him a chance, and rants and blusters about assumed slights and imaginary injustices when drunk. His is always hard time because it's always someone else's fault that he's in jail; his brief is always incompetent and the screws always have it in for him. Anyway, he didnae do it. His life is one continuous failure to recognize that actions have consequences. One of the old rules of thumb of sociology way back in the heady days of the sixties and seventies was that the working class was separated from the middle class because it didn't know how to defer gratification. This was never true, of course: the working class had nothing to defer. It's even less true since credit cards so proudly took the waiting out of wanting and the middle class no longer defers anything either. Doubtless, all kinds of new ad hoc rules have been coined in sociology departments the length and breadth of the land and I'm willing to bet that one of them draws a distinction between those on the shady side of the law who recognize and accept the consequences of their actions and those who don't, thus giving rise to the concept of the responsible criminal. I suppose it's already there in the old adage, 'If you can't do the time, don't do the crime.'

Billy MacPhail was my nearest neighbour and had been so for two and a half years, of which he had been in residence for only eight months. The rest of the time, as his four children had learned to say, 'he was a long way away' and, once a month, the children would, until the car was repossessed, be dressed up by his amiable slattern of a wife and get dragged off to Edinburgh to see him.

I wasn't exactly clutching at straws when my thoughts strayed to Billy, but I was definitely focusing on the only possibility I could come up with and he was worth more than a passing thought. He was certainly not a responsible felon and he had been out for more than six weeks. Which meant that, quite apart from the fact that his wife was probably pregnant again, he'd be bored and broke, and getting into mischief. When Billy got into mischief, it usually meant that someone's property went missing. The disappearance of the briefcase and Billy might well be completely unrelated but I didn't think so. Anyway, I didn't have any other options. Billy MacPhail would have to be visited and questioned closely. My already less than buoyant heart sank even further at the prospect.

I'd dried myself down, put some cotton wool and a plaster on the cut and started to apply witch hazel to any obvious signs of bruising when the phone rang. A towelling robe was hanging on the back of the bathroom door. I lifted it from the hook, struggled into it and half ran, half limped off to the study to pick up.

It was Carole.

She sounded furtive, as though she was afraid of being overheard.

'Iain,' she said, 'Duncan appears to know nothing about those two Irishmen who were arrested.'

'Really,' I said. 'He told you that, did he?'

'Not exactly,' she said. 'But he doesn't seem at all concerned. Except, of course, that we were broken into. That, and the fact that you were here. And I was coming back to meet you. That does seem to concern him . . .'

She trailed off and there was a short silence. I didn't know what to say and she didn't seem to have anything to add. I'd never thought of Duncan as much of an actor and he'd certainly known all about the events at my house that morning when he'd spoken to me before lunch. So I supposed that he must have lied to Carole very convincingly.

Or she was not being entirely honest with me.

I hated myself for the thought immediately.

'Did he know they'd been picked up?' I asked.

'Yes,' she said slowly, 'but only because the police contacted him about it.'

'Why did they do that?'

'To let him know, I guess.'

'Not because Liam and Dermot said that he'd invited them to the house?'

'No,' she said. 'At least, I don't think so.' She paused. 'Anyway, if they had said that and he'd confirmed it, they'd have been released, wouldn't they?'

'They have been,' I said.

'What?' she said. 'How do you know?'

'I've just seen them.'

'Where?'

'Here. They paid me a social call.'

'Are you all right?'

'Yes,' I said. 'I'm fine.'

'Thank goodness. Anyway, I just wanted to let you know that you're wrong about Duncan,' she said. 'He isn't part of this. Whatever it is.'

'Carole,' I said, 'I love you for your loyalty. Don't change.'

Her voice dropped a few decibels to a faint and warm whisper. 'When will I see you? I really want to. I'm worried about you.'

'Believe me,' I said, 'so am I. Can you make it to the hotel restaurant for eight thirty? We could meet then. I'll be there.'

'I'll try,' she said. 'I will try.'

She cut the connection, leaving me with a vague feeling of unease and a warm urgent desire to see her.

Chapter Eight

The bar was much busier than it had been earlier. I had to force my way to the counter past some fishermen still clad in their bulky working clothes.

I saw Dougie, sitting at the same table, reading a battered paperback book, absentmindedly holding an empty pint glass in his right hand. The residue of white froth smearing the inside was turning the yellowish-brown of a nicotine-stained finger.

Fiona was not behind the bar: she must have gone off to collect her weans from her mother. She'd been replaced by a gaunt, unsmiling, sparsely bearded man I didn't know who, silently but efficiently, poured another pint of Guinness for Dougie and handed me my whisky. I drank it straight down and asked for another while the Guinness still flowed. The barman didn't even raise an eyebrow and quietly obliged.

I carried the drinks through the little throngs of drinkers and sat down next to Dougie. He looked up and noticed me for the first time.

'This is a belter of a book, you know,' he said, placing his black-jacketed copy of *The Crow Road* on the table. 'I've been meaning to read it for ages.'

'Aye,' I said, 'it's one of his best. They filmed the TV series around here.'

He pushed a key across the table towards me. I left it where it was and sipped a little whisky.

'I checked you in. Room seventeen,' he said.

I nodded my thanks.

'You all right, Iain?' he said.

'I'm fine,' I said.

Dougie looked unconvinced but he let it drop, stood up and picked up his fresh pint.

'Let's take these off to the restaurant and order,' he said.

'Yeah,' I said, rising to my feet, pocketing the key and following him into the hallway and up the stairs to the dimly lit and completely empty restaurant.

It didn't take the IQ of a Goethe to work out which was our table. There was only one set, a candle spilling a little golden light on the crisp white tablecloth. We sat in silence and looked out over the harbour at the streaks of reflected light smeared on the surface of the black and brooding sea until a slim waitress who looked as if she was still at school came over and presented us with two large, leather-bound menus and a wine list. Dougie told her that we'd take a few minutes to decide and she dutifully disappeared.

He studied me thoughtfully.

'So,' he finally said, 'how did you enjoy the play apart from that, Mrs Lincoln?'

'What?' I grunted at him.

'Och, Iain, you're even more out of sorts than usual. What's up?'

'Nothing,' I said.

'And grumpier than a bear with a sore bum. Something happen up at the house?'

'Aye,' I said and, backtracking rapidly on my earlier decision not to tell him about it, I recounted as concisely as I could my discovery that the briefcase was missing and that I'd been visited and given a perfunctory warning beating.

'Shit,' he said. 'You all right?'

'Yeah, just a couple of bruises and the cut. It's tomorrow I'm worried about when they turn up and I still don't have the briefcase.'

'Any ideas?' he said.

'Just one. But it's a good one.' I told him about Billy MacPhail.

He nodded thoughtfully but didn't have time to say anything as Carole appeared, nervous and skittish, by my side. She leaned down and kissed me warmly on the cheek. Then she looked across at the big man.

'Dougie,' she said. 'I'd forgotten you were coming.'

Dougie half got up.

'Carole. How nice to see you again,' he said.

She hesitated for a few seconds, then stepped across to him and they embraced awkwardly. She pecked him on the cheek and he sat down again. Carole remained standing. They both looked faintly embarrassed.

'I'll get the waitress to set you a place,' I said.

'No,' she said. 'I've already eaten. I'll just stay for a few minutes.'

She looked around helplessly.

Dougie lumbered to his feet and hauled a chair over from another table. Carole favoured him with a tight little smile and sat down.

'So, Dougie, how have you been?' she said.

'Good,' he said, his head nodding vigorously, 'I've been good. *Muy bueno*, as the Spanish say. You?'

'Well,' she said, 'not so great, really. What with Mum and all.'

'Aye,' he said, 'I was really sorry to hear about that.'

As I watched them and listened to their stilted conversation, a thought formed. There was something about their studied formality, about the way they didn't really look at each other, about the awkwardness, that wasn't right. They were both being so careful not to say anything untoward, so anxious to be scrupulously polite. Theirs was an uneasiness that implied a one-time intimacy in the not so distant past. They were like a couple meeting up unexpectedly for the first time since the divorce.

In Iain Lewis's impoverished equivalent of a Joycean epiphany, I suddenly understood what Carole had really been trying to tell me over lunch. It had been Dougie she'd had the affair with. I'd also completely misinterpreted Dougie's embarrassment about her, and her reticence about him. They'd both been trying to protect me and my feelings. I felt like fool.

I stood up, murmured something about having forgotten to take my bag up to my room and needing the bathroom.

I was conscious of them both watching me as I walked very slowly out of the room. I went into the cold, damp toilet and stayed there for a few minutes, trying to make sense of it all, staring at my pale reflection in the speckled and distorting mirror until one of the local fishermen came in and gave me an unsettling look, disturbingly at odds with the bright cheerful yellow of his rubber boots.

I fled down to the car and then carried my bag up to the safety of my room.

I switched on the TV and lay on the bed not watching it, preferring to stare at the strange patterns I could make out on the ceiling. The phone rang twice but I ignored it. Then there was a light tap on the door and Carole called out my name.

I opened the door and she came in.

The TV burbled quietly in the background as she sat on the bed. She patted the space next to her.

'Iain, come and sit next to me,' she said. 'I want to explain.'

'What's to explain?' I said sullenly, but I sat next to her.

'Everything,' she said. 'Everything.'

There was a sadness in her eyes and a weariness in her voice that I hadn't seen or heard before. I felt guilty for my petulance.

'Where do I start?' she said and looked helplessly up at the ceiling.

I just wanted to hold her.

'Why not explain why you didn't tell me?' I said.

'I'll come to that,' she said. 'When I first moved back here, I wanted to get in touch with you but I didn't know whether I should or not. I thought that Dougie might be able to help me make that decision. We met up. To discuss you.' She paused. 'The truth was that Dougie had no more

176

idea than I did if any overtures I made to you would be welcome or not. You're a difficult man to read. But he's a big, gentle, amusing man. I hadn't seen that in him before and, surprisingly I suppose, given what I'd always felt about him, we became friends. We met up whenever I went to Glasgow. Went to the movies, to art galleries, had lunch, even went shopping. He's a good companion. Very kind and understanding. But you know that already. Deep down, he's also lonely. I suppose it was inevitable that we'd eventually sleep together. Of course, in the meantime, Mum arranged for you to come over for that ghastly lunch. It was then that I understood that I really had to get together with you again. Dougie and I agreed that we had to finish. It was all completely over eight or nine months ago. We both sort of regret the affair. Me, because I lost a friend: him, because he thinks that he betrayed his friendship with you. That means more to him than you probably realize.' She paused again but I said nothing. 'He thinks of you as one of his few real friends.'

She hadn't looked at me while she had been speaking. Now she did, and I saw vulnerability, concern and compassion in her eyes and in the thin frown lines that tightened across her forehead. There was also the hint of tears.

I didn't know what to say. I did feel betrayed, even though I knew that I had no right to. I had had no claims on Carole. Still didn't. Dougie hadn't betrayed me. And nor had she – not recently. I hadn't been in the picture at the time. I leaned against her and kissed her cheek.

'Go down. He feels just awful. Get drunk with him. Show him that he's forgiven.'

'What's to forgive?' I said. 'We're all grown-ups. We all, even me, make bad decisions. We agonize about them. We move on.'

She looked up and narrowed her eyes in mock anger.

'What was the bad decision here?' she said.

'Not telling me about it, of course,' I said. 'Which you still haven't explained.'

She pursed her lips. 'And what would you have done if he had told you about it?'

'Don't know. Run away. Become a recluse. Joined the circus as yet another sad-eyed clown with a broken heart. Written another book of mediocre verse.'

'There you go,' she said. 'Dougie saved the world from a fate worse than death. There's already quite enough bad poetry out there.'

'You're right about that, at least,' I said.

'Go down and see him,' she said.

I kissed her gently on the lips, got up, smiled down at her and left the room.

I wandered back along the dowdy corridor and down the stairs feeling confused and uneasy. Carole's concern, honesty and warmth reassured me, but I wasn't happy about my own adolescent reaction: self-obsessed, self-dramatic. I smiled at my faintly ridiculous posturing as I entered the restaurant.

It was still empty apart from the one table. Dougie sat at it, morosely, looking like something out of one of Edward Hopper's gloomier paintings: *Deserted Restaurant with Large Scottish Male*, in the muted, dark colours of *Automat* or *Night Hawks*, with the same sense of isolation and quiet hopelessness.

I sat opposite him and he looked up.

'She told you then,' he said.

I nodded.

'I'm not going to apologize, Iain. It happened and it was good. Now, it's over and that's not so good. But that's my problem.'

'Nothing to apologize for,' I said, reaching for the menu. The little schoolgirl waitress was waiting patiently by the door that led down to the kitchen. 'Lamb for me. And I'd suggest some Burgundy. What about you?'

'The lamb as well, I think,' he said, 'and you're more of a wine buff than me. You choose and don't stint. This is on the paper. What about starters. Queenies?'

178

I shook my head. 'They'll not be fresh and they don't freeze well.'

'Marinaded herring,' he said. 'No one even pretends that's fresh.'

He closed his menu with a flourish and looked around. The waitress was on us in an instant and we ordered. I knew that he had to be feeling bad, or distracted, when he didn't banter with her. I asked for two glasses of Sauvignon, which was the only white wine they did by the glass, to go with the herring, and then for a bottle of Fleurie to follow.

The evening passed quickly in amiable companionship. We drank our way through two bottles of the wine and then lingered over brandy while we talked about everything except Carole. Dougie had called his policeman friend but he expected to be tied up in court for at least another day. He'd offered to call someone but Dougie had declined the suggestion on my behalf, thinking, quite correctly, that I wouldn't have been happy about it. Then he'd said again that I ought to go to the locals myself. I thought about it but didn't see the point without the briefcase. What could I show them? What could I say? Dougie sighed and quoted the old maxim about when in a hole the best thing to do was to stop digging.

In spite of his misgivings, he agreed to come and see Billy MacPhail with me the next morning. He's a big man and Billy wouldn't know that he's as soft and mushy as an overripe avocado. Anyway, he's got an NUJ card and Billy might think he'd write a sympathetic story about the hard-done-by petty villain dumped in the middle of nowhere, three miles from his nearest neighbour who, usually, doesn't have anything worth stealing.

'What if he doesn't have the briefcase, though?' Dougie said.

'I'll visit the bank, take out as much as I can and head off to the sun,' I said.

'Why not just bury your head in what has to substitute

179

for sand around here, the mud?' he said. 'They're not going to forget about it just like that.'

'Och, it'll turn up,' I said. 'Anyway, Billy MacPhail *does* have it.'

'How do you know?'

'Poet's intuition,' I said. 'And he's got my strimmer and my old bike.'

'Tell me,' he suddenly said, 'about Carole's family.'

I looked at him sceptically, wondering what he wanted to know and why. I decided that the quickest way to find out was to ask him.

'What do you want to know?' I said.

He shrugged. 'I don't know, really. It was just that she talked about her father's suicide a lot, and it never added up. I couldn't put my finger on it but something wasn't right about her account. I wondered what really happened. You never talked to me about it. You were too pished most of the time immediately afterwards.'

I told him what I knew of what happened and he asked some questions about Peter and his relationship with Margaret.

'That's it,' he said, when I finished. 'Suicides don't do that. They take their shotguns off to some isolated spot or wait until they're alone. They don't shoot themselves in front of their fourteen-year-old sons.'

I shrugged.

'So, Peter Crawford wasn't your average suicide,' I said.

'No,' he said, 'he certainly wasn't that.'

'What do you think?' I said.

'I really don't know enough to hazard an opinion.'

'Ignorance has never inhibited you in the past.'

He smiled.

'Go on,' I said, 'tell me I did it. Carole thinks her mother killed him, Martin thinks that he did.'

'All right,' he said, 'you did it. Or Carole did.'

I laughed. 'And there was me thinking the pope did it. He killed himself, Dougie.'

He shrugged.

'Of course,' he said.

I left Dougie to his brandy at five past eleven, offering up my thanks that Carole had sent me down to see him.

She was stretched out on my bed, reading a bilingual edition of Rilke's Duino Elegies that I had brought with me.

'So?' she said.

'Everything's fine. We rebonded. Tomorrow we're taking off for the woods with nothing but a copy of *Iron John*, to dance naked, beat drums and pee communally,' I said. 'But shouldn't you be at home?'

'Probably, but I thought I'd wait. I wanted to know that everything was OK.'

'You're an angel,' I said.

'*Jeder Engel ist Schrecklich*,' she said, holding the book out to me.

'I've never known what that means,' I said.

She shrugged.

'All angels are terrifying,' she said.

'I know what it means,' I said. 'I've just never known what it *means*.'

'That's because you've never met an angel,' she said. 'Until now.'

She sat up, scrabbled across the bed and glared at me before poking me forcefully in the stomach. She hit the cut and I recoiled in pain.

'Now you know what it means,' she said, laughing. Then she realized that I really was in pain and looked horrified. 'I'm sorry,' she said. 'I didn't mean to hurt you.'

'You didn't. Someone else did. You just happened to hit exactly the same spot,' I said.

'Who?' she asked.

'As I told you, I bumped into some old friends earlier this evening. Quite hard. I should look where I'm going,' I said and laughed, holding my hand to my stomach.

I fell asleep in Carole's arms and woke suddenly, still fully dressed. The bright red display on the clock/radio said it was just after two. I knew that she had gone but

I called out for her anyway. There was something comforting in saying her name out loud in the deep, almost tangible darkness.

The heavy frost covering the yellowing grass on the verges was like make-up on a geisha's face, thick and unnatural, an artifice. The rising sun was inching slowly but inexorably over the horizon in front of me, streaking the few wispy clouds and the pale, clear, winter sky a disconcerting pink. The dark shadowed hillsides were turning a reddish brown. When the sun hit it at the wrong angle, the dirty windscreen of the car became opaque.

I saw the scruffy school bus coming towards me in good time and I pulled over, leaving tyre tracks in the virgin frost that covered the passing place. The bus roared past and the driver acknowledged me with a raised hand, as in, 'Thanks for courteously pulling over and allowing me to pass.' I acknowledged his wave by raising my own hand. As in, 'No problem – I'm just happy to have been able to move out of your way before you were on me, you crazy, one-vehicle accident cluster.' I hoped that he didn't hit a patch of ice and end up in a ditch.

Dougie kept fiddling with the car radio, trying to chase the news on Radio 4 as the weak signal faded in and out, while we snaked along the road to Billy MacPhail's house, seemingly headed towards the ice-topped mountains of Arran and the blinding sun beyond.

'You need a digital radio,' he finally said, switching off the radio and sitting back in his seat with a long sigh.

'Wouldn't make any difference, Dougie,' I said, 'unless it was beamed down from overhead. It's something to do with the landscape. You see those pointy things in front of us that stick up? Well, they are called mountains and they get in the way of the signal. Anyway, digital radio hasn't come to us yet.'

He sighed again and sniffed.

'I have to admit, Iain, that you do live in a beguiling part of the world.' He paused and sniffed again, for dramatic effect. 'Thirty per cent less rain, one hundred per cent less midges, a quality curry house, a decent Chinese, three movie houses, a classy tailor and decent TV reception and it would be close to paradise.'

'At the moment,' I said, 'I'd settle for a few less felons. Anyway, the local chippie sells very good pizza – not deep fried. And there's the Screen Machine.'

'What's that?'

'A mobile cinema. It's a specially commissioned truck that folds down into a hundred-seater movie house and tours the Highlands, taking Hollywood to underprivileged rural communities.'

He harrumphed.

'Well, nowhere's perfect, Dougie.'

'But seriously, Iain, how can you live without the bare necessities, like hearing the news?'

'I guess it's just a different way of life,' I said.

'Oh,' he said sceptically.

'There's an old joke about a Spaniard trying to explain the concept of *mañana* to a west coast Scot. He describes it as essentially a philosophy that entails never doing today what you can put off until tomorrow. The Scot nods wisely and then says, "Aye, we have something like that here. But without the sense of urgency."'

Dougie laughed amiably, although I must have told him the joke before. Unlike most Glaswegians, he was too polite to tell me.

'The phrase here, though,' I continued, 'isn't *mañana*: it's "I'll come next Wednesday." Your roof has blown off in a gale, your pipes have all burst, and the tradesman you call will say, "I'll come next Wednesday." At the time he means it but he probably won't turn up. You get used to it.' I paused. 'Actually, there is an exception to that. The man who repairs TV aerials always says, "Och, you canna be withoot your telly," and turns up half an hour later, clatters about and restores some sort of reception. But I don't think it's news deprivation that bothers him. The last time he said that I didn't have the heart to tell him the aerial had fallen down three months before.' I paused. 'I guess that his is another of the old skills, like thatching, that will soon be a thing of the past. Now that we have cable and satellite TV.'

'You should get satellite,' he said. 'In your line of work it's tax deductible.'

I shrugged and pulled into another passing place to let the post van – another vehicle driven with homicidal intent – overtake me, but it didn't. Instead, the postman drew alongside, stopped and wound down his window. I did the same.

'Not much today, Iain. No parcels, so it all fitted in the box,' he said. 'Saw himself hanging around your gate on my way home yesterday afternoon.' He nodded towards Billy MacPhail's house. 'Just thought I'd let you know.'

I gave Dougie a meaningful look.

'Thanks, David,' I said. 'Was he carrying anything?'

'I don't think so,' he said.

'On his way in then,' I said.

He laughed and shook his head.

'Guess so,' he said. 'There was another lad with him, though. Not local. Looked a bit rough. Even rougher than himself.' He paused and stared off into the distance. 'I love it when it's like this – cold and bright. You can see the mountains to perfection.' He looked wistfully off at Arran. 'See you later,' he said. 'Oh, by the way, did Mrs Ferguson catch up with you yesterday? I saw her on her way to your place as well.'

'She didn't say,' I said, 'but I did see her lunchtime yesterday.'

'Aye, well, that'll be right,' he said and roared ferociously away.

I wondered what Carole had been thinking. She must have forgotten that we were meeting up at her place for lunch and had only remembered when she'd not found me at home. I'd have to ask her.

Dougie looked around at the empty, sugar-sprinkled landscape and shook his head in bafflement.

'What was the council thinking of, sticking an essentially urban beast like Billy MacPhail in the middle of nowhere?' he said.

'Oh, I don't know. It must have seemed inspired. The authorities know where to find him, except when he's off working, of course. Miles away from anyone, he can't threaten the neighbours when he's drunk and who's he going to thieve from? There's only me and the forestry ranger.' I paused. 'Mind you, he has had a go at both of us. Necessity though, not gain: the strimmer, a pair of shears, an axe, my old bike. That sort of thing. Anyway, it gives the old wifeys something to gossip about. They always know what he's up to. Sometimes before he does. And if they don't, David the postie will be happy to tell them. And, incidentally, he just confirmed that he was hanging around my place yesterday.'

'I know,' he said. 'Disregard a poet's intuition at your peril.'

I pulled out and followed the post van. It receded into the distance, lost in the glare of the low, winter sun, not stopping at my neighbour's house.

I parked by what would have been the MacPhails' fence if Billy hadn't torn it down in a drunken rage on one of his previous brief vacations from prison. One thick post still stood, defiantly pointing at the sky. The rest lay scattered all around, broken and irreparable, mulching down into the peaty earth.

There was a newish, green Ford Mondeo that I hadn't seen before just in front of me, and a black BMW in front of that. The Beemer looked very sleek, very big and grown up. In short, very unBilly. If he was going chic and expensive, he'd opt for a Chrysler Neon or an Isuzu Trooper, a proper redneck drive. Anyway, I didn't see how, assuming he had relieved my septic tank of the briefcase the day before, he could possibly have found time to put a down payment on one car, let alone two, since then. I had to assume that he had company but, even so, decided that I didn't have any choice but to confront him. Colm Kelly hadn't left me any leeway or room to manoeuvre. I only had a few hours to find the briefcase. Guests or no guests – and I didn't much care to imagine the kind of person who'd be visiting Billy MacPhail, although one young incomer, clearly away with the fairies, had once described him as witty and sensitive – Billy had to be confronted.

'Well,' Dougie said grimly, 'let's get it done.' He nodded at the cars. 'It looks like he's home and the relatives are visiting.'

I suddenly felt an enormous surge of love for the big man. He looked pale and tense. He wasn't a complete physical coward but he was close. He hated this kind of confrontation and he was only there because of me. Greater love hath no man and a' that . . .

We both climbed out of the car and made our way across the rubbish-strewn garden, past the scrofulous hens pecking at the frosty ground, to the back door. I saw my strimmer, its casing split and cracked, the wiring spilling out like desiccated entrails, lying discarded on a pile of household refuse. There was, however, no sign of my bike.

I had thought to catch Billy at a distinct disadvantage by arriving early. He had never been known to rise before noon unless there was a good reason and I had assumed he'd still be asleep. It hadn't occurred to me that he might have visitors or, as turned out to be the case, actually be up because he hadn't yet gone to bed.

The reek of stale cigarettes and sour beer that rushed at me when he blearily opened the door forced me to take a step back. Billy was swaying slightly, like a stumpy high-rise building in a gale. It took him a moment to focus, but when he did, and he realized who it was, the vacant expression was replaced by a narrow-eyed, thin-lipped look of ugly and naked suspicion and dislike.

Billy MacPhail was a short man but he was powerfully built with a thick, fleshy neck and shoulders, and strong hands and forearms covered with hair and thin, blue prison tattoos. However, the burgeoning beer belly did militate against the general impression of strength. As he

186

stood in the doorway, his face was at the same height as mine and I had retreated to the bottom step to escape the worst of his rank breath. I found myself staring straight into his pale, unshaven face with its shapeless blob of a nose and the soft, rheumy brown eyes with their unnaturally dilated pupils. It was not a face informed by intelligence, or wit or charm.

He was clearly completely out of it and had been for some time. I decided that there was not much point in adopting a subtle approach and that I might as well get straight to the point.

'Just give me the briefcase, Billy, and that'll be the end of it. No police, no problems.'

'What makes you think I've got it?' he managed to slur out.

I shrugged as nonchalantly as I could. 'Well, for a start, the fact that you know exactly what I'm talking about.'

'I haven't got your fucking briefcase,' he said. 'Now, fuck off off my property.'

He made to slam the door in my face but he was clumsy and slow with the drink and the drugs and I had plenty of time to jump on to the top step, brace myself and put my foot up. The flimsy door bounced off my boot and smacked back into his face.

Dougie, standing just behind me, groaned.

'Assault and battery,' he muttered. 'Terrific.'

I readied myself for Billy to come charging back out at me, but he didn't. Instead, when he stepped unsteadily out from behind the door he was holding his hand to his face and dark blood was dripping steadily from it down the front of his grubby, worn T-shirt. He didn't appear to be seriously hurt – just a little bash to the nose and mouth – but I thought at first that he was crying. In fact, behind his hand, Billy MacPhail was sniggering, like some malign cartoon character.

The man who suddenly appeared behind him in the doorway went a long way to explaining his otherwise, in the circumstances, inexplicable mirth.

He looked like a real Glasgow hardman, complete with bottle-scarred face and a nose broken so often that it was flat to his face. And he towered over wee Billy. His stature was much enhanced by the blue-black Colt .45 automatic he was pointing at me. As he pushed his way past Billy and stood looking down at me from the top step as I backed away, I couldn't help noticing that the gun looked vaguely familiar.

I tried to look on the positive side. The fact that his companion had the gun definitely pointed to Billy having taken the briefcase. All I had to do was convince him and his equally inebriated friend to give it to me.

Unfortunately, I didn't have any idea how to do that.

And I didn't even want to think how much of the contents they had already managed to consume or spend.

I held up my hands placatingly.

'Billy,' I said, trying to keep my voice level and reasonable, 'you don't know what you're into. The briefcase isn't mine.'

'No,' he giggled, 'it's mine and there's not a fucking thing you can do about it. You know you can't go to the law.'

'It's not the law you have to worry about,' I said. 'Not initially, any road. Just give it to me and I'll see that it gets back to its owner. With any luck there won't be any unpleasant ramifications for any of us.'

'Just fuck off,' Billy said, and the pair of them walked slowly down the steps and into the garden.

At the kitchen window, I could see three faces peering out. I'd forgotten about his kids. I'd thought they would be in school but clearly that wasn't the case. His wife was also presumably inside somewhere, holding the smallest.

I took another step back, my hands still held up in front of me, palms towards them. Behind me, I heard a car glide slowly past, tyres crunching across the gritted surface of the road. The sun was glinting off the windows of the house and the slates of the roof were starting to steam gently as they warmed up. The hens were still strutting around and a robin hopped about on one of the upstairs windowsills. The thick frost sparkled in the sunlight and even the MacPhails' usually squalid backyard managed to take on a slightly magical air under the clear blue sky. I didn't think that this was where and when I was going to die, in spite of the gun waving in my direction. It was all too unreal. I had an insane desire to grin at them.

'OK,' Dougie said very quietly, 'we're going, but it would be simpler all round if you just gave us the briefcase and its contents. Before anyone gets seriously hurt. At the moment we can guarantee that this is where it will end. But, if you don't hand it over now, the consequences could well be considerable and severe.'

'Is he threatening us?' the big bruiser said incredulously. 'Is he threatening us?'

He looked genuinely confused, but that probably had a lot more to do with the cocktail of drugs and alcohol he'd been ingesting for the past twelve hours than with the inherent complexities of the situation.

He pushed past Billy and took two long strides that put him nose to nose with Dougie, who looked less than happy.

'Are you threatening us?' he barked into Dougie's face.

Dougie flinched and took a step back. The bruiser followed him, the gun dangling down at his side.

'Look,' Dougie said, 'all I'm trying to do is explain things. This isn't pleasant for any of us. But it has to be faced. If we don't return that briefcase, with its contents, there are consequences. For all of us. I mean, take Danny McGovern.'

The bruiser turned back to face Billy. I couldn't see what passed between them but there was a short, apparently meaningful silence and then the hardman spun around and faced Dougie again.

'That's not down to us,' he said, his face looking decidedly animated for the first time since he appeared, as if he was alive after all. He even looked as if he might be making a determined effort to sober up. 'No one's gonna say that's down to us. We were here when it happened. We didn't do it. That was someone else. Definite.' He paused. 'What do you know about it? What are you saying?' His thick, blunt-ended finger stabbed at Dougie, emphasizing every word.

Dougie retreated backwards under the assault. I took a step towards them, thinking to save Dougie a lump or two, when another figure appeared in the doorway.

'Hold your whisht, Oscar,' the newcomer barked out. 'And put that toy pistol away before someone thinks it's a real one. This man is a well-known and respected journalist. He doesn't want to be bothered with your hardman games. Do you, Dougie?'

The bruiser took a step away from Dougie who shook his head.

'No,' he said, 'I don't. I'm just taking a break away from it all in the country.'

'Is that so? Just like myself, enjoying the delights of late autumn in Kintyre, is that right?' the newcomer said.

'Sorry, Mr Nugent,' Oscar the bruiser said.

'That's all right, Oscar. Dougie's already forgotten every word. Isn't that so, Dougie?'

'I guess it must be, Archie,' Dougie said.

Archie Nugent strolled calmly down the steps and into the garden, and looked around, as though he were window-shopping in Buchanan Street. His suit was Armani or Hugo Boss, or something else equally expensive, fashionable and well cut, and his polished black shoes were Church's. But, somehow, he didn't look out of place emerging from Billy MacPhail's back door. You can take the man out of the Gorbals . . .

He was compact and looked to be about my age, maybe a year or two older, and he moved with a feline grace that suggested he was very fit. Either he was just back from the Caribbean or he had a sunbed in his personal gym. But the golden tan couldn't hide the pockmarked complexion or the thin, bone-white scar that sliced all the way down his right cheek from just under the eye to the edge of his jaw. His bright blue eyes glittered unnaturally. Although he was more in control than the others, he was obviously strung out too.

There are some men you know instinctively to keep away from. Even my grandfather would have considered his options very carefully before mixing it with Archie Nugent. There was about him an indefinable air of insouciant danger. He didn't swagger but he oozed confidence from every pore. You just knew that if he decided to hurt you, he'd really hurt you. I didn't know who he was, and I didn't much want to, but clearly Dougie did and, equally clearly, Dougie was wary of him.

He stood next to Dougie for a moment and looked up at the blue winter sky and then he put his arm around Dougie's shoulders.

'Let's take a walk, big Dougie,' he said. 'You have a little to tell me. And I have a little to tell you. A pleasant morning stroll in the sunshine should blow away the cobwebs. That's what my mother always said, you know?'

'Aye, mine too,' Dougie said. 'But, Archie, I really am on holiday. Visiting Iain here. He's an old friend. I'm not working.'

'I do believe you, Dougie, but when is a good journalist genuinely not working? Let's walk.'

He steered Dougie towards the road.

Dougie was hunched over, whether against the cold or against the force of Archie Nugent's personality or reputation I didn't know, and he seemed diminished in size and awkward next to this controlled and icy man.

As I watched them, I suddenly recalled seeing Nugent's name somewhere, in the depths of some impenetrable article about business activity in the new Scotland or about the way the new parliament worked. He was some kind of lobbyist at the Scottish Executive, or a special adviser of some description, or just a wheeler-dealer. I couldn't remember exactly but I was sure that he was on the gravy train somewhere. And he clearly wasn't afraid of getting his hands dirty by the look of things.

I stood uncomfortably in the cold for the ten minutes or

so that the two of them prowled up and down, talking. Billy, still dabbing his hand to his nose and mouth, and his mate shivered sullenly in silence by the back door, smoking. Billy stared viciously at me.

Archie Nugent smiled pleasantly at me when he strode back, Dougie a pace or two behind him. Nugent stopped next to me, still smiling. I felt vaguely threatened.

'Dougie's explained everything in his usual admirably succinct style,' he said, turning to cast a smile on Dougie. 'I'll see to it that you get the property in question back without any more fuss. And there'll be no comebacks from this quarter.'

Dougie stood by my side as Nugent marched briskly up to Billy, leaned towards him and started talking very quietly. Billy started to remonstrate with him but Nugent simply held up a warning finger and wagged it at him. Billy meekly went into the house.

'Don't ask,' Dougie breathed in my ear.

After a couple of minutes, Billy appeared at the doorway, carrying the black briefcase. He handed it to Nugent who opened it and indicated to the man he'd called Oscar that he should drop the Colt in. The big feller did so and Nugent closed the case, walked over and presented it to me with a tight, smug little smile on his face. My guardian angel. And suddenly the line from Rilke made perfect sense.

'I'm afraid there's a few hundred quid missing and inroads have been made into the nose candy but almost all of it's still there.' He shrugged. 'But, what can I tell you? It's an imperfect world. Good luck, Mr Lewis. I hope this solves your little difficulty. Maybe we'll meet in more salubrious circumstances and we can have a drink.' He turned to Dougie, all business. 'Dougie, I'll see you in town. Soon.'

I had the distinct feeling that we had been summarily dismissed from the presence, and no longer impinged on his consciousness. *Jeder Engel ist Schrecklich.*

He turned away from us and went back into the house, followed by the big thug. Billy remained outside, staring malevolently at me until we were in the car and driving away.

'So,' I said, as I executed a clumsy and noisy three-point turn that mysteriously metamorphosed into a very clumsy and very noisy five-point turn, 'why don't you tell me what was said.'

Dougie sighed. 'It's a favour. He'll seek his pound of favourable coverage at some time when it suits him. It's how he works.' He paused. 'Archie Nugent thinks he's a power in the land. And, to be fair, he has made the jump from small-time crook to Mr Fix-it for a number of polit-icos and a few industrialists of the shadier persuasion. Some of them find him indispensable. He has a certain reputation for keeping things quiet and, sometimes, for getting things done. I can't begin to think what he's doing here, and he didn't tell me. In fact, he made it abundantly clear that it would not be in my interests to speculate. Whatever it is, it's bound to be unsavoury, probably not what you or I would regard as entirely legal and probably involves largish sums of money. But I rather doubt it involves drugs. Just be grateful you've got most of the contents of the briefcase back. And that *you* don't owe him anything for them.'

'Yeah,' I said. 'Thanks for that, Dougie. But, come on, someone like that doesn't just turn up at the house of a Billy MacPhail for no reason. He must have said something to explain his presence here.'

'Gods move in mysterious ways and explain themselves to no man, if they can help it. Never apologize, never explain and all that. And that rubs off on the coat-tailers. But, my, the gods do like to gossip. And that rubs off, too. He did say something that set off a distant peal of bells.'

He tapped his nose knowingly.

'Dougie, that is an infuriating habit, and it tells me that you don't have a clue,' I said. 'Anyway, I've been thinking, I really ought to go straight to the police and hand them the bloody briefcase.'

'That wouldn't be such a good idea now,' he said. 'Not

now Archie Nugent's involved. He wouldn't like it much. And he'd take it out on me. Anyway, I've started to smell a story.'

'And if I left Nugent out of it?' I said.

'I don't see how you could do that,' he said. 'If I read your sleazy little friend MacPhail right, he would drop Archie's name faster than he can down a pint of heavy, and then your life, and, more importantly, my life, wouldn't be worth living.'

'My life doesn't seem to worth much at the moment. Anyway, I'd leave Billy out of it.'

'Then you wouldn't have much of a story to tell, would you? So, this all happened on Friday, did it, Mr Lewis? And this is Tuesday, is that right? So, what were you doing all weekend and that dope looks as if it's been got at . . .' He tailed off and stared at the road for a moment or two, then he looked up. 'Iain, Archie Nugent is not good news. There are all kinds of rumours about him but he's highly litigious, which tends to inhibit journalists just a bit. It's the Maxwell approach: make it clear that you'll sue over anything and nothing gets said.'

'I'm sure I read something about him once,' I said.

'Aye,' he said, 'that's possible but I bet it didn't say anything about him and you can't remember a thing from the piece.'

I stopped at my gate and Dougie climbed out to open it. He grabbed my mail from the wooden box and dropped it on the rear seat before swinging the gate open and allowing me through. He closed it, struggled into the car and we drove down to the house in silence.

Chapter Nine

The mail was mainly catalogues and unsolicited offers of financial services. But there were a couple of depressingly large bills as well, which I dutifully wrote out cheques for.

However, there was an interesting message on the answerphone from my agent. She had exciting news. Work on a new, exciting project. A pilot episode. A thrilling *and* exciting series about Inspector Lestrade. What did I think? Well, I thought that maybe someone had already done it but the memory was only a vague one. Could I call her soonest? Well, I did but she was unavailable. Her whereabouts were unknown and so was the reason why she'd been in the office at so unfashionably early a time. I left a message with her patrician assistant who I remembered as being rather tall and attractive with a formidable intelligence hiding ineffectually behind her languid manner. The message was simple: Send me the details.

Dougie was in the kitchen, messing about with the coffee grinder, the cafetière, his mobile phone and the radio – to no real purpose or effect. I took the grinder and the cafetière away from him and left him happily fiddling with the radio, after he'd put his phone away. I made coffee and noticed that the cat had been and gone. His dish was empty.

Dougie exhausted all the radio's possibilities very quickly. I can only receive six channels and, since one of them is the local Gaelic programme, one of them is from Northern Ireland and one is Belgian, he wasn't having much luck finding the news at nine forty-five on a Tuesday morning. He gave up and slumped down at the table, waiting for the coffee.

'OK, so what do I do?' I said, handing him a mug of Colombia's second biggest export.

He shrugged. 'Give the Irishmen back their briefcase, apologize for the shortfall, hope they're not too pissed off and pray that they don't beat you to a bloody pulp. Then, in spite of what I said earlier, tell Ali the policeman everything when he eventually turns up.'

'If he turns up,' I said gloomily.

'Aye,' he said, 'if he turns up. But everything means everything, including Archie Nugent's involvement. Ali's very bright and savvy: he'll know how to handle things, what to follow up and so on and, with any luck, he'll square it with the locals. Then you should write some more bloody poems. Oh, and sweep Carole off her feet. It's what she wants and it's what you need.'

'Well, that's a plan,' I said. 'I might have to work on some of the detail, though.' I drank some coffee and looked at him over the rim of the cup. 'Dougie, is it me, or has the situation just taken an even more serious turn?'

'How do you mean, serious?' he said, not looking at me and peering into the depths of his mug as though he might find the secret of the universe in there somewhere.

'Och, you know fine well. It can't be coincidence that someone like Archie Nugent, someone with connections, shows up here and now, just when some dodgy Irish "businessmen" are passing through. Can it?'

'Don't ask me. Ask Arthur Koestler,' he said. 'Iain, I don't know coincidence from conspiracy. And I don't, as you've probably guessed, know what's going on here any more than you do.' He paused and looked up from his coffee, straight at me. 'But I can smell a story, though, and I do know that I'd like to find out what it is. Whether it's got anything to do with your problems, I can't say, and whether I can publish it or not is another matter. But there are a few enquiries I'd like to make.'

'Like what?' I asked.

He shrugged.

'Again, as you've probably guessed, I won't know until I start making them,' he said gnomically. 'But Archie Nugent did drop a name. He did it ostensibly to warn me off but I'm not so sure that's what he really intended.'

'Whose name?'

'All in good time. Point me to the telephone. My mobile doesn't seem to be working too well. Could it be something to do with those mysterious pointy things that you drew my attention to earlier?'

I handed him the cordless phone, left him to it and went off to my study to find a copy of *The Adventures of Sherlock Holmes*, so that I could claim to be on the case when my agent rang back.

I heard Dougie make several short telephone calls and I heard him pecking away at his laptop, and I sat at my desk, stared at the first page of 'A Study in Scarlet' and thought, about Carole, about what I was going to tell Colm Kelly, about Archie Nugent, and just a little bit about Inspector Lestrade.

My agent didn't call me back and I decided to drive into the village to post the cheques I'd written out earlier.

There was the usual, slow-moving queue in the post office: people collecting benefits and paying bills, and one or two taking so long I assumed they must be changing their nationality. By the time I realized that I only needed a couple of stamps and I could have bought those in the newsagent I was at the counter and it was too late to save any time.

It was a beautiful day and I strolled over to the harbour to look out at the few yachts still moored there and watch the fishermen tinkering with their grubby and smelly little boats. I stood there for a while, trying to take in the cold blue of the sea, the muted winter browns of the deeply shadowed hills and the harsh calls of the malevolent-eyed gulls, remembering a line from Gerard Manley Hopkins who had described to his correspondent, probably Robert Bridges but I couldn't quite recall, how he'd looked out on a scene and 'inscaped the lot'. I envied him that ability.

'Grand day, isn't it?' a voice said behind me.

I turned and saw Archie Nugent staring out to sea, a contented smile on his face. Martin Crawford was standing next to him, looking less at ease, nervously shifting his weight from one foot to the other.

'Aye,' I said, 'it is.'

'I'm glad we've met up again,' he said, turning his gaze on me. 'You might have got the wrong idea about me earlier and I wouldn't want that. I'm really just here to relax for a day or two and see Mr Crawford and Mr Ferguson on some trivial business matters and I thought I'd take the opportunity to drop in and see Billy MacPhail while I was here. I know him through some voluntary prison work that I do. The other bad boy who was there I know for the same reason. I'm afraid some people – and Billy and Oscar are among that number – are incorrigible, but one does what one can. Don't misunderstand. I'm not a bleeding heart liberal but I do believe that people should be given a crack at rehabilitation. Don't you agree?'

I nodded.

'Anyway, I was glad that I was able to help.'

'Yeah, thanks,' I said.

'What happened?' Martin said. I wondered if he really didn't know.

'Oh, nothing much,' Nugent said. 'You know Billy. He'd been up to his old tricks. He had something of Mr Lewis's and I suggested it would be better all round if he gave it back.'

As if anyone ever saw things any other way than his, I thought. Including Martin who clearly took the hint that this wasn't something Nugent wanted discussed.

'Well, I'm very grateful,' I said, making to walk away.

'Think nothing of it,' Nugent said, putting a restraining hand on my shoulder. 'Martin here has been telling me all about you. You're something of a local celebrity, I understand.'

'I don't know about that,' I said. I found myself staring at his scar.

'Don't be modest, Mr Lewis, Iain. Anyway, I didn't say everything I've heard about you was good.' He took his hand from my shoulder and reached into the inside pocket of his suit jacket, under his overcoat, and took out a leather business-card holder. He extracted a card and handed it to me. 'If there's ever anything I can do for you, give me a call. I know that there isn't much money in poetry and poets always need grants and bursaries. I'm not saying that I can necessarily swing things but I'd be more than happy to put a word in for you.'

'That's kind,' I said, taking the card and studying it. 'But I don't write verse these days.'

'Pity,' he said. 'What do you do now?'

'Write for television mostly,' I said.

He nodded sagely, implying that was very sensible of me.

'All the same,' he said, 'give me a call if you need anything. You never know.'

'I will,' I said and made a show of carefully putting his card into my wallet. 'Thanks again. It was nice meeting you.'

'Just one more thing, Iain, before you go,' he said. 'If I were you, I'd sort that spot of bother of yours out as quietly as possible.'

The slight emphasis on the word 'quietly' was all the warning he was going to give me. As sticks go it was fairly subtle, but I had been expecting something like it after he had dangled the juicy carrots in front of me.

I nodded my understanding.

'I'll certainly try to settle things as quietly as possible,' I said. 'I just hope that the other parties cooperate.'

'I'm sure they will,' he said. 'It's not really in anyone's interest to make a fuss.'

He looked at Martin and smiled, but it wasn't an expression of warmth. Martin looked away and followed me for a few paces.

'Iain,' he said, 'about our conversation the other day . . .'

'Forgotten,' I said.

'I know,' he said, 'but I just wanted to say that none of it meant anything. Mum's death had got to me more than I thought. It was all nonsense.'

He looked very pale and tired, but the lower lid of his left eye was no longer trembling. He hadn't shaved that morning and the blond stubble weakened the line of his jaw, made him look slightly out of focus.

'As I said, it's all forgotten.'

'Thanks, Iain,' he said, putting his hand on my arm.

Dougie was humming tunelessly and looking particularly pleased with himself when I returned. He asked if he could go online for a while as there were 'things he needed to check out'. He was being infuriatingly mysterious and had added a patina of smugness just to irritate me even more. But I got him his connection anyway and, feeling decidedly superfluous, went off to make some more coffee and do some heavy duty brooding in the kitchen.

As I rinsed cups out in the sink, I had a painfully vivid recollection of my father washing up after dinner, singing 'Miss Otis Regrets' in his clear, pleasant tenor.

I stared bleakly out of the window at the dun.

One of the more lugubrious poems I'd written about Carole's disappearance from my life had been dressed up in clothes borrowed from a fanciful myth about the abduction of the fairy queen. Deliberately unromantic and studded with understated images of casual violence, it had generally been considered one of the more powerful pieces from my first book.

It came into my head flat and false and reminded me of one of the exchanges between Oscar Wilde and Edward Carson during that tragic court case. Wilde had defended an explicit description of Bosie in a letter on the grounds that it couldn't simply be read as a letter because it was art and it was beautiful. Carson read the offending piece to the court, turned to Wilde and said archly, 'Is that beautiful?' To which Wilde had replied, with almost regal disdain, 'Not as you read it, Mr Carson.'

Nothing that I had written sounded beautiful to me, not even when I read it.

I took my coffee out into the garden. It was very cold outside and I shivered. But, where the weak sun had touched it, the frost had disappeared, leaving the sick-looking grass damp and the ground slick and muddy.

Beyond the urgently rushing burn, still in something approaching full spate, a stand of majestic old beech trees, bare now and silhouetted by the bright winter sun, cut out the view to Arran. Chaffinches brawled noisily and swaggered and bullied each other in the hawthorn hedge that lined the driveway.

I recalled my father patiently cutting that hedge back on days like this, his face reddened by the cold edge of the wind, laboriously hacking at the tougher branches, smiling encouragingly at my brother or myself as we struggled to gather up the cuttings and lug them to the huge pile that awaited burning sometime before spring.

Suddenly, I realized that I wanted to hit something, very hard. The heavy punchbag beckoned.

I strode into the musty garage, which smelled richly of moist earth, splintered, rotting wood and furtive, wary rodents. The old leather bag hung from its crossbeam, a solid shadow caressed by a single ray of sunshine that emphasized its cracked, scuffed, dull surface.

I put down my cup and slammed my fist savagely into the bag, sending dust motes dancing wildly in that bright, slanting slice of light. I stepped aside as the bag swung back at me, my aching ribs, cut stomach and bruised knuckles reminding me sharply to take a little more care with a damaged body.

Cursing quietly and sucking a sore knuckle, I stooped to pick up my coffee.

I whirled around at the sound of my name and knocked over the cup. The dark-brown fluid flooded out and was immediately blotted up by the thirsty earth floor. No harm done.

I knew it was just Dougie calling out to me – I'd recognized his voice immediately – but the sound had still startled me. I hadn't realized Colm Kelly had me that much on edge.

'Here, Dougie,' I said, bending down to retrieve the cup.

I saw something white sticking out from the priceless collection of dusty old wine bottles that I keep in the darkest, most distant corner of the garage.

I wandered over, picked it up and looked at it. It was a sealed envelope with no name or address on it. I was pretty sure that it hadn't been there when I'd sneaked in after my night vigil on the hill. Which meant that it had been dropped – or carefully placed – there since.

I was still holding it, reflectively tapping it against my chin when Dougie crunched across the driveway and came in, wrinkling his nose and gasping like a gaffed fish.

'Is there a meaner smell than cat's piss?' he said. 'Always excepting the reek given off by a politician on the make.'

'That's not cat's piss,' I said. 'The cat doesn't pee in here. The smell that I think you're alluding to could be bat shit or the faecal matter of some other small rodent or secretive, scurrying creature.'

'Ah,' he said, 'the lore of the country. It's what I leave the city for – to learn such potentially life-saving skills as how to differentiate between the smell of bat shit and cat's piss.' He nodded towards the envelope in my hand. 'What's that?'

'Don't know,' I said. 'I just this second found it over there among the bottles.'

Dougie looked across at the great pile and shook his head, aghast. 'What is that, a month's worth?'

'Two years, more like.'

'You have to take those down to be recycled, Iain. What are you? Some kind of ecological Luddite?'

'I guess I must be,' I said. 'The trouble is that every time I go to the bottle bank, the doctor is there, dumping his newspapers, and when he hears the apparently interminable sound of breaking glass he looks at me in that concerned, professional, deeply irritating way they all have. You know, the one that says, "You have a problem. Come and talk to me about it."'

'Och, you're misinterpreting him. He just recognizes you as a fellow fiend for the drink. And you probably do have a problem,' Dougie said.

'I don't have a problem,' I said. 'I just like a drink.'

'Anyway, the envelope, what is it?'

I looked down at the white rectangle. It was heavy and crisp, slightly smudged from its contact with the bottles, but of a very good quality. It hadn't been nibbled, crapped on or molested in any way, so I was right, it hadn't been there very long. I tapped a finger against it absentmindedly. If it had been dropped accidentally, which wasn't very likely, then I needed to open it to find out who it belonged to. If it had been left for me to find, then I had to open it to find out why.

'Let's have a look,' I said and tore it open.

Inside were a cheque and a single sheet of paper. The cheque was drawn on a local bank and signed on behalf of Crawford's (Main Account) by Duncan Ferguson and Carole Ferguson, though both signatures looked like stamps to me. It was made out for thirty thousand pounds and was payable to Alan Baird. The sheet of paper was just a payment record and indicated that the money was a 'consultancy fee'. I passed them both over to Dougie who whistled.

'I'm in the wrong business,' he said. 'I should be a consultant.'

'Whatever that is,' I said. 'But what advice could you offer that's as valuable as that of an MSP? I doubt there's all that much call for consultants on the correct speed to down a pint of Guinness.' His comment about my drinking had stung.

'Baird isn't your local MSP. His constituency's over in Fife somewhere,' Dougie said.

'He's got a big house here, though, just down the coast. He's had it for years,' I said. 'He spends a fair bit of the summer here. Braves the midges and the rain rather than making the trek to Tuscany or Umbria with the rest of the Barolo-swigging plutocrats in New but rapidly ageing Labour.'

'Now, now, Iain, don't let your prejudices show. We all know that you come from solid working-class stock whose memory and struggle have been betrayed.'

'Anyway,' I said lamely, 'he comes over for Christmas and Hogmanay, as well.' As I spoke, I recalled the big white house with its little boathouse, nestling in the bay. 'That's funny,' I said. 'I hadn't thought of it before, but Baird's house is very close to the Old Mariner's Grave, where Danny was killed.' I shook my head, trying to dismiss the thought. 'It's probably only coincidence. I don't suppose he's there at the moment.'

'No,' said Dougie, 'he's far too busy building a New Scotland.'

He looked puzzled and stared at the cheque for a few seconds. 'You're right, though, there is something odd about this. And it ties in with what I've been looking into this morning. But I'm not sure how.'

'What's so very odd about a politician taking money from businessmen?' I said. 'Most of them seem to do it all the time.'

'Yes,' said Dougie, 'and, doubtless, their wisdom, sagacity and care for the community and environment shine through in every decision our corporations make. But politicians have to register their interests. I was just looking up Mr Baird and I don't recall seeing any mention of a relationship with Crawford's. Let's go in and check him out again. It's cold out here.'

I followed him back into the house and busied myself

washing up while he went off to my office and plunged into the world of half-truth, ignorance, myth and bona fide information that is the world wide web.

Dougie returned surprisingly quickly and plonked himself down at the kitchen table

'Nope,' he said, 'no mention of Crawford's in any of Baird's disclosures. Still, it might be a recent thing that he'll declare in due course. Now, where did you find the body?'

'I told you,' I said, 'down on the beach, by the Old Mariner's Grave.'

'And who owns that stretch of land?'

'The Crown owns the foreshore, doesn't it? So, the Crown Estate, I suppose.'

'Well, who owns the land round about, the area that leads to it? Access?'

'Well, there's some Forestry Commission land around there and there's Baird's house. But I don't know how much land he owns. I think the Crawfords own most of it,' I said.

'Do the Crawfords own much else?'

'A farm, a couple of small forests. Quite a lot, I suppose.'

'And it all borders on the sea?'

'Most of it. It'd be difficult for it not to on an isthmus this narrow. Where's all this going, Dougie?' I said, sitting down opposite him.

'Patience, I'm not one hundred per cent certain myself.' He paused. 'The Crawfords aren't exactly thriving, are they?'

'Word is that things haven't been too good over the last three or four years,' I said.

'And yet they're writing out cheques for thirty grand to "consultants". I bet that's more than young Martin Crawford gets paid. In fact, I know it is.'

'Yeah, that is odd,' I said. 'Not to mention that the cheque itself ends up in my garage. That needs explaining.'

'Indeed it does but I can't help you there,' he said.

'I'm going to have to ask Carole about all this,' I said.

'Don't bother,' he said, 'a pattern is beginning to form.'
He paused. 'What would you do if you had a large sum of
money that had been gathered through illegal means?'

'Personally, I'd use it to disappear from the forces of law
and order who would, presumably, be in hot pursuit. But
I suppose you want me to say that I'd find a legitimate
business to launder it through,' I said. 'Preferably, one
which would generate large and completely legitimate
profits, on paper. That, of course, cannot be said of the
Crawfords' various enterprises.'

He beamed.

'Exactly,' he said. 'So, why then do our Irish friends –
whom we assume not to be entirely legit – seem to be more
than happy to pour money into the leaky vessel that is
Crawford's?'

'I really can't say, and I didn't know that they were,'
I said. 'In fact, I had rather assumed that they were just
checking out Crawford's ability to transport "fish". But
I imagine that you're about to tell me that isn't the case,
and expound some theory.'

He tapped his nose in that irritating manner again.

'Supposition only, Iain,' he said.

'Go on,' I said.

'A large amount of money has been put into Crawford's
over the last couple of months. Some of it since Margaret's
death but the bulk of it before. Overdrafts have been paid
off. Mortgages renegotiated and transferred.'

'Some of it might have been insurance payouts on
Margaret's death,' I said.

'No,' he said, 'I doubt that any of those would have
come through yet, given the circumstances. Anyway,
Crawford Holdings is a new company, only set up in
August. And that's where the money has been coming
from. The family has a controlling interest, and the rest is
owned by a property company based in the Netherlands.
I'm having more than a little difficulty finding out just who
owns that, but it's early days and I can hazard a shrewd

guess. The purpose of Crawford Holdings seems to be to exploit the land owned by the Crawfords.'

'You've lost me, Dougie. I just don't see where all this is going,' I said.

'How much is this house worth?'

'What's that got to do with anything?'

'Quite a lot, actually. What's it worth?'

'I really don't know, Dougie.'

'Well, hazard a guess.'

'Like all things, it's worth what anyone is prepared to pay for it. In any event, not much by national standards. Eighty, ninety thousand, maybe a hundred, if I'm lucky.'

'How would you like to sell it for three hundred thousand?'

'Love to, Dougie, but I didn't know you had that kind of money.'

'I don't,' he said.

'So, how am I going to find another mug like you?'

'Suppose you told him that there's gold in them thar hills.'

'But there isn't.'

'Or oil in that thar sea?'

'What?' I said.

'Currently, no fewer than three oil companies are seeking permission to sink exploratory wells a few miles off the coast. If they find oil, this is one of the places that it will be piped ashore and this area will be booming.'

'Dougie, ever since I was a wee boy and oil was found over in the North Sea, folk here have been dreaming about this coast being transformed by a similar discovery. It's not going to happen. Even if they do a little bit of exploration, what if they don't find oil or if they work out of somewhere else, like Ireland?'

'You make a killing during the speculation.'

I shook my head dismissively.

'No one around here is going to fall for that,' I said.

'But they might collude,' he said.

'Some might,' I said, thinking of the small local retailers

and the hoteliers who'd seize the opportunity. 'But most don't have anything to collude with.' We fell silent. 'Anyway,' I finally said, 'it can't be for real.'

Dougie gave an expressive shrug.

'Well, it is and it isn't,' he said. 'The oil companies are ready to rumba. Tax write-offs for exploration and some government and EU grants make it a fairly attractive proposition for them. They can't really lose. Which is just as well, because all the surveys carried out are a bit iffy. The price of crude would have to rise substantially to make exploitation of whatever's out there viable. And these days there's an environmental lobby to consider – all those cuddly seals and lickle Arctic terns. It's quite a thorny problem. It could, as the saying goes, turn into something of a political hot potato.' He grinned. 'Care to guess who the energy minister who has to make the decision about licences and so on is?'

'Alan Baird,' I suggested, with a very heavy heart.

'Bingo,' Dougie said, 'the very same. And would you care to guess the name of one of the smaller companies subcontracted by one of the major companies employed by the oil men to lobby on their behalf? You have to dig a bit for this one.'

I struggled to recall the name on the card that Archie Nugent had given me.

'I don't know,' I said. 'Nugent Communications.'

'Very close,' he said. 'Very close indeed. It's actually called Nugent Associates. Though no one knows who his associates are. Or wants to, for that matter.'

'As always, Dougie,' I said, 'you are a model of lucidity. But I don't entirely follow. Now I hate to sound insular, self-obsessed or completely egocentric but, if you are even remotely close to the truth – which is by no means certain – why am I in the middle of all this? If it's all about a bung to influence a politician, why is cocaine and cash badly hidden in my house, and a potentially incriminating cheque dropped in my garage? Why isn't it all taken ten miles down the road to the politician's house? Or handed over to him in an Edinburgh bar?'

Dougie didn't reply immediately. He leaned back in his chair and stared at the ceiling.

'I think I'll have to call a friend on that one, Chris,' he finally said. 'Or maybe ask the audience.' He paused. 'By the way, the name that Nugent dropped was that of Alan Baird. And, as I said, I don't think it was really to scare me off. I can't help feeling that Archie and his masters think Baird may not be coming down their way and that they want him out. A little whiff of scandal would probably do the trick.'

'Hm,' I said, 'I thought the preferred method of paying bungs was in brown envelopes delivered by private chauffeur, rather than by cheque.'

'Yeah,' he said. 'It's a puzzle, isn't it?'

'I *have* to go the police now, don't I?' I said, thinking of Nugent's suggestion that all be resolved quietly.

'Good golly, Miss Molly! Are you fou, man? This is a story. It is begging to be investigated. The polis and politicos will bury it. And Special Branch will be all over you. We have to get the story and then go to the polis.'

'And your tame policeman? What do I tell him when he turns up?'

'The story about the briefcase. Nothing more.'

Well, I thought, you're nothing if not inconsistent, big man.

'Dougie,' I said, 'anyone can write a cheque out to anyone. I could write a cheque out to the first minister but it doesn't prove he's on the take.'

'It might if he cashed it,' Dougie said.

'You just implied that Nugent might be trying to get Baird out. The cheque would fit in with that: someone setting him up and using me, the complete political innocent with a journalist friend, to do it.'

Dougie leaned forward and stared at me intently.

'Exactly,' he said. 'There's the story, Iain. Who?'

'I don't know,' I said. 'It would have to be someone at

Crawford's, wouldn't it? Someone with access to the chequebook. Ferguson?' And then it occurred to me. 'Carole? I don't know?'

'Their signatures are on the cheque,' Dougie gently pointed out. 'Why would they drop themselves in it?'

'I don't suppose they would,' I said. 'But then I can't really make much sense out of any of this.'

Dougie thought for a few seconds and then smiled.

'Well, let's go and talk to someone who might be able to. Put your suit on and saddle up Rover.'

'Why?'

'We're off to Auld Reekie.'

'Why?'

'To baird a lion in his den.'

'I can't, Dougie. I've got to be here when that Irishman turns up. I've got to give him the briefcase.'

'Och,' he said, 'you don't really want to be here when he shows, do you? Leave the gear somewhere he'll find it easily with a note: "Sorry, unexpectedly called away to Ulan Bator on important cultural business, a crucial poetry summit on the rhyming couplet crisis." Something like that. Believe me, it's what he'll be expecting.'

I nodded glumly, recognizing that being absent when Colm Kelly arrived had its advantages, and went out to the car. I opened the boot and peered in at the briefcase. I realized that I hadn't checked the contents since Nugent had handed it over.

I hesitated a moment and then popped the latches and lifted the lid. The neat packs of cash were more than a little dishevelled but they still seemed substantial. One of the bags of cocaine had been opened but it was still more or less intact.

I stared at the gun. Hesitantly, I reached out and touched it, then, shaking slightly, I picked it up. It was colder and heavier than I had imagined, a serious chunk of metal. I held it loosely and stared down at it. It glistened dully in the pale sunshine and smelt of oil and leather. It occurred to me that I'd never held a real gun before, although as a

210

young boy I'd been photographed, listing badly to my right, with a sideshow cowboy at a funfair, holding his fake Peacemaker in my hand.

The Colt was not as elegant. In fact, it was rather ugly. It looked like what it was – a machine-tooled precision instrument for hurling lethal hunks of lead at people at a high velocity. It was unattractive but curiously fascinating. I waited for the feeling of power, the buzz that I'd been told by gun nuts you got from just holding one, but it remained a cold, inert weight dangling from the end of my arm.

I repacked it in the briefcase and then carried that into the storm porch and placed it prominently among my walking boots and mud-covered wellingtons. That would have to do. Colm Kelly couldn't miss it. Nor, of course, could Billy MacPhail, should he come prowling around. But I didn't think that even mad Billy would risk the wrath of Archie Nugent.

Chapter Ten

Edinburgh is not my favourite city. Sure, it's beautiful and a' that, but it has a railway line where it ought to have a river, it's not very nice to motorists and it's always cold, with that cutting wind blowing in from the Firth of Forth. And then there are the Edinbuggers. There are many honourable exceptions, of course, but, if the wind is cold, then the good people of Edinburgh are positively icy. Mercifully, they hibernate for the three weeks of the Festival but they make their frosty presence felt for the rest of the year. If ever a city deserved a dyspeptic duke it was Edinburgh.

A few years ago, before mobile phones were ubiquitous, I found myself in a long queue for a payphone in a bar in Edinburgh. The middle-aged woman behind me tapped me on the shoulder and, in a slightly slurred Morningside accent, told me peremptorily that the city boasted many fine public telephones and that I should take myself off and find one forthwith. I mildly said that I hadn't seen one in the immediate vicinity of the hotel and turned back to do some serious queuing. She tapped my shoulder again and somewhat loftily informed me that she begged to differ. I asked her, a little acerbically, why, if that was the case, she didn't go and use one rather than waste her no doubt valuable time in that extremely long queue. At which she became black affronted and expected her large but flabby and equally drunk consort to intervene and deal with me. He swaggered over, took one look at me and saw immediately that I was extremely pissed off and wisely thought better of pushing his luck.

Anyway, that made it official: Edinburgh wasn't very keen on Iain Lewis, and it was mutual.

I found myself thinking sourly of that day as Dougie and I boarded the bus bound for Waverley Station. I'd parked at the airport because I really didn't want to drive into the city centre. Dougie grumbled about it and sulkily refused to pay for a cab, even though he was on expenses, but I was adamant. I wasn't going to drive into Edinburgh. The city was rich enough. It could live without any more parking fines from me. Dougie was just as adamant. So, the bus it was. A compromise that made neither of us happy.

Dougie had phoned Alan Baird's office and, to my astonishment but not his – 'I am a well-known and respected journalist, Iain, and he owes me a favour' – Baird had agreed to meet us for a drink. I had pondered, with a mixture of pride and incredulity, this striking reminder of just how small a country Scotland is, and how even friends of mine are able to masquerade as important movers and shakers.

As the bus roared through the dull afternoon, Dougie slumped uncomfortably on a double seat, shifting his position constantly and sighing audibly. Apart from his far too theatrical attempts to communicate his considerable discomfort to me, we travelled in silence.

I found myself marvelling again at Dougie's inconsistency and strange logic. If I couldn't go to the police because his 'story' would be sat on by the authorities, where was the sense in seeking out the very man who had most to gain by burying it in order to question him? I was close to uttering the thought once or twice but a quick glance at Dougie's contorted posture in a space designed for someone half his size suggested that the very best I could hope for by way of an answer would be a baleful look.

The light had long since faded by the time we jumped

off the bus in Princes Street into the damp, murky November afternoon. The wet, mucky pavements were still thronged with shoppers, and Christmas music and lights flooded out from all the shops as we negotiated the crowds and made our way to the warmth and peace of the George Hotel.

It was just after four and, apart from the barman and two businessmen who had lunched well and were, presumably, still lunching, the place was deserted. Dougie chose a table by the window, away from both the entrance and the bar, and ordered whisky. He still hadn't completely forgiven me for the indignity of taking the bus into town. He sat in silence, drinking his Glengoyne, not responding with so much as a monosyllable to anything I said.

He nodded a question at my empty glass and I handed it to him as he stood up. While he was at the bar, ordering more whisky, Alan Baird came in, followed by a minder who looked carefully around and then sat at the opposite end of the room to me. Baird saw Dougie leaning on the bar and the two shook hands. Dougie summoned the barman again and ordered Glengoyne for the minister.

I disliked Alan Baird on sight. He was blandly good-looking with prematurely silver hair and expensive designer frames to his glasses. His dark-blue suit was impeccably cut to hang elegantly on his spare, gym-honed frame, and his crisp white shirt was probably the third one he'd put on so far that day. The understated red silk tie was from somewhere I should have heard of – like Milan, which the minister probably pronounced with an 'o' at the end. He exuded vigour and a sense of purpose and he wore his pager at his waist like a badge of office. In short, every inch of his five feet seven was pure New Labour.

Dougie ushered him over and I stood and shook hands. His grip was practised, firm and dry. To his credit, he affected not to notice that mine inclined more to the limp and slightly damp. Dougie smiled at me beatifically and I assumed I'd been forgiven.

'It's good of you to meet with us at such short notice, Minister,' Dougie said as we sat.

'It's always good to see you, Dougie. And it was an intriguing invitation,' Alan Baird said. 'Needless to say, I was, as you no doubt intended, intrigued.' He raised his glass to us in salutation. '*Air do shlàinte.*'

Dougie and I also lifted our glasses and we all drank.

'Just for form's sake, Dougie, I'd like your assurance that you are not recording this conversation.'

'I'm not,' Dougie said.

'That's good and, just for form's sake, nor am I,' Baird said.

I must have raised an inquisitive eyebrow because he gave me a long, appraising, but not unfriendly, look.

'The reason I ask, Iain – I hope I may call you Iain – is that I intend to be, as I always try to be, frank. But I need to make it clear that this conversation is off the record and what I say is unattributable.'

'You mean that "sources close to the minister" or "friends of the minister" actually means the minister,' I said in mock horror.

'It depends what's being said,' he said. His smile was tight and unfriendly.

'Or denied,' Dougie said.

'Or denied.' He paused and sipped a little whisky. 'And, of course, the other point about this conversation not being taped and being off the record is that means it is also completely deniable. Right, Dougie?'

'Right, Minister,' Dougie said.

I told myself the fact that I didn't like him and that he was a prissy little man didn't necessarily make him corrupt. But some very unattractive trait deep in me, that aspect of my personality that didn't just delight in the uncovering of hypocrisy in public figures but revelled in it, really did want him to be. I heard my father's voice telling me to trust my first impression. But, Dad, what do you do when your first impressions are based on nothing but blind prejudice?

215

Dougie asked casually about an Executive initiative to combat juvenile crime and the minister frankly admitted that it was nothing but window-dressing but that he didn't see that it could do any harm. He then asked me a little about myself and, among other things, I told him we were near neighbours. He said that that was no longer the case as he had been forced, reluctantly, to give up the house on the coast. He asked after the Crawfords who, he said, he had got to know quite well over the last ten years or so. He was sorry that he had not been able to attend Margaret's funeral but ministerial business had not permitted it. He then asked how Martin had taken the death of his mother, as he knew that he'd been deeply disturbed by the death of his father all those years ago. He then looked pointedly at his watch.

'Well, Dougie,' he said, 'what do you have for me that is important enough to call me away from Parliament?'

Quietly and succinctly, Dougie relayed to Baird what he suspected about Crawford Holdings and the reasons behind it. Significantly, he didn't mention the briefcase or the cheque, but he did speak at some length about Danny McGovern's murder, emphasizing the location, to underline the serious turn that events had taken. The minister didn't respond to that at all. Clearly, either he had sold the house some time before or he wasn't a man to play poker with. I watched him closely but his face didn't give anything away. He leaned forward intently and his posture gave the impression that he was concentrating entirely on Dougie, but his eyes gave him away. Occasionally, I was aware that his gaze briefly alighted on me, that he was appraising me while I was appraising him.

Dougie wound up by saying that he knew, what with the lobbying that always accompanied such potential money-spinning enterprises as oil exploration, that the minister must be under intense pressure to act one way or another and he was wondering about any dirty tricks that may have been attempted or any undue influence.

When Dougie had finished, the minister sat silently for

a few seconds with his lips pursed and his fingers steepled, then he sat back in his chair.

'Well,' he began, 'I'll repeat what I said earlier about the house. I sold it some time ago and I must say that I'm relieved that I did. A murder almost on the doorstep is something I can live without.' He paused and looked at me and then back at Dougie. 'Interesting though what you've told me is, there has to be a little more to it. Otherwise you wouldn't have come to me. You'd have concocted a story, floated it and seen what transpired. And I don't understand what Iain's involvement is. Why is he here?'

'He found the body,' Dougie said.

'And?' Baird said.

Suddenly, I was fed up with his calm and unperturbed demeanour and I really wanted to unsettle him just a little.

'And he found something else,' I said. 'Something that touches you very closely.'

He favoured me with his tight little smile and I was aware that I had his full attention.

'Ah,' he said, 'now we will perhaps get somewhere. What, exactly, did you discover that touches me so closely?'

His snide tone and manner served only to piss me off even further, and I decided that I'd enjoying denting his *amour propre*.

'A consultancy fee,' I said. 'From Crawford's.'

He frowned and Dougie looked up at the ceiling, but whether in exasperation or amusement I couldn't tell.

'I'm afraid that I don't understand,' the minister said. And he did look genuinely puzzled.

'I found a cheque from Crawford's made out to you, for consultancy work,' I said.

'But I've never done any consultancy work for Crawford's,' he said. 'Or for anyone else for that matter. Not since I've been a minister. I can't. Show me the cheque.'

'I didn't bring it with me,' I said.

He sat in silence for a moment and then he drummed his fingers on the table impatiently. Then he leaned forward and addressed us both.

217

'I understand,' he said very quietly, obviously struggling to control his anger. 'You don't trust me. You suspect me of taking money. You think that I'm bent.'

'Not at all, Minister,' Dougie said smoothly. 'I honestly would not have brought this to you if I thought that. I would have attempted to prove it.'

The minister looked suspiciously around. His minder appeared to have been alerted to something and was staring at us.

'So, what do you think?' the minister said.

'I rather think that someone might be trying to set you up. If you were perhaps inclining to a decision that some powerful party didn't like, that party could be preparing to compromise you.'

Baird didn't appear to be noticeably mollified. The fingers of his left hand continued to drum on the table and he gave me a savage look.

'I hardly think so,' he said. 'We are a long way from making a decision. In any case, it's all been very genteel. There hasn't been any undue pressure. I've been subjected to the usual lobbying, of course.'

'What about personal pressure?' Dougie said. 'Has anyone from Crawford's spoken to you about it?'

'Naturally,' Baird said. 'Poor Margaret talked to me about it last summer, over dinner. She said that it would be a shame if there were oil derricks, helicopter pads and roughnecks spoiling the place. I said something bland about progress and economic regeneration.'

'What about your own feelings?' Dougie said. He seemed determined to keep the minister's attention away from me. 'After all, you have had, for a number of years, a relationship with one area that could benefit from any development. Isn't there the merest hint of a conflict of interest?'

Baird shook his head vehemently.

'No,' he said. 'That was one of the reasons that I sold the house . . .' The pager at his belt must have started to throb because he looked down at it like it was something very unwholesome. 'Dougie, I have to go. There's a vote that I have to attend. I would very much like to take that cheque with me.'

His manner was overbearing. I imagined him browbeating junior civil servants.

'I don't have it with me,' I said.

He stood up and stared at me.

'Don't be unnecessarily obdurate,' he said. 'I know that it's unfashionable and I know that you don't believe me, but I am not in politics for what I can get out of it. I won't deny that I enjoy the power and the trappings of power, but that doesn't make me corrupt or susceptible to corruption. Contrary to popular belief, not all politicians are on the make. We may be incompetent and fallible – some of us may even be party hacks and timeservers – but most of us do our honest best. You may not like me, Iain, and I sense that you do not, but I cannot be bought. Now, the cheque, please.'

I added pompous to prissy, and reflected that this was a man who was used to being obeyed. And to bluffing. I even realized that it worked. If I'd had the cheque with me, I would have handed it over.

'I really didn't bring it,' I said.

Baird turned to Dougie. 'Dougie, I resent this. I suspect a cheap trick to elicit information from me, and I won't forget it.'

'The cheque exists,' Dougie said. 'And I – we – wanted you to be aware of it. Naturally, I'll make it available to the police immediately. If that's what you'd like.'

The atmosphere didn't lighten perceptibly but Baird managed a tight little smile and directed it at Dougie.

'This is most awkward,' he said, clearly having calmed down but looking decidedly uneasy, even a little shifty. 'Listen, I really do have to go. Damned divisions. However, I don't think that either of us has anything to gain by the involvement of the police at this stage. As you're only too aware, you'd lose your story for the moment – and just maybe completely. And I could well find myself under

219

utterly unwarranted suspicion. Let's meet later.' He took a card from his wallet and wrote an address on the back of it. 'I'll be there at eleven or soon thereafter.' He nodded curtly to both of us. 'Perhaps you'd be kind enough to remember to bring the cheque this evening,' he said sharply and then strode off. He stopped and spoke to his minder who ambled casually over to us.

'The minister would like to pick up the tab for the drinks,' he said amiably and nodded to the barman, who appeared to understand.

'That's very kind of him,' said Dougie.

'Aye, well,' said the minder, 'that's the man he is.' And he turned quickly and followed the minister.

'That went well,' Dougie said drily. 'And we got a free bevvy. You know, Iain, for a very bright person you do act impulsively and behave like a horse's arse. I love you for it, of course. It's one of your more endearing traits. But why in the name of all that you hold sacred did you have to mention the cheque? This is an intricate game of give and take.'

'So that's how high-powered investigative journalists get their scoops. I've often wondered,' I said and drank some Scotch. 'I'm sorry. I didn't know the rules we were playing under. I didn't know we were keeping the information from him. I thought it was to be a full and frank discussion.'

'Don't be daft,' he said. 'He's a politician. Still, at least you had the sense not to hand the damned thing over.'

'I didn't hand the damned thing over because I don't have the damned thing on me,' I said. 'Jesus, was I the only person in that conversation telling what we used to call the plain, unvarnished truth?'

'Probably,' Dougie said. 'So, where is it? Why don't you have it on you? You haven't lost it, have you?'

'No, I haven't lost it. It's in the car. I put it in the glove compartment and didn't think to bring it. Sorry.'

'What's to be sorry about?' Dougie said. 'Apart from the fact that some little toe-rag has almost certainly broken into your car by now and stolen everything in it, and we have to schlep out to the airport and back before meeting Baird tonight. And then we'll have to explain to him why a thirteen-year-old's dad is offering the cheque for sale to the tabloids.'

I looked at my watch. 'I am sorry, Dougie. I should have remembered the cheque. But I have a lot on my mind at the moment. In less than an hour some Irish "businessmen" will be arriving at my house. If I'm lucky, they'll take what they've come for and go. If I'm not, they'll torch the place just for badness.'

I hadn't exactly forgotten about Colm Kelly's twenty-four-hour ultimatum while we'd been talking to Alan Baird, but I had put it to one side, I suppose. However, that kind of threat does come back with something of a bang. I can't say that I was sorry not to make the appointment – I was sure that it was better not to be there – but I suspected that I'd have to face him sooner or later. In the meantime, I just hoped that he wouldn't take any frustration out on the cat. I'd hate to find him nailed to the door.

Dougie didn't make any comment about my troubles but he did signal to the barman for some more drinks and I knew that he'd forgiven me for the bus ride and that our interview with Alan Baird hadn't gone quite as badly as he'd implied. The drinks arrived and the barman told him that, from now on, we were drinking on our own account and not Baird's. Dougie nodded his understanding, raised his glass and beamed at me.

'You know,' he said when the barman was safely back behind the bar, 'methinks the laddie doth protest too much. Not that I've ever met a politician who sat a high horse comfortably. We're so used to seeing them fake sincerity and concern that it always looks wrong when they are genuinely indignant about something. In any case, genuine indignation doesn't necessarily equate with genuine innocence. Aitken and Hamilton both frothed

221

splendidly. But I have to say that Baird's always seemed straight to me.'

I wondered if he hadn't rubbed shoulders with the wrong sort for too long and was too inclined to give the rich and powerful the benefit of too much doubt.

'I don't know,' I said. 'He looked shifty to me. When you mentioned the police.'

'Well, straight in a devious sort of way,' he said.

'So, what do we do?'

'Go and see him tonight. And, maybe, just maybe, hand over the cheque.'

'OK,' I said.

'But we'll perhaps keep a wee photocopy of it.'

I didn't drink any more that night, but I did watch enviously as Dougie inhaled a pint of Guinness in a pub in the old town and then consumed two margaritas and three pale-blond Mexican beers while we ate chicken enchiladas and refried beans in a dark and intimate little restaurant. I sipped water, having been firmly told by Dougie that we were returning to the airport to collect the car and the cheque and I would be driving back. Parking meters, he declared, went to sleep after dark, even in Edinburgh.

I'd been ruminating all day on the reaction of Oscar the bruiser at Billy MacPhail's house to the mere mention of Danny McGovern's murder. He'd seemed much too keen to deny everything when no accusation had been made. Dougie simply said that a certain kind of criminal, like a certain kind of politician, just denied everything as a matter of policy and that I shouldn't read anything much into it.

I wasn't so sure but I kept my own counsel as Dougie launched into a number of very funny and highly actionable stories about the incompetence and peccadilloes of high-profile politicians. Stories that he swore were common currency among newspaper folk. He was particularly scathing about the quality of the Members of the Scottish Parliament.

While he paused in mid-rant and drank from his bottle of beer, I found myself in the odd position of being less sceptical than he was as I mildly intimated that I thought that might be a harsh judgement and that they had put in place some decent legislation. Dougie had the grace to concede that was true.

'But,' he said, wiping the froth from his moustache, 'after their first year, the only way was up. Och, they even managed to turn Brian Souter and the late and not much lamented Cardinal Winning into heroes of the people over some legislation about gays.'

'Well,' I said, 'you'd have to admit that does take a certain kind of genius.'

'Yeah,' he said, 'if that's the word you use for Jerry Lewis and the Three Stooges.'

'Some do,' I said. 'Mad French semiologists and the like.'

Dougie moved his lips in a little camp moue of pained distress and I paused to allow him time to rinse the bad taste out of his mouth at the thought of what he considered to be academic charlatans and their preposterous and out-rageously cynical theories with a clean, astringent swig of beer before continuing.

'Anyway,' I said, 'forget the rest. Tell me about Baird.'

Dougie banged his bottle down on the table, the remains of the beer frothing mutinously, and he looked up at the ceiling and considered.

'Bright guy,' he finally said. 'Bit of a party hack, of course, and all that implies. He was tipped for real success at Westminster. High office beckoned but he blotted his copybook over the euro. Far too gung-ho for the Iron Chancellor's taste. Became a born-again devolutionary. Going places up here now. Gave up his Westminster seat very early to concentrate on Scotland. Ambitious and able. And much more careful now. Politically, that is.'

'Not likely to be trousering bungs, then?'

'Not really, he has too much to lose. But who knows? Of

course, giving up the Westminster seat meant giving up the Westminster salary and expenses as well. And then there's the plain and simple fact that politicians are just like the rest of us in one important respect: they don't always think straight.'

'And?' I said.

He shrugged. 'I don't know but there was something not quite right about his performance this afternoon. I can't put my finger on it, but it wasn't kosher somehow. He shouldn't have agreed to see me at a couple of hours' notice. He's a busy man: he has meetings up to his wazoo. He wouldn't cancel them for a second-rate hack with Guinness stains on his suit who just happens to mention Crawford's.'

'But, Dougie,' I said, 'I always thought that you were a shaper of public opinion and politicians ignored you at their peril. At least, that's what you always told me. Of course he dropped everything and rushed off to see you.'

Dougie grinned. 'Much more likely that he couldn't resist the invitation to meet a living legend, one of the country's foremost poets.'

'Fuck off, Dougie, he gently remonstrated,' I said mildly and sipped more water, my mind on the Irish thugs who had probably moved into my house by now, to await my homecoming. I had the feeling that I would be returning to a very unhappy cat.

The part of Colinton that I drove into, in search of the address that Alan Baird had given us, was full of small, neat houses in unfathomable cul-de-sacs and roads that described arcs that curled back on themselves. The particular crescent that we were seeking didn't appear to exist.

Eventually, in sheer frustration, I parked in a road with a similar name and suggested that we walk up and down it in the hope that the crescent would miraculously reveal itself. Dougie sighed theatrically and, grumbling, deposited himself on the pavement. I locked the car and joined him.

It was dark, quiet, misty and cold. The streetlights seemed dull and ineffectual. The little halo that surrounded the top of each hardly seemed to penetrate the damp, gloomy atmosphere. Our footsteps echoed loudly in the otherwise silent street. In the distance, I could hear the dull roar of the traffic on the motorway. But that was all. No dogs barked, no raucous music boomed, no babies howled with the gripe, no drunks sobbed or bellowed in existential rage, no muggers, vibrating like tightened violin strings, high on some drug-enhanced tension, leapt out from behind the neat hedges and demanded our wallets. It was a lifeless part of the city, a strange, dead place.

Dougie and I walked in complete silence, looking carefully around and, after maybe six or seven minutes and several turns, we found the address we were seeking.

It was an unpretentious, two-storey, terraced house with a Renault Megane wedged into the concrete parking lot that took up most of the front garden. A little light seeped out from the small bay window and I could just hear the TV murmuring quietly. It didn't look to me like the house that Alan Baird would have chosen to live in.

'I'll get the car,' I said to Dougie. 'You go on in. I'll be back in ten minutes.'

He ran his tongue around his lips nervously, hesitated for a moment, then nodded, marched up to the front door and rang the bell. It shrilled like a lost soul.

I was already thirty yards away when I heard the sound of the door being opened and muffled voices.

The car was just where I'd left it, unmolested, and, to my amazement, I found it easily, retracing my steps perfectly. I sat in it for a moment or two, opened the glove compartment and took out the cheque and payment record. I slipped both pieces of paper into my suit jacket and started the car. Dougie had found somewhere in the terminal building to photocopy them and had mailed the copies to himself.

True to my word, ten minutes after I'd left Dougie I was parking only twenty yards or so from the house. I heaved myself out of the car and stood in the street for a couple of minutes, feeling the damp and chilly mist seep into me, and I looked carefully around.

I wondered if Carole had left the cheque in my garage. She seemed the obvious suspect. The postman had even spotted her. Billy MacPhail wasn't the sort to leave anything behind, apart from a mess, when he'd been visiting.

A black and white cat padded silently past.

'I don't like it, Carruthers,' I said in my best 1930s upper-class English accent to the erect tail and pink, puckered anus as they swayed sinuously into the night, 'it's just too damned quiet.'

I walked up to the front door, pressed the white button and the bell burst into life, harsh and strident after the quiet of the street. The sound effectively jolted me out of the muted reverie that I'd slipped into.

The woman who opened the door to me was no longer glamorous. But, clearly, she had been. She was still slim and her thin, elfin face was both dramatic and pleasing. Her short, greying-blond hair was expensively cut and framed the elegant planes of her face to great effect. She looked to be about Baird's age, in her late forties, and was dressed in worn, faded jeans and an expensive lilac sweatshirt. Her feet were bare.

She smiled at me and I changed my mind. She was still very glamorous.

'You must have come to see Alan,' she said, 'no one calls to see me at this time of night.' She affected the kind of aristocratic drawl that always suggests, even now, hunting pink, stirrup cups, off the shoulder ballgowns and casual promiscuity.

'I'm afraid that it is Mr Baird I've come to see. How do you do? Mrs Baird?'

'No,' she said imperiously, but with a slight smile, 'I'm not Mrs Baird. Nor am I the housekeeper. Come on in. They're in the living room.'

226

'I do apologize,' I said. 'I shouldn't have made the assumption.'

She gave me a shrewd look.

'You don't know Alan, do you?' she said.

'No,' I said, 'not at all.'

She tilted her head slightly and looked at me again.

'But I know you from somewhere,' she said.

'I don't think so,' I said. 'I would have remembered.'

'Maybe,' she said, smiling sadly and turning into the house. I followed her into the small hallway. Directly in front of me was a staircase and a narrow corridor leading to the back of the house, which was in darkness. She indicated, with a little offhand flourish, that I should go through the first door on the right and then she moved fluidly up the stairs, clearly aware that I was watching her. She was humming the first few bars of 'As Time Goes By'. When she reached the landing, she turned, leaned over the banister and gave me a little wave. Then she laughed throatily and was gone.

She didn't belong in that small, suburban house any more than Baird did. I thought of the walls closing in on her, her laughter becoming brittle and then hysterical. And I thought of my mother.

'Here's looking at you, kid,' I murmured before turning, steeling myself and opening the door that she'd indicated.

I went into a cramped, overheated living room stuffed with more furniture than it could easily accommodate and with three more people than I'd been expecting, and none of them was a welcome sight.

Archie Nugent was standing by the mantelpiece, to the right of the large electric fire, his thin, white scar standing out starkly in the subdued lighting. There was a glass of whisky in his hand and he smiled expansively at me. His florid complexion and the sheen of sweat on his forehead suggested that this certainly wasn't his first drink of the evening, and probably not his second.

Colm Kelly was standing, like the other half of a set of particularly unattractive bookends, to the left of the fire.

He wasn't drinking and he definitely wasn't smiling. I tensed at the sight of him and the wound in my stomach started to throb painfully.

Martin Crawford was standing next to Nugent. He was looking extremely unhappy.

I nodded at him and at the others and looked around for Dougie. He was sitting stiffly on an overstuffed green sofa, and he appeared to be a little chastened.

'I think everyone knows everyone else,' Alan Baird said from an armchair which seemed to be a very close relative of Dougie's sofa. There was another just like it behind me. Baird was facing the television set. The volume was very low and it was tuned to some twenty-four-hour news programme. Baird dragged his attention away from it and smiled.

'I suppose you're all wondering why I called you here this evening,' Nugent said and laughed. 'I'm sorry, Alan. I just couldn't resist.'

'Yes, well,' said Baird. 'I think we all know why we're here. I was a little worried that you, Iain, and Dougie had been left with the wrong impression earlier on and so I thought I'd bring in some others to explain.'

I wondered briefly what kind of explaining Kelly had in mind, but the minister quickly went on.

'I rather thought that you and Dougie would like to hear from the horse's mouth, so to speak, that nothing untoward had been going on. Archie is here in his capacity as an independent adviser to me; Martin, of course, is company secretary at Crawford's; and Mr Kelly, who I hadn't met until this evening, is a major shareholder in one of Crawford's subsidiary companies. They can explain.'

I waited for Dougie to say something. When he didn't, I thought that I had to respond.

'I can assure you that none of this is necessary, Mr Baird. I certainly have no reason to disbelieve anything you tell me.'

'Well, that's very reassuring, Iain,' Baird said. 'So, perhaps you'd like to give me the cheque?'

I didn't react immediately. I wasn't thinking of with-holding the cheque, I was just taken by surprise at the trouble Baird had gone to and the speed at which things were going. I had been hoping for some guidance from Dougie but it didn't look as if I was going to get it, and I didn't want to give up our only bargaining tool without his agreement. It was Colm Kelly who broke into the short silence.

'Mr Lewis,' he said in that ugly accent of his, 'you are a regal pain in the arse. I'm relieved to see that your ob-duracy doesn't seem to be aimed at me personally but extends even to senior figures in your own government. But, believe me, that in no way mitigates my feelings towards you.'

'I can't think of anyone whose animosity I'd rather culti-vate,' I said, turning to face him.

He stepped away from the fire towards me but Baird held up his hand and he stopped.

'Do I take it you two have a history?' Baird said.

'Yes,' I said. 'Short and far from sweet.'

'Have you got that cheque on you?' Martin said quietly.

I nodded.

'Why don't you just hand it over to Mr Baird, then?' he said.

'Yes, Iain,' Dougie said, 'give the minister the cheque.' He carefully and deliberately emphasized the last word.

I nodded towards him.

'Sure,' I said. 'In spite of what Mr Kelly thinks, I never had any intention of not handing it over.' I slipped my hand into my jacket pocket and found the cheque with a minimum of effort and slowly extricated it, between my thumb and forefinger, carefully leaving the flimsier state-ment where it was.

Alan Baird's attention had been called back to the flick-ering screen but he held out his hand and I laid the cheque on his palm. His fingers immediately curled around it and, after no more than a cursory glance, he stuffed it into a

229

pocket in his baggy cardigan, which had an incongruously festive reindeer motif running around the bottom.

'And there are no copies of this?' Nugent asked.

Dougie shook his head.

'No copies,' he said untruthfully.

'Good enough for me,' Nugent said amiably. 'Thank you both for being so cooperative.'

'You're more than welcome,' I said. 'Is that it? No explanation? What's it all about?'

'Nothing really,' Nugent said and he turned to Martin.

Martin shuffled forward a foot or so and cleared his throat.

'It's all a bit of a misunderstanding, Iain,' he said, sounding as if he was reading from a prepared statement. 'There was a plan that Mr Baird should become a non-executive director of Crawford Holdings. But, of course, he then became a minister and it was no longer possible – perceived conflicts of interest and ministerial codes of conduct and all that. That's really all there is to it. Unfortunately, the cheque for the first year's remuneration was already in the system and was duly drawn up.'

'Oh,' I said, aiming for the non-committal and missing by a nautical mile. Even to my ear the innocent exclamation sounded deeply sceptical. 'And how did it end up in my garage?' I decided not to mention that the cheque was drawn on Crawford's main account and not on Crawford Holdings, that it was more normal to pay salaries on a monthly basis and in arrears, and that the minister had been a minister for quite some time whereas the cheque had been dated only a few days earlier.

'Now there's a question,' Nugent said.

The ensuing silence probably only lasted fifteen seconds but it seemed to go on for much longer.

'Yes, indeed,' I said eventually. 'There's a question. Things just keep on turning up at my house.'

'Don't push your luck,' Colm Kelly said, pointing a meaty finger at me. 'We're all prepared to forget this very crass attempt to blackmail Mr Baird if you leave it right now.' He paused. 'Of course, there are other matters that you and I need to discuss, but they can wait for the time being.'

'Really?' I said. 'So, what does that mean? You came unprepared and you don't happen to have a flick-knife in your pocket at the moment, or a pair of goons drinking tea in the kitchen?'

He took another step towards me, his finger still pointing at me.

'Come on,' I said, beckoning to him, 'I rather fancy sinking my fist in your gut and watching you puke on Mr Baird's nice carpet. Cracking a rib or two would also give me great satisfaction.'

'Oh, Jesus,' I heard Dougie moan from his sofa, but I didn't take my eyes off Kelly and watched as his breathing became more laboured and his upraised finger started to tremble. I didn't think he'd take me on there without back-up, but I wanted to upset him a little, embarrass him in front of Nugent. However, I also knew that if he did come as much as a step closer, I'd relish the opportunity to hurt him. He'd scared me and he'd humiliated me. I'd decided that wasn't going to become a habit.

I was aware of Archie Nugent looking on with interest and of Martin Crawford, just behind him, scarcely breathing. It flashed across my mind that Martin had probably never seen a fight as an adult, whereas Nugent probably saw grown men hurt each other all the time. I stared hard at Kelly, willing him to either back down or take that fateful step towards me.

It was Archie Nugent who broke the moment. He stepped easily between us, smiling his expansive, whisky-fuelled smile.

'Come on,' he said, 'we're all friends here. Colm didn't mean anything. Did you, Colm?'

Kelly didn't say anything, just stood, with his mouth open, in that ridiculous, Lenin-like pose, his wavering finger still pointed in my direction. I didn't take my eyes off him.

'Like he didn't mean anything last night when he brought a couple of his little bum-boys over to my house to give me a poor imitation of a beating?' I said.

'Doesn't look like he did you too much harm,' Nugent said wryly.

'He didn't,' I said.

'Well, maybe we'll have better luck next time,' Kelly said, safe behind the solid bulk of Archie Nugent.

Baird suddenly turned to face us all and stood up. The television still droned on, waffling heads waffling quietly to themselves, but it no longer had his attention.

'I am growing more than a little weary of all this macho posturing,' he said. 'Mr Kelly, is that true? Did you have friends of yours administer a beating to Mr Lewis?'

'It was a misunderstanding,' Kelly said through clenched teeth.

'There seem to have been a lot of misunderstandings lately,' Dougie said quietly.

'Indeed,' Baird said sharply, in his best ministerial manner, 'and there will be no more. At least, not here.'

'I'm still game for one more,' I said. 'With Mr Kelly here. If he's got the balls for it.'

Dougie groaned again and Kelly said, 'You little gob-shite.' But he made no move towards me.

'You talk an awful lot, Mr Kelly,' I said, 'but I don't see you swinging those dainty fists of yours. Frightened you might break a nail or pop a knuckle?'

This time he did take a hesitant step towards me, lurching clumsily around Nugent, his right arm swinging in a half-hearted haymaker.

I'm sure it was intended to be all threat and that he expected Nugent to block him off. But Nugent was slowed by the drink, and it presented me with just the opening I'd been looking for.

I stepped neatly inside his arm and the blow merely grazed my shoulder as I clipped him firmly on the chin with a straight right. When he stepped back, surprised and a little stunned, I followed up immediately and, as I'd more or less promised, drove my left into his solar plexus. He wasn't nearly as well muscled as he looked or as I'd expected and the punch took all the wind out of him. He doubled up, gasping for air, and sank to his knees. For one triumphant moment I thought he really was going to heave all over Baird's green Axminster. Dougie started out of his seat and Baird gasped but neither seemed to know what to do.

'That's for last night,' I said, stepping back from Kelly.

I was breathing heavily and feeling that strange mix of emotions that I always experienced after violence: there was elation there and relief, but there was meanness and an uneasy sense of shabby and unworthy behaviour too.

'Violence doesn't solve anything,' my father always used to say after another of my altercations at school and, as a kid, I'd accepted his words at face value. But I'd grown to discover that he wasn't entirely right. Not very often, but sometimes, there was in me some vicious and malignant thing, sown by someone else, that would grow and grow, like a tumour. An eruption of violence against the originator was the only surgery I knew that would remove the growth.

Archie Nugent, who had again stepped between us, was looking at me in astonishment and with some amusement.

'I thought you said he was a poet, Dougie,' he said.

'He is,' Dougie said, 'but he used to box a bit too.'

'Like Lord Byron,' Nugent said as he leaned forward and patted Kelly on the shoulder. Then he put his hand under his oxter and helped him to his feet.

'Come on, Colm, up you get,' he said. 'No real harm done. From what I've heard, you had that coming. Let's shake hands and forget all about it.'

'I don't think so,' Kelly rasped out between ragged breaths. 'The little gobshite is really going to regret that.'

'That's enough,' Baird said, regaining his voice and some of his authority. 'Archie, I'm holding you responsible for ensuring there's no more unpleasantness or violence. This is just outrageous.' He paused. 'Mr Kelly, Iain has been very cooperative and I can see no reason for any more trouble. Whatever is between you – and I don't want to know what it is – finishes now. I hope I make myself clear to both of you.'

I looked at Kelly who was plainly not in a conciliatory mood, and I couldn't say that I blamed him. He scowled as he tried to regain his breath and his composure, smoothing down his thick, wavy hair. He looked as if he still might heave. In the background, Martin Crawford looked almost as sick.

My right hand was numb and I knew that it would be stiff for a few days, but it had been worth it. I tried to flex the fist as unobtrusively as possible as I turned to Baird.

'I'd still like to know what's going on, and why I've been involved. And I'd really like to know why an acquaintance of mine is dead. If you have any explanation whatsoever, I'd love to hear it.'

Baird shrugged and sat down again, as if this was nothing at all to do with him. Dougie took this as his cue to sink back into the depths of the sofa.

'I can't enlighten you, I'm afraid,' Baird said. 'I know nothing about any of these matters. Nor, what's more, do I want to. I can assure you, however, that I have no further interest in you but, of course, I can't speak for these other gentlemen.'

I glanced back at Colm Kelly and, through the pain evident on his face and in his gritted teeth, I thought I detected the ghost of a smile. It reminded me of a schoolkid making a promise with his hands behind his back and his fingers crossed. Nugent just smiled enigmatically, and Martin looked very worried.

'I'll be honest,' I said. 'I had hoped for more of a dialogue this evening but, if that's all I'm getting, I'll assume that our business is concluded and I'll be off.'

'I'm sorry to disappoint,' Baird said.

'You coming, Dougie?' I said.

Dougie nodded and slowly rose from the sofa. I turned back to Colm Kelly.

'I take it you found your property out at my house?'

'We did,' he said, 'but I was hoping to see you too. Some of my "property" seems to be missing.'

'If you have further business,' Alan Baird snapped, 'take it outside.'

'Care to step outside, Mr Kelly?' I said.

He held up his hands.

'Oh, no,' he said, 'I'm not coming outside with you.'

'No need to worry,' I said, 'I'll only hit you if it's really necessary. Anyway, Mr Nugent can come and ensure fair play. He was, after all, instrumental in recovering your property and can shed some light on what happened to it.'

Still holding his stomach, Kelly looked at Nugent who shrugged and nodded. I wondered when Kelly would realize that the bruise on his chin was going to make shaving both painful and difficult for a few days. My right hand started to throb a little and I reached across and massaged it with my left.

Baird turned back to the television, aimed the remote and pointedly raised the volume. The rest of us assumed that meant we'd been unceremoniously dismissed from the minister's presence and slowly shuffled out of the room and into the small hall without bidding him farewell. I looked back up the stairs as Dougie opened the front door, but there was no sign of the woman, although I could hear Billie Holiday mournfully singing 'Don't Explain'. I imagined the woman quietly mocking all of Baird's late night guests by playing it and wondered again who she was.

I lingered for a moment, listening to Lady Day's beautiful phrasing, before following the others out into the damp, cold Edinburgh night.

We didn't speak but, by mutual consent, walked away from the house and trudged along the road to the car, the sound of our steps echoing menacingly along the quiet street. When we stopped, Kelly and I stared at each other for a while.

'Well,' he said finally, 'where's the missing money and the C? Dip your hand in the till, did you?'

'I know it's not all there,' I said, 'but Mr Nugent can probably explain that better than I can. In any case, there's a greater chance of you actually believing him.'

Kelly looked at Nugent with narrowed eyes and Nugent smiled. Martin Crawford was standing a few yards off, trying to disappear into the night, looking wretchedly unhappy.

'It's just a few quid short, and a few grams shy,' Nugent said. 'An unfortunate occurrence and absolutely nothing to do with Mr Lewis here.'

'Oh?' said Kelly.

'One of my contacts, fairly low level,' Nugent said. 'Just didn't know the provenance. How could he? It's as simple as that.'

Kelly looked at me with undisguised hate.

'I'd like the rest of it, or some recompense,' he said.

'And I'd like to know why you planted it on me in the first place,' I said.

'I already told you,' Kelly said. 'We needed somewhere for it to rest for a while and someone thought it would be amusing and convenient to leave it at your house.' He paused. 'He was wrong on both counts. What can I say?'

'That you're sorry and it won't happen again,' I suggested.

He snorted.

'Thought not,' I said. 'You could tell me whose idea it was.'

He strode away without a glance at me but I followed him down the street back towards that cramped little house.

'So, whose idea was it?'

He didn't look round but gave a low, rumbling laugh.

'And this is all over now?' I said.

This time he didn't laugh, but he did stop, turn and stare at me. I halted a few yards from him, waiting for him to say something. But he shook his head, his coppery hair glinting as it caught the subdued light from one of the streetlamps, his upturned face a bland, featureless moon in the soft, pale radiance, and he just stood, big, confident and menacing, in front of the little garden of what I still couldn't bring myself to think of as Baird's home.

As I turned away to walk back to the car, the knife wound started to itch and throb again.

Chapter Eleven

I was determined to sleep in my own bed that night and I drove through the darkness with grim purpose.

Baird would probably have categorized it as macho posturing and he may have had a point, but it was my house and I wasn't going to be kept from it by a cheap thug in expensive clothing. I hoped no one else understood that it was about not admitting to fear.

Dougie knew me well enough not to argue and he restricted his comments to exclamations of disbelief that I could do anything as stupid as to attack Kelly in front of Baird. To be fair to him, that was after he insisted that he come with me and sleep in the guest room, and his various mutterings about my shortcomings as a civilized human being were more than matched by the vehemence of his anger at Nugent and Baird for daring to lie to him about what was going on and about their implicit threats should he investigate further. I merely observed that it would be a good idea to get Martin Crawford on his own and have a full and frank discussion with him, and expressed my intention to do just that.

In the event, I did sleep in my own bed, but not well, and I awoke early from fractured dreams featuring Danny McGovern and Colm Kelly with a bad headache and a worse sense of foreboding. It was pitch black and I could feel the darkness pressing in on me and my breathing becoming laboured.

I forced myself to sit up and turn on the light. It was seven and I'd been asleep for less than four hours. The little wave of panic subsided and I stumbled to the bath-room and swallowed down some paracetamol. The pills caught uncomfortably at the back of my throat but I forced them down. I went back to bed and waited for them to take effect. I left the bedside lamp on.

On the table next to my bed, there's an old black and white photograph. It's one of the few of our entire family. I found it next to my father's bed, after his death. It must have been taken after my brother's christening, as he is in my mother's arms, wrapped in a long, white shawl, and we are standing outside the front porch of the kirk. It's a curiously timeless photograph, although, of course, I can date it exactly. My mother looks down lovingly at Rory, the plump, blond baby, her thick hair falling across her face. She is wearing a simple, cotton dress in the warm sunshine and my father, proudly looking across at his new son, has taken off his dark suit jacket and is standing in his crisp white shirt and waistcoat. He's an unselfconsciously hand-some man, with alert eyes, a full head of hair and a charming smile. The little boy squinting unsmiling into the sun is me. My unruly hair has been slicked down with something and I'm wearing a little striped tie.

I have no memory of that day and the only resonance the photograph has for me is that my father kept it. That gives it great poignancy somehow.

I stared at it that morning until it became an abstract image, a series of shapes and lines, blocks of light and shade, with an ungraspable meaning.

The great Charles Trenet song, 'Que reste-t-il de nos amours?', went round in my head.

After thirty minutes, the headache had abated a little but the 'vieille photo de ma jeunesse' had not revealed any blind-ing insights into my family, and my feelings about my mother remained as ambivalent as ever.

I showered listlessly, letting the water wash over me as I leaned against cool tiles, and then, clad in dressing gown, I slumped at the kitchen table.

Dougie found me there a little later. He looked as if his

quest for a decent night's sleep had fared no better than mine. He yawned and stretched, peering out of the kitchen window as the sluggish dawn lightened the sky to a dark grey.

'Any chance of some tea?' he said. 'I have a feeling this may be a three-cup sort of morning.'

'Sure,' I said. 'I'll get the kettle on.'

I filled the kettle.

'I shouldn't have hit him, should I, Dougie?'

He was a strange, faintly comical sight in his Calvin Klein underpants and his white T-shirt, pale, hairy and bulging. He thrust out his lower lip and put his hand to his brow, as though in deep thought.

'No, on balance, to state the transparently obvious, it was probably a bad move,' he said. 'But there's no real point in feeling guilty about it now and, if it's any consolation, in spite of what I may have said last night, it made me feel very much better after the verbal pasting they'd given me before you arrived. The look on Baird's face when you decked the bugger was a joy to behold.'

'Any more thoughts on what's going on?'

'Not really,' he said. 'I'm no further on than I was yesterday. Going to see Baird wasn't such a good notion.'

'Oh, I don't know,' I said. 'At least we know he's involved in something. We just don't know what.'

'Och, it'll be some deniable shenanigans that will make them all a lot of money,' he said. 'If I can find out what it is, I'll write about it, if the paper lets me. But they'll weather the storm, though. They always do.'

'All I want is a quiet life,' I said. 'I'm hoping to be able to return to that today but the look in Kelly's eye last night suggests that I might have to wait a while yet.'

Dougie didn't answer and I turned back to the teapot. As I did so, his mobile phone chirruped into life from somewhere in the living room.

'That's odd,' he said. 'It didn't appear to work yesterday. Could those tall, pointy things you drew to my attention have moved in the night?'

He went off to locate the phone and I heard him mumble something monosyllabic and then he reappeared.

'It's for you,' he said with a little half-smile.

I took the phone from him uneasily. I wasn't entirely certain that I would want to speak to anyone who had to contact me on Dougie's mobile phone.

'Hello,' I said hesitantly, looking at Dougie, who merely smiled.

'Mr Lewis, Iain, it's Helen Baxter.'

I recognized that haughty English languor immediately.

'Oh, hi,' I said, 'what can I do for you?'

There was a brief pause and I could hear Ella Fitzgerald singing 'Why Can't You Behave?' in the background.

'I understand that you were something of a naughty boy last night,' she said.

'Oh?' I said, wondering if her choice of music was just happenstance and deciding that it was not.

'Alan tells me most things,' she said, 'and he's a little worried about you. Which made me think that there might be reprisals.'

'From Baird?' I said.

'Good heavens, no,' she said. 'From the Irishman you hit. Alan says that Archie Nugent says he's not a very nice man. And if Archie Nugent thinks he isn't very nice, then he's probably a reincarnation of Attila the Hun. Actually, dangerous was the word that Alan used and I thought that I'd warn you.'

'That's very kind of you, Ms Baxter, but not really necessary. I'd already worked out that Colm Kelly was unlikely to become a soulmate.'

'Helen, please,' she said. 'You must call me Helen. Especially if you're taking me out to lunch today.'

'I'm not sure that I can manage that,' I said.

'Oh, but you have to,' she said. 'I promised myself an entertaining lunch today.'

'Well, I'm a little too tired to drive to Edinburgh today,' I said. 'I didn't get back until very late last night. Perhaps some other time. I'm very grateful to you but –'

'Oh, but it has to be today,' she said firmly. 'I'm a great believer in seizing the moment. Where do you live?'

'Kintyre,' I said.

'How charming! I'm more than happy to meet up half-way,' she said. 'I know. Loch Fyne Oysters at one. I'll see you there.' And she broke the connection before I could remonstrate with her.

I handed the phone back to Dougie.

'Well?' he said.

'That was Helen Baxter,' I said.

'Who she?' he said.

'She was at Baird's place last night. The mistress or girlfriend, I suppose. She was the one who let me in.'

'Right,' he said. 'Got her. I thought I recognized that voice. What did she want?'

'Lunch,' I said.

Dougie waggled his eyebrows in a very bad imitation of Groucho Marx.

'Ah, the infamous Lewis charm,' he said. 'Thirty seconds alone with a woman and he wins her heart.'

'And to warn me that Baird thinks Colm Kelly will be after me.'

'Must be serious then – if even Baird noticed,' Dougie said. 'Perhaps I should try to raise Ali again. If he can't make it, maybe he could have a word with someone sympathetic around here.'

'Shit!' I said.

'What?'

'I just remembered that I was supposed to go to the police station yesterday and see the detective in charge of the investigation into Danny's murder.'

He thrust his phone at me. 'Ring him now. Apologize and go in to see him this morning. And, Iain, if you're at all tempted to make a clean breast of it, in spite of any advice I may have inadvertently given to the contrary, it might not be such a bad idea.'

I nodded and took the phone.

But the inspector wasn't available and wouldn't be until

the following day. I left a message, apologizing profusely and saying that I'd be at the station at nine the next morning come hell or high water.

'Come hell or high water, eh?' Dougie said as I started to scramble some eggs. 'That's an interesting coinage. I'll have to remember that and maybe use it myself. It's amazing how much an uninspired hack like me can benefit from just being around a genuine and original wordsmith like yourself.'

I ignored him and put some slices of stale bread in the toaster.

The reception area at Crawford's was very small, brightly lit and overheated. I sat on one of the only two chairs, sweating uncomfortably, waiting for the friendly receptionist sitting behind a counter piled high with mail to track down Martin Crawford. She gave up after a few minutes and told me that he wasn't in and wasn't expected.

I silently cursed myself for not having realized that, as I'd left him in Edinburgh at only a little before midnight, he was unlikely to be back yet. Not everyone was crazy enough to drive through the night just to sleep in their own bed.

I asked if Carole was in. The receptionist made a quick call and told me that Mrs Ferguson would be right down.

I ran a finger between my itching neck and my shirt collar. Then I looked up and saw Carole standing a few feet away. She was smiling. My heart lurched at the sight and I knew I was as hopelessly in love with her as I'd been twelve and more years ago.

I hastily extracted my finger from my collar and jumped up.

'It's hot in here,' I said, gesturing futilely at my neck. 'That's why . . .'

'It's always hot in here. Shall we take a stroll outside?'

I nodded and followed her to the door.

It hadn't brightened noticeably since I'd left Dougie at

the hotel to, as he said, earn his expenses. I took that to mean speak to a policeman or two and some fellow barflies and file some copy. The cloud was still dark and threatening but at least it wasn't raining.

Carole starting walking towards the little green patch that lay just behind the office and masqueraded as the school's playing field.

'So,' she said, slipping her arm into mine, 'what are you doing here?'

'I came to see Martin and, failing him, Duncan.'

'I'm mortally offended,' she said.

'You shouldn't be. I didn't want to talk to them about anything pleasant.'

'Oh?'

'It's nothing much.'

'It must be something. Maybe you don't think I should be bothering my pretty little head with it.'

'Do you know anything about a payment to Alan Baird? A payment from Crawford's. Baird's a minister in the Scottish Executive,' I said.

She shook her head.

'Only I found a Crawford's cheque made out to him up at my house.'

She gave a quizzical sideways look.

'I don't suppose you dropped it when you were up there on Monday?'

'I wasn't there on Monday.'

'The postman saw you on the road.'

The dark sodden field had bare muddy patches in the areas around the goals.

'Yes,' she said, 'I was nearly at your place before I remembered we were meeting at home. Silly of me.'

I peered through the gloom at the sombre hills that seemed to surround us.

'Why do you think your mother killed herself?' I said.

She sighed.

'I wish I knew, Iain,' she said.

'Was there anything bothering her?'

'The company, of course. And Martin. She was uneasy about the money coming into the business. She and Duncan rowed about it constantly. She didn't like our new associates and she particularly didn't like the way they seemed to influence Martin. He's always been, as she would say, easily led – even by Duncan – and she just hated seeing him go along with what she considered scams.'

'Scams?' I said.

'There are some attempts to manipulate property prices. Someone – I'm not sure who – thinks that it's possible to make a killing in advance of a decision about oil exploration.' She looked up. 'Of course. That's Baird's connection, isn't it? He's the minister who makes the decision. You don't think that Duncan or Martin is trying to bribe him, do you?'

'I don't know,' I said. 'If they are, leaving the cheque in my garage is not the best way of doing it.'

We walked around the field in silence for a couple of minutes. Two plump-bodied, spindly-legged sheep trotted, sure-footed, over the brown and decaying bracken on one of the hillsides, like dingy, off-white blemishes on film.

'Did your mother suspect anything about the money that was coming into the company?' I said.

'What do you mean?'

'That it wasn't legitimate.'

She shook her head. 'I really don't know. Isn't it?'

'I doubt it,' I said. 'Not if what I found in the briefcase left in my study offers a clue.'

'Let's go back,' she said, tightening her grip on my arm. 'I'm starting to get cold.'

We turned around and walked more briskly back to the narrow road. Before we reached the office, she stopped and kissed me hard on the lips.

245

'Iain,' she said as she pulled away, 'I think I'm falling in love with you all over again.'

At ten to one, I jolted my way across the uneven car park that surrounded the restaurant, loose stones pinging against the underside of the car and mud spraying the wings and mirrors as the wheels found every water-filled rut and puddle.

I could only see three other cars as I crunched my way through the wet gravel. Unless a member of the waiting staff had a private income, or tips were considerably better than they'd been when I'd waited on tables in one of the more middle-brow hotels in the area, the mud-splashed dark-blue BMW convertible parked at an insouciant angle across two of the spaces reserved for disabled drivers suggested that Helen Baxter had already arrived. The three-year-old Fiesta didn't look to be her style at all, and the eight-year-old battered Peugeot 205 wasn't even in the running.

I wondered, not for the first time since I'd set out, what I was doing there, why I hadn't just stood her up. She didn't mean anything to me and she hadn't even waited to confirm that I'd meet her before hanging up. I guess that I was just too polite for my own good; and too intrigued to refuse; and only too happy to accept any invitation that meant I wasn't at home to receive the unwelcome attentions of Colm Kelly. I was very aware that he and his two associates were very much at liberty and had a couple of fat, meaty bones to pick with me. Fifty miles suddenly didn't seem anything like enough distance between me and home.

The light rain that had been threatening all morning had started to fall as I passed through Furnace and was now more persistent. The low, grey cloud suggested that the weather was set for some time.

It was a day without hard edges, every angle and vertical softened by the moisture in the air, every bright colour

246

dulled, every strong emotion compromised by the damp and chilly atmosphere. But the cool rain was refreshing after the overheated and stuffy car, and I stood in the car park for a minute or two, looking out at the still, shining, gently dimpled waters of the loch and the damp, brown hillsides cut by the foaming, swirling white burns in full spate, until the accumulated water ran steadily from my hair, down my face and dripped from my chin to my jacket. I thought of Carole and that surprising, firm kiss. Then I walked briskly into the restaurant.

A small puddle formed on the polished pine floor at my feet as I stood waiting by the bar for someone to notice me. The bar itself was fashioned like half a Viking ship, which should have looked decidedly cheap and downmarket but, somehow, didn't. The dragon head carved on the prow stared proudly out towards the shop and the rest rooms.

I don't eat in the restaurant anything like often enough for anyone there to know me but everyone is always unfailingly polite and charming, and the woman who guided me past the creels, nets and other fishing paraphernalia heaped decorously around to the table at the far end of the long, thin building, where Helen Baxter sat waiting for me, was no exception.

Helen Baxter smiled as I sat down and didn't, as I feared she might, offer a cheek to be pecked as though we had known each other for years. A quick glance at her was enough to confirm what I'd remarked the previous night. She was still a very attractive woman with a mischievous glint in her eye.

'I do hope you've brought your biggest credit card with you,' she said. 'I've just ordered champagne.'

'Champagne?' I said.

'Yes, I was feeling guilty that they seem to have opened just for us.' She looked sadly around at the empty tables. 'So I naughtily ordered their finest.'

'Is there any other kind?' I said, attempting to sound gracious, which I didn't altogether feel.

'I knew I was going to like you,' she said.

247

I pulled my chair closer to the table and the back legs shrieked alarmingly in the empty restaurant as they scraped across the floor.

'Is it always this empty at this time of year?' Helen asked. 'I don't remember it being like this in the summer.'

'No,' I said, 'it's usually buzzing then. Maybe it's the weather. Anyway, a couple of cars have just pulled in. I don't think we'll be lunching in splendid isolation.'

'Thank goodness for that,' she said.

I leaned forward slightly.

'So,' I said, 'why is it so important that we meet today? I don't usually have that effect on sophisticated and glamorous women.'

'Thank you for the compliment,' she said, 'but you're being far too modest, I'm sure.' She turned her head slightly, arched her carefully shaped eyebrows and looked at me coquettishly.

Our waitress arrived with the wine, champagne flutes and ice bucket. The dull explosion as the cork was removed echoed as unnervingly as my failure to recognize the label. While the waitress fussed with the bottle and a white cloth, I risked a surreptitious glance at the wine list and noted that Helen had just spent eighty-five pounds of my money. As nonchalantly as I could, I ordered a large bottle of water to accompany it and, reconciling myself to a sizeable bill, hoped that Helen would not prove to be too thirsty. I reminded myself that we were both driving and that one bottle of champagne would be more than enough.

We touched glasses and sipped.

'So,' she said, 'you must tell me all about you.'

It hadn't escaped my notice that she hadn't answered my question and I decided not to let her off that lightly.

'First, you have to tell me why we had to meet today.'

'Oh, I'm just very impulsive,' she said breezily. 'That's all. I liked the look of you last night and decided that we had to meet. Especially after I asked Alan who you were. And I'm a great believer in striking while the iron's hot

248

and all that sort of thing. I sort of collect interesting people. And you looked very interesting.'

'Really?' I said, raising my eyebrows. I was trying to convey my scepticism about 'collecting' interesting people in general, and, in particular, about whether I could lay any claim to a place in such a collection. Obviously, I failed on both counts as she completely disregarded any edge that I had endeavoured to give to the comment and the gesture.

'Yes, Alan's always teasing me about it but I get very bored with all his tedious political and business friends. Not all of them, of course. And it's a bit difficult sometimes, not being the wife . . .' She trailed off.

'I suppose it must be,' I said, not really wanting to tread that particular path, and picking up the menu. 'Shall we order?'

'Poor Alan,' she said, ignoring my attempt to steer the conversation away from that subject. 'He can't divorce. Not at the moment. His career, you see. He worries about it all the time. Being a public figure can be very burdensome.'

'I'm afraid that my withers are generally unwrung about the burdens of public office. At least as far as politicians are concerned,' I said, a little more icily than I'd intended. I hurried on. 'Since we're drinking champagne, I'm going to start with the smoked salmon and then move on to the mussels.' I closed the menu firmly. 'What about you?'

She laughed.

'It's all right. You don't have to worry about Alan. He knows I'm lunching with you,' she said. 'He has no reason to be jealous. And he's not as bad as you may think.' She paused. 'Actually, it was his idea that we meet. He was concerned about you.'

I looked up but she pointedly studied the menu and started to hum. It was a few seconds before I recognized the tune.

'Do you always provide a soundtrack to your life?' I said.

She cocked her head on one side and smiled. 'Sorry?'

'It was just something I noticed last night and then again

this morning,' I said. 'On the phone you were playing "Why Can't You Behave?", which seemed to be making some kind of pointed statement about me and my conduct. And last night, when I left, you were playing "Don't Explain", which was a pretty good comment on the conversation I'd just had with the minister.'

'It usually is,' she said, 'for one of Alan's late night meetings.'

'And just now,' I said, 'you were humming "Always true to you, darling, in my fashion" after mentioning jealousy. So, do you? Always provide a soundtrack, I mean.'

She laughed. 'Doesn't everyone?' She paused and looked thoughtful. 'It's wasted on most people, though.'

'Well, I'm something of a fan of both Billie Holiday and Cole Porter,' I said, 'particularly *Kiss Me, Kate*. So I tend to notice.'

'I played in it once, opposite darling Harry,' she said, taking it as read that I knew just who 'darling Harry' was. 'No prizes for guessing which role.'

'No,' I said, imagining that, as a young woman, she would have been a devastating Lois Lane. 'I didn't know that you acted.'

'Darling, I'm shocked that you didn't recognize my name immediately,' she said, looking very far from shocked. She smiled engagingly. 'The truth is that I've never been very famous. Just honest, journeyman stuff in rep mainly. Bristol and Birmingham.' She paused and looked at the menu again before closing it decisively and laying it down. 'These days I'm a drama teacher.' She sighed. 'I kid myself that I don't miss it. You know, all those silly theatre superstitions, like not whistling in the dressing room and only referring to "the Scottish play", and all the tantrums and the bitchiness. But I do.' She paused again and then smiled wanly. 'I think that I'll have the smoked salmon too, and then the lemon sole,' she said. 'And I promise that I won't bore you any more with talk of Alan Baird and his problems in clawing his way to the top of the heap.'

Lunch lasted until three twenty largely because, from two forty-five on, Helen kept ordering coffee, claiming it as a necessary prerequisite to driving after consuming half a bottle of champagne.

She had proved to be an extremely pleasant and entertaining lunch companion, waspish and amusing. I learned about her brief television career – 'My finest hour, darling' – in a very short-lived soap opera. She pretended to be appalled that I'd never heard of it – 'And you in the business.' And she told me about her three ex-husbands and her mildly eccentric family. But it was all froth. I discovered nothing of substance about her. She managed to be, in fact, exquisitely discreet while masquerading as quite the opposite. I was also no wiser at the end of the meal about her reasons for insisting we meet than I had been at the beginning. I decided that I might as well take her at face value and put it down to boredom.

We parted in the car park, the best of friends, kissing each other theatrically on each cheek, and passing hastily scribbled phone numbers, promising to meet again soon, though both of us were aware that that was unlikely.

I watched and waved as she roared away, engine over-revving, her tyres spitting gravel, hoping that the coffee and the time spent drinking it had sobered her up sufficiently, as I couldn't see her getting back to Edinburgh without being stopped by the police.

I sat in the car for a few minutes before starting the engine, feeling vaguely melancholy, then I pulled slowly out on to the road. I drove carefully and listened to a tape of Bill Evans' *Conversations With Myself*, the quiet, intricate, introverted music somehow appropriate to the gloomy afternoon and my mood.

The journey took just over an hour and I was back well

before five, thinking of a quiet evening with Rochester's poems and a little Mozart.

The door to the storm porch was open, which was surprising as I remembered closing it before leaving. Even more disconcerting was the open front door beyond, which was hanging at an unnatural and alarming angle. I was getting decidedly pissed off with people entering my house or rummaging around in my garden whenever the fancy took them, but I controlled my anger and stepped cautiously past the damaged door that led into my living room, turning on the lights as I went.

The place was a mess, but Dougie and I hadn't exactly waltzed the Dyson around before leaving. On the other hand, I didn't recall us tipping the armchair over, or throwing most of the crockery on to the floor. Nor had we finished off the bottle of Macallan ten-year-old that lay, empty and forlorn, in a reeking pool of vomit in the fire surround. And I certainly didn't remember Dougie carrying the video under one arm and the TV under the other as he bade me a fond farewell when I left him at the hotel. Still, the computer was in place, which meant I hadn't lost any work, such as it was, and so, somewhat surprisingly, was the CD player and all my CDs, which meant that I could still play music, and suggested that the thief hadn't thought much of my musical taste.

All in all, if I was going to be the victim of a burglary, then this was the kind I'd choose. The vomit excepted, it was as close to painless as they come: I could live quite happily without a TV, and the broken crockery was hardly Royal Doulton. I resented the wasted Macallan, though.

I rang the police and reported a break-in. I was told that someone would be with me the next morning. I asked if I could clean up the vomit and the desk sergeant said in a deadpan voice that he would if he were me. I took that to mean that he believed in good old-fashioned police work and had no interest in a perpetrator's bodily fluids, unless they were spattered up a cell wall after an invigorating exchange of opinions.

I righted the armchair and plonked myself down in it. I felt very weary.

The obvious suspect was Billy MacPhail. But Billy could hold his drink – in the sense that he didn't usually spew it back up – and Billy hadn't been known to break into any of his neighbours' houses recently. Sure, he'd snap up the odd disregarded trifle he happened to find lying around in the garden if there was no one at home, but breaking and entering was a different matter. On the other hand, he could have been harbouring a seething resentment in what passed for his mind about our recent confrontation.

But, lurking in the cobwebbed recesses of my own mind, there was a decided feeling of unease about it all. Alan Baird had encouraged Helen to have lunch with me. Maybe it had even been his idea and he'd asked her to make sure that I wasn't at home between twelve and four. She'd certainly endlessly prolonged lunch by ordering coffee after coffee. Perhaps Baird knew that Colm Kelly had something planned, suspected that he'd be sending a couple of young thugs with a score to settle who, when they didn't find me at home, would be content to half-heartedly trash the place. An outcome that he perhaps regarded as preferable to me being knocked about a bit. Or, more likely, a lot. I couldn't get a handle on Baird. Why would he bother to keep me from a beating? If that had been his intention.

It was all a little too convoluted for me. Billy still had to be, as one of my London friends would say, favourite.

I looked around the living room. The place suddenly seemed very shabby. I felt like I wanted to redecorate immediately, buy new furniture, curtains and rugs, get a Dobermann and feed it nothing but raw and bleeding testicles ripped from the pale and useless bodies of whining, dishonest idlers and vicious, scrawny would-be gangsters – with tempting morsels torn from plump lobbyists and sleek and lying politicians to add a little spice, fat and variety to that otherwise poor and dull diet.

I struggled wearily to my feet when I saw a brief flash

of headlamps as a car swept past the living-room window. It bumped across the uneven, cracked paving stones that my father had put down so many years ago and slithered to a halt just behind my own Rover. I assumed that the police had decided to drop by this evening after all.

But it was Duncan Ferguson who stood in the bright glare of my outside light, his pale face gleaming like a full moon, the features all but lost in the brilliant gleam. He nodded to me.

He must have heard my loud sigh, and he certainly saw me shake my head.

'I wondered if we might have a word,' he said.

'Now's not a good time, Duncan,' I said weakly.

He took a step towards me and raised a hand to his face and rubbed at his chin. His tongue flicked around his lower lip.

'All the same . . .'

He looked uneasy, almost shifty, but there was also an air of quiet desperation about him that transmitted a certain determination. He did not look as if he would be easily dissuaded and so, reluctantly, I beckoned him in.

'Looks like it was some party, Iain,' he said, looking around at my dishevelled living room and wrinkling his nose at the all-pervading smell of sour vomit.

'Aye,' I said, 'it's just a pity I wasn't here to enjoy it.'

A frown creased his forehead and crinkled his puffy features.

'There was a break-in,' I said. 'This afternoon when I was out. Let's talk in the kitchen, away from all this mess.'

He followed me in and then stood, big and uncomfortable, in the doorway.

'Much taken?' he said.

'Not as far as I can see,' I said. 'The telly, the video . . . Listen, I'm going to make some coffee. Can I get you anything?'

He didn't respond immediately and I lifted the kettle from the counter, raised it to head height and pointed at it.

He shook his head dismissively and then ran his hand reflectively over his heavy jowls.

I filled the kettle, switched it on and emptied the coffee grouts from the cafetière into the mulch bin. It was all displacement activity and I certainly didn't want to encourage him to talk. I could hear him behind me, his foot squeaking against the floor, his hand rasping against his late-afternoon stubble, the little, wet, throat-clearing noises. He seemed to be made up entirely of nervous tics and his presence was beginning to irritate me.

He coughed loudly and I turned.

'I had a call this morning,' he said, staring at the ceiling.

'From?' I prompted.

'A mutual acquaintance. Alan Baird?'

'I've met him,' I said warily. This was not at all what I'd been expecting.

'Yes. He asked me to go and see him. And I did. He wanted to talk about you.'

'Me?'

'That's right. He wanted me to make a few things clear to you. It didn't seem important enough to take me away from the office for a day. But it must be important to him and wasting other people's time doesn't seem to bother him.'

'I guess not,' I said and busied myself at the counter, warming the cafetière and rummaging around noisily in the cutlery drawer for a spoon for the coffee. I'd been expecting a confrontation about Carole and I had to admit that this was something of a surprise, not to say a relief.

'I didn't really want to come to see you. For obvious reasons . . . But he was most insistent. You know these politicos. They can be very demanding and persuasive. And he's not someone you want in the opposite corner. He did go as far as to make some unfriendly noises. So, here I am.' He cleared his throat noisily. 'He wants you to know that he has absolutely no connection with Crawford's, and that any suggestion to the contrary would be quite wrong-headed, and possibly actionable. And he wanted you to

255

hear that from me.' He paused again. 'I don't know what you've done or said to him, but he was very keen that I personally explain this to you, from the company's point of view. Officially, as it were.'

I made no comment.

'I told him, of course, that to describe you as a loose cannon is to defame loose cannons, but he still wanted you told.'

'And is it true?' I said.

'Yes,' he said. 'Of course it is. Alan was a personal friend of my mother-in-law's: a very personal friend at one time, I believe,' he said. 'But I only know him slightly from that connection, and I can assure you that I have never made any kind of approach to him, of a commercial nature. Nor, as far as I'm aware, has anyone else at Crawford's.'

I shrugged and turned around to face him.

'Call me a jaundiced old cynic with an axe to grind, if you like,' I said, 'but your assurances don't explain the cheque I found, made out to Alan Baird and bearing your and Carole's signatures.'

'Cheque?' he said, looking genuinely nonplussed. 'What cheque? Alan didn't say anything about a cheque.'

'A Crawford's cheque made out for thirty thousand pounds.'

'Show me,' he said.

'I can't. I gave it to Baird last night.'

'How convenient,' he said.

'But I can show you the remittance advice that was with it.'

I reached into my jacket pocket, pulled out the flimsy slip of paper and handed it to him. He read it very quickly.

'But that's not possible,' he said. He read it again. 'I can't explain this. It makes no sense. No wonder Alan was concerned. This can't have passed through the books. I'd've spotted it. How did you get it?'

'I found it in my garage. It had been dropped there. I can't think that it could have been left there other than deliberately.'

256

'Deliberately or accidentally, what was it doing in your garage? It shouldn't even exist.'

I shrugged and we lapsed into silence.

'Iain,' he finally said, 'I really know nothing about this. But I'm going to bloody well find out. The signatures could have been stamps or we signed blank cheques. That sometimes happens.'

'They looked like stamps to me,' I said.

He nodded. 'Can I hang on to this?'

'It's your company,' I said.

'I wish,' he said. He left the kitchen and stalked into the living room, clutching the remittance advice firmly, heading for the front door.

'I'd be a little careful,' I said when I caught up with him and we stood by his car. 'There do seem to be some unsavoury characters hovering over this particular pile of ordure.'

'Like who?' he snapped.

'Colm Kelly and his little friends,' I said.

'I can handle Kelly,' he said dismissively.

I rather doubted that and I was sure he couldn't handle Archie Nugent but I said nothing as he slipped behind the wheel of the BMW and started the engine.

I stood in the pool of cold, bright light thrown by the halogen bulb mounted above my storm door, surrounded by a profound darkness, watching the red pinpricks of Duncan's tail-lights disappear as he turned off my driveway and on to the road, accelerating away.

I'd never liked him but I had to admit to a sneaking sympathy for him as he'd been forced to admit that he didn't know what was going on in the company he was supposed to be running. It couldn't have been easy. He had always struck me as essentially a weak man who clothed his weakness in bluster, mistaking a bullying manner for authority. But something seemed to have dripped at least a little iron into his soul.

I stood in the cold long after he'd gone, watching my breath condense, listening to the sounds of the night: the rush of the burn, the creak of the hawthorn hedge, the scuttling of tiny feet in the garage, a deer bellowing in the distance, and the eerie cry of a ghost owl as it swooped low over the field. All that was missing was the bark of the big dog fox that lurked on the other side of the road. It was too early for him.

The cat slunk out of the shadows and rubbed up against my leg. I hunkered down and ran my hand along his cold fur.

I felt as if I'd taken up far too much of Alan Baird's time for one day. Helen Baxter and Duncan Ferguson had both been sent out in his name. I couldn't work out why a busy and apparently distinguished politician should expend any energy at all on me. It ought to have been suspicious, and maybe it did indicate that he had something to hide. Who doesn't? But I didn't think it was that at all. I had the feeling that he desperately wanted me to think well of him, even to like him. Which, of course, had quite the opposite effect and made me think that he was a sad little prat.

The cat followed me into the kitchen and I opened a can for him and dumped the foul-smelling contents into his dish. He purred like a high-speed train.

I turned on the radio and the rich, pure sound of Elisabeth Schwarzkopf singing the last of Strauss's 'Four Last Songs' filled the room with a deep melancholy.

I went back to the front of the house and shut and locked the storm door, then pulled the front door to. Its lock was bust and one of the hinges would have to be fixed.

When I returned to the kitchen, the cat had gone, leaving half of his gourmet rabbit in rich gravy, and Elisabeth Schwarzkopf had run out of notes.

I realized that I didn't have anything in to eat and that I didn't want to stay in alone, anyway. I left all the lights and the radio on and went out of the kitchen door, carefully locking it after me.

Chapter Twelve

Dougie wasn't in the almost deserted bar, a half-consumed pint of Guinness on the table in front of him, quietly contemplating the follies of man or energetically listing them to a circle of equally boisterous listeners. There was something unnatural about his absence; it amounted to the violation of an immutable law of nature.

Fiona was pulling pints for a couple of fishermen and I patiently waited my turn as she exchanged friendly, if slightly barbed, banter with them. Eventually, she turned towards me.

'Just the man I wanted to see,' she said.

'Och, I bet you say that to all the boys,' I said.

'No, I don't. Not to all the boys. Anyway, it was your bank manager friend who said you'd be in. What can I get you?'

'Just a lemonade and orange juice, Fiona. I'm driving,' I said. 'And what did big Dougie have to say for himself?'

'He left you a message,' she said, pouring bright yellow liquid from a small bottle and then directing a clear stream from a small hose into the same glass.

'Oh, aye?' I said, handing her a five-pound note.

She went to the till and returned with my change and a white envelope.

'I expect it'll be telling you why he had to leave,' she said.

'I expect it will,' I said, pocketing the change, picking up my drink and message.

Fiona leaned on the bar and smiled at me.

'Aren't you going to open it then?' she said, nodding at the envelope.

'Aye, I am,' I said, moving away towards a free table. 'Thanks, Fiona.'

She gave an exasperated sigh that I wasn't planning to share the contents of the message with her and bustled along to the far end of the bar, busying herself with dirty glasses.

I sat down and opened the envelope. By any standards, Dougie's handwriting was neat and attractive. For someone who spent most of his life hunched over a computer screen, tapping away at a keyboard, there was about it something beautiful and miraculous. I read the note quickly.

Iain,

I've been recalled to active service – well, desk duty, really. The news editor is about to go into hospital to have his hip replacement replaced (it's the only recorded case of a plastic joint rejecting a human being) and I'm apparently his deputy. Which is definitely news to me. So how suited am I to the job?!

Reading between the lines, my illustrious editor (may all the gods preserve him) has been nobbled. And I'm not offering any prizes for correctly guessing who by. I'll just say that he went to school with a certain minister.

Anyway, the modesty board and ergonomic bum receptacle beckon and the intention is clearly to keep me too busy checking other hacks' stories and expenses, and writing emails about the abuse of the coffee machine and the lamentable grammar of the graffiti in the ladies' loo to investigate anything myself. We shall see!

I'll phone when I can.

Dougie

PS How can anyone possibly live a £105 taxi ride from civilization? Either civilization has to move or you do!

I suddenly felt very alone and vulnerable. I'd been relying on Dougie just being there. I wasn't expecting him to solve all my problems (though that would have been nice). I just needed him to listen to them sympathetically. He didn't really have to do anything, apart from drink Guinness and be big and friendly. Which came naturally to him.

Feeling deflated, decidedly sorry for myself and let down in some vague and unspecified way, I went back to the bar and ordered lasagne, declining Fiona's cheery offer of chips. The weeks I'd spent in Florence as a student just wouldn't let me eat chips with pasta, any more than they would allow me to drink cappuccino after midday. That brief, golden time had left me with a smattering of Italian, a love of Dante, Leopardi, Petrarch and di Lampedusa and those two inflexible cultural rules.

The evening spread out in front of me bleak, barren and miserable and I couldn't face even thinking about my violated house just then, and I certainly couldn't face any more orange juice and lemonade. So I asked for a glass of the filthy pub red wine.

It proved to be not at all filthy but surprisingly smooth and pleasant: a Merlot or a Pinot Noir, I decided.

It was, of course, neither and when Fiona waved the bottle of Rioja at me I made a mental note not to enter any blind tastings in the future. I was clearly in need of a lot more training. In the event, the wine was good enough to ask for another glass.

I'd finished that and all of the lasagne that I wanted when Martin Crawford came in, blinking and sweeping his wind-tousled hair from his face. He peered around the bar, looking for someone. The sour look that crossed his face when he saw me made it clear that that someone was definitely not me. He looked around again and it seemed that whoever he was to meet wasn't there because he forced a weak smile on to his face, bobbed his head in acknowledgement and made his way over to my table.

I'd been sure that I'd wanted to see him in the morning but now I was far from certain that I could face him. The only Crawford I really wanted to see was Carole. Still,

I realized that I'd have to talk to him sometime and steeled myself. He stood in front of me looking awkward.

'Iain,' he said, 'I'm glad that I ran into you.' He ran a hand through his blond hair. 'I wanted to explain about last night. And apologize for Colm.' He looked tired and pale. There was about him a worn look that suggested someone much older than his twenty-six or so years. And the little tic had again started to tug at the soft, surprisingly dark and plump pouch under his left eye. 'What are you drinking?'

'The pub Rioja. It's pretty good.' I said.

'Let me get you another,' he said, sweeping up my glass and striding back to the bar.

I wasn't about to be less than polite or unfriendly to him in public and I let him go without a protest, reasoning that I could move on to coffee when it was my round and then I could leave.

A minute or so later, he handed me a glass of wine and sat down opposite me. He raised his whisky and then sipped at it.

'So?' I said. 'What was last night all about?'

'Business,' he said. 'What did you think?' His hand brushed at his hair again. 'It's necessary to keep politicians sweet sometimes, whatever you may think of them. Alan Baird asks me to jump and Archie Nugent tells me how high. To be honest, I don't really know what was going on.' He looked around the bar while he spoke, avoiding my gaze.

'So, you were just telling me what he wanted me to hear?'

'Oh, no,' he said, looking away from me. 'There's no financial arrangement between Crawford's and Alan Baird. I have no idea what that cheque was all about.' He looked back at me and gave a tight little smile. 'And no idea at all how you got hold of it . . .'

I nodded politely. A thought was forming. It had occurred to me that Colm Kelly had been in my garage the night before I found the cheque. It was more than possible that he'd left it there, following instructions from someone.

'Now, I know that you and Colm don't get on, and I'm really sorry that he needled you last night,' he said, 'but I think it would be a good idea if you apologized to him. You've pissed him off regally.'

'Have I?' I said.

'Yeah,' he said. 'Apologize and it'll all be forgotten. Colm's not so bad. Deep down.'

'Martin,' I said, 'I suspect that deep down, as someone once said, Colm Kelly is a very shallow man.'

'Someone said that about Colm?' he said, forcing a nervous laugh.

I shook my head.

'Only me,' I said. 'It's not original, though. And, for the record and onward transmission, I don't think that I've anything to apologize to him for.' I picked up my glass and gulped down some wine.

'Maybe not,' he said, 'but I'd just point out that you're not a businessman with some very good connections.' He paused and pursed his lips. 'And some very bad ones.'

'No,' I said, 'I'm just a scribbler with the soul of a thug.'

'Well, you said it. But don't be too modest. You've got the features of a thug too.'

He forced out that high-pitched nervous laugh again.

'Well,' I said, 'that does have the merit of being much less embarrassing than the description one female journalist once used.'

He looked the question at me.

'She said that I had the face of a fallen angel.'

'Very nice,' he said and smiled. Then he looked thoughtful for a few seconds before saying, 'But it isn't just Colm. You seem to be making a habit of pissing people off. I saw Duncan and he was looking even more sour and disagreeable than usual. When I asked him what was up, he said that he'd been to see you about something. I don't wish to pry, and what you and my big sister get up to is, for the most part and with the obvious exception of Duncan, just between you, but I'd suggest that the two of you make a decision soon.'

He raised his whisky to his lips again and peered at me over the rim of the glass in his faux jejeune manner, coy, flirtatious and knowing all at the same time. He reminded me of Carole in her most irritatingly Princess Diana mode.

'Thanks for the advice,' I said, 'but it's more for Carole to decide than me. She's the one with the commitments.'

'I guess,' he said.

'So, you know nothing about the cheque or how it ended up in my garage?' I said.

He looked away again and started picking at the back of his right hand.

'I told you,' he said, 'I know nothing about it. And I didn't even know that Colm Kelly knew Alan Baird. His presence there was a complete surprise. I just went because Archie told me I had to.' He looked down at his hands and, with obvious effort, forced himself to stop scratching, clutching his left hand in his right.

We lapsed into silence for a few moments and sipped our drinks. He wasn't going to tell me anything and I had nothing more to say to him. Somehow, my wine didn't taste as good as it had.

The bar was starting to fill up and Martin looked around every time someone stomped in. Even so, I saw him first.

We both missed his entrance, though. He didn't seem to have swung through the noisy, creaking door; he just materialized at the bar, his elegant, understated, dark-blue overcoat open and revealing a charcoal-grey suit and a crisp white shirt. A blue cashmere scarf hid his tie.

He looked like his wardrobe probably cost more than my house.

'Archie,' Martin said, rising to his feet when Nugent came over to the table.

'Martin, Iain,' Nugent said, nodding to me.

'Excuse us, Iain, but we have a little business to discuss,' Martin said.

'Aye,' I said. 'No problem. You go and discuss European grants for Crawford's or whatever it is you have to discuss. I have to be off anyway.'

'Where's Dougie?' Nugent said. 'I thought he was staying here.'

'He was,' I said. 'But he was called back to the office.'

'Pity,' he said. 'It would have been good to have a drink with him later. I was talking to his editor only this morning, telling him what a good man Dougie is.'

'Were you at school with him too?' I said.

'Who?' he said.

'With Dougie's editor. Everyone seems to have been at school with him.'

'Not me,' he said. 'But I do know him socially.'

'Well enough to recommend Dougie for promotion?' I said.

'I wouldn't have thought so,' he said. 'Why? Has Dougie been promoted?'

'It seems so,' I said.

'That's very good news. Incidentally,' he said, tapping the side of his nose, 'a word to the wise: I would be careful around Colm Kelly for the foreseeable future, if I were you. He's more than a little miffed about last night. You don't just deck him publicly and get away with it. He nurses grievances. Now might be a good time to take that winter holiday you always promised yourself.' He gave me a thin, slightly disturbing smile and then he and Martin wandered off to a table in the far corner of the room.

Everyone suddenly seemed very concerned about my health. Although, I had the distinct impression that Archie Nugent wasn't all that concerned.

I looked over at the two of them, then contemplated the dregs of my wine. I wondered what they were cooking up.

I went to the bar and asked Fiona for some coffee. I took it back to my table and brooded over it. Unlike the wine, this really was authentically filthy – weak and slightly burned.

Suddenly, there were too many possibilities, and none of them made any sense. If Nugent wanted Baird discredited, he certainly wouldn't want Dougie taken off the story, but the minister would. If a bribe was involved, they'd both want him out of the way, but Nugent was surprised by the news that Dougie had been promoted, which suggested that he knew nothing about it. If Kelly had been taking the bribe to Baird (and why would he?), would he be so careless as to drop it?

I looked again at Martin Crawford and Archie Nugent, speaking earnestly on the far side of the room, and I thought about asking them straight out what was going on. But I didn't know what question to ask. Maybe there was no conspiracy, and the thirty thousand pounds was entirely innocent. And there really are angels in America.

The TV in the bar was tuned in to the news, presumably before the soccer match started, and one of the prime minister's egregious attack dogs was snarling soundlessly.

Suddenly, I realized that I didn't care much about Baird, Crawford's, Nugent or snarling ministers who could turn on the anger when it suited them. All I wanted was to clean up my house, repair the lock on the front door, replace the TV and video (perhaps with a DVD player), listen to *Der Rosenkavalier*, maybe start to write something, and forget about the outside world for a while. I also realized that the outside world, in the shape of Colm Kelly and his thugs, wasn't likely to allow that. I thought back to the first time I'd seen Kelly and the flash of anger out of all proportion to the offence and shuddered to think what he might have in mind for me.

I was beginning to find the bar gloomily oppressive. But I didn't want to go home.

I thought about ringing Carole but I made no move to the public phone. Instead, I went to the bar and ordered whisky. Fiona raised an eyebrow at me and I said I'd be getting a cab home. She looked sceptical but I reassured her and she took down the bottle of Ardbeg.

By nine thirty, I was relaxed and talkative, positively bubbling over with words. The only problem was, there was no one to talk to. Dougie was in Glasgow; Archie Nugent had left at eight, my question unformulated and unasked; a haunted-looking Martin had joined me for five or ten minutes but he had left well before nine. Fiona had reminded me that I was calling a cab when I wanted to go home, angled again to find out what Dougie had written to me and who he was, and then waved me a cheery goodbye just after Martin had gone.

I'd once been at the bar in the Hilton on Sixth Avenue in New York late one Friday afternoon when the staff had been changing shifts. The outgoing barman had been briefing the man just coming on duty. He quietly and coherently explained who was who around the bar and when he came to me and the English poet I had come upon by chance in MOMA, he paused and, choosing his words carefully, had said, 'And the two gentlemen at the bar are quietly drinking,' which had amused me. It wasn't untrue – we were perfectly well behaved at the time – but it carried with it the hint of a warning.

I had been 'quietly drinking' for nearly two hours and I knew that another whisky could well change all that. And I was very talkative. Both of which were very good reasons, I decided, for calling Carole.

Duncan answered the phone, sounding as if he had spent the last few hours doing much the same as me. He didn't seem at all fazed when I asked for Carole, and he just bellowed to her that the call was for her. He didn't even make any rude reference to who was calling. I wondered if his apparent indifference was real or assumed, but then found that it didn't bother me either way, just as long as it meant that he didn't give either Carole or me any grief.

267

Carole, however, was fazed. I wasn't sure if she was mad at me for calling her, or for calling her when I'd been drinking. The conversation was short and not at all sweet.

More than a little chastened, I went back to the bar and ordered the whisky I knew I shouldn't have. The taciturn barman put the glass down on the dark counter, filled it and took my money as if I was buying just another drink, and not the one on which the entire evening hinged. I was staring, fascinated, at the whorls and black knot-holes in the wood when he returned and plonked my change down into a little golden puddle of beer next to my glass. I pocketed the damp coins, splashed a little water into the whisky and carried the drink carefully over to the table I'd not long vacated. I just looked at it for a few long moments then, slowly raised the glass to my lips. One small sip and I could feel myself slipping from talkative to morose, but that may have had more to do with the brief, acerbic conversation with Carole than to the tiny amount of alcohol I ingested.

Then there was a yell across the din in the bar, over the chants from the game on TV. It took me a few seconds to register that the barman was calling my name and waving the telephone receiver in my general direction. I held up a hand to acknowledge him and walked across to take the phone from him.

It was Carole.

'I'm really sorry about just now,' she said. 'I was mad at Duncan and I took it out on you.'

'That's OK,' I said. 'I expect I deserved it.'

'No, you didn't,' she said. 'Anyway, grab your coat and get outside. I'm in front of the hotel in the car. I'll run you home. You sound as if you need a ride.'

'I do,' I said. 'Thanks. I'll be right there.'

My mood lightened immediately and I was grinning like a mad thing when I emerged from the hotel bar almost immediately, my last fateful glass of Ardbeg barely touched, standing in glorious, golden isolation in the centre of the table where I'd left it, almost forgotten. I hauled open the passenger door of the Golf and fell into the seat.

Carole leaned across and kissed me lightly on the lips, her long, cool fingers stroking my cheek.

'I *am* sorry about earlier,' she said when she pulled back, 'I really am.' She then straightened up and smiled. 'But this won't do at all, creating a scandal in public. Let's go somewhere we can do it in private.'

'I'd better warn you,' I said, 'my place is in a bit of a mess.'

'So what else is new?' she said.

'Well, it's worse than usual,' I said. 'I was burgled some-time this afternoon.'

'Oh, no, Iain, I'm so sorry. Anything much taken?'

'No, no, not really. Just the TV and the video as far as I can tell,' I said. 'Fortunately, they didn't touch the computer.' I made a disgusted voice as I remembered the vomit. 'One of them puked in the living room, though. I'm afraid I didn't clear it up before I came out.' I paused. 'It's strange: I just didn't want to be there on my own. I don't know why.'

'It's perfectly understandable,' she said, in her best psychology-major voice. 'It's all to do with violation. Even macho poets can feel violated.' She paused. 'And now I feel even more wretched about being so vile to you on the phone. Are you sure that you want to go home now?'

'Got to do it sometime,' I said.

She looked in the rear-view mirror, signalled and pulled smoothly out into the empty street.

'So,' I said, 'why so mad at Duncan?'

'He was drunk, and ranting about some fraud he thinks he's uncovered in the firm,' she said carefully. 'I decided to leave him to it. I honestly don't think I can bear to spend any longer under the same roof. I'll have to move out.'

My mood lightened even further but I decided to be careful about making the obvious offer.

'But it's your family's home,' I said.

'Yes,' she said, 'but it's full of terrible memories.'

It must have been just about the time that Carole and I finished restoring my living room to some semblance of order that Duncan Ferguson lurched out of the house, climbed into his BMW and somehow, without running into anything or swerving off the road, drove the six miles to the isolated house that Colm Kelly was staying in.

The house had once been a small hunting lodge and so it must have seemed appropriate to Duncan to take his shotgun and a handful of cartridges with him.

He parked, or abandoned, the car at a crazy angle by the gate and walked the hundred or so yards up the driveway, the gun broken and carried in the approved fashion.

It was very dark and Duncan was very drunk, and he had only the distant lights from the house to guide him but he managed to stumble his way almost to the front door without mishap. At that point, the sensor on the security light detected him and the bright, white bulb clicked on, flooding the area immediately in front of the house with a brilliant, intense illumination. Duncan was temporarily blinded and froze. After a few seconds, he could just make out three shadowy figures in the doorway. Swaying a little and closing his eyes against the glare, he called out.

'Kelly, I have to talk to you. I don't like being played for a sucker.'

There was no answer and Duncan tried again.

'This is my company, my life. You can't do things behind my back. Especially if they're illegal. *I'm* the one who goes to jail. And bribing government ministers is illegal. And using company cheques drops me in it up to my neck.'

There was still no response from the shadowy figures in the doorway.

'Come on, Colm. Talk to me.'

'No, you're drunk,' Colm Kelly barked at him, before turning back into the house.

For a moment, Duncan was confused. Why wouldn't Kelly talk to him? This was important. He had to make him talk. Then the door was slammed on him and his booze-fuelled anger kicked in. He snapped the shotgun shut and started walking towards the doorway. He fired one barrel straight into the solid, oak door, splintering wood. The second barrel he discharged at the irritating light, but he missed.

As he fumbled in his jacket for more cartridges, he was smiling. He was starting to enjoy himself.

His third shot took out a small window on the upper floor and his fourth shattered the light. Duncan yelled in triumph as darkness overwhelmed the driveway again.

Kelly opened a window at the side of the house, safely out of range, and yelled, 'No more shooting, Duncan, and we'll talk. Yeah?'

Duncan was having too good a time to respond immediately but somewhere in his alcohol-wasted brain he knew it couldn't go on.

'OK,' he said hesitantly and he lowered and broke the gun. It spat out the cartridge cases and Duncan watched, fascinated, as the light-grey smoke leaked from the barrels.

He was still smiling when the spring-loaded cosh thudded into the back of his head.

At least, that's how I imagined the scene later.

At what stage Kelly decided to use the situation to take me out as well, I don't know, but it was some hours before the two cars came jouncing down my driveway.

I heard them in a vivid fragment of a dream. I was in the Botanic Gardens in Glasgow, looking for Dougie in the fern house. The delicate plants were dying as I walked by, changing from lustrous green to golden-brown instantly in the gentle breeze that my passing created. Dougie was somewhere ahead of me, elusive, the Green Man. There were cars outside the fern house, their engines growling, their lights reducing the ferns to dust.

I was still a little drunk and I lost a minute or so as my addled brain tried to cope with what was happening. Carole was standing at the window, naked, peering out.

'It's Duncan,' she said, 'and there's another car. That black Audi.'

I joined her at the window. We both watched as the driver's door of the Beemer opened and we knew that something wasn't right when it wasn't Duncan who emerged but Kelly's cousin.

'This looks like it might get ugly,' I said. 'It might be better if we weren't here.'

Carole looked puzzled for a few seconds.

'Kelly and his thugs don't like me much,' I said. 'And I don't suppose that Duncan is my best friend just at the moment.'

She frowned at me and then burst out laughing.

'So, what are they going to do? Shoot you maybe? Nail your head to the floorboards?' she said.

'Maybe,' I said, 'I don't know.'

'Don't be silly, Iain,' she said.

She cocked her head to one side and looked at me like I'd just suggested we cross the road to avoid some aggressive drunks. She was daring me to mix it with them.

I nodded.

'OK,' I said, 'I'll go see what they want. But you stay here, out of the way.'

I pulled on some jeans and a T-shirt and decided that sturdy shoes were a good idea too. By that time, they were already hammering at the storm door.

Carole was still standing by the window and she turned away from me to peer down into the gloom. Her pale body was almost luminescent in the dark room and shadows scooped alluring hollows in her side and back.

I stepped across and held her, running my hands over her smooth, cool belly. She leaned back against me and I looked over her shoulder. I saw Duncan sagging against the black Audi, the little rat-faced Dermot standing at his side, and I was aware of the delicate perfume of Carole's

272

body, apples masked by a musky sweat. Her flesh was starting to goosebump.

There was a renewed banging on the door and Colm Kelly yelled up, 'Lewis, get down here before we smash this door in.'

'Your man's getting impatient,' Carole said gently, her voice a quiet, calm contrast to Kelly's.

'Yeah, I'd better get down,' I said, stepping away from her. 'And, Carole, you might put some clothes on, by the way.'

She turned around and smiled enigmatically as I left the room.

I stopped by the listing front door and called through, 'What do you want? It's a little late for a social call.'

I heard an ugly sound that I realized must have been Kelly laughing.

'The manifestation of Mrs Ferguson's car in your driveway suggests that you're already receiving visitors, Mr Lewis. Just let us in and save us the bother of splintering your fine door,' he said. '*Mr* Ferguson is very anxious to join the party. He's even brought his own firecracker.'

There was some subdued sniggering that I assumed came from the rat, Dermot.

'Why don't you go away now?' I said. 'If you've got anything worth saying to me – which I doubt – I'll see you in the hotel at twelve tomorrow.'

'Won't do, Mr Lewis. Just won't do. It has to be now.'

Someone kicked ineffectually at the big door and the dull sound resonated throughout the house.

'Why?' I said. 'Why does it have to be now?'

'Because, Mr Lewis, if the desperate and outraged husband is to catch his erring wife in the arms of her raffish lover, there couldn't be a more opportune moment, now could there?' he said.

It was a chilling statement and, as the implications sank in, I felt weak. I crouched down until I was sitting. It may have been the adrenaline rush or just the cold realization that Colm Kelly intended to kill me – and Duncan and

273

probably Carole as well – but I was definitely light-headed and a little weak-kneed. I breathed deeply and stood up.

'You expect me to let you in so you can rig it to look like Duncan killed me and then, presumably, killed himself.' I raised my voice a little. 'Do you know what they have in mind, Duncan? Do you? They plan to kill us both, Duncan. And they'll have to kill Carole, too. To cover themselves. Do you understand that, Duncan?'

I didn't have great hopes of Duncan in his what I assumed had to be fuddled state, but I did hope that Carole could hear me and was busily phoning the police on her mobile.

The assault on the door was more sustained this time and I found myself wondering why they didn't just go around to the back and the kitchen door, which was much less solid. I also remembered that there was a fourteen-pound axe in the garage which would make short work of even the storm door.

But it was dark. I could only hope that they wouldn't spot the axe and wouldn't want to venture around to the back of the house. I wondered what they were armed with. Certainly, they'd have the .45 automatic.

I eased my way past the damaged front door and looked into the storm porch, which was lit by the headlamps of the two cars.

Among the boots and anoraks that littered the storm porch, there were two old tennis rackets and a hefty cricket bat.

I chose the cricket bat and slipped back into the house, moving as silently as possible to the kitchen door. The storm door would hold for a lot longer and I just couldn't take the chance that they wouldn't investigate other ways in.

I stood by the kitchen door and waited. I couldn't quite believe that there was no one there and I listened for about thirty seconds. But, even as I opened the door, I could hear someone scuffling through the gravel at the side of the house, picking his way cautiously, his hand sliding along the wall.

I crouched down in the shadowed doorway, my heart thumping as he turned the corner. As soon as he appeared in front of me, I wielded the bat like a scythe and cracked it across his shins. For some reason, he suppressed his yell of pain but he did fall heavily. I stood up and brought the bat down on his shoulder. This time he did start to yell but, before he could really make any noise, I fell on his back and knocked all the breath out of him. I thought about jabbing him in the kidneys but decided not to risk damaging my hand. I just lay on him for a few seconds, attempting to immobilize him. He'd overdone the lemony aftershave and it was sharp and aggressive. I sneezed violently and shifted my position, allowing him some movement.

It was Liam, Kelly's cousin, and he had been carrying the .45. It now lay on the ground where he'd dropped it. He reached slowly out for it with his left hand but, in spite of the sneezing, I spotted the move, stood up and just jabbed his wrist hard with the toe of the bat. He recoiled, gasped, rolled up into a ball and started to sob violently.

I couldn't bring myself to hit him again. If he didn't have a broken leg or wrist, then his dislocated shoulder would probably inhibit his movements for a while. I bent down, picked up the gun and walked around to confront the other two.

The gun felt heavy and cold, dangling uselessly from my clammy hand as I sidled around the corner of the house, my back pressed hard against the stone wall, and looked out on to the driveway. The rubber-covered handle of the cricket bat, tightly gripped in my left hand, was an altogether more comforting presence.

I was shivering but sweating under the worn old T-shirt. It was an odd sensation.

I could hear the unfortunate Liam, who seemed only to

have walked into my life to be battered and bruised, groaning quietly. I briefly thought about going back and hitting him again to shut him up completely but I didn't have the time. If the others hadn't heard him by now they would have in the minute or two it would take me to silence him. Anyway, I knew that I didn't have the stomach for laying him out in cold blood.

I found it difficult to believe that no one at the front of the house could hear him whimpering but it seemed so. I assumed that the rodent-faced Dermot was too concerned with propping Duncan up to hear, and that Kelly was so enraged at me and my obdurate door that all he could hear was the angry blood pounding in his temples.

It was a strange sight to look out on. The headlamps of the cars lit up the front of the house in a harsh, blinding light, turning the area into a flat, two-dimensional film set, rendering it curiously unfamiliar, almost alien. The lights obscured two figures who slumped in the shadows by the rear of the BMW, one of them muttering incoherently while the other held on firmly to his arm, and silhouetted another, who was posed dramatically on the step.

Kelly had found the axe, which was not a comforting thought. However, he clearly didn't know how to handle it and, for one glorious but brief moment, as he raised it inelegantly above his head to savage the wooden obstacle in front of him, I thought he might save me any further trouble by missing the door entirely and embedding it in his thigh, severing his femoral artery and establishing himself as a vivid and memorable, but very temporary, fountain feature.

It transpired that his short arm stab worked well enough: the axe head bit deep into the wood and stuck fast. Kelly cursed as he tried to pry and lever it loose, struggling to work the long handle up and down. I thought of the logs I had failed to split in one go and the effort involved in extricating the axe for another blow.

As he wrestled with it, Duncan yelled something incoherent but spiced with audible obscenities at him. Kelly turned towards Duncan and faced the light with a strangely beatific smile on his face. The beam from the headlamps haloed his thick hair around his head and it occurred to me that he must have been a choirboy at some Catholic school once upon a time, with an adoring mother.

I called to him without stepping into the light.

'Kelly, you're a very violent and angry man and I want you off my property before you do any more damage.' I was trembling and could hear the fear in my voice. I just hoped that he couldn't.

He didn't reply but left the axe where it was and stooped down. Too late, I saw the shotgun propped against the wall. In the same moment as he snatched it up and pointed it in my direction, I realized that I didn't have a clue whether the .45 was loaded, if the safety was on, or how to switch it off. But then, he didn't know that I'd never handled a gun before. I could almost hear Dougie murmuring, 'Be bloody, bold and resolute, but, if at all possible, do try to avoid the bloody.'

The barrel of the shotgun was waving around as he tried to locate me in the shadows at the side of the house.

I raised my arm and extended the gun from behind the wall and let him see it.

'I wouldn't do that, if I were you,' I said, stepping out into the light. The beam of the headlamps glinted dully on the blue-black barrel. 'Get in the car and take the weasel over there with you. Duncan stays here, and so does the other one. As insurance.'

'What have you done with Liam?' he said, without lowering the shotgun. I had the feeling that he knew I was bluffing.

'A little less than he would have done to me,' I said. 'He's just bruised.'

'You little gobshite,' he said. 'You don't know what you're into, mixing it with me.'

There was a low murmur of inarticulate rage from the direction of the cars and suddenly Duncan was lumbering towards Kelly, the unfortunate Dermot hanging on to him like a rat clinging tenaciously to a maddened black labrador. Kelly swivelled and pulled both triggers in rapid succession.

The blasts were deafening and the effect immediate. Duncan stopped like he'd run into a wall and both he and Dermot collapsed to the ground in an untidy, bleeding heap.

Kelly broke the gun and I realized that, if I couldn't stop him reloading, I was next.

I ran at him, the gun still hanging from my right hand, swinging the cricket bat with my left. It caught him on the neck and shoulder and he lurched sideways. The impact juddered up my arm and I nearly dropped the bat.

He was still on his feet but he was swaying from side to side. I'd learned enough in the ring to know that a groggy fighter is still a dangerous one and I stepped closer in order to follow through. I used the heavy old bat like a pickaxe handle and chopped down on the back of his head. The contact was sickening and he crumpled over and stopped moving.

The bat was in as bad a shape as he was and would never drive a ball through the covers to the mid-on boundary again (not that it had done it all that often in my playing days). I was holding just the handle and the little wedge that fitted into the bat proper. The blade was lying next to Kelly.

I thought at first that I must have killed him and I started to panic. But then I forced myself to lean over him and I thought I saw his chest move slightly and I was sure I could hear a little air rasping its way into his lungs.

I straightened up and closed my eyes. I was breathing hard and trying to gather my thoughts when I remembered Duncan and the thin runt of an Irishman. I walked haltingly across and knelt beside them.

Kelly's blast had caught Duncan high up on the shoulder, and it was dark and wet with sticky blood. He was still conscious and cursing quietly. The Irishman was a head shorter than Duncan and had been less lucky. The shot had taken him above the eye. His forehead was a terrible mess, and I wasn't sure if he was alive or dead.

I called out to Carole and she was almost instantly at my side.

'Can you call for the police and an ambulance?' I said.

'I've already done it,' she said. 'Jesus, Iain.'

She was pale and trembling, her arms jerking in an exaggerated way. I looked down at my own hands and realized that I was trembling almost as much.

'Jesus, Iain,' she said again, staring down at Duncan, at Kelly and at Dermot. 'Are they all right? Is Duncan going to be all right?' Her voice was rising into a wail. Then she started sobbing uncontrollably and I stood up and took her in my arms.

'I think Duncan's going to be OK,' I said as reassuringly as I could manage. 'At least he's still swearing robustly which has to be a good sign. Kelly's still breathing. I think. The other one . . . I just don't know about.'

I stroked her hair and kissed her forehead. She was still crying but she calmed a little.

'Let's see if we can make Duncan more comfortable,' I said, thinking that if we did something we might stave off shock. She nodded and we went into the house and up to my bedroom where we found blankets and towels.

The towels were all dark with blood by the time I heard the first emergency vehicle, siren blaring, roaring along and looked up to see the distant flash of lights.

Neither Kelly nor Dermot had stirred when I'd covered them with blankets but a white-faced Duncan continued to babble away.

Bruised, battered and limping heavily, Liam had dragged himself around to the scene of the carnage but, after just murmuring 'Jesus Christ', he had hunkered down next to his cousin and said nothing. I draped a blanket around his shoulders but he didn't seem to notice.

The young police constables who were first on the scene immediately asked for back-up, the clatter of the radio and the flash of their blue light irritating and obtrusive, their attempts to ascertain what had happened uncertain and ineffectual.

Eventually, I stood silently, my arm around Carole, holding her close, until the first ambulance arrived.

She left with Duncan. I saw her in the interior of the ambulance, before the paramedics closed the doors, sitting next to her husband, tightly clutching his hand between both of hers.

Chapter Thirteen

The interview room where I was held wasn't exactly cosy, but it wasn't as bleak as the *policiers* and the TV detective series all suggest. The table *was* grey and grubby and it was covered in dark stains. So were the walls. The furniture *was* all bolted to the floor and the place *did* smell of stale cigarettes and staler human beings. But there were two small watercolours of local scenes on one of the walls, and someone with a broad sense of humour (or perhaps with no sense of irony at all) had even pinned up a police recruitment poster.

After an hour of waiting, drinking the machine coffee that the duty sergeant kept bringing me and studying the two indifferent paintings, I was beginning to think about applying to join myself.

I'd gone voluntarily to the police station but I had been left in no doubt at all that, if I hadn't, I would have been arrested on suspicion of something.

I knew I was in shock. The interview room was overheated and underventilated but I couldn't stop shivering. And I kept seeing the shotgun blast and Dermot's ruined forehead, and the dark, sticky blood oozing from Duncan's shoulder. I also found myself having to repress an inappropriate desire to giggle every so often. I could just imagine some glib lawyer characterizing me in court as deeply psychotic on the basis of that alone.

When the tired and sad-looking detective inspector I'd first seen on Sunday finally came in at a little after three, it seemed at first as though he was as light-headed as I was.

'I wasn't expecting you until nine, Mr Lewis,' he said.

I smiled weakly but didn't reply and he switched on the tape recorder and formally started the interview, mumbling his name and that of his sergeant into the machine.

While I'd been waiting, I'd had plenty of time to go over everything that had happened and prepare a story. But I'd finally decided that I had no choice other than to tell the truth about everything. And I did. It was something of a relief to do so. I began with Margaret Crawford's funeral and the black briefcase, worked my way through the various confrontations with Kelly, my encounter with Nugent at Billy MacPhail's, the mysterious appearance of the cheque in my garage and the subsequent meetings with Alan Baird. I finished with as concise an account of the events of the evening as I could give.

I was as precise as I could be about the injuries I'd inflicted on Liam and Colm Kelly, and the sergeant raised his eyebrows and muttered something about how right Prince Philip had been about cricket bats when I explained how I'd broken mine over Kelly's head.

The inspector and the sergeant both asked shrewd and searching questions throughout my account, double-checking points or seeking clarification. They were methodical and thorough, scrupulously polite and even-tempered. Apart from the one occasion, there were no raised eyebrows or exclamations of incredulity, and there were certainly no thumped tables. In fact, there were no histrionics from any of us. It seemed that they accepted that my story was too preposterous for me to have invented it. They'd even both smiled when I explained why our history made it difficult for me to expect a fair hearing from Sergeant Darling.

It was a little after three forty-five when they called in the uniformed man to stand with me while I was left to stew a while. Anticipating a long wait, I tried to engage the young, bleary-eyed policeman in conversation, but failed miserably. My ill-informed and clumsily framed comments about Rangers and Celtic elicited nothing but a non-committal cough.

But I needn't have worried; the detectives were only out of the room for ten minutes.

Neither of them sat down when they came back and the inspector chewed his lip and stared down at me. Eventually, he shook his head.

'Well, Mr Lewis, do you want the good news or the bad news?' he said.

I shrugged. 'I guess I'd better hear the worst.'

'OK,' he said. 'Well, we haven't yet decided what to charge you with but, as sure as eggs is eggs, we will be charging you with something. And it's unlikely to be trivial. Unless the prosecution service can be persuaded that they have little chance of securing a conviction, in which case it'll be some Mickey Mouse charge and you'll be admonished and fined.'

I nodded in what I hoped was a suitably resigned way.

'In the meantime, you can bugger off somewhere and get some sleep. Is there anywhere you can go? You won't be able to return home until tomorrow afternoon when the forensics boys have finished up.'

'I don't know,' I said. 'I hadn't thought about it.'

'Well,' he said, 'Mrs Ferguson is waiting for you. Could you go home with her?'

'That's a possibility,' I said.

'Let the desk sergeant know,' he said, looking at me in as neutral a way as he could manage.

I slowly lumbered to my feet.

'Any news on Duncan Ferguson? And the others?' I said.

'The quacks are picking shot out of his shoulder even as we speak, but he'll be OK.' He reached into his pocket, pulled out a notebook and flipped through it. 'Colm Kelly has a suspected depressed fracture of the skull, is still unconscious and in intensive care; Liam Kelly has some very serious bruising and a broken wrist but nothing

283

worse; Dermot O'Brian is described as "gravely ill". I can't tell you any more.'

'Thanks,' I said and walked to the door. Just as I opened it, he spoke again.

'Don't you want to know the good news?'

I turned back, puzzled.

'Sorry?' I said.

'I told you there was good news and bad news. I've told you the bad. Don't you want to hear the good?'

'I guess so,' I said, giving a weary shrug.

'We've recovered your TV and VCR.'

'That was quick,' I said. 'How did you manage that?'

'Good, honest police work, sir. How do you think we managed it?' He did seem genuinely pleased with himself.

'That's great,' I said unenthusiastically.

'I thought you'd be a bit happier about it,' he said, sounding a little put out.

'I'm sorry,' I said, 'but it's difficult to get too excited, in the circumstances.'

He nodded understandingly.

'It was two bad Glasgow lads,' he said. 'We picked them up when they tried to offload your telly in one of the bars down the road. Tried to sell it to an off-duty sergeant!' He paused and looked at me shrewdly. 'Now, clear off. We'll be in touch.'

I nodded to him and the sergeant and made my way to the door but, just as I reached out for the handle, he spoke again and I stopped and turned back to face him.

'One more thing, Mr Lewis, Iain, if I may,' he said. 'I'd take it as a great personal favour if you made some attempt in the immediate future not to obstruct my enquiries and to share with me any relevant information you have. Of course, I'd also appreciate it if you didn't wield a cricket bat with lethal intent or otherwise cause mayhem, but I imagine that's too much to hope for.'

I gave him a tight little smile and quickly left the inter-view room.

The harsh strip lighting was hurting my eyes and I felt

bone-weary as I plodded along the corridor, across the scuffed blue linoleum, past the dirty cream walls to the front desk.

Carole was waiting there, sitting demurely on a black, moulded-plastic seat. She looked very pale, as though the bright light had leached all colour from her. Her eyes were flecked with red from weeping and there were dark smudges of fatigue under them. But she was a beautiful sight.

She looked up as I approached and slowly rose. Her mouth was set in a thin, hard line but she relaxed a little when she saw me and she tried to smile.

She didn't even get close. By the time I was at her side her face had contorted into something ugly and the tears and uncontrolled sobs had begun.

I wrapped my arms around her and held her to my chest until she calmed a little. I told her that I couldn't go home just yet and asked if I could come back with her. She nodded and I turned to the desk sergeant, who had discreetly busied himself with some paperwork while we embraced, and told him where I'd be. He made a note of it.

Then I put my arm around Carole's shoulders and led her out. We eventually found her car and I drove her home.

We slept surprisingly well for two people just lying on the sofa holding each other.

The sky had lightened to a dark, dark grey by the time I woke and sluggishly stirred myself. The arm under Carole had lost almost all feeling and I eased it away from her and tried to massage some circulation back into it without waking her. She stirred as I pulled away from her and got off the couch.

I padded on bare feet to the big kitchen, aware that rain was falling steadily.

Martin was pouring himself a cup of tea from a huge

285

brown pot, a piece of toast clenched between his teeth. He put down the pot, grabbed the toast and put it on his plate.

'What the hell are you doing here?' he said. 'Duncan'll throw a blue fit if he finds out.'

'I don't think he'll find out,' I said. 'Unless you tell him.'

He looked puzzled, and I suddenly realized that he had no idea what had taken place during the night. Or else he was a consummate actor.

'There was a spot of trouble up at my house last night,' I said. 'I had to sleep on the sofa here.'

'What happened?'

'You and Nugent were right to warn me about Kelly. He showed up with a shotgun, a handgun, two friends and a very drunk Duncan.'

'And you're here to tell the tale?'

I nodded.

'And the others?'

'In hospital. Mostly,' I said.

'You put them all in hospital?'

I shook my head.

'No. Kelly's responsible for half the casualties. I'll own up to hurting him and his cousin, though.'

'Jesus, Iain. What happened?'

'I'm sorry, Martin, but I'm not really in the mood for long explanations. Ask Carole. Or go and visit Duncan in hospital. I'm just too tired. I'm sorry.'

He slurped his tea and chewed his toast, thinking. He blinked and then stood up, nervously moving from foot to foot.

'How serious is it? Are the police involved?' he said. He started to pick at the skin on the back of his right hand.

'It's serious, Martin, and the police are definitely very involved.'

'Shit,' he said and he marched briskly out of the kitchen. I heard him stride to the front door and then heard it open and close. A few seconds later his Jag roared into life.

I stared out of the window at the bedraggled trees and wondered about my cat and whether he had been driven away permanently by the activity of the night. I doubted it but I had no doubt that I could add him – and probably Martin, as well – to the list of those very pissed off with me. At least I could buy the cat's affection with a little fresh fish.

I heard the fridge open behind me and turned to see Carole peering into it.

'No orange juice,' she said, yawning.

'That's OK,' I said.

'I can probably manage tea. Or coffee, if you'd prefer it.'

'Tea's fine,' I said.

'Do you think you could organize it?' she said. 'I just don't seem to be able to stop trembling.'

'Sure,' I said and moved to her side. 'You're still a bit shocked, I expect. I know I am. Tea's probably just the thing.'

It was her turn to stare out of the kitchen window at the rain sluicing across the bleak bare garden while I filled the kettle.

'It's enough to make you believe in the pathetic fallacy, isn't it?' she said quietly.

'Oh, I don't know,' I said. 'It rains a lot up here. Remember? It even rains when you're happy.'

She made a little dismissive snort, as though being happy wasn't something she easily associated with life.

'I said I'd be at the hospital by twelve,' she said. 'The doctor wasn't sure that Duncan would be in any state to see anyone, but I think I'd better be there, just in case he is.'

I nodded at her as I gently warmed the old teapot, nursing it as I remembered my father doing.

'He's going to be very sore for a while, they said.'

I nodded again. She was chewing furiously at a ragged nail.

'Nothing to worry about, though, except infection. They'll be keeping him in for at least a few days. Just for observation. They said.'

'That's good,' I said.

I put the teapot down on the counter, walked over to her and wrapped my arms around her. She leaned back against me.

'If they say he's going to be all right, I'm sure he will be,' I said.

She pulled away from me and turned back to the window.

'It's funny, isn't it?' she said. 'You think you no longer care about someone and then something happens that makes you think again.' She paused and sighed. 'I don't think I love Duncan any more. I haven't loved him for a long time. Sometimes I wonder if I ever did love him. But I do care.'

'That's not so strange,' I said. 'You live with someone for six or seven years, or whatever it is, and they become part of your life, I guess. Of course you care about them.'

'But,' she said, 'seeing him, lying in the ambulance, pale and bleeding, I kept on thinking that this could solve so many problems. If he died.' She turned back to face me. 'Iain, that can't be right. Not wanting him to die, just so that some of my problems would disappear and my life would be that much easier.'

'I don't know if I can help you on that one, Carole,' I said. 'But, for what it's worth, I don't think the fact that such a thought crossed your mind makes you a bad person, just a more than averagely complex human being.'

'Did it cross your mind?' she said.

'I don't think that it did,' I said. 'But I had other things to worry about at the time. And, in any case, I'm a relatively simple soul.' I ran my tongue over my dry lips. 'And I just don't see Duncan as an obstacle to anything.'

She turned away again and stared out of the window. She raised her right hand and tried to ease some of the tension out of her neck and shoulders, her long, strong fingers probing at the knotted muscles.

I stood looking at her for a few seconds, awkwardly wondering whether there was something I should say or do, wishing that I could take the single step that would put me next to her, knead the stress away, whisper words that would make her feel better. But I didn't stride over, just turned back to my tea-making.

I handed Carole her tea as the phone rang. She indicated that she'd rather I answered it and so I left the kitchen to do so.

'I called the cop shop and they told me you'd been released and that this was where you'd said you'd be,' Dougie said. 'The fact that they've let you go with no strings attached – assuming there are no strings attached – bodes well. I just got in and heard the news.'

I looked at my watch. It was only ten to nine. It had never occurred to me that Dougie could be moving early enough in the morning to be at the office by that time.

'How?' I said.

'It's my job. I'm a journalist, remember? I have reliable sources. I work in a news room. We get the news. But are you all right?'

'Yeah,' I said. 'I guess so. Physically unscathed anyway.'

'The one on the critical list? You didn't shoot him, did you?'

'He's not dead, is he?'

'No. Not yet, anyway. Was it you?'

'No, it wasn't me,' I said. 'It was Ke –'

'I don't want to know who did it,' he broke in. 'Not yet, anyway. I'm just relieved it wasn't you. Now, listen to me: it's not going to take other journalists long to track you down. In fact, I'm surprised they haven't managed it already. I am the first, aren't I?'

'Yes, Dougie, you are.'

'Good. Now, you're going to have other calls, possibly even visitors. A word of advice: be polite, give 'em tea, but don't say anything. No comment. Nothing, *nada, nichts, rien, niente.* Don't say anything that will piss the police off. Be as silent as the grave. From this day forth you never will speak word.'

'Except to the police, of course,' I said.

'Of course,' he said.

'And to Uncle Dougie, of course,' I said.

'I didn't say that, Iain, and I didn't mean that. In fact, I'm black affronted that you should even think such a thing.'

'Sure you are, Dougie,' I said. 'You don't want a nice big exclusive or anything.'

'I don't,' he said. 'Not at the moment. I was just concerned for an old friend who has more than his share of woes. But if that's what you think, I won't take up any more of your time. You know where I am, if you think you need me.'

'I'm sorry, Dougie, I didn't mean anything,' I said quickly, before he could ring off in a huff. 'I'm not thinking too straight at the moment. I know you wouldn't dream of exploiting a friendship just to get the inside track on a story.'

'Of course I would,' he said, 'but I'd rather wait for the complete story. Things are still more than a bit fuzzy round the edges at the moment. Which is partly why we don't want anyone muddying the pool with comments that can be traced back to you. What did you tell the police?'

'Everything.'

'Everything?'

'Everything.'

'So a certain prominent politician and a discreet but tough-minded lobbyist have both had their names raised?'

'They have,' I said.

'So the Sundays will probably get a sniff of it.'

'How?'

'Someone – probably a policeman – will leak it. How do you think? But don't let it be you. OK?'

'OK, Dougie.'

'Was I mentioned?'

'Yeah, your name came up.'

'OK, I'll expect a visit. At least I can corroborate some of your story.'

'Yes,' I said. 'But do you really think the papers will be crawling all over this?'

'I'm afraid so. It's potentially a big Scottish story. Of

course, if a big scandal involving our much loved First Minister breaks, or if the Pentagon extends the war on terrorism to include the Swiss, you might get a day or two respite. But if things are slow in the news room, it'll be smeared all over the front pages. Just be prepared for it.'

'I will, Dougie. And, Dougie, thanks. I do appreciate the call and I'm more than grateful for the advice.'

'You're welcome and don't worry, I'll claim my kilo of flesh in due course.' And he broke the connection.

Carole was still staring out of the kitchen window when I returned. The mug of tea was in her hand, untouched. She didn't ask who had called.

'Drink your tea before it gets cold,' I said, 'and then, after a quick shower, I'll drive you to the hospital.'

'Thanks,' she said. 'I don't think I'm up to the drive. But, Iain, I have to see Duncan alone. I don't imagine he'll want to see you.'

'No, I don't suppose he would,' I said, more to myself than her.

She wrapped both hands around the mug and raised it to her mouth. She sipped absentmindedly, never lowering the mug, still staring out of the window.

The bright, crowded waiting area at the hospital was as uncomfortably overheated as the reception area at Crawford's. I'd long since taken off my waterproof and my jacket and the sweat was still trickling in little rivulets from under my arms and down my back, and beading on my forehead.

I sat, drinking coffee and reading the *Guardian*, waiting for Carole to reappear. It seemed that she'd been gone for an age but, in reality, it was no more than thirty or forty minutes. We'd sat together for about twenty minutes before a doctor had come to explain to her how Duncan was and then taken her off to see him.

The coffee was muddy instant and served in the kind of polystyrene cup that sent the same tremor down my spine as the rasp of an ice-lolly stick when I'd licked one as a kid. But the caffeine was giving me the buzz I needed to keep going. I was on my third cup and my second time through the *Guardian* when the sad-faced and taciturn detective inspector and his sergeant suddenly appeared.

'Mr Lewis,' the inspector said, 'what are you doing here? Just having your cholesterol checked out, or is it the special clinic you're visiting?'

'Afternoon, Inspector,' I said. 'No, I'm not here on account of anything that ails me. I drove a friend here.'

'And who would that friend be?' he said, making it sound as if he was highly doubtful that I had any friends.

'Mrs Ferguson,' I said. 'She's visiting her husband,' I added unnecessarily.

'Can I have a word?' he said, nodding towards the door. 'Somewhere a bit quieter.'

He and his sergeant ambled off and I followed, grabbing my jacket and waterproof as quickly as I could.

The rain was still lashing down and we stood under the concrete shelter over the hospital entrance and looked glumly out on to the flooded car park.

The sergeant lit a cigarette and a little plume of grey-blue smoke drifted lazily away. The harsh, acrid smell from the spent match lingered in the atmosphere. The air was cold and damp but it was refreshing after the stuffy, oppressive feel of the interior. I shrugged my jacket on and then hauled the waterproof on over the top of it.

The inspector stared off into the distance and I had the feeling that he was relying on his sergeant to gauge my reaction to anything he said.

'Things have taken a bit of a turn in the last couple of hours,' he said. 'Dermot O'Brian died of shotgun wounds to the head. It looks like this might be a nice juicy murder enquiry after all.'

'I don't think so,' I said. 'Kelly wasn't aiming at O'Brian. He was aiming at Duncan. Which makes it attempted murder. And manslaughter, I guess. Doesn't it?'

'Colm Kelly is still very sick, and Liam Kelly isn't saying anything,' he said.

He turned his weary face towards me and I saw for the first time that he had kind, brown eyes.

'I'm not sure, but I don't think Liam Kelly saw what happened,' I said.

'Of course, Mrs Ferguson has confirmed some of what you told us about what happened. One of our men spoke to her here at the hospital last night. We haven't interviewed Mr Ferguson yet. That's what we're here for now. I do hope his story agrees with yours.'

'Why wouldn't it?' I said.

'You tell me, Mr Lewis.' He looked off into the distance.

'Well, he was very drunk,' I said.

'Exactly,' he said.

'Look,' I said, 'I've told you what I know and, as far as I can, what I did and what I saw. I imagine the forensic evidence will bear out what I've said. I didn't shoot anybody. Colm Kelly did. All I did was act in self-defence.'

He nodded understandingly.

'OK, Iain,' he said. 'Don't let us keep you. We'll be in touch. When we've spoken to Mr Ferguson, we should have a clearer idea of what happened. Who knows? Mr Kelly may regain consciousness and admit everything.'

'But I wouldn't hold your breath on either count,' the sergeant said very quietly and chuckled.

'Don't take any notice of Gordon here,' the inspector said. 'He's just an old cynic. Mr Kelly has every chance of regaining consciousness and he will, as an honest and upright citizen, explain what happened. It should be an interesting story.'

The sergeant chuckled again as I went back inside.

My seat had been taken and so I just stood there, waiting for Carole.

I was in an odd state. I seemed to be beyond tired. I'd slept for only about four hours but it had been deep and dreamless.

I risked another cup of coffee and stood staring out of

the glass doors at the pouring rain, thinking about nothing at all, sipping at it. I wasn't sure if my problems were over or just beginning. I didn't know whether I wanted Kelly to make a full recovery or not. I certainly didn't want him on the loose with vengeance in his heart. But I didn't want to serve time for manslaughter either.

The inspector and his sergeant nodded at me as they strode purposefully past in the direction of the wards. I assumed that they were heading off to see Duncan and so I wouldn't have to mooch around waiting for Carole for very much longer.

It was late afternoon and already dark by the time I arrived home, having left Carole and reclaimed my own car.

The inspector had been right: the police had gone, having taken their measurements and removed their samples, cartridge cases and whatever else they needed. There was still some blue and white tape fluttering in the breeze. Mercifully, there was no horde of journalists camped outside yet.

The morning's weather forecast had promised that the wind would shift from the south-west to the north during the day and, as we'd driven back through the bleak, grey mountains, their bare sides shining and awash with rushing water, and past the lush, waterlogged farmland, littered with pale standing stones, strangely luminous and ghostly in the winter gloom, and the mysterious, truncated stone circles, so it had. And, as the wind changed direction and the cloud broke up, lifted and ran before it, the rain stopped, the sky cleared, and it started to turn bitterly cold. The standing water on the road would be frozen by the early hours of the morning and the saturated fields, churned to a dark, viscous, primeval mud by sheep, cattle and tractors, would glitter coldly with a diamond-hard frost.

Carole had been silent in the car for most of the journey back, occasionally dozing off only to start suddenly, and violently, awake a few seconds later. But, as Dunadd, the ancient home of the Dalriada kings, brooded darkly off to our right, she had started to talk.

At first, what she said seemed inconsequential – a series of statements about the fiscal position of the company and some references to what Duncan had told her about what he remembered from the night before. But there was a pattern to it and slowly the hesitant monologue became more coherent and gave me some of the background that had been missing from my knowledge of recent events.

Her mother and Martin had decided some nine months before that it was important to wrest control of the company from Duncan. She – loyalty to the spouse and all that – had refused to go along with the plan and the board had been irreconcilably split. Martin had been sullen and resentful at first that he wasn't going to get his way but had then knuckled down to some serious intriguing and, via Archie Nugent, had come up with a much needed injection of cash in the shape of two Irish investors. Since those two investors had insisted on being appointed to the board, Martin had his majority.

It was then that Margaret Crawford had become bothered all over again, and Carole had shared her misgivings. Large sums of money were being channelled through the company without the company seeing any apparent benefit, and there were no satisfactory answers to their questions about what was going on. Duncan was airily happy that the company was still afloat, complicit in what Martin had organized and suddenly a close ally of the man who had so recently been on the other side of a bitter boardroom battle. Martin had just been evasive when asked pertinent questions. And it was impossible to pin either of the Irishmen down.

She lapsed into silence again just as I turned into the village and parked the VW next to my old Rover, which was still sitting on the edge of the harbour, opposite the hotel, where I'd left it the night before, apparently unmolested.

I looked out over the dully glinting ribbons of rainbow smeared across the oil-streaked water towards the Cowal peninsula for half a minute and then leaned across and kissed her soft cheek lightly, stroking her hair. I muttered some anodyne nothings about how it was all going to be all right. She nodded but said nothing and didn't really look at me as I opened the door and wearily and gracelessly squirmed out of the car. She was still sitting in the passenger seat, staring into the far distance, or possibly the past, as I drove off.

Once at home, I ignored the flashing red light on my answerphone that told me I had received eleven calls and put Janáček's string quartet 'The Kreutzer Sonata' on the CD player: restless, urgent music to brood by.

I tried to fit what Carole had told me about Crawford's and its internecine battles and what had happened to me, and I couldn't. I assumed that Duncan, out of some malicious desire to do me harm because of his, at the time, misapprehension that I was having an affair with his wife, had been responsible for the clumsy attempt to spike my drinks at Margaret's wake. I imagined that he'd been hoping to have me picked up by the police for drunk driving and kept out of the way while the black briefcase was hidden and then retrieved. It had always been, and still was, the most likely explanation. But had Duncan known what was in the briefcase? I suspected that he had more than an inkling. On the other hand, his apparently genuine surprise at the existence of the cheque made it highly unlikely that he had planted that on me. Which left Martin.

The phone rang just as 'The Kreutzer Sonata' finished and 'Intimate Letters' began, reminding me of all those messages. Sluggishly, I rose from the armchair and walked into my study to stand by the phone, listening to the reporter from the *Record* asking me to call him urgently.

What may have been urgent to him didn't seem so to me and I stared out of the window, searching vainly in the darkness for the hill and the dun. Then I played back the messages.

Dougie had been right: it hadn't taken the newspapers long to find out my name and my telephone number. Every call was from a reporter, five from the same, obviously very determined man from the *Record*. I didn't know whether to be impressed by his doggedness or dismayed that he had so little to do. I erased everything but left the machine on. I had decided to follow Dougie's advice and not to speak to the media at all. Maybe the bitter weather would keep them away from the house.

I realized that, in fact, I had no desire to speak to anyone. Telling all to the police had left me talked out. I felt as if I had nothing meaningful to say. It was oddly satisfying.

I walked to the kitchen, the distant, agitated sound of the Janáček perking me up like a jolt of caffeine, and the phone rang again. This time the caller elected not to leave a message and hung up as soon as the recording kicked in.

Again, I stared miserably out into the darkness, my reflection a sequence of pale, abstract hollows in the kitchen window. I was too weary to think about the Crawfords and their clandestine business dealings. I closed my eyes and almost dozed off standing there but the sudden ringing of the phone clattered me awake.

The soft, threatening sound of Archie Nugent slowly and carefully enunciating every syllable as he told me that Alan Baird was very, very unhappy that his name had been dragged into last night's tragic events, and that Archie himself wasn't best pleased at having been mentioned either, by the way, and that I should call him immediately and this was his mobile number, which he repeated twice, very slowly indeed, echoed throughout the empty house.

I opened a can of food for the cat, spooned the foul-smelling mess into his dish and decided to go to bed early.

Chapter Fourteen

I awoke suddenly in pitch darkness, completely disorientated and panic-stricken. The darkness had weight and substance and pressed against me, forcing me flat against the bed. It took a moment to realize that it was my own bed I was on and another moment to locate the alarm clock and discover that it was six thirty in the morning and I'd slept for over ten hours.

I lay quietly and tried to relax, breathing deeply until my heartbeat slowed and thoughts organized themselves into a coherent pattern. Then I turned on the bedside lamp and levered myself out of bed.

It was still very dark outside when I emerged dressed in sweatshirt and pants, and very chilly. The car windscreen was opaque with a hard frost and my breath whispered away into the night.

I turned on the light in the garage and spent the next forty minutes stretching, bending, skipping and dancing around the heavy bag, lightly tapping it from time to time.

It was twenty past seven and I was steaming, my head and face slick with sweat, when I crossed the cold, dark, quiet driveway and went back into the house to take a shower. The moon was the colour of a very pale and mild cheddar cheese in the greyish light, just about discernible, hanging over Arran like a thick shard of glass.

By eight fifteen, I was shaved, showered, dressed and on my second cup of coffee. I was wearing a heavy white linen shirt from one of the more upmarket mail order catalogues, a pair of black wool slacks from the same source and my best pair of black Church's Oxford shoes, picked up in London on sale a mere three years before.

And I was feeling pretty good. A decent night's sleep, a little exercise, a clean shirt and a lot of caffeine will do that for me. The sickening violence seemed a very long time ago.

The news on Radio 4 was all politicians sounding off on the economy, and on Radio Scotland it was fishing quotas and teaching standards. My misadventures merited no mention.

I turned off the radio, checked the answerphone to make sure that no one other than Nugent had called me overnight, put on my black leather jacket, picked up my wallet and car keys and was ready to go.

I'd never been in Carole's office before. It was small and neat, with a few personal touches carefully placed. A photograph of her mother in a plain aluminium frame and a simple crystal vase with no flowers in it occupied a place to the left of a small pile of work on her scrupulously tidy desk. Her black laptop lay unopened next to a large grey telephone.

I sat in her comfortable black leather guest's chair and waited for her to arrive. On one wall there was a nineteenth-century photograph of the fishing fleet sailing into the harbour, and another, just below it, of a group of women expertly gutting a mountain of herring. There were too many boats to count. They were an impressive sight, jockeying for position, forcing their way into the safety of the harbour, solid and substantial, like the women, who beamed disconcertingly coquettishly at the photographer, offering up fish heads and entrails for him to inspect.

I wasn't sure if Carole was going to turn up or not. In fact, I thought it unlikely as she had a sick and truculent husband in hospital fifty-odd miles away but I hoped she would. I had a few questions for her. But it didn't really matter if she didn't show because I had a few questions for

Martin as well. I hummed '*E lucevan le stelle*' tunelessly and waited for one of them to appear.

At about twenty past nine, Carole's secretary came in and coughed apologetically.

'I'm really sorry, Iain,' she said, 'but it doesn't look as if she is coming in, after all. She's usually in before me and she hasn't rung, which is not like her. Only, I don't like to call her. What with all the trouble and that.'

She was only nineteen or so; a tall and pleasant-looking girl with dark-brown hair. I smiled at her. I knew her from somewhere.

'It's OK, Kirsty,' I said. 'I'll hang on for a few more minutes. Just in case she's overslept. She was very tired the last time I saw her. Will that be all right?'

'I'm sure that'll be fine. Can I get you anything? Some coffee? Or tea?'

I smiled again and shook my head. 'No thanks, I've already had my quota of caffeine for the day.'

She nodded and looked thoughtful.

'Are you writing anything at the moment?' she asked suddenly.

That was it. She had been one of the only five students who had turned up at the ill-fated creative writing course I'd been asked to teach a year or so before. Argyll had proved not to be as full of potential poets as the organizers had hoped and the project had been abandoned as a financial disaster after only two weeks.

'Sort of,' I said. 'I do the occasional script for TV. I haven't been writing any verse lately, though.'

She still stood there, in the doorway, looking a little coy and nervous.

'I've been writing a bit,' she said and blushed. 'But I don't know if it's any good or not . . .' She looked away. She was obviously hoping that I would make some kind of gesture and I knew that I couldn't delay it too long. I've always been something of a sucker as far as earnest young writers are concerned – I remember being one myself – and I duly responded.

300

'Why don't you let me look at what you've been doing?'
I said. 'I'd be happy to give you my opinion.'

'Would you really?'

'Sure,' I said. 'But I'll be honest. And don't get your
hopes up. I'm not a publisher or an editor or anything
important or useful. Though I do still have a few contacts.'

'Well, it's probably no good anyway,' she said.

'If you want me to have a look, just ask. Faint heart
never won book contract.'

'Thanks,' she said, 'I will.'

'By the way,' I said, 'I don't suppose Martin's in, is he?'

'I think so,' she said.

'Maybe I'll pop my head around his door and say hello,'
I said.

'I'll check that he's free,' she said and immediately left
the office to return to her desk outside.

I heard her on the phone, asking Martin's secretary
about his availability in that strange, conspiratorial voice
secretaries sometimes adopt when they are self-conscious
about being overheard.

After she put the phone down, she came back in.

'Mr Crawford's on the phone at the moment,' she
said unnecessarily loudly, 'but he should be free in five
minutes.'

I raised my eyebrows a little and frowned quizzically at
her formality and she took a step closer, leaned towards
me and started to whisper.

'He's been like a bear with a sore bum all week,' she said,
'flying off the handle at the least little thing. Even more than
usual. I expect it's everything that's happened. His mother
and that. And now Mr Ferguson in hospital . . .'

She broke off and looked embarrassed as if she'd just
remembered my involvement.

'I expect that's it,' I said. 'Just give me a yell when
he's free.'

'I will,' she said and left.

I contemplated the photograph of the jolly fishwives
again. They were all plump, well-made lassies, their faces

301

shining with dirt and mischief, fish scales glittering like diamanté on their hands and arms. No doubt the photographer had been forced to put up with coarse and good-natured enquiries about his propensities and virility. If he had been English or from Edinburgh – more or less the same thing to these women – their accents would have been so broad that he probably wouldn't have understood them. They'd maybe even been speaking in the Gaelic. But he would have been fully aware that he was the butt of some off-colour and very personal jokes.

It was a good picture, though, vibrant and vital, slick with silver fish, dark with cloud and drudgery. I stood up and peered at it more closely.

'You can almost hear "The Shoals of Herring", can't you?'

I turned and there was Martin, standing in the doorway, frowning at me, limp blond hair drooping over his forehead.

'I heard you were in and thought I'd better come and make sure you weren't prising open the filing cabinets or hacking into the computer system,' he said.

'Good of you to spare the time,' I said. 'I imagine that you must have a pile of work, with Duncan incapacitated and Carole looking out for him.'

He made a curious, deprecating gesture with his hands, like he was shaping a clay pot on a wheel.

'To tell you the truth,' he said, 'the place is easier to run without the pair of them bickering away. Duncan never does much except shout at Carole after his first drink of the day, which usually coincides with his first coffee break, and Carole only deals with advertising, which we have no budget for just at the moment. God knows what she spends her time doing.' He looked around the neat and tidy office, and shook his head dismissively. 'Coffee?' he said. 'I'd like to have a chat. I was just talking to a mutual friend who asked after you.'

'Who was that?' I said as he escorted me to his office, further along the corridor.

'Archie,' he said. 'Archie Nugent.'

Compared to Carole's, Martin's office was a tip, with piles of papers and ring binders everywhere. His working practices and filing system bore a strong resemblance to my own. He picked a large heap of invoices off a chair, deposited them on the floor next to another hummock of invoices and indicated that I should sit down. He manoeuvred his way behind his desk, sat down himself and then rang the secretary we had just passed outside to ask for coffee. I wondered why he hadn't mentioned it to her then. It flickered across my mind to ask him but it was probably some boss/secretary ritual that I was incapable of understanding.

'Yes,' he said, looking at me very intently. 'Archie was wondering if I'd seen you or heard where you were.' He paused. 'He's very anxious to talk to you, apparently.'

'Really?' I said.

He leaned forward.

'Yes,' he said, 'really.'

'I wonder what that can be about,' I said.

Martin started scratching at the back of his hand.

'I really can't imagine,' he said knowingly. 'But, in my experience, it's always worth talking to Archie when he wants to talk to you.'

I smiled.

'I'll give him a call sometime,' I said. ' I don't suppose it's all that urgent.'

'That wasn't the impression he gave me,' Martin said.

'Well, I'll call him this morning,' I said.

'I would,' he said, 'if you want the Arts Council grants to keep flooding in.'

He leaned back in his chair and put his feet up on the corner of his desk, staring at the ceiling, still worrying at his hand. I assumed that he had lapsed into silence because he wanted me to contemplate all that Arts Council money I would never now have. As I'd never received any in the past, I wasn't particularly anxious at the thought.

His secretary knocked and bustled in with a pot of coffee, a jug of milk, two cups, a bowl of sugar and a small

303

plate of biscuits on a tray. She looked around for somewhere to put it. Martin continued to stare up at the ceiling, apparently oblivious to her dilemma.

I took the tray from her and put it on the floor, thanking her. She nodded an acknowledgement and rolled her eyes up to heaven. I didn't know her but she seemed to take it for granted that I shared her exasperation with her boss.

She left, and Martin and I sat in silence for a few minutes. He was still considering the ceiling when I started to pour myself some coffee.

'Black for me,' he said suddenly, taking his feet from the desk and leaning forward purposefully. 'A word of advice, Iain. I really would take Archie more seriously than you appear to be doing. I'd sort something out with him if I were you. He and Baird are far from overjoyed that you shopped them.' He paused and leant back in his chair. 'Between you and me, I think Archie rather enjoys the thought of Baird being interviewed by the boys in blue. Especially if he can extricate him from whatever brown and sticky stuff is threatening to engulf him. But what bothers Archie is that he doesn't see how he can do that if the same tide of effluent is licking at his own Gucci loafers.' He paused again as he took the cup of coffee from me. 'The only thing that really concerns Archie is influence. For him, everything else flows from that.'

I looked at Carole's little brother and realized for the first time that he'd grown up. He wasn't a troubled fourteen-year-old any longer. He was a troubled twenty-six-year-old who thought he knew more about the ways of the world than he did. The glib and sophisticated cynicism, the affected worldliness, were just a little undercut by the constant movement of his eyes as they shifted focus, and the self-inflicted damage on the back of his right hand. Of course, none of that meant that his judgements about Nugent were necessarily wrong. For all I knew, they were spot on. I just had the feeling that they were someone else's.

I studied him thoughtfully for a few seconds as he

sipped at his coffee, his eyes studiously avoiding mine. I decided to get to the point.

'Martin, do you really know nothing about that cheque? I ask because your presence at the little meeting with Baird makes little sense to me if that's the case.'

'Well, it is,' he said. 'I know nothing about it. Honestly. I was there because Archie wanted me there. He seemed to think that you would be happier hearing it from me. I have no reason to pay Baird thirty grand. He has nothing I want. It doesn't make any difference to the company what he decides about oil exploration. Whatever you or your journalist friend think.' He stood up very suddenly. 'Now, if you'll excuse me, I've got a lot to do.'

I stood up too. I couldn't think what else to do. It had seemed so simple at seven that morning: ask Carole what was really going on; if she didn't know, and I didn't think she did, confront Martin and find out. It hadn't occurred to me that he wouldn't tell. I didn't have a plan B.

'Martin,' I said, 'the police and the press are going to find out pretty soon what's going on. Why not just tell me?'

There was a thin smile on his face and he shook his head slowly from side to side. I suddenly realized what I should have understood some time before – he really didn't like me very much.

'There's nothing to find out,' he said.

I turned to go but he spoke again before I was out of the door.

'Call Archie,' he said, 'soonest.'

I wandered along the corridor towards Carole's office and the stairs that led down to the street, dawdling behind the post boy until he stopped and I was able to slip carefully around him, wondering at my naivety in hoping to gain anything from talking to Martin.

Kirsty was sitting at her desk and she smiled shyly as I approached.

'Iain,' she said, 'Carole's just called. She's planning to go to the hospital and so probably won't be in today.' She paused and I nodded. 'By the way,' she continued, 'if you were serious about looking at what I've written, I've got it here . . . and you could take it with you . . .'

She was holding a reassuringly slim sheaf of papers close to her breasts and staring at me with a wide-eyed look of optimism.

'Sure,' I said, holding out my hand.

She stood up and nervously passed the manuscript across to me. I flicked through it very quickly and was relieved to see that it seemed to consist of three short stories and no poetry.

'Wait a minute,' I said. 'You do have a copy of this, don't you?'

'It's all on my computer at home,' she said.

'Of course,' I said. 'Do you have an envelope or a file or something I can put it in?'

'Sure,' she said and started to rummage in her desk drawers. She looked up after a few minutes of frantic searching. 'I don't seem to have anything big enough. Can you hang on while I go to the stationery cupboard?'

I smiled and handed over the manuscript just as the post boy – who was, of course, no more a boy than pot boys in pubs are – limped up to the desk and plonked a pile of mail on Kirsty's desk. She thanked him and then turned to me as he lumbered off, pushing his trolley.

'I'll only be a couple of minutes; stationery's on the next floor,' she said and left me at her desk.

I glanced down at the jumble of brochures, magazines and letters.

The envelope on the top of the heap immediately caught my eye. It was of good quality, heavy and a buttery yellow. It was addressed, of course, to Carole in a firm, confident and legible hand, clearly marked 'personal and confidential'. But none of that was what attracted my attention: it was the logo and address of the sender engraved in the top left-hand corner. It had been struck through with a single strong line, but it was easily legible. It was from Nugent's company.

I glanced quickly up and down the corridor. The post

boy and his little red trolley were at the far end, just about to turn the corner, and no one else was around.

I'm not in the habit of interfering with Her Majesty's mail – in fact this was the first time I'd even thought about it – but some sudden compulsion had me reaching out, picking up the envelope and slipping it guiltily into my jacket pocket. I had to know what Nugent had written to Carole.

Kirsty reappeared almost immediately and handed me a large brown envelope.

'Thanks,' I said, grinning nervously. I was surprised at just how tense I was. Beads of sweat had suddenly materialized on my forehead. It was out of all proportion to any risk I was running.

'Thank *you*,' she said.

'I don't know when I'll be able to get back to you,' I said. 'A week, maybe two.'

'That's OK,' she said. 'Whenever. I've put my mobile number in there.'

'Great,' I said, 'I'll call when I've read them.'

'See you,' she said.

'Yeah,' I said, 'see you.'

I started off towards the stairs, expecting her to notice that she was missing a letter and come storming after me, demanding its return. I forced myself not to hurry away.

But Kirsty didn't pursue me and I made it down the stairs and into Crawford's little car park without anyone else raising the hue and cry either.

I sat in my car for a moment or two, fiddling with the radio, exaggerating my nonchalance and unconcern, and then I assumed that Kirsty hadn't, after all, as I'd hoped, even glanced at the mail when it had been handed to her.

I was trembling slightly as I opened the envelope.

It wasn't much of a letter. There was no address on the single sheet of paper, just Wednesday's date. The boldness and clarity of the writing was matched by a certain bluntness of expression. It read simply:

307

C.,
Earlier is better for me. Four, not four thirty.
A.

Thoughtfully, I stuffed the letter back into the envelope and returned it to my pocket. Then I put the Rover into first and slowly, and with a hissing of tyres, pulled out of the car park and on to the muddy lane that led down to the main road.

My agent once said, a propos of just what particular feud I had embarked upon I can't recall (which must mean that, although it impressed her, it was a trivial affair, a poor and unconsidered irritation), that I held a grudge better than anyone she'd ever met. I told her that that was only because she hadn't met my mate Ron, who was the undisputed heavyweight champ of grudge bearers, but that I *was* still waiting for that bastard Walsingham to get his for what he did to Christopher Marlowe. She didn't know what I was talking about and just smiled sweetly and sipped her Chardonnay.

She had a point though. I can, as Dougie might say, smile and smile and be a vindictive sod. And I intended putting that particular trait to work for me.

In spite of what he'd said about his availability, Archie Nugent's mobile phone did not respond to my calls and the office number simply rang and rang. I was finally forced to conclude, after breaking the world record for the number of frustrating and unanswered phone calls made in twenty-five minutes from one draughty phone box, where brutal-looking seagulls congregated to strut their stuff and wind skirled around the ankles, that the recorded message repeatedly informing me that the Vodaphone I was calling may be switched off probably contained an essential truth. I also had to concede that it was far too early in the day to expect chic, cosmopolitan PR staff to be at their desks.

I decided to drive to Edinburgh anyway and call Nugent again en route or when I finally arrived. The fact that I was that anxious to see him would probably convey to him that I was taking seriously his request of the night before to make contact. Which might wrongfoot him a bit, because I wasn't.

I left the bright, cold morning behind me after passing through the mountains at the Rest and Be Thankful and hit heavy cloud. By the time I was sweeping across the Erskine Bridge towards the M8, Benjamin Britten's sea interludes from *Peter Grimes* gently subverting tonality on Radio 3, the Clyde beneath me the colour, and apparently the obduracy, of gunmetal, the rain was a nagging, persistent presence. Spray issued from the heavy log lorries like ectoplasm from the orifices of a particularly fecund spiritualist, enveloping everything, and giving the great lumbering vehicles a vaguely ethereal look.

The steady flick of the windscreen wipers and the constant need to concentrate was giving me a headache. I decided to park at the airport again.

It was ten to twelve when I stepped off the bus on to the damp, crowded pavement of Princes Street. The wind had picked up and little gusts threw squalls of rain at me as I threaded my way between the heavy-laden shoppers towards Waverley Station.

I was uncomfortably damp and chilled by the time I settled myself at a bank of telephones, but at least my headache had been blown away by the cold wind.

Archie Nugent was still, it seemed, incommunicado. His mobile phone was switched off and his office, in the person of a somewhat haughty PA, was doggedly unhelpful. It was all sunshine and gentle showers to the tender shoot I was nurturing into a giant, grudge-bearing redwood. After fifteen fruitless minutes I decided to abandon temporarily my efforts to reach him directly and rang Helen Baxter.

She sounded genuinely pleased to hear from me and was only too happy to meet up for lunch. She suggested a trendy brasserie conveniently, for me, situated just outside the station and I fortified myself with an espresso from one of the kiosks in the station before going.

The coffee was hot and strong, and I sipped at it while watching the world hurry by, rehearsing what I was going to say to Archie Nugent when I finally caught up with him.

Suddenly, I saw a blond head that I thought I recognized walking towards the taxi rank. She was a long way away and it was dull and dark in the station but I was reasonably sure. I started towards the taxi rank myself but got caught up in the rush of passengers leaving a newly arrived train. By the time I reached the cabs, Carole was nowhere in sight.

The brasserie was all glass walls, luxuriant potted plants, bamboo furniture and bright young things, but a genuinely friendly and efficient waiter found me a quiet corner table and a huge glass of Pinot Noir in record time.

Rain spattered against the glass wall next to me and ran in little irregular rivulets down to the pavement. The wind drove the fluttering pages from a discarded newspaper past. The big chair was comfortable and the restaurant was warm. I sipped my wine – which was delicious – and I settled back to wait for Helen.

I wondered if I really had seen Carole and, if so, what she was doing in Edinburgh. There could have been, and probably was, an innocent explanation but the thought that the message from Nugent and her appearance in the city were not coincidental nagged at me. The note had, after all, only been confirming the appointment.

I made further inroads on the glass of wine and decided to act as if I was mistaken. It couldn't have been Carole. Carole was at the hospital, visiting Duncan. Carole was not in Edinburgh. And if she was, so what? She was Christmas shopping.

I had a volume of Tom a-Paulin's (poets were calling

him that long before anyone at *Private Eye* had spotted him
rubbishing, by implication, Terry Pratchett on *Late Night
Review*) poetry in my pocket and I took it out. I came across
a-Paulin once but I doubt made any impression. It was at
a poetry reading down on the south coast of England.
Frankly, he didn't make much of an impression on me
either. In fact, all I can recall with any clarity from that day
is lunch. Insalata caprese followed by sea bass, washed
down with far too much Pinot Grigio, in a light airy Italian
restaurant looking out over the restless grey sea, which
was *un peu agité*. He's certainly no Yeats and he doesn't, for
me, pass the Ian Hamilton memorability test, but a-Paulin
is at least an interesting poet. I lost myself in his verse for
a while.

Then Helen arrived. And she wasn't alone.

The woman she was with had a strong, intelligent face
with a short, snub nose, bright eyes and a smile tugging
at her lips. She was younger than Helen, but not that
much, which made her six, maybe seven, years older than
me. There were a few spikes of iron grey in the wild thicket
of dark hair and a couple of her teeth were slightly
crooked, which, somehow, made her just right to play
Lady Macbeth.

When I stood up, I realized that she was quite small,
which was not the impression she gave. Helen introduced
her as Mary Elgin and the name rang a vague bell. She had
long, strong fingers and her hand was warm when she
took mine in greeting.

We sat and, while our waiter gathered up an armful of
menus and prepared to amble over, Helen told me that
she'd just bumped into Mary in the street outside and had
persuaded her to join us. She said that she knew Mary
from way back as Mary had written the music for that
television show she'd been in. 'You remember,' she said,
'the one you don't remember.'

And I did remember – at least in the sense that she
meant it – and I remembered where I'd heard the name
Mary Elgin.

'Ah,' I said, 'I didn't realize that you were *that* Mary Elgin.'

She smiled.

'Which one did you think I was?' she said.

'Sorry,' I said, 'that came out slightly wrong. I meant that I hadn't expected to meet a famous composer today.'

She coloured a little.

'I don't know about being famous,' she said.

'Of course you're famous, darling. Even I've heard of you,' Helen said. 'Now, would you mind powdering your nose for a minute? I have to have a private word with Iain. Don't worry, I'll order you a big gin and tonic.'

Mary smiled again, shrugged, looked up, spotted the sign for the rest rooms and headed off towards them.

Helen leaned forward conspiratorially.

'Two things,' she said and paused. 'Well, three things, really. One, Alan is after blood and I suspect he rather wants yours. But I wouldn't worry. There doesn't seem to be too much he can do at the moment. But you might just ring him up and apologize a little bit. He needs his ego stroked. Reassure him a little. Tell him exactly what you told the police. It'll make him feel a lot better, just knowing exactly what they know. He's a great believer in the knowledge-is-power theory of things. He's a dear, sweet thing really but he does rather try to upstage everyone. At the moment, it's the end of his political career. Not that I'd mind all that much if it was, not really, darling. And I've heard it all before, of course – after a speech that didn't go down as well with the party faithful as he thought it should, or when a senior minister hasn't invited him to a party. He'll think of something and call in a favour or two, I expect.' She paused and studied me carefully before continuing. I assumed that she was making sure I'd got the point. 'Talking of favours brings me to point two, which is far more important than Alan's tenuous grasp on the slippery pole.

'Mary wants to write an opera and is looking for someone to write the words. Well, I, of course, thought of you.

312

And three, Mary also wants a new English translation for a production of one of Mozart's operas she's putting on somewhere: *Cosi fan tutti*, in Toronto, I think. Well, I remembered you saying something about speaking a little Italian, so I thought of you again. You do speak Italian, don't you?'

My barely perceptible and wary nod masked the fact that I hadn't opened an Italian grammar in anger (and I do mean anger) in thirteen years and that it was more than two years since I'd even visited the place, and that trip had been to Sicily and so didn't really count. Needless to say, none of that could possibly have registered on Helen and she hurried on.

'She's got funding for both projects. Try to make a good impression, there's a good boy. And ring Alan. And that awful Archie Nugent as well. I rather think that when he's after blood, someone ends up bleeding.'

'OK,' I said. 'I'm on my best behaviour now and I'll call both Baird and Nugent this afternoon. But I don't imagine that either of them will be all that reassured. If the minister has been taking backhanders, he's in deep trouble.'

'I wouldn't worry about that,' she said, smiling indulgently. 'He's such a drama queen. And to think how dismissive he is of my theatrical friends.'

I didn't have time to ask any questions about Mary Elgin and her two undertakings as she and the waiter both arrived at the table at the same moment.

'Where's my G and T?' Mary said.

'On its way?' the waiter said, arching an eyebrow. I had the feeling that Helen had been in this restaurant before.

'And mine?' Helen said, raising an eyebrow archly in return.

'I'm sorry,' the waiter said, 'my psychic powers seem to have temporarily deserted me. I'll bring it now.'

'And you can bring me another glass of this,' I said, holding up my glass.

'Aye,' he said, over his shoulder, 'I can.'

I beamed a big, ingenuous smile at him, the sort that

implies that such willingness deserves considerable lar-
gesse when calculating the gratuity. Then I extended the
same soppy smile to include the two women opposite and
decided to have venison sausages and mash for lunch.
I banished for a while the insidious thought that Alan
Baird and favours had something to do with Mary Elgin's
unexpected appearance at lunch.

Chapter Fifteen

My alcohol intake over lunch, if not modest by medical or hypocritical-politician standards, was lighter than it might have been. I kept it to three, admittedly rather large, glasses of wine, thinking of a possible forthcoming confrontation with Archie Nugent. And, anyway, I had to keep a reasonably clear head because Mary Elgin, encouraged by Helen, kept up a low-key, but nonetheless serious, interrogation about what I was working on and why I wasn't producing much at the moment. It was difficult, under her intelligent questioning, to be evasive for very long and eventually I found myself admitting to serious doubts about my abilities and to a complete lack of inspiration. She suggested that the best way forward was to start working again, maybe in collaboration with someone.

Helen was right about one thing at least. Mary Elgin was definitely looking to write a major opera and she was actively seeking a suitable subject. 'Something classical, something Scottish,' she said at one point, wistfully and enigmatically. *Ossian* had been firmly rejected, though I wasn't quite sure why. I privately determined to send her a copy of Henryson's *Testament of Cresseid* and see what she made of that.

Apart from that, we swapped deliciously implausible stories about television producers and programme controllers we had known and loved. Helen's were better than mine (which were scant and not very funny), and Mary's were better than Helen's.

At five to three I made my excuses and left Mary and

Helen at the table, still drinking coffee and gossiping about some elderly Lothario and his *amours*. I paid the bill as discreetly as I could, adding a generous, though I hoped not flamboyant, tip, and made my way out into the wind and rain of a depressingly bleak late afternoon. My accountant would be proud of me: I had even thought to write this down as a business expense. It might actually turn out to be a legitimate one.

I took up residence by the same bank of phones in Waverley Station that I had occupied before lunch, wondering for the first time if I might possibly need a mobile phone. I rang Dougie and got through at the first attempt.

'Hello, big man,' I said.

'Ah, the damned elusive Mr Lewis,' he said. 'They seek him here, they seek him there . . . Where are you?'

'Edinburgh,' I said.

'Why?' he said.

'What do you mean?' I said.

'Why?' he said again. *'Pourquoi? Warum? Perché?* What's not to understand? Why are you in Edinburgh?'

'Oh,' I said. 'Important business lunch appointment. With Helen Baxter. And Mary Elgin. The composer.'

'Good,' he said. 'Only it would be a terrible idea to attempt to make contact with Archie Nugent or Alan Baird. Inspector MacPlod might well take that amiss. Poor Archie is a much interviewed man. And Mr Baird is keeping a very low profile. Rumours of his imminent resignation abound.'

'You can hardly keep the glee out of your voice,' I said.

'I'm not trying to,' he said. 'I will confess to taking more than a modicum of pleasure in their discomfiture. They haven't been very nice to me over the last couple of days. And I am going aff ma heid sat at this desk, having to decide how many tampon dispensers there should be in the ladies' rest room. There's news out there, waiting for me to uncover it. Contrary to common belief, news is a shy, retiring beast; it has to be sniffed out, stalked, seduced and coaxed out of hiding. Och, I'm bored, Iain. Tell me you're going to do something stupid and classically Lewis, like stomp Nugent's heid, or something.'

'I'm going to stomp Nugent's heid,' I said.

'Seriously?'

'Seriously.'

'You shouldn't, you know.'

'I know.'

'But you're going to anyway?'

'That's right.'

'Can I come and watch?'

'Can you tell me where he is?' I said. 'I can't find him.'

'Give me half an hour,' he said and hung up.

I fumbled around and finally found the mobile number that Carole had given me and rang it. I was told to leave a message but didn't.

Then I tried the number for Alan Baird that Helen had given me and got BT callminder. This time I did leave a message, apologizing to him at one remove. This seemed to satisfy my promise to Helen without compromising me too much.

I tried Nugent's mobile again, with no luck. And then tried his office number. There was a suspiciously long pause before some PA told me he couldn't be contacted and would I like to leave a message. I imagined her staring at her immaculately manicured and painted nails for the ninety or so seconds that would convince me she was trying to contact him. I told her to tell him I'd called.

Well, if Dougie was able to track him down and confirmed that he was in his office, it wouldn't take me ten minutes to get there. The envelope that I had taken – stolen, I reminded myself – from Carole's in-tray told me he had an address just off Hanover Street.

Only seven of the thirty minutes that Dougie had asked for had elapsed and, since no trip to the big city would be complete without running up a major credit card bill in a bookshop, I loped up the steps to Princes Street in pursuit of a Waterstone's.

The rain was falling steadily, propelled by a vicious north-easterly wind, and I turned up the collar of my jacket against the gusts, wishing I'd thought to wear something more suited to late November in the coldest city in Britain.

Fortunately, the shop was no more than a hop, skip and a jump away and I only suffered because the traffic lights were against me and at least one bus and a taxi went through after they had changed in my favour. I shook myself like a dog and shed water in the foyer, smiling apologetically at a stony-faced security guard who stared at me like he knew I had four kilos of semtex strapped to my chest. I expected him to tell me to go and drip/detonate somewhere else. He sniffed as I walked past, rolled his shoulders and turned down his mouth.

'It's no very nice,' he said.

'No,' I said.

'Try the café,' he said. 'It's warm and dry in there. Good Black Forest gateau.'

'Thanks for the tip,' I said and slipped into the shop and stood under the powerful heaters in what felt like suffocating heat for about forty-five seconds until I couldn't stand it any longer. By that time I was steaming nicely, like an old compost heap, and another coffee was an appealing prospect. But the sight of all those books was too much for me.

In less than an hour I had piled up quite a haul: a Michael Dibdin Aurelio Zen mystery (my subconscious suggesting that I ease myself back into things Italian without the pain of having to read any), an anthology of contemporary American poetry (a pitiful attempt to pretend that I was still interested and engaged), Peter Ackroyd's biography of London (brilliant quotes and I'd been promising myself that I'd read it for at least a year), Peter Robb's *Midnight in Sicily* (my subconscious urging me on again), James Lee Burke's *Purple Cane Road* (someone – it might have been Dougie – had told me that we finally find out what happened to Robicheaux's mother,

318

and it had a great cover), an English National Opera guide to *Cosi fan tutte* (no explanation necessary), and the latest Discworld novel by Terry Pratchett (no explanation possible, according to a-Paulin). I was reasonably content.

The friendly young guy at the cash desk said there wasn't a payphone in the shop but he offered to let me use his mobile. 'Got to use up those free minutes,' he said, declining my offer to pay for the call. I found myself positively warming to Edinburgh and its good people: first, an amusing and helpful waiter, then a talking security guard, now this. Of course, none of them were actual Edinburghers . . .

Dougie hadn't managed to locate Nugent, which he found strange, and he told me to call back in an hour.

So, I found myself in the café after all, a cup of coffee (my seventh of the day, I noted with some dismay) in front of me, the Pratchett open next to it. They were all out of Black Forest gateau, which was just as well for the sake of my waistline.

The coffee was good, although my stomach was definitely rebelling and turning a little acid, and the book was entertaining in a charming Wodehouse kind of way. (I found myself wondering what a-Paulin and the other pundits on *Late Night Review* would manage to splutter out if anyone dared to suggest that Jeeves and Wooster lived in a world every bit as fantastical as Granny Weatherwax's.) In the same way that I pretend to myself that I'm still in touch with trends in recent poetry, I do, in my very limited fashion, try to keep abreast of some aspects of popular culture. I may not be able to hold my own with TV producers when they wax what passes for lyrical in media circles about reality TV programmes, but I can at least speak with a little knowledge about the Discworld.

In fact, I was so absorbed in it that I barely registered that someone had sat at my table. It wasn't until half a bar of the toreador aria from *Carmen* warbled out tremulously from a few feet away that I looked up.

It seemed that Archie Nugent's mobile phone was switched on again.

I finished my coffee and watched as he murmured into the phone in a softly modulated voice that meant I only picked up one word in five. He was obviously well practised. Nugent clearly didn't use his phone to ring home and boom out that he was at the airport, or to call the office and announce that he was in the lift.

He looked worried and tense – there were pronounced lines around his eyes that I hadn't noticed before and his usually immaculate hair was slightly dishevelled – and nowhere near as dangerous as some people had told me he was, and as I had felt him to be. But I could still feel the anger in me.

He ended the call and acknowledged me with a nod.

'Dougie told me you would be here,' he said. He sounded tired, and he looked it. 'You wanted a word.'

'I thought you did,' I said.

He nodded again, in an oddly dispirited way. He was badly out of sorts and it didn't suit him at all. I stared at that thin scar, but he didn't appear to notice.

'Must be strange for you, finding yourself in here,' I said. 'You don't strike me as the bookish type.'

He shrugged.

'Oh, I read a bit,' he said. 'But I can do some early Christmas shopping. Also the coffee's good and I can sit and think untroubled thoughts. I'm not usually bothered by people here.' He paused. 'Lobbyists, advisers and other assorted hangers-on tend to send their researchers and PAs to bookshops, and most of the politicians I know don't read much, whatever they say. They prefer succinct briefings. Preferably with a bland but sound opinion attached.' He paused again before saying, 'They do buy political autobiographies, of course.'

'Well, I suppose someone has to,' I said.

'But they don't read them. Just look in the index to see if they're mentioned.'

'Like journalists,' I said and reached into my pocket,

pulled out the envelope and billet-doux and slid it across the table towards him.

'Yeah, journalists do that too,' he said, picking up the envelope and studying it for a moment. He turned it over a few times in his hands before taking the note out and reading it. He looked unconcerned. He peered at the address on the envelope and raised his eyebrows.

'A purloined letter,' he said.

I nodded.

'Didn't Conan Doyle write a story with that title?'

'No,' I said.

'No? I thought he did.'

'Edgar Allan Poe. A different detective,' I said.

'Oh,' he said. 'You're sure?'

'Yes,' I said.

I could almost see the thought process flicker across his face as he struggled to dredge up the plot.

'Something about a lady's honour, wasn't it?' he said.

'That's right. And not just any old lady,' I said. 'The queen of France, no less.'

'Indeed,' he said. 'So, whose honour does this have anything to do with?'

'It's not so much about honour,' I said. 'More about self-respect. Mine. So, what have you got to talk to Carole about?'

He didn't say anything for a few seconds, just looked a little puzzled, then his face relaxed into a grin, his shoulders heaved slightly and his body shook in a soundless and largely humourless laugh.

'Ah,' he said, 'you think I've been making assignations with your sweetie.'

'It's on your notepaper and it's signed with an A,' I said.

'Yes,' he said, nodding, 'a reasonable assumption would be that I wrote it. But I didn't.' And he slipped the note back inside the envelope and slid it back across the table.

'You didn't?' I said.

'No,' he said, 'I didn't.' He sighed. 'A number of other people have access to my stationery and some of them, well, one or two, have the same initial.' He paused and looked thoughtful.

'For instance?' I said.

There was a long, long pause and I could read nothing on his impassive face. Just when I thought he wasn't going to answer me, he shrugged, as though dismissing a considerable burden.

'Alan Baird, for instance,' he said quietly.

'Baird?' I said. I felt like I'd been remarkably obtuse.

He nodded and glanced at his watch. 'He's probably in the bar at the George even as we speak. If you want a word with him about this.'

'Jesus,' I said. 'Alan Baird! That's his writing?'

Nugent nodded again.

'Before you go,' he said, 'perhaps we could discuss what exactly you told the polis about my role in the affairs of Crawford's.'

It was my turn to pause and nod.

'Well?' he prompted me.

'Well, nothing,' I said. 'What could I tell them? I know nothing about your role. All I know is that you've been around. And that's the sum total of what I told them.'

'Is it now?' he said. 'That's very interesting, because that's not what they've been implying. They've been talking about – if my understanding is not deficient – bribery and corruption. Not in so many words, of course, which would be ill advised if they've no proof. But that's what I took them to be looking into.' He pursed his lips. 'So, the sum total of what you told the polis is that you've seen me twice in this connection.'

'And there's the small matter of you recovering the briefcase for me,' I said.

'Ah,' he said. 'So, they know about the case. Funny, they haven't mentioned it.'

'Of course they know about the case,' I said. 'Without it, I wouldn't be involved in any of this.'

'No,' he said sadly, 'you wouldn't, would you?' There was something a little bleak about the look he turned on me. His eyes flicked down to his watch again. 'The soon-to-be ex-minister – if my intelligence network is up to its usual high standard – will probably be in the George for another hour . . .'

He looked very weary, with red-rimmed eyes under-scored by dark pouches and sagging shoulders, a little punch drunk, as if he'd just gone a round or two with Mike Tyson. I thought maybe Alan Baird wasn't the only one whose career had taken a setback. I almost felt sorry for him. Almost. But then I realized that he was resilient and would bounce back. And Baird would take up all those directorships he'd no doubt be offered, and become a newspaper columnist, or a radio pundit. There's no such thing as enduring disgrace any more, just a different kind of publicity that offers a different kind of opportunity.

Nugent raised his eyebrows at me as if to ask what I was still doing there, and I felt as if I'd been dismissed from his presence and, very self-consciously, stood up and gathered my things together, my books and the letter, as though I was leaving a private meeting in his office.

'Thanks,' I said.

He inclined his head graciously in a 'you're welcome' gesture.

I was about to leave when he spoke again.

'A word of advice, Iain, if I may.'

I stopped, turned and looked down at him.

He didn't look up and spoke to the table. 'Go back to Argyll and your rhyming and TV writing. Keep your head down and, most important of all, trust no one. Or, at least, trust no one to behave like an intelligent adult.'

I grinned at the top of his head. I suddenly felt full of energy.

'I wouldn't know what an intelligent adult behaves like,' I said.

'No,' he muttered. 'I don't suppose you would.' He paused and looked at me thoughtfully, then he leaned forward, obviously having made a decision. 'Sit down.

I'm going to tell you a story that was told to me by Billy and Oscar.'

The odd, orange light from the streetlamp outside seeped through the thin curtain and smeared the bare room with shadows as he crouched over the single bar of the electric fire, hoarding the heat. He stood up carefully, walked slowly to the window, pulled the filthy, mildewed curtain aside and peered out. A black cat padded along the road, weaving between the parked cars, its raised tail swaying gently.

There was nothing else to be seen and he turned back into the room, patted the reassuring half bottle of Scotch in his back pocket and then bent down to turn off the heater. Slowly, he walked into the small hall where he took his old, greasy waxed jacket down from the peg and wrestled himself into it, zipping it up carefully, pressing each of the studs together very precisely. Then he stepped out into the chilly night.

At least it was dry, and the big winds from a day or two back had died away. But it was far from warm and he shivered. Again, he reached around and touched the bottle in his back pocket, as if it contained some holy relic which could impart warmth, hope and comfort.

He walked silently past his neighbours' houses to the main road and trudged steadily away from the town and into the darkness, feeling every pebble through the thin, worn soles of his cheap shoes.

It was four ten and pitch black and it was so quiet that he ambled along the middle of the road, taking out the bottle and sipping from it at carefully considered landmarks: the silent and empty caravan site; the floodlit lorry park; the deserted ferry terminus; the red house that marked the turn-off from the trunk road; the slim, grey standing stone, barely visible in the bleak, black field; the dark, brooding hill that shouldered the dun, which was silhouetted against the night sky; and, finally, the Old

Mariner's Grave. Not a single vehicle passed him on his three-hour journey.

His feet, slipping about in the ill-fitting shoes, were blistered and bruised, but he was used to that. His throat was dry and he could do something about that. He stood at the back of the beach and took a long, satisfying pull on the bottle, which was now less than half full. The cheap whisky trickled down his throat and burnt its way into his gut.

He narrowed his eyes and stared at the boat anchored about thirty yards out. It wasn't one of the sleek yachts that sailed around in the summer and overnighted in any cove that took the captain's fancy. This was a blunt-ended, working boat. He could smell the diesel. He sniffed the air again. It wasn't a fishing trawler. It lacked that unmistakable, pungent aroma.

It was not much more than a dark shape at that time, but the sky was growing grey and soon he'd be able to see it properly, find out its name, maybe see where it was registered, what flag it was flying.

When he heard the distant rumble of an approaching truck, the whisky was three-quarters gone and a weak sun had started to rise behind him. Light from it touched the silent sea, raking it with flashes of amber and streaking the clouds above with pallid pink. He squinted hard at the boat, trying to read the name, but the lettering was flaking and indecipherable in the half-light.

As he watched, a hard-looking man, buttoned up against the cold, grey November morning in a dark-blue reefer coat, clattered on to the deck of the rust-stained boat, and, for some reason he could not articulate, Danny McGovern thought it expedient to slip quickly into the broken-down caravan at the rear of the beach before he was seen.

He'd slept in it two or three times in the past on cool summer nights and he'd listened to the murmur of the sea and the gentle drumming of the soft rain in the early morning when he woke. The caravan was starting to smell bad – rot, decay, the musk of animals and the urine of humans – but he didn't mind that so very much. The last storms, though, had taken their toll, cracking and warping panels and littering the surrounding sand with door handles and struts plucked off by the winds. One of the plywood panels from the warped and battered door was missing. He tried to pull the door closed behind him but it was missing a hinge and hanging at a strange angle. It no longer fitted between the jambs and swung open.

The squeal of brakes and the throb of an idling engine told him that the truck he'd heard had stopped not far away, and he peered at it through one of the torn-out windows. It was a big, white Crawford's lorry. Suddenly the engine died.

Four men got out. Two of them were wearing dark, city suits and overcoats and they walked slowly past the caravan towards the sea, heading for the boat. One of them was constantly muttering, complaining. He sounded, Danny thought, like a Fenian. The man with him had a shock of auburn hair. He said nothing.

The other two were just boys, dressed in trainers, jeans and cheap leather jackets. They leaned against the side of the truck in silence. One of them lit a cigarette.

Danny felt the need for one himself but took another gulp of whisky instead. That made him feel a lot better about the lack of nicotine and so he took another long swallow. The bottle had very little left in it.

Snatches of a shouted conversation between boat and shore carried to Danny in the caravan, a few odd words that drifted on the wind and meant nothing to him. However, it was obviously unsatisfactory because the two city men turned and stomped unhappily back to the truck. As they did so, a flicker of movement on the boat caught Danny's attention.

The hard-looking man in the reefer coat was leaning on the rail, watching the two men as they walked away from him. He was chewing on the thick, glossy, black moustache that drooped under his crooked nose. Behind him, a slight figure dressed in dark trousers and white shirt emerged from a hatch, looked furtively around and, seeing the man, backed away, climbed unsteadily over the rail at the far side, making no sound at all, and then slipped out of sight into the sea. Danny stepped into the doorway of the caravan in order to see better.

A minute or two passed, then another crew member ran to the master, said something to him and the two of them strode the length of the deck, peering into any potential hiding place. The search didn't take very long.

The master looked over the side. As he did so, Danny saw a head bobbing on the surface of the water at the stern, swimming weakly for the beach. The master spotted the head at the same moment and he yelled at it. It was just a sound to Danny, a muted and meaningless bellow, but it carried authority and menace.

The two men Danny thought of as the Fenians turned back to face the sea, and the auburn-haired one called out to the ship, 'What's up?'

'A girl. One of the girls. In the water,' the master yelled back, slowly and carefully enunciating every word.

The Fenians looked at each other and then ran down to the sea. The two boys followed on, sauntering very slowly.

The girl was only a few yards out now and had found her feet on the gently shelving beach. She scrambled her way towards them, falling several times, calling out in a language Danny didn't know. But the sound – a shrill keening, a desperate cry for help – cut through him. Danny thought how cold she must be. Involuntarily, he shivered. He was still holding the bottle of whisky. Absentmindedly, he raised it to his lips and emptied it. He shivered again as the harsh spirit hit the back of his throat. He laid the bottle down on the floor behind him.

By the time he looked back, the girl had stumbled out of the water and Danny could see her properly. She was just a skinny kid, dark-haired and tawny-skinned, with huge black eyes. Her clothes were plastered to her, emphasizing her scrawny build. She had no more meat on her bones than Danny.

The ferret-faced, complaining Fenian grabbed the girl roughly by the arm and hauled her upright. She looked puzzled and hurt, and then she hung her head in resignation. Her body was shaking violently.

'Well,' Danny heard the Fenian say, 'we've got one of them. And for nothing.'

Without realizing it, Danny had stepped out of the caravan.

On the boat, two members of the crew appeared alongside the master, and each of them was carrying a heavy rifle.

'You will hold her for us,' the captain called to the Fenians.

'Give us a few more hours and we'll have your money,' the auburn-haired Irishman yelled.

'No,' the captain said. 'You told me it would be here this morning. So I waited. But you do not bring it. I cannot stay.'

'One more hour,' the auburn-haired man said.

'No more time. I will find another client. I have stayed too long. The coastguard came by yesterday. I told him I was making repairs. That we were a little damaged in the storm. He will check on me again. I must go. Give me the girl.'

The two Irishmen turned away, dragging the shivering girl with them. Danny saw the master nod to one of his men who immediately raised the rifle to his shoulder. The gun cracked once and the Irishmen sprawled on the beach as the bullet whined past them and smacked harmlessly into the sand. Then they slowly turned towards the boat, their hands raised, leaving the girl lying there. Danny thought that she was sobbing.

'OK, OK,' the auburn-haired Irishman called out, his voice more than half an octave higher than it had been, 'the girl stays.'

The master nodded to his men again and they scurried

off and lowered an inflatable dinghy into the sea. Then they followed it, climbing down a ladder and leaping sure-footedly aboard. The engine roared into life and the prow of the dinghy lifted out of the water.

'No,' Danny muttered, 'no.'

He walked down the beach towards the three figures, taking off his coat. He tried to put it over the shaking girl's shoulders but the thin-faced Fenian, suddenly aware of his presence, pushed him away and called to the two boys who had retreated to the edge of the beach when the rifles had been produced.

They trotted down, grabbed Danny and started laughing and punching him lightly on the shoulders and chest, knocking him over. Then they backed off.

Danny wasn't hurt, just puzzled. He didn't know what was going on. The girl lifted her head and stared at him with her huge, liquid eyes. Danny offered her the coat he was still holding. She crawled across the sand to him and took it. She was shivering uncontrollably and he helped her into it. Then she put her trembling hand in his and started to sob. Her hand was so cold that Danny thought he had been touched by a corpse, or by death itself.

She started talking, in her strange, harsh tongue, plead-ing with him, her free hand moving gracefully about, describing beautiful geometric figures in the air. Danny reached out and patted her shoulder as reassuringly as he could. But, even as he did so, he saw the two sailors leap out of the dinghy and bustle ashore and he knew he couldn't help.

The two men strode up the beach, ripped the girl away from him, and half-dragged, half-carried her back to the dinghy. They threw her in, jumped after her and man-oeuvred the little craft back towards the boat. The girl tried to stand at one point but she was pulled down.

It was only a matter of minutes after they were aboard that the engines started and Danny saw the anchor, streaming water, rise out of the sea. Then, painfully slowly, the boat pulled away.

Danny was sitting on the beach, drunk and puzzled. The thin-faced Irishman kicked him viciously in the side. Danny groaned and fell back.

'What the fuck we going to do now?' the Irishman said in his thin, complaining voice. 'What we going to tell Colm?'

The other one shrugged but didn't answer.

'It's not our fault,' the thin-faced one continued to whine.

The other one shrugged again. Then he looked at Danny and called to the two boys.

'Deal with him,' he said, when they had wandered closer, and then he walked away.

'What you want done with him?' one of the boys said.

It was strange. Danny knew they were talking about him, but it didn't seem that way. He was a long way off, looking down. He wondered what would happen to the girl. The men had been very rough with her.

'What you think we want done with him? We want you to take him off and give him a slap-up breakfast,' the thin-faced Fenian said and followed his companion back to the truck. 'I've got some stuff in the cab you can use. You can do it when we're gone.' He stopped and turned to face them. 'And make some effort to hide him. We don't want him found too soon.'

'You leaving us here?' said the boy who'd spoken before. He was pure East End of Glasgow. 'How we supposed to get back?'

'Resourceful boyos like you will find a way,' the thin-faced man said over his shoulder as he walked away.

'Wait a minute,' the boy said.

The Fenian turned to face them again. This time he didn't say anything, just stared.

'Right,' the boy said very quickly and he lifted the unresisting Danny to his feet. As the Fenian went to rejoin

330

his companion in the truck, Danny was hauled back to the caravan.

When Nugent had finished, he just stared off into the far distance for a minute or two. Then he spoke again.

'You do understand what I'm saying, don't you, Iain?' he said.

'I'm not sure,' I said.

'I'm advising you to act like an intelligent adult,' he said. 'Keep your head down and your mouth shut. The more close-lipped you are, the better. Colm Kelly didn't act like an intelligent adult and look where that's got him. Going to the police is pointless, incidentally. Nothing can be proved against him. I'll deny this conversation ever took place, and Billy and Oscar aren't going into the dock as prosecution witnesses. Don't tell Dougie. It would put him in the firing line as well and I don't think you'd want that. You'd better hope that Colm Kelly doesn't recover. But, if he does, remember you'll be in a stronger position with me on your team. Do you understand me now?'

'I think so,' I said.

'Good,' he said. 'Now you should still find the minister with a glass in his hand.'

It only took me five minutes to walk to the George, but the rain was coming down in heavy flurries, propelled by the bitter wind, each drop of water glinting like sharpened steel in the soft light from the streetlamps. Although I hurried, rain was trickling from my head and down my neck in icy streams by the time I got there.

I went through the heavy door and into the warm lobby and just stood there for a few minutes while the chill left my hands and face. I knew that I really shouldn't be there, that I should just leave well enough alone. But I couldn't. Although Nugent's account of Danny's last hours was still fizzing in my head, confusing me, I'd come to Edinburgh for a purpose.

331

The gentle chink of afternoon teacups and the soft whisper of muted conversations lulled me, and the pleasant warmth and comfortable upholstery of the lobby almost convinced me that I should forget about Baird and Carole and sit, drink tea and reflect. But the handle of the carrier bag holding my books cut into my hand and reminded me that there was something to be settled.

I hesitated a little longer and then strode to the bar. The first person I saw as I entered was Baird's minder. And he saw me too and was on his feet immediately.

He stepped in front of me and put his hand on my chest.

'If you're looking to talk to Mr Baird,' he said calmly, 'I'm afraid that's not possible this afternoon.'

I closed my eyes and counted to ten. Then I looked down at the restraining hand he had on my chest and stared at him. He lowered the hand.

'I just wanted a quick word,' I said.

He shook his head.

'Not possible, I'm afraid,' he said.

He was a neat and compact man, and he held himself and spoke with complete assurance. He was slightly smaller than me but he had that look in his eye that said he knew he could take me. I assumed that he was recently retired from some elite regiment – an NCO, not a rupert – and that he probably could deal with me but that he had, nevertheless, underestimated me a little. I also realized that even if I did, temporarily, get past him, I wouldn't get very far and that I'd be arrested before I even got a chance to speak to Baird. Anyway, I didn't really want to talk to Baird. All I wanted to know was if he was with Carole.

'OK,' I said, 'no problem. I'll just have a glass of orange juice at the bar and I'll be on my way,' I said.

'I'd rather you didn't,' he said.

'Are you going to stop me?' I said.

He looked me up and down and took a step back.

'Are you going to try to get close to Mr Baird?' he said.

'No,' I said. 'I'll sit quietly at the bar and when I've finished my drink, I will leave even more quietly. If, on the other hand, you elect to try to eject me, I can promise you a noisy and unbecoming struggle. Which may not make the minister happy.'

He didn't look particularly bothered at the prospect of a fracas but he pointed to the far end of the bar.

'The back of the bar,' he said. 'And I'll be watching you every second.'

'Thank you,' I said and turned towards the bar. However, as I moved away from him, I looked back into the room and saw Baird, on his own, staring miserably into a glass of whisky. It looked as if whoever he was waiting for hadn't shown up. I glanced at my watch. I was surprised to see that it was still only twenty-five past four.

I settled on a bar stool and ordered an orange juice which I drank as quietly as I'd promised. Then, just as quietly, I slipped down from the stool, nodded at the minder and made my way out. Baird never looked up and didn't even see me.

I was conscious that the minder followed me to the door of the bar and watched to make certain that I left the hotel.

It was still raining heavily and, glumly, I set off towards Princes Street where I hoped to find either a bus or cab to take me back to my car. As I turned the corner, I glanced back at the hotel and saw, unmistakably, Carole, lowering her umbrella before entering. She backed into the door, shaking water from her umbrella, and she looked across the road, straight at me. She must have seen me but she gave no sign of recognition and immediately disappeared into the hotel.

I stood in the rain for a couple of minutes, considering following her. But I knew I wouldn't get past the minder, and that she'd never forgive me. And I wasn't in the mood for confrontations any more. The story of Danny's death was weighing heavily on me. I turned back towards Princes Street.

Queen Margaret Drive was eerily quiet. A damp, clinging November mist draped itself in ragged, swirling scarves around the naked trees of the Botanic Gardens and insinuated itself through the cold railings, leaving icy droplets on the heavy iron. My footsteps resonated and echoed loudly as I scrunched my way towards the Byres Road. There didn't seem to be anyone else about. It was not long past seven, but it felt much, much later.

My mood hadn't changed at all on the drive from Edinburgh. I felt bleak and puzzled, completely at home in the subdued and chilly atmosphere that Glasgow exuded. There was something profoundly melancholy, elegiac almost, about the evening. Even the roar of traffic on the Great Western Road couldn't dispel it, and the isolated figures, buttoned up and hunched over, scurrying along outside the shuttered shops on the Byres Road, only emphasized it.

The bright lights and loud, raucous crowd in the bar should have stopped me brooding, but didn't. Especially when I realized that Dougie wasn't there yet.

I wasn't quite sure why my response to the news that it had been Baird who had written to Carole and not Nugent had been one of relief and good humour. I supposed that it was because there was something hard and edgy about Nugent that I took seriously but, while people soft-shoe-shuffled around Baird, it was the office and not the man they were wary of. Baird was not someone who was ever going to command respect. Not mine, anyway. And, I thought, not Carole's. But Nugent's story about Danny's death and the clear implication that the only person who could keep Kelly and his boys off my back was Nugent was enough to turn my mood sour. In return, he'd want my silence about him and the minister.

I half-heartedly forced my way through the early evening drinkers, and a young, lean and fit-looking barman I didn't recognize finally served me, neglecting to ask if it was fresh orange I was wanting.

'You Iain Lewis?' he asked as he handed over my change.

'Aye,' I said.

'Dougie rang,' he said. 'He's gonna be a little late. He said something unintelligible about a man and a dog.'

'He would,' I said. 'Thanks.'

A table had just become free as a large group of youngsters left for a movie or a restaurant and I managed to commandeer one of the chairs.

'You all right, pal?' a small, thin-faced drunk said as he sat opposite.

'I'm fine, thanks,' I said.

'Only you look a bit wrong, you know?'

'I'm fine,' I repeated. 'Just a bit tired, I guess.'

'Only that looks like orange juice,' he said. 'And that's definitely all wrong.'

'I'm driving,' I said, 'and when I'm driving I don't drink. OK?'

'You should go to a coffee shop or a milk bar, if you don't wanna drink. You don't belong in a pub.'

'I'm meeting someone here,' I said.

'I'll get you a drink. A wee dram is what you need,' he said and got up unsteadily.

'No,' I said, 'I don't want a wee dram. It's kind of you but, like I said, I'm driving.'

'You refusing a drink, pal?' he said.

I could see him bridling, and his shoulders stiffened and his fists tensed. He was at a dangerous stage in his drinking.

I stood up.

'No,' I said in as calm a voice as I could manage, 'I'm not refusing. I'll just take a rain check. I'll have one next time I'm in.' I looked around for some excuse. I really didn't want to have to whack him and I could see him boiling up to a fight. Nothing much occurred to me, so I said, 'I just have to speak to the barman for a minute. I'll be back directly.'

I ambled over to the bar but he followed me.

'You refusing to drink with me, pal?' he said.

Fortunately, I was waiting for it and brought my right arm up smartly just as he grabbed for the lapels of my jacket. Instead of shattering the bridge of my nose, his forehead hit the point of my elbow, not very hard. He hadn't had time to gather any real momentum. I was very glad he was drunk and slow.

He executed a very theatrical doubletake as he stepped back and couldn't seem to understand why I wasn't lying in a crumpled heap with blood pouring from my mouth and nose. He shook his head vigorously, as though he was trying to remove water from his ears, and took another exaggerated step back.

'That's one hard heid you've got, pal,' he said. There was a note of awe in his voice. 'Let me buy you a drink.'

'Och, don't waste your money on him, Gary. Buy me one instead. A pint of Guinness.'

'Right you are, Dougie,' Gary said and leaned across the bar, looking for service.

I turned around and grinned at the big man.

'The Seventh Cavalry, I presume,' I said.

'You should have taken the drink,' Dougie said.

'I didn't want one.'

'Even so.'

'Aye, you're probably right. Who is he, anyway?'

'A lonely drunk who likes to buy drinks for people. His name's Gary.'

'Anything else known about him?'

'Not a thing,' said Dougie. 'Let's sit down.'

I followed him back to the table I had just vacated.

'This what you were drinking?' Dougie said, indicating my orange juice and tonic water.

I nodded.

'No wonder Gary was upset. We know what boys, men and heroes drink. But who the hell drinks this?'

'Drivers who don't want to lose their licences,' I said defensively.

'Och, you know you can always stay the night.'

'I know that, but I'm intending to go back home. I just need some advice,' I said.

'Auntie Dougie is at home to visitors – or, at least, he will be when he has his pint – and will dispense wisdom to all who seek it. But you must write to the column care of the editor.'

Dougie's pint was slid across the table towards him.

'Ah, thank you, Gary,' he said. 'Now all is right with the world.'

I wasn't sure about that, but I said nothing.

'You're welcome, Dougie,' Gary said. 'It's always a pleasure to drink with you. But I can see you're busy, so I'll leave you to it.' Gary turned his red-rimmed gaze on me. I noticed a faint, yellowish tinge to his cheeks and the whites of his eyes. 'That's one hard heid you've got there, pal. One hard heid.' He shook his own and walked slowly away.

'You've made a friend for life there,' Dougie said and took a long, satisfying slurp on his pint.

'That may not be such a long-term thing,' I said, 'judging by the state of his liver.'

Dougie ignored me and took another pull at his beer. He gave a tiny grunt of pleasure, put down his glass, loosened the neat knot of his dark-blue silk tie and undid the top button of his still-crisp white shirt.

'That's better,' he murmured. 'Now the beer can flow more freely. There's nothing like a pint after a hard day spent curbing the worst excesses of subs.'

I must have looked puzzled, though I didn't mean to, because he decided to explain.

'They come up with more and more preposterous headlines. It's expected.'

I knew it was a mistake to encourage him but I couldn't resist.

'Like what?' I said.

'Oh, you know the sort of thing: "Super Ali, Sonny listless!"'

'Ali wasn't Ali when he fought Liston,' I said pedantically, not entirely sure I was right. 'He was still Cassius Clay, I think. And had the movie of *Mary Poppins* been released by the time of the fights?'

'Exactly,' Dougie said. 'You're exactly the kind of humourless, boring, old fart I have to protect from that kind of thing.' He paused and took another long drink. 'Anyway,' he said, 'I've checked. And it was all in 1964. Movie release, fights, name change.'

'Beside the point,' I said. 'As a headline, it stinks. And it's not original. The song's been used in a football headline.'

I'd known Dougie for more than fifteen years, since the second year at uni when I'd watched this gangling, awkward engineering student dye all his clothes a subtle and becoming shade of lavender in the local laundrette. I'd been particularly impressed by his attention to detail: handkerchiefs and shoe laces had been included and, when he'd finished, he'd started the wash cycle on the machine again without any clothes in it, so, he told me, that the next person to use the machine wouldn't end up with a faint light-blue tinge to their undies. I still think that he was trying for a deferral of his forthcoming Part Ones, which he didn't have a prayer of passing, on the grounds that he was just the tiniest bit barking. He has always resolutely refused to confirm that but he did, at the same time, make the eminently sensible move over to the philosophy department, which didn't involve him in eight-hour days in the lecture room and workshops and prolonged his time at uni by another year. I guess that Dougie counts as my oldest and dearest friend. If he'd just spent all day thinking up truly awful headlines, I owed it to him to be suitably dismissive.

'Tell Uncle Dougie everything,' he said.

I looked into that shrewd and good-natured face and told him most of what I'd discovered that afternoon. I left out Nugent's story about Danny's death. I hadn't weighed up all the implications yet and Nugent's advice had been specific. All I wanted from Dougie was advice about Carole. One thing at a time.

He didn't interrupt me and didn't respond immediately when I'd finished. Instead, he went to the bar for a refill and then sat down again, looking thoughtful.

'So?' I said when he'd drunk about a third of his pint. 'What do you think?'

He shrugged. 'Nugent's a canny bastard. You did come here straight after ringing me?'

'More or less,' I said. 'I did take a wee walk.'

'But not a wee walk that took you anywhere near Baird and Carole?'

'No, I couldn't see any point. I'd never have got anywhere near them.'

'I can just see Nugent's thinking: you arrested for assault, Baird involved in a public brawl over a woman. It wouldn't let Archie off the hook but it would undermine what little credibility you and Baird have. Bad blood between you and all that. For once, and probably inadvertently, Iain, you've done the right thing.' He paused. 'Word is, Iain, that Baird was going to veto any oil exploration on your part of the coast. Archie wouldn't like that. Which gives a bit of substance to the discrediting theory.'

I sat in silence for a few minutes.

'So, what about Carole and Baird? What do you think?' I finally said. When it came down to it, that was all I really cared about.

Dougie thrust out his lower lip. 'What's to believe? So, they meet up secretly for a drink. That doesn't mean they're having an affair. Do you think they are?'

'I wouldn't have thought so,' I said slowly. 'Not really. He doesn't seem her sort.'

He leaned back in his chair.

'I wouldn't have said that Carole's taste in men was anything to write home about. Duncan, you.' He paused for a long moment. 'Me,' he finally concluded, sadly.

'So, you think they are having an affair?' I said.

'I didn't say that,' he said. 'There's only one way to find out. Talk to her. Ask her. She knows you saw her, she'll be expecting it.'

'That's your advice?'

'That's my advice.'

I was about to worry at it further when I felt a tap on my shoulder. I turned and looked into Gary's sad, gaunt, strangely hued face.

'So, pal,' he said, 'what's your name?'

'This, Gary,' Dougie said grandly, 'is the famous Iain Lewis.'

An odd, puzzled look flickered across Gary's face.

'You Welsh then, pal?' he said.

'No,' I said.

'Then how come you've got a Welsh name?'

'I haven't,' I said. 'My great-grandfather came from Lewis and changed his name when he realized how many MacDonalds there were in Glasgow.' There was certainly something more to it than that – my father had often told me stories passed down from his grandfather – but I couldn't see any point in telling Gary the dark secrets of my ancestors.

'Oh,' said Gary, 'right.'

He turned to go and then swivelled round to face me.

'I'll tell you what, pal,' he said. 'Welshmen have hard heids.'

Then he swayed gracefully away, slipping between the little copses of drinkers like a jaundiced wraith.

Chapter Sixteen

I arrived at the Crawfords' house shortly before eleven, the full beam of the Rover's headlights hitting the little swirls of mist that rose from the driveway and the lawn and bouncing back at me. The house looked dark and deserted but a faint gleam from one of the upstairs windows suggested that it wasn't. And Carole's Golf was slewed across the driveway near the door. I couldn't see Martin's Jag.

I parked the Rover near the entrance and hauled myself wearily out into the chill night air. I patted the bonnet of Carole's car as I passed. It was still warm. She hadn't long been back herself, which was hardly surprising.

I walked very slowly to the big door and paused before climbing the steps and I looked up at the big, ugly pile, which was just a featureless shape in the darkness. It loomed over me, obdurate, louring and about as welcoming as a Wee Free meeting.

I knew that Dougie was right and that I had to talk to Carole. But I didn't much want to and I didn't know what to say. I was afraid that if I asked what I really wanted to ask, I might not like the answer.

As I steeled myself to knock, a light was turned on in the hallway and I heard someone shuffling about inside. Then Carole called out in her most imperious voice, 'Who's there? Is that you skulking out there, Martin?'

I coughed apologetically and told her that it wasn't Martin but me.

Nothing happened for several seconds and I began to think that she didn't intend letting me in but then the door opened very slowly and Carole stood there, the light behind burnishing her blond hair but turning her face into a single plane of dark shadow. It was a strange and disconcerting effect.

'Come on in,' she said. 'I thought you'd show up sooner rather than later. I gather that you were at the office this morning, as well as Edinburgh this afternoon.'

'Yeah,' I said, following her in, 'I just wanted to see you.'

She led me into the kitchen and sat at the big table.

'I'm not long in myself,' she said.

I took a seat opposite her and saw how fatigue had etched lines into her face. She looked thin and just a touch haggard. It was a look that suited her.

'How's Duncan?' I said.

'Not too good,' she said. 'He's contracted some infection which is making him feverish. They're not too worried about him but he'll have to stay put for another few days.'

I nodded.

'He's talking up a storm, though,' she continued. 'About what he's going to do to Martin and the crooks he brought into the company.' She sighed. 'If there still is a company . . . Can I get you something to drink?'

'Coffee,' I said.

She rose sluggishly and shuffled over to a cupboard where she rooted around for a few seconds.

'It'll have to be instant,' she said over her shoulder.

I gave a non-committal grunt which she chose to interpret as assent. She spooned freeze-dried crystals into a mug and, leaning on the counter, waited for the kettle to boil.

'What's going on, Carole?' I said.

She didn't turn around.

'You tell me,' she said.

'I would if I could,' I said, 'but there's too much that I don't understand.'

I fished in my pocket for the note from Baird and put it on the table. When she did turn to face me, I pushed it towards her. It rasped loudly on the rough surface.

She looked down at it, and then she looked at me. There was pain on her face and I thought that she was about to cry, but she didn't.

'I'm afraid that I took that from your desk this morning,' I said.

'You had no right,' she said. But her voice was thin and there was no conviction behind the statement.

'I know,' I said. 'I'm sorry. Very sorry. I shouldn't have done it.'

'Not that it matters,' she said. 'But why did you take it?'

'I don't really know,' I said. 'I thought it was from Nugent. He's a deeply unpleasant and dangerous man. Even Dougie is wary of him.'

She made a dismissive face and went back to the kettle, which had just switched off. She poured boiling water into the mug and stirred it vigorously.

'Archie's a pussycat, next to that snake Baird,' she said.

She plonked the mug down in front of me and I watched a little circle of bubbles accumulate in the middle of the thin, aroma-free beverage. This was what I wanted to hear. She hated him.

'What's he up to?' I asked.

'You mean you haven't found out? You didn't just go and beat it out of him?' There was a contemptuous edge to her voice.

'It did cross my mind,' I said. 'But he had his minder with him in the George and I didn't feel that it was the time or place to force the issue. Anyway, I only found out it was Baird because I happened on Nugent quite by chance. Nugent seemed to want me to go and beat it out of Baird. And what Nugent wants is usually only in his interest, and not necessarily in mine, so I decided against. So, what is he up to? Baird, that is.'

'What do you think?' she said a little pugnaciously, leaning across the table.

I shook my head.

'I really don't know what to think,' I said, 'as I told you.'

343

'You mean that you never thought we might be having an affair?'

'That did occur to me,' I said. 'Of course it did.'

She sat down and bent her head over the table. Her jaw was working, like she was chewing. After a few seconds, she sat back in her chair, a look of determination on her face.

'I wouldn't dream of having an affair with that man,' she said. 'He's contemptible.'

She stared down at the surface of the table again, as though, if she looked hard enough, she'd discover the answers to all her woes in the stains, scars and whorls of the old grain. When she looked up, there were tears in her eyes.

'Years ago – nine or ten – when he first moved up here, he and Mum had an affair. For her, it was the real thing – a grand passion. Dad had been dead a couple of years, and she was still very attractive. Baird was a little younger than her, charming and obviously on the way up, not long elected to Westminster. For him, it was, I suppose, just a fling with an older woman. Anyway, it came to nothing but they were very civilized about it all. Except that Mum had felt very close to him. I don't know: she was lonely and she needed someone, I guess. I wasn't around, and Martin was a problem. During their relationship, she confided in Baird. In particular, something that lay pretty heavily on her conscience. Just recently, he saw some advantage in that knowledge and reminded her of it. It was all very subtle but he was clearly after money to keep quiet about it.'

'But that's blackmail,' I said.

'That's right,' she said.

'But what could he possibly know about your mother that he could use in that way?'

'The truth.'

'The truth about what?'

'Dad's death.'

'I don't understand,' I said. 'I thought this was all about some scam involving property prices.'

'Some of it might be,' Carole said, 'but not the part that includes Baird. That's only coincidental and doesn't suit him at all. It does mean that there's money being pumped into the company and he's obviously decided he wants some of it.'

'Hold on. Why does he want money? And, anyway, the truth about your father's death is well known. There's no secret about it.'

'Apparently there is. As for the money, I don't know. Running a mistress as well as a wife and family can be expensive. He did sell his London flat but he still has a house in the constituency, a house for the other woman and a respectable flat in Edinburgh that he can take the wife to. All that costs money. And the wife's parents are both in expensive residential care in England, and she's as poor as the proverbial church mouse – and about as adventurous, I gather.'

'And the secret?'

Carole sighed. 'Mum did leave a suicide note. I didn't hand it over to the police because of what was in it. She was clear that Baird should be paid off if he came to me and she said that he knew the truth. She told me that I should protect Martin at all costs.'

'What did that mean?'

'I thought it meant protecting him from the truth. And it did. But not in the way that I thought. I went to see Baird today to find out what it was all about, and he told me.'

'Told you what?'

'What I suppose we all should have known, worked out for ourselves. Martin did kill Dad.'

Suddenly what Martin had said to me the other day made complete sense. The memories of the event that he had recounted were too vivid, too detailed, not to have something behind them. But then I remembered that he'd more or less said that he'd killed his mother as well.

'There's no question mark over your mother's death?'

345

I said. 'I mean, there's no doubt that she killed herself, is there?'

'None at all,' she said. 'She was sick with worry over what it would do to Martin if Baird told, and she didn't know how to find the money. I think she killed herself hoping that it would end with her death. But it didn't. Baird rang up the day after her funeral. I didn't know what to do. I drew up the cheque and then I had second thoughts. That's why I left it where you would find it.'

She started to weep. Great sobs racked her body, her nose started to run and her eyes looked swollen and bloodshot. Even so, she looked lovely to me. I tried to ignore that.

'Why didn't you just tell Duncan?' I said.

She pulled herself together and blew her nose on a tissue.

'Because he's completely useless,' she said, 'and, anyway, we hardly ever talk about anything any more. Whenever I try, he's hopelessly drunk. You've seen him.'

'Why me, then?'

She shrugged.

'I don't know,' she said. 'I just hoped you'd be able to do something.'

'What?'

'Just something.'

'Thanks for the vote of confidence,' I said, trying to make light of the fact that she hadn't chosen to confide in me and had, instead, sent me to Baird in ignorance of what was really going on. 'That's me: knight errant extraordinaire, by appointment to the local gentry. No quest too small, no dragon too big.' I tried my most charming, self-deprecatingly wry smile on her. 'I'm sorry if I temporarily mislaid my white charger.'

She smiled back. 'Anyway, I was pretty sure that you'd tell Dougie about it. I knew that he'd be interested in Baird and a payment from Crawford's. I thought the threat of exposure might embarrass Baird, but apparently it didn't. Do you know, he even express-cashed that cheque?'

346

The thought that Archie Nugent hadn't only been referring to Colm Kelly when he'd spoken about no one acting like an intelligent adult flashed into my mind. 'That's proof of something, I suppose,' I said.

'He did it straight away. He must be regretting it now. After the events of the other night.'

'Well, he couldn't have anticipated Kelly turning up at my place. And if he did, he would have assumed that I'd come off a poor second from any confrontation and would be in no condition to be making statements to the police.' I smiled at her again. 'Well, what do you want me to do now?'

She smiled back but there was no conviction in it.

'That's just it,' she said. 'I still don't know. Part of me would like you to go and sort him out. But another part knows that that would be wrong and wouldn't solve anything.' She paused. 'If the little rat had left it for a while, I think I'd've ignored him and let him do his worst – which is what I should have done. But I wasn't thinking straight. I was thinking of Mum and what she wanted.' She gave a bitter little laugh. 'He knew just when to strike.'

'So?' I said.

'So, let's let it run its natural course,' she said.

'OK,' I said. 'I'm not sure that, even if Baird did find some way of accusing Martin, anything would happen. He wasn't there and your mother isn't around to corroborate his story. And I rather think that Martin knows what he did. He more or less told me as much the other day.'

'What did he say?'

'Just what I told you at lunch – that he still had clear and vivid memories of doing it.'

'So, Mum wouldn't have been protecting him from anything? And nor would I?'

I shook my head.

'I don't think so,' I said. I decided to keep quiet about his equally vivid memories of feeding his mother sleeping pills. It would only muddy the water.

Carole stood up and walked away from the table to

stare out of the window into the deep, deep blackness of the night.

'If only Mum had confided in me,' she said in a quiet, faraway voice.

I followed her to the window and put my arms around her. Our pale faces were reflected in the window, overwhelmed by the intense and impenetrable darkness that surrounded them.

'You weren't around, Carole,' I said. 'Remember?'

'I meant immediately. When it happened. If she had, I wouldn't have gone away. Or she could have told me when Baird first approached her.'

'She probably thought that you had problems enough of your own. Grief for your father at the time, a failing marriage now.'

We both stared out through the window, beyond our reflections in the glass, into the all-consuming blackness of the night, where the intangibles of memory and of what might have been seemed to reside.

'Would you like me to stay?' I eventually said.

She turned around to face me, still nestled in my arms, but, before she could speak, the phone rang, echoing harshly through the empty house. She broke away, shrugged and went to answer it.

I remained at the window, not listening, although I could hear the quiet murmur of her voice coming from the hall.

I heard her put the receiver back on its cradle and walk into the kitchen. When I turned to face her, she was standing by the Welsh dresser, apparently lost in thought. She looked at me bleakly and shrugged again.

'That was the hospital,' she said. 'Duncan's taken a turn for the worse. His temperature's shot up and he's a bit delirious. Nothing to worry about, really, they said, but they think I should go in.'

'I'll drive you,' I said automatically.

'No,' she said. 'I'd rather go alone.'

'Are you sure?'

She nodded.

'Yes, I'm sure. And I'd better be going,' she said.

'Yeah,' I said. 'Me too, I guess. How all occasions do inform against us.'

'They do rather, don't they?' she said. 'But maybe it's for the best.'

I walked across the kitchen to her and brushed her cheek with my lips. She didn't respond.

At least the cat was pleased to see me, rubbing urgently against my leg and purring like a Ferrari with a bust muffler.

We went straight to the kitchen together, him weaving between my legs, and I opened a can of something noxious, murmuring, 'Out, vile jelly,' as the glistening lump of congealed offal slurped and slithered on to the dish.

I felt slightly nauseous but the cat didn't seem to mind.

I left the cat to his meal and went into my study. I'd turned off the answerphone when I'd left in the morning, so there were no messages to sidetrack me as I sat at my desk. It was only a little after midnight and I didn't feel like going to bed. I was too full of the day and coffee and undigested thoughts to sleep. I decided to work for a couple of hours.

The computer fizzed into life and I called up the short story loosely based on the death of Caravaggio that I'd been working on for months. Originally, I'd had a notion of entering it in some short story competition or other but it resolutely refused to be told in the three thousand words that most competitions looked for. At the last count it had reported in at eighteen thousand and still rising. Pretty soon I'd have a novella on my hands.

I was enjoying writing it but, somehow, I couldn't finish it, couldn't stop tinkering with it. There was always something that didn't convince me, or that needed a lot more detail, always a little more research to do. Of course, I knew that it was all displacement activity and that I just couldn't bring myself to send it to my agent for her to tell me what I already knew – that there was no market for it and it was completely unsaleable. So, I put off the fateful day by planning a trip to Malta, although I'd already seen the awful hole in the ground masquerading as a dungeon that the Knights Templar had put Caravaggio in. And I couldn't think what else I was going to research while I was there. After Malta, I think that I would have discovered a desperate need to visit Naples, just to see (again) the spot where he was attacked and nearly killed. After that, I'd probably think of somewhere else that I'd simply have to go to.

That night, I decided to recast the story completely, and tell it from the viewpoint of a travelling companion. I was three pages in and it was two thirty before I knew that it wasn't going to work and decided to make my way slowly to bed.

The cat was nowhere to be seen, but I could hear faint sounds coming from the garage, the usual hunting ground. I hoped that I wouldn't wake up to find a dead vole lying on the pillow next to me.

Claudio Arrau playing a few Chopin Nocturnes seemed the right music to relax to for fifteen or twenty minutes and I put on the CD, poured myself a small glass of cognac and sat quietly, letting the subtle music ease the knots of tension out of my aching brain.

The sounds of the night – the steady murmur of the burn, like so many distant conversations, the shrill scream of a rabbit as the talons of a hunting owl fastened on its back and dug in excruciatingly painfully, the incessant rustles of restless creatures – receded as the brandy burned its way into my empty stomach and the music slid effortlessly into my too-full mind.

It was still dark when I awoke, but that wasn't too surprising. At the tail end of November it was dark from four in the afternoon until close to eight the following morning.

The telephone was squawking horribly downstairs and I fumbled for the switch to turn on the bedside lamp before floundering out from under the duvet. A couple of books precariously balanced on the top of the mountainous pile of unfinished bedtime reading material slid slowly off and thudded on to the carpet: Peter Robb's biography of Caravaggio and Evelyn Waugh's *Decline and Fall*. Both had been there for some time, I noted guiltily. I made a mental note to take the Peter Robb to my study, where it would be to hand.

The small alarm clock, startled by the bright, golden glow of the lamp, showed seven thirty-five. I, startled by the shrilling of the phone and the chill of the morning, showed bare, white feet.

If it was a double-glazing salesperson conducting a 'survey' on which two windows I would like replaced free, or a charity asking me to sell raffle tickets to my friends and neighbours, I was prepared to be very grouchy indeed. If it was a journalist, I'd just hang up.

It wasn't.

It was a tired-sounding Carole calling from the hospital.

'Iain,' she said, 'I hope I didn't get you up.'

'No bother,' I said, happy that she was calling. Then I remembered that I had to ask, even if was only for form's sake. 'How's Duncan?'

'Well, his temperature is down and he's resting. The doctor says he's going to be fine in a day or so. I only hope I will be after another night with hardly any sleep. But how are you?'

'Oh, I'm fine too. Nothing wrong with me that a few hours' sleep won't sort out.'

'That's good.' She sounded reflective and there was a short pause before she continued. 'I just wanted to apologize. For last night. I wasn't at my best, I'm afraid, and I'm very sorry.'

'There's nothing to apologize for,' I said.

There was another pause, a long one this time, and the

351

ether whispered slyly. The only other sound was the heel of my hand rasping against my unshaven chin.

Eventually, she spoke very quietly, as though she'd been steeling herself to it and couldn't quite bring herself to say it out loud.

'I think maybe I do want you to have a word with Alan Baird.'

I didn't say anything. I couldn't think of anything *to* say – either to her or, more particularly, to Baird.

'Will you?' she said.

'I guess so,' I said, trying not to sound quite as reluctant as I felt. 'What would you like me to say to him?'

'I don't know. I just want him to leave me alone.'

'OK,' I said, 'that's what I'll tell him. He's to leave you alone.'

'Thank you,' she said. 'I'm really grateful.'

'It's OK,' I said. 'It's no problem.'

'Come to dinner tonight?'

'I'd love to,' I said.

'About seven?'

'I look forward to it.'

And the line went dead.

I sleepwalked through shaving, showering and the orange juice that passed for breakfast, then I sat down at the computer and lost myself in the sun and intrigue of early seventeenth-century Italy.

It felt good to be working, after so much time lost, even if I wasn't sure that I was really getting anywhere.

I'd been writing for two hours when the phone rang again.

A pleasant-sounding police sergeant introduced himself and asked me if I could possibly come into the station that afternoon to see Detective Inspector Stewart and his sergeant. He made it sound like a request.

I asked him what it was about and he murmured something about developments in the investigation into the murder. He resolutely refused to be drawn further.

Reckoning that even if they kept me waiting for an hour

and then the interview took another hour, I'd still have time to get to Carole's by seven, I told him I'd be there at four.

The call disturbed me more than a little and I found it impossible to settle to work. I could see again Danny's pale, distorted face and the dried blood on his hands where his fingernails had lacerated the skin in his final, awful moments. And then I saw myself, as though in a film, hitting Colm Kelly with the cricket bat, and heard the sickening crack as it connected with his head. I also found myself restlessly speculating on what the 'developments' in the case could be. I also wondered if I could safely tell DI Stewart what Nugent had told me. I decided I had to.

I also decided that my edgy mood was perfect for calling Baird and, at least, keeping my promise to Carole.

I grasped the phone and punched in the number that Helen Baxter had given me. I waited for the answerphone to kick in but, to my astonishment, a very efficient-sounding aide answered immediately and, very politely, without asking any questions except my name, put me straight through to Baird.

Unlike his aide, he wasn't scrupulously polite. If I'd entertained any doubts as to just how popular I was, they were put to rest when he growled down the line at me. This wasn't the egregious politician on the stump, glad-handing the voters. This was the narrow-eyed backstabber who lurked in the corridors of power, waiting for his opening, straight out of a Jacobean tragedy.

'What, exactly, do you want?' he said. 'You've already ruined my career with your fantasies. Apart from a public flogging, I can't think what further entertainment I can possibly provide.'

'I was just talking to Carole Crawford,' I said with a firmness and a resolve I didn't altogether feel. I could well understand why he wouldn't want to hear from me. I even felt a slight sympathy for the guy. 'And she asked me to have a quiet word with you. I think you probably know what about.'

'I don't know anyone called Carole Crawford,' he said

icily. 'Are you trying to link my name with cheap hookers now?'

'No,' I said, 'Carole is not a cheap hooker. And her name is, of course, Carole Ferguson these days. I apologize for the slip of the tongue.'

'Oh,' he said, 'and what did the fragrant Mrs Ferguson wish you to impart to me that she couldn't say herself?'

'Well,' I said, 'she really would like you to leave her alone.'

'Would she?' he said sarcastically. I wondered just how sarcastic he would be if I was in the same room as him.

'Yes,' I said.

'Well, that won't be difficult as I have never had any dealings with Mrs Ferguson and have no intention of having any.'

'That's not what she says and I'm inclined to believe *her*, rather than you.'

'I repeat,' he said, 'I've had no dealings with the lady in question.'

Someone in the Labour Party had once told me that a very prominent and influential member of the same party was the only person he knew who could look you in the eye and lie to you knowing that you knew he was lying. I had always been inclined to think that he was under-estimating the number of politicians for whom that was as natural as adultery. Baird was certainly supporting my view.

I knew it was pointless but I felt that I had make a show of resistance.

'Of course,' I said, 'and you weren't in the George Hotel at four yesterday afternoon and she didn't come in to see you at about half past.'

'That's correct,' he said.

'OK,' I said, 'I'll just say this once: make sure that you do leave her alone.'

'That's a threat, is it?'

'That's not how I'd put it,' I said, discovering that a politician lurks even within me when I think there's a distinct possibility that whoever I'm talking to may be recording the call, 'not how I'd put it at all . . .'

Mercifully, he hung up.

'Well,' I said aloud to the dead phone, in the very best sitcom tradition, 'that seemed to go well.'

I knew that I still wouldn't be able to settle down to work again and so I started rummaging in the loft.

My old, slim and battered, Faber & Faber copy of Henryson's *The Testament of Cresseid* proved as difficult to locate as I thought it might. But I eventually found it languishing at the bottom of a mouse-nibbled box, oppressed by obese, overripe tomes of fantasy that I'd never quite got around to reading or to disposing of as I'd forgotten I possessed them. Indeed, I had no memory of even acquiring them. Which made me think that maybe they belonged to someone else. But I couldn't think who.

I took the Henryson, and a Penguin edition of some Icelandic sagas, down to my study and put them both in a small, padded envelope, added a carefully chosen postcard (a Sisley snowscape) that just happened to be lying on my desk (the care and the choosing had been lavishly expended some time before in an art gallery in London or Paris) scrawled with my best wishes and the request that they both be returned, added my name, and then addressed the package to Mary Elgin. I wondered what she'd make of them. And then I wondered if Helen Baxter would still be talking to me after Baird told her that I'd just threatened him. Probably not. But I hoped she would.

I hauled on a coat, tucked the envelope under my arm and went out to the car, making a note to call the joiner as I wrestled the front door open.

It was dull and cold in town, with wisps of fog still hovering over the harbour in the still air. Everything was damp, grey and murky, with the smoke of a hundred coal fires swirling slowly about. Even the usually bustling pensioners who were milling around the Co-op were strangely listless.

The Christmas tree had been erected that morning on its

usual corner of the harbour, opposite the Co-op, the butcher and the pharmacy. As colourless in the bleak afternoon as the surrounding paving stones, it signally failed to impart any seasonal cheer to the lacklustre scene.

It hadn't registered with me that it was Saturday until I went to the post office and found that it had shut at noon, and so I failed to post the package to Mary Elgin. It suddenly occurred to me that I'd been doubly lucky (or unlucky) in managing to get hold of Baird in his office on a weekend morning. The thought that maybe he was clearing his desk put a little spring into my step.

My parcel tucked under my arm, I went into the Co-op and picked my way between the little clumps of wifeys swapping symptoms and gossip, and I gathered up some groceries. A poster in the window reminded me that this was the last night of the musical society's production of *Me and My Girl*. What a choice! Dinner with Carole or a night spent watching some prat in a boater and a red-and-white-striped blazer singing 'The Sun Has Got His Hat On'? It didn't even cross my mind to ask Carole if she'd like to go.

Ah well, the musical society hadn't exactly turned out in great numbers for my last poetry reading. In fact, I didn't think that any of the seven people who had sat on bum-numbing chairs while I uneasily read verse I no longer cared about had been a member. In any case, I felt sure that the two principals, the debonair, twinkle-toed bank manager and Argyll's very own, utterly beguiling, divine Miss M (well, this being Scotland, Mrs McM), *chanteuse extraordinaire*, wouldn't even register my absence.

As I stowed the groceries on the back seat of the car, I recognized the brown envelope that Carole's secretary had put her short stories in. Guiltily, I decided to read them after lunch, and drove home.

I tuned the radio to Classic FM, and miraculously managed to find a signal, as I warmed through a Co-op pizza and prepared some salad. Someone was playing Fauré's Dolly Suite when the phone rang. Whoever was on the line hung up as soon as I answered. I punched in 1471, but the caller had withheld the number.

I returned to the kitchen, a little uneasy. Fauré had been replaced by the news, and a brief item about Alan Baird resigning from the Scottish Executive amid allegations of corruption, which he strenuously denied, vowing to clear his name, immediately caught my attention. It went a considerable way to explaining his frosty, and curiously self-pitying, tone when I'd called. Well, it wasn't exactly unexpected.

I settled down to eat pizza and salad, hoping that the phone would ring again and the call would be explained. But it didn't ring. I tried to put it from my mind but the events of the last eight days made that very difficult. Even a simple wrong number or a cold call from a salesperson who decided from my one-word greeting that I was not a likely mark made me jumpy and suspicious.

After lunch, I settled at my desk again.

The short stories weren't bad. They weren't that good, but they weren't bad. Two of them were wistful little pieces about lost or missing love, and the third was a sentimental account of the death of a pet dog. I made some coffee and wrote notes on plot, content and style, offering a few bland comments and a little advice.

I then went online and picked up my email: my brother telling me how much I'd be missed at Christmas – even on my computer screen the message heaved a big sigh of relief that I wouldn't be there – a small poetry press seeking subscriptions not submissions, an expatriate Scottish poet living in Michigan who'd taken to sending me reviews of his work for reasons that I couldn't fathom, and an offer from Amazon.

Life seemed curiously normal. The savage violence of Wednesday night had moved slowly into the background, a sequence of jagged, grainy, inchoate images that would, I hoped, eventually fade.

Suddenly, it was time to head off to the police station.

Chapter Seventeen

The reception area was very bright, after the November gloom outside. But it was just as stark and harsh a place as it had been in the early hours of Thursday morning. I announced myself to a large and completely uninterested sergeant and was waved to a black plastic chair which lurched alarmingly when I put my weight on it, and sat and waited.

After about five minutes, Angus Darling walked in, briefly bringing the damp, chilly afternoon with him into the fuggy heat. He raised a hand to the duty sergeant who barely acknowledged him, which seemed to me to mean that either he liked Darling about as much as I did or he treated everyone equally. Either way, it cheered me up slightly.

Darling saw me and a tight little smile lifted the corners of his mouth for a fraction of a second, as if he was imagining taking me off to the cells with a couple of his larger mates to give me a perfectly executed kicking. I was reminded of how difficult it had been for him at school to get through a single day without some altercation when he was teased about his name, whereas a sweet-natured and affable lad called Dearie had managed the trick easily.

'Good result, eh?' he said.

I looked at him quizzically.

'Good result, no?' he repeated.

'Oh, aye,' I said, not having the stomach for a long explanation of just what he was referring to and reckoning that agreeing with him would shorten any conversation considerably, 'a very good result.'

He looked at me with sad eyes, as if I'd disappointed him yet again, shook his head slightly as his right hand moved involuntarily to his face and his thick forefinger gently stroked the kink in his nose, and then he strode on down the corridor towards the back of the nick. I honestly couldn't remember if any of our fights had been over his name. I hoped not.

I hadn't got a clue what he'd been talking about but he had, in spite of any intentions to the contrary, managed to cheer me up. The fact that he was talking to me at all suggested that I wasn't about to be arrested on suspicion of being Jack the Ripper in a timely attempt to tidy up the figures on unsolved crime.

The heat was making me a little drowsy and I leaned back against the wall and closed my eyes. A dark image of Colm Kelly, a mad anger blazing on his face, turning the shotgun on Duncan stabbed across my inner vision and I sat up, eyes wide open, immediately. The big duty sergeant was looking at me indulgently, benevolent world-weariness written on every aspect of his creased features.

'Room four,' he said. 'Detective Inspector Stewart is waiting.' A wry smile crinkled his face. 'I believe you've been there before.'

He was right. It was the same interview room I'd been questioned in.

The laconic Stewart was sitting at the table, busily filling in forms. His detective sergeant was leaning against the wall behind him, smoking. To his right was the police recruitment poster.

Stewart looked up as soon as I came in, put his pen down and closed the file in which he'd been writing.

'Ah,' he said, 'Mr Lewis, Iain. Sorry to keep you waiting.' He waved his right hand airily over the files and smiled.

'That's OK,' I said, meaning it. I felt a certain sympathy

for him and his obviously heavy workload, which I had added to considerably.

There was a small watercolour of picturesque and colourful fishing boats tied up in what I took to be Carradale harbour just above the sergeant's left shoulder and I gazed at it, not sure that I was looking at the place I had visited so often.

'Anyway, good news,' Stewart said briskly. 'We've just formally charged Danny McGovern's murderers.'

'What?' I said.

'The two bad lads from Glasgow who turned over your gaffe have admitted doing it,' he said.

'Really?' I said, my heart lifting. I wasn't going to have to tell him about Nugent.

'Yes,' he said, patting the file in front of him, 'I have two signed statements right here.'

'Probably out of their brains on something,' the sergeant said. 'According to them, they were on the beach for an early morning walk and your friend turned up and there was an altercation.' He paused and stroked his chin for a moment. 'It's amazing what a few hours without access to dope will do to a dope-fiend's memory.' He scratched his right ear. 'Horrible little bastards they are. Truly unpleasant.'

'You're sure?' I said.

He looked puzzled for a second.

'Sure enough,' he said. 'I've seen some horrible wee bastards in my time and these certainly qualify for the description.'

'That was all there was to it,' I said.

He shrugged.

'As sure as you ever can be,' Detective Inspector Stewart said. 'There are some discrepancies in their stories but nothing's ever as tidy as it ought to be.' He looked up at the ceiling. 'But, yes, I'm confident that these are the guys who did it. For a start, they know how he was killed, and we haven't given that information.' He sniffed. 'Anyway, I expect that the body will be released sometime next week: Tuesday or Wednesday probably.' He looked at me with sad brown eyes and raised his eyebrows. It was an unspoken question.

'I'm sorry,' I said, 'but I don't understand.'

'Will you be arranging the funeral?' he said.

'Oh,' I said. 'I don't know. I haven't thought about it.'

'I thought you were a friend of his,' he said.

'No more than anybody else,' I said. 'Did they say what Danny was doing there?'

'Why would they know? But didn't he say something to you about a boat pulling in down there? I think you mentioned it.'

It was my turn to shrug.

'Yeah,' I said. 'Could there have been anything in it?'

Stewart nodded.

'We checked with the coastguard. There was a boat there on the Saturday morning. But it was gone by Sunday,' he said. 'Now about the body . . .'

'I'll take care of the funeral arrangements,' I said. 'What happens?'

'In this case? If you find a funeral director and let the duty sergeant know who it is, he'll take care of it.'

'And that's it?' I said.

'That's it,' he said.

'Right,' I said.

I stood there for a moment in silence. I wondered whether to push it further but couldn't see the point.

'Incidentally,' the sergeant said, 'I thought you might like to know that the guy you whacked with that strange sassenach instrument of torture is out of danger now. He's no very well, but he's out of danger. On the basis of your testimony, and that of Mr and Mrs Ferguson, he's going to be facing some very serious charges, and, with any luck, a long stretch inside. There's a school of thought here – actually, someone's opened a book on it – that leans towards the view that you won't. What exactly does constitute reasonable force when someone turns up at your house with an automatic pistol and a shotgun? Most of us

361

reckon we'd've whacked him too. Harder than you did. It's possible that you'll face an assault charge. It's up to the procurator fiscal. But we're not pressing for it. I just thought you'd like to know. Make sure you've got a decent brief, Iain.'

'Thanks,' I said, 'I will and I appreciate you telling me the score.'

He lit another cigarette.

'There's still the other stuff, of course,' he said, smiling sympathetically. 'The briefcase, the cheque and so on. The stuff you didn't tell us about when it might have done some good. Before the events of the other night.'

'Aye,' I said, 'there's always the other stuff.'

'If it's any consolation,' Stewart said, 'I can understand why you might not have wanted to impart any of that information to Sergeant Darling, but others might not be so sympathetic, and I'd appreciate you not repeating that. By the way, did you hear the news about the minister?'

'Aye,' I said.

'You might be amused to know that he's admitted to cashing your cheque, which was pretty dumb of him,' the inspector said, 'if it is dodgy. The thing is, he can't quite remember what it was for. But he thinks that he will, given time and access to his records.'

The sergeant grinned.

'I wish,' he said, 'I could afford to be quite that forgetful about a year's salary.'

I arrived at the big house in good time, my hair still wet and gleaming from the shower, a more than decent bottle of Georges Duboeuf Fleurie, picked up at the off-licence three hundred yards from the police station, firmly grasped in my hand. Nothing untoward had happened on my return home, no more unnerving phone calls.

Martin opened the door before I had a chance to knock. He looked very tired and worried, constantly trying to blink away the tic under his left eye.

'Iain,' he said. 'What a surprise. Come to see my big sister, I take it.' He opened the door wide and gestured extravagantly. 'Enter, enter. While Duncan the cat's away and all that . . . I wondered what all the activity in the kitchen was about. It's baked beans mornay, by the way. I'm just on my way out, so I won't be joining you. Wasn't invited, in fact. But I'm glad to have seen you.' For a moment, he looked like the unhappy boy he had once been, then he ran down the steps past me and turned, pointed his hand at me, forefinger extended and thumb raised behind it like the hammer of a gun, clicked his tongue in imitation of a misfire, turned the gesture into a wave of farewell and walked swiftly towards his car, his feet crunching on the gravel.

I stood and watched him go, wondering if he meant anything by it, then went in.

I found Carole in the kitchen, looking remarkably cool, poised and rested, sipping at a glass of red wine, leaning against one of the counters. Her smile was bright enough when she saw me, but there was something a little brittle about it, as if she were on display at some social event she took no joy in, and she made no move towards me.

I placed my bottle of wine on the table and grinned at her. The kitchen was filled with the smell of roasting lamb, garlic and rosemary.

'Hi,' she said. 'Drink?'

'I don't know,' I said. 'Am I driving back later?'

'Probably,' she said, nodding thoughtfully, eyes slightly narrowed.

I saw no future in arguing.

'OK,' I said. 'Then I'll have one glass of wine with dinner, but water now.'

'Help yourself,' she said.

I opened the fridge and found some Highland Spring water. Carole handed me a tumbler and I filled it with ice and water, chinked it against her wine glass and smiled.

'Salut,' she said.

'Salut,' I said and sipped some water. 'Did you hear that Baird has resigned from the government?'

She nodded.

'I can't say that I'm exactly heartbroken,' she said.

'It's because the stupid bastard cashed your cheque,' I said.

She nodded again, absentmindedly, as if the matter was of very little interest. I couldn't think why that should be the case, as it touched her and her family's company closely, but I decided that there was no future in pursuing it. She clearly didn't much want to discuss it.

'So,' I said, 'how is Duncan? You said his temperature's down.'

'Yes,' she said, 'it is. And the infection seems to be under control. But he threatens to burst a blood vessel whenever he thinks about Colm Kelly and the company.' She laughed and sipped a little more wine. 'Actually, I think the wound hurts quite a lot and his painkillers make him just a touch woozy. Which is just as well. It means that he's only tetchy part of the time. The rest he's sleeping or away with the fairies. He'll be staying in for another couple of days, according to the doctor. Just for observation.'

I nodded thoughtfully. 'And then?'

'"And then" what? He comes home,' she said.

'I realize that,' I said. 'I meant, what about you and me?'

She turned away, took a step or two towards the sink and stared at her reflection in the window.

'I haven't really made up my mind,' she said quietly. 'I really don't want to rush into anything, Iain. I'm terrified of making another mistake. To tell you the truth, I'm thinking about going back to Glasgow, or maybe Edinburgh, and living on my own for a while.'

'I see,' I said and glugged down some ice-cold water, wishing it was something with a high alcohol content and that I'd never started the conversation along this course.

'I doubt it,' she said, turning towards me with that tight little smile on her face. 'You're probably feeling all hurt and abandoned. But I'm not abandoning you. It's Duncan

I'm abandoning. That probably means leaving the area. I don't think I could put up with seeing the great lumbering ox drinking himself into an early grave.'

'He's doing that, anyway,' I said, 'as far as I can see, with you still around.'

'Even so,' she said.

I didn't say anything, just smiled wanly.

She walked back across the kitchen and put her hand on my chest.

'You big softy,' she said. 'You can always come and visit me in the city, you know.'

'I guess so,' I said, 'but only if you live in one of the big apartments in the West End. I'm not interested in any trendy new flats down by the river.'

'I don't suppose I'll be able to afford either, the way house prices are,' she said, patting my chest. 'You'll just have to come to wherever I end up. Now, supper'll be ready in a few minutes. I thought we'd eat in here.'

'Fine by me,' I said.

'Good,' she said. 'I'll get the lamb out of the oven and you can carve after we've set the table and the lamb has rested for a few minutes.'

'I spoke to Baird,' I said as she bent to open the oven and a great blast of hot, fragrant air filled the kitchen. 'Before I knew he'd resigned. He wasn't best pleased.'

'No,' she said, straightening up, holding the roasting tin, 'I don't suppose that he would have been. In the circumstances. Did he have anything interesting to say?'

I related my conversation with Baird more or less verbatim as we put out cutlery, glasses and napkins, and I opened the wine I'd brought. She made no comment but I couldn't help feeling that she thought I'd let her down, that she'd been hoping for some definitive comment from him.

At first, dinner was a civilized affair and I tried to remain cheerful, but I soon found myself brooding over Carole's statement of her intention to move away and, every so often, little spasms of self-pitying gloom would threaten to overwhelm me.

She was right; I was feeling hurt and abandoned, and none of her reassurances could change that. She'd gone away from me before and that had not worked out well.

My responses to her conversational ploys became increasingly monosyllabic, and I swallowed more wine than I had intended by way of punctuation. I was halfway down my third glass before it even registered that I had exceeded my self-imposed limit by a considerable factor.

Carole's conversation kept returning obsessively to the violence at my house on Wednesday night, reflecting on how much worse it could have turned out for us. She was obviously still very shaken about it, still a little shocked. I was suddenly aware that my reassurances were sounding more and more casual and less and less convincing. But it was the realization that I didn't really care that was the more unsettling.

It was as if I had already accepted the fact of her imminent disappearance from my life, that our futures were going to be separate, and I was viewing her emotional state with indifference, worrying only about my own.

It had taken me depressingly little time to adjust and distance myself from her. I knew that it was entirely defensive but I also knew that I wasn't going to waste any emotional effort in an ultimately unsuccessful fight to keep her. I hated myself for it.

I interrupted her in mid-sentence.

'Carole, what did you hope that Alan Baird was going to say to me? When I told him to lay off you?'

She looked a little nonplussed and then composed herself, deciding to ignore my rudeness.

'I don't really know,' she said slowly. 'I suppose I just thought that if he understood that I had someone looking out for me, someone who wasn't afraid of him, that he might back down.'

I nodded, barely listening to her reply, ruminating on just how shallow, self-absorbed and sceptical I had become over the years. What I really wanted to know was why she'd left Baird's cheque for me to find, rather than just tell me what was going on, rather than confide in me. But I could see no point in asking her. She probably didn't know herself. And if she did, she was unlikely to tell me now.

I absentmindedly finished the glass of wine and reached for the nearly empty bottle.

'I thought that you were taking it easy on the booze tonight,' she said.

Something about the prim, prissy, disapproving way she said it irritated me.

'Yeah, I was,' I said. 'But somehow the news that the woman you love doesn't love you is a little difficult to take sober.' I thought of Duncan, though, and left the bottle where it was and put my glass down.

'I knew that's what you'd think,' she said. 'That I don't love you.'

'It's a difficult conclusion to escape,' I said and looked down at my plate and concentrated on sawing at a piece of lamb.

'I do, you know,' she said. 'Love you. I always have – in my way. But it's very difficult for me. Somehow, you and horrible, violent events in my life go together.'

'Carole, it isn't my fault that your father died of a gunshot wound,' I muttered angrily. 'Nor did I invite a shotgun-wielding Irish psychopath into my life. These things have much more to do with your family than with me. I may not be an innocent bystander exactly, but I am the next best thing.'

'And what is that?' she asked, her head cocked on one side, her eyes narrowed.

'Oh, I don't know: a guilt-ridden bystander,' I said.

'You're not,' she said. 'You're not a bystander, innocent or otherwise. You're an integral part of things. Violence seems to happen around you. I don't know why, but it does. And I can't cope with that.'

'That's not true,' I said. 'You could just as easily say that

367

a lot of the violence in my life has happened when you're around. But I don't blame you for it.'

'That's the way I see it,' she said. 'For me, you and violence go together.'

'That doesn't make it true,' I said.

She stared at me fiercely.

'It makes it true for me,' she said.

There was a short, tense silence as we looked at each other. I could see a real anger in her, tugging at her mouth and the corners of her eyes, and it seemed to be directed at me. I didn't understand it, but I no longer cared.

'OK,' I said, in a placatory gesture, 'I guess I can understand that.'

'I don't think so,' she said, and there was an edge to her voice. 'I really don't think that you're capable of understanding me. Or anybody else for that matter.'

I thought of the Graham Greene line about no one ever understanding another human being, and I thought of my father living for more than twenty years after my mother had left, never knowing why she'd gone, never knowing where she was or what had happened to her. I thought of her mother living with the knowledge that her son had killed his father, attempting to protect him from the knowledge. And I knew that Carole was right. I didn't understand her or anyone else. I said nothing. I couldn't match or answer her anger. Anyway, she was planning to vanish from my life again. Why should I make any effort?

I stood up and dropped my napkin on the table.

'Maybe I'd better go,' I said.

She nodded.

'Maybe that would be best,' she said.

As I walked out, I looked around the big, empty house. I wasn't expecting to be back inside there again anytime soon. And I wasn't sorry.

It had been a poor excuse for a quarrel, a very lame affair really, but it had been enough. It suddenly seemed as if we'd both been looking for a little spat. Maybe she was right, maybe we really were very bad for each other.

I stood outside on the bottom step for a moment or two. I wasn't really expecting Carole to come after me, but I thought I'd give her the opportunity.

She didn't disappoint and stayed firmly behind the closed door.

There was a damp and clinging chill in the air and I felt cold after the warmth of the kitchen. I also realized that, while I wasn't even close to being drunk, the third glass of wine had probably taken me over the alcohol limit for driving and I decided to stroll around for thirty or forty minutes before climbing into the car.

I walked slowly down the steep hill into town and wandered aimlessly along by the harbour, feeling the cold from the sea on my face, staring out across the heavy, dark water towards the twinkling lights on the other side of the loch, my hands thrust deep into my pockets. The smell of diesel and decaying fish caught in my throat, and the crowded hotel bar at my back spat out raucous laughter and little gobbets of light every time someone opened the door to enter or leave.

It was a wretched way to leave things with Carole, and I determined to speak to her and apologize for my behaviour and insensitivity when I went back to collect the car. Only a few minutes away from the quarrel and it already looked completely insignificant. It had only happened because I loved her and didn't want to lose her. I had to make some effort, however small, to keep lines of communication between us open.

I also suddenly realized that I didn't need to cast around for a lame excuse to knock on her door again. I had bone fide information to impart to her. For some unknowable reason buried deep in my subconscious, I had completely forgotten to tell her about my trip to the police station, and so I hadn't given her the news about the arrest of Danny's alleged murderers.

I kicked a small white stone into the sea from off the harbour wall. It described a simple arc and there was the faintest of plops as it slipped beneath the oily surface. The glistening sea reflected back a few dull lights from the hotel and the streetlamps, and the red, green and gold lights from the Christmas tree shimmered and danced, but there was barely a ripple from the passage of the stone.

I turned and walked back up the hill to see Carole. I wasn't expecting much. All I was hoping for was a relatively civilized parting this time, instead of no parting at all as twelve years ago, or an acrimonious one as forty minutes before. And to part with just a glimmer of hope.

Sleek, dark and predatory, Martin's low-slung Jag was parked at an acute angle to the bonnet of my old Rover, blocking my exit. A new black BMW I was sure I'd seen before was discreetly tucked in behind the Rover, effectively stopping me from reversing.

I stood quietly for a while in the driveway, to the left of the steps that led up to the door, watching my breath evaporate in a thin, pale, insubstantial stream, listening to the distant sounds of the village, wondering, not too hard, if the parking was haphazard or by design.

Martin was known in the village and beyond to be notoriously casual about who he boxed in or double-parked – and he was always disarmingly polite and charmingly apologetic and ready to move when he could be found and tackled about it – but there was something a little too planned, too contrived, about this.

I shook my head. I was starting to see threat and conspiracy everywhere. But that wasn't so surprising, given what had happened to me, and others, in the last week. And the looming presence of Archie Nugent's big Beemer, glinting expensively in the faint, yellow light from the living-room window just above it, wasn't altogether reassuring.

I wondered where he'd come from. He hadn't had time to drive from Edinburgh in the hour and half or so since my arrival at the house. So, if Martin had tipped him off, then he must have been fairly close at hand. I wondered what he could possibly have to say to me that couldn't have been said in Waterstone's and started to worry. He must have heard about the arrests earlier in the day and assumed it was down to me.

The situation didn't bode well. If Martin Crawford and Archie Nugent wanted to talk to me badly enough that they felt they had to ensure that I stayed around to listen – and that did seem to be the implication of their parking – then I probably wasn't going to like what they had to say.

Whenever I'm presented with an opportunity to consider options, I've never been the most decisive of men. I'm acutely aware that my judgement is fallible. I usually dither until I'm fed up and then act impulsively. I could save a lot of time if I plunged immediately. Some, those who didn't rightly see me as just stupidly rash, might even regard me as a man of action. Which I am not.

The best course here was probably a swift retreat back to the hotel to phone for a cab home. But that would only put off the inevitable. They knew where I lived and I'd be stuck there without a car.

As I stood there, undecided, I heard muffled sounds from inside the house. But I stayed where I was.

The door opened and a little, pale light issued out on to the steps, accompanied by the insistent beat of an over-amplified bass guitar. The two of them were silhouetted in the doorway.

In spite of the fact that they were unlikely to see me as I was in the shadows, well away from the weak beam from the hallway, the old cliché about a rabbit caught in headlamps and paralysed by fear and indecision, coupled, oddly, with the image of a sweet little bunny with a bloodstained mouth from the terrible old movie *The Night*

371

of the Lepus, shimmered across my mind's eye and I slipped quietly away to the left side of the steps and further into the shadows.

Then I hunkered down with my back against the cold stone, wedged into the angle that the steps made with the house. I felt slightly foolish but I was certain that they'd be unlikely to discover me there.

One of them shuffled forward.

'Anything?' I heard Nugent ask.

'Nothing, but I thought I heard something,' Martin said.

Their voices, from just above me, carried clearly on the still night air.

'Ach, it was probably a cat. Anyway, I don't know how you can hear anything over the racket of those CDs,' Nugent said impatiently. 'The scunner's at the pub, getting rat-arsed. He may make it home tonight or he may not, but he's no coming back here. He'll get a cab back. And if he does show here, he's no going anywhere, is he?'

'Let's go down to the bar. Roust him out.'

'Not the best idea you've had today. What'll we do? Walk in, point him out and have Billy and Oscar frogmarch him out? People tend to remember things like that, even if he doesn't kick up such a fuss that they feel they have to intervene. I don't think he'll come quietly, do you? Anyway, we don't know for certain he's there. No, we'll let it be for tonight, unless he turns up here. Maybe we'll pay him a call first thing tomorrow morning while he's still hung over. He's no hard to find. He's no hiding. Why should he be? A popular man like him? What's he got to hide from? He doesn't have an enemy in the world: except for you, me, Alan Baird, Duncan Ferguson, Colm Kelly, Colm's pathetic cousin and probably a few hundred others.'

At least, I thought, Carole's name was not on his list.

'What is the latest on Colm?' Martin asked.

'He's conscious and out of danger, apparently. He's still under police surveillance, though. I guess they'll arrest him when he's well enough.'

372

'And Baird's still the same as this morning?'

'Aye, he's still having to change his trousers every half-hour. Definitely in need of a little stiffening. If only he hadn't been stupid enough to cash that cheque, he'd be in the clear. There's nothing else against him. Still, all is not lost. I just have to find some plausible reason for the payment.' He paused and sniffed. 'Oh, and take care of the odd witness, of course. And after I warned him to behave intelligently . . .' He paused again. 'Talking of stiffeners, how about some more of that good malt whisky of yours?'

I heard them shuffle back inside, still talking. The door closed and I was left in the darkness and cold, feeling a little less foolish. This wasn't the tired and jaded Archie Nugent I'd seen in Waterstone's the day before. This was the old, fearsome Archie Nugent, ruthless, no-nonsense, determined, attempting to take some control of his own destiny.

I was still crouched down, my legs starting to stiffen and complain, when I heard someone coming stealthily around the side of the house. Thinking of Billy MacPhail and his ugly pal, Oscar, I stood up and stretched my pain-racked muscles, trying to ready myself for some kind of physical encounter. But it was a small, blond-haired figure that hurried past me without so much as a glance in my direction.

I allowed her to get well ahead of me and then went after her, catching up when she'd passed the gate and was on the road into the village where I was confident that we couldn't be seen or heard from the house.

Nevertheless, I still whispered when I spoke her name. She whirled around at the sound.

'Iain, thank goodness. I was just coming to look for you.'

She stepped towards me and wrapped her arms around me and I held her tightly, realizing just how pleased and relieved I was to see her.

'What's going on?' I said.

She looked anxiously back at the house.

'Let's get away from here,' she said. 'They're waiting for you.'

'Yeah, I rather gathered that,' I said. 'I just wondered why.'

She stepped away from me and I reluctantly released her from my embrace.

'I'll tell you what I know later, when we're well away.'

'Where's your car?' I asked.

'Garage. I couldn't risk alerting them to the fact that I'd left,' she said.

'How many of them inside?'

'Martin, Nugent and two thugs. One of them's Billy MacPhail. I don't know who the other one is. The thugs are drinking. Heavily.'

'Nugent and Martin?'

'Just drinking.'

'Let's give them an hour to marinade, and then we'll take your car and roar off into the night,' I said.

'Where to?'

'Home, sweet home.'

'But that's the first place they'll look.'

'I don't think so,' I said. 'Not if we make a lot of noise and it's obvious I'm with you and know they're after me. And we cause them a little trouble.' I paused, then added, 'Anyway, if they do come, we'll be expecting them.'

I took her hand. As I reassured her, I understood that that wasn't what I was doing at all. She remained apprehensive, but I felt a lot better. Partly, it was because I now had a plan, of sorts, but mainly it was just seeing her, not being alone. Carole tended to think of me as decisive, resourceful and resilient – or so I liked to think – and so, when she was around, that was what I endeavoured to be.

'Come on, let's go get a drink or a cup of coffee or something and you can tell me what you know.' I paused and looked at her. 'And I'm sorry for being such a prick earlier.'

She looked back at me and grinned.

'Yeah,' she said, 'I'm sorry you're such a prick, too.'

'But there is an upside to the defect,' I said.

She raised her eyebrows.

'Which is?' she said.

I shrugged. 'It means I wasn't there for the thugs to practise their thuggery on when they arrived.'

She hugged me fiercely.

'Iain,' she said, 'I'm sorry as well. I shouldn't have said some of the things I said. And I should have been more careful about how I told you what I have in mind for my future. I was acting as though it's nothing to do with you. And it is. You are part of my future. Whatever happens.'

We kissed lightly and sauntered arm in arm down to the hotel, as though we didn't have a care in the world.

We settled down at a corner table, between the Christmas tree, which had miraculously appeared since my last visit, and the fire, and waited for coffee. Carole told me that Martin had arrived back about twenty minutes after I'd left and Nugent and the others had turned up five or ten minutes later. They'd asked her where I was and things had nearly turned nasty when she'd told them for the fourth time that I wasn't there. But Martin had eventually calmed everyone down and then explained that Nugent just wanted to talk to me, to point out that it was in my best interests to disappear for a while. Nugent had then chimed in. Basically, what it came down to was that, without me, there was nothing much, he seemed to think, that could be proved against him or Baird. He was even prepared to offer a financial inducement. A substantial financial inducement, he said.

Carole said that she hadn't believed him and she'd told him so, pointing out that if that was what he had to say there had been no need for him to bring anyone – particularly hired muscle – with him. Martin and Nugent had both laughed and pooh-poohed the very idea that respectable businessmen such as themselves would even contemplate violence. Carole had pointed out that these same respectable businessmen had just admitted that they were proposing to bribe a potential witness in a possible court case. At which point everyone had gone very quiet and she'd announced that she was off to her room to read.

Our coffee arrived and we stopped talking. I thought for

a little while about what Dougie had told me about Nugent lobbying for oil exploration and Baird being the minister who would make the decision about whether it went ahead or not.

'Is Dougie right?' I asked Carole. 'Is this about the property values in the event of a go-ahead to look for oil?'

'Of course he's right,' she said. 'Partly. I think that Kelly was up to something else, and so did Mum, but Martin and Duncan had certainly talked non-stop to Nugent about what the farms, the factory, the houses and so on could be worth. And Nugent was really lobbying hard. He thought it could happen. But, of course, it wouldn't have to actually happen for land values and property prices to soar. People just have to think it's going to happen. And then the speculation will start. That's Martin's view, anyway.'

'If that *is* what this is all about,' I said, 'I don't understand why I'm involved at all. Oh, I know why you left Baird's cheque and a' that. But why should Kelly leave a briefcase with money, drugs and a gun at my house? He said it was all a joke. But that doesn't make any sense to me.'

Carole shrugged. 'Who said everything has to make sense? Duncan can't stand you because he thinks we're having an affair – which, of course, we are, now. The briefcase, the contents of which Duncan steadfastly claims to know nothing about, is going to be collected and it has to be stored somewhere. Duncan doesn't want it in our house – he may not know what's in it but he knows enough to know it's not a good idea for it to be left there, just in case. After all, we're having a funeral and holding a wake. Lots of people coming and going. Someone might find it. If it's discovered at your place, so what? Who cares? Apart from you. Certainly not Duncan.' She paused and shrugged. 'I don't really know, I'm just speculating, but that's a possibility, isn't it? Who knows why people do things?'

'Not me,' I said.

She looked down and stared into her coffee.

'Do you really think it was Duncan's idea?' I finally said.

376

She didn't look at me, she just made a dismissive moue.

'And Martin?' I said. 'Do you really think he shot your father?'

This time she did look directly at me before she nodded decisively. She was silent for a while and then suddenly said, 'By the way, did they ever try to make you an offer for your house?'

'No,' I said. 'Were they going to?'

'I told them it would be a waste of time and that you'd never sell,' she said. 'They did buy a few of the other places, though.'

'Like Baird's house?' I said. 'The one down near the Old Mariner's Grave.'

'The big white house?' she said.

'That's the one. He's had it for years,' I said.

'I think you'll find that he's been renting it from Crawford Holdings since September,' she said. 'At a peppercorn rent.'

'Crawford Holdings bought it?'

'I believe so,' she said.

'Do you know what they paid for it?'

'No,' she said. 'Mum and I were carefully excluded from the board of Crawford Holdings and the minutes of their meetings are never circulated. That's the Irishmen's territory.'

'That's more evidence against Baird, isn't it?' I said.

'I imagine that the deal has been backdated some distance,' she said.

'And there was me thinking that blind trusts were set up to stop this sort of thing happening.'

'I guess some trusts are not quite as blind as others,' she said.

'And my house?' I said. 'Why would they want that?'

'Oh, I don't know the ins and outs,' she said, 'but the dun at the back of your house is listed somewhere as a low-grade monument, so it can't be touched. And the road would have to stay where it is. So, in the event of anything being piped ashore, it would have to bypass the dun and would probably end up going through your living room.'

'Ach,' I said. 'Nothing is going to be piped ashore because it's not worth exploring out there. I told Dougie, people have talked about this since I was a lad. In any case, there must be hundreds of alternatives to going through my back door.'

'You're missing the point,' she said. 'This is mainly about speculation.'

'You mean it's South Sea Bubble time in Argyll! I just don't see it.'

'That's why you'll never be rich,' she said.

'It's not going to happen. People will never fall for it.'

She made another dismissive moue.

I shook my head and then started to think about more immediately pressing problems.

'Do you happen to have a manicure set, or anything like that, with you?' I asked.

Carole picked up her handbag and rummaged around in it before pulling out a small leather case and handing it to me.

'Funny time to want to do your nails,' she said.

It was my mouth's turn to form a dismissive moue. I opened up the case and found the sharp, pointed instrument I was looking for.

'May I borrow this for half an hour or so?' I said.

She nodded and I slipped the case into my jacket pocket. Then I stood up, asked Carole if she wanted another coffee and held my hand out for her car keys when she declined the offer.

'All being well, I'll be back in twenty minutes,' I said.

'Don't be silly,' she said. 'I'm driving. You'll never get the car out of the garage fast enough to get away. It's a tight fit and a tricky manoeuvre. Anyway, I'm a much better driver than you are.'

I couldn't argue with that really, but I tried.

'Come on, Carole,' I said, 'I can't ask you to take the risk.'

'What risk?' she said. 'What are they going to do to me?

378

And my presence might just stop them doing something to you. If we're caught.'

I stood there looking stupid for a few seconds, but I knew she was right about the driving.

'Iain,' she said, standing up, 'I'm coming, so you might as well be a little bit gracious about it. And you might be a touch grateful as well.'

I didn't know what else to do so I shrugged, smiled as brightly as I could, nodded, picked up our empty cups and put them on the bar as I left.

Chapter Eighteen

It was surprisingly difficult to puncture the front tyre of Martin's Jag. I knelt down on the cold, damp gravel and worked the nail scissors back and forth until, with a loud gasp, the side wall split and air poured out. The Jag sank alarmingly and I scuttled back swiftly as it leaned over towards me.

Carole mimed a question at me as I strode to the other side of the car in order to set to at the rear tyre. I pointed to the scissors, then to the rear tyre and made a stabbing motion, then I knelt down again. I'd got the hang of it and this time I jabbed the scissors viciously through the tough rubber.

I stepped quickly to Nugent's BMW which presented no problems at all.

There was something oddly satisfying about such vandalism and I found that I had to restrain myself from running the scissors the length of the Beemer's paintwork. I wanted to but I knew that I'd have a tough time justifying it, even to myself. I almost wished that I had a couple of bananas to shove up the exhausts. I'd seen Eddie Murphy do it in one of the *Hollywood Cop* movies on the telly and it worked pretty well for him. It just seemed that it would be nice to have one more surprise for them after they'd finally managed to replace the tyres, which wouldn't be that easy.

Sadly, I imagined that they'd take it out on the Rover and I patted its bonnet affectionately, and apologetically, as

I slipped past, indicating to Carole that we should move quickly to the garage.

There were a few lights on in the house and the occasional sound of raucous laughter carried above the long, low beat of the heavy metal CDs that pulsed and whined out from the stereo at a volume that should have rattled the windows. I wondered that Nugent and Martin could bear it. But I reckoned that it gave us a very good chance of getting clear away.

The garage was set back to the right of the house, and reversing out of it at speed, without lights, and swinging around without crashing into either the wall on the right-hand side or Martin's Jaguar on the left would not be easy. I was glad that Carole was going to be driving, and I hoped fervently that she could do it with her eyes shut, because it was that dark.

In the event, I needn't have worried about that because, as we approached the garage, a motion-sensitive light mounted just above the door responded to our movement and flooded the entire area with a bright beam that was almost unbearable after the darkness.

I heard Carole swear apologetically as we both hurried forward, completely forgetting any need for silence, certain that the light must have been seen from inside the house and that someone was bound to investigate. We wrestled with the up-and-over door, which creaked alarmingly as it swung up.

I bashed my thigh painfully on some sharp corner as I struggled into the passenger seat in the dark and narrow space between the garage wall and the door. Carole was already in and had started the car.

We roared out of the garage and Carole neatly manoeuvred the little Golf around and had us hurtling along the driveway before anyone appeared at the door.

I imagined that Oscar and Billy MacPhail must have been catatonic with the drink by then, and Nugent and Martin slowed considerably.

Carole turned on the lights as we hit the road. I looked back but I could still see no sign of pursuit.

'They probably didn't notice the light, or assumed that a cat had set it off. They're always doing it,' Carole said. 'And the music must have been too loud for them to hear anything. And they're almost certainly drunk by now.'

She was talking a little too quickly, the adrenaline still pumping.

'Yeah,' I said, feeling slightly hysterical myself but fighting it, 'it looks as if we've made it. Maybe you should slow down a little. Just in case we run into a police patrol.'

'Och, Iain,' she said, 'don't be so daft.'

'You never know,' I said.

She dutifully slowed down just a little and turned and beamed at me.

'Iain Lewis,' she said, 'you're such a boring killjoy.'

'I know,' I said. 'Life with me is just one long dreary day after another.'

I was staring moodily out of the kitchen window at the drear grey dawn, waiting for Carole to finish in the bathroom, when I saw my Rover bouncing across the ruts in the long driveway that led down from the road to the house.

I should have been expecting them, but I wasn't. I had rather hoped – indeed, expected – that it would take them all of this Sunday morning to replace the tyres and come looking for me.

Not being at all mechanically minded, it had not occurred to me until that moment that most jails run courses in Starting Automobiles Without Ignition Keys or Permission, and that both Oscar and Billy MacPhail had probably graduated with ease. For all I knew, Archie Nugent and Martin Crawford had both achieved a certain proficiency in the trick as well.

I was also surprised that this was their first port of call. I had completely disregarded Carole's scepticism when I'd said that, if they knew we'd gone off together in her car, this would be the last place they'd look and so had rejected her suggestion that we drive to Glasgow. I'd have to remember to apologize to her for that – if I got the chance. I wondered if they really hadn't heard us leave the night before. It didn't seem possible.

I was momentarily aggrieved at the violations suffered by poor old Rover, especially as she was being handled particularly roughly. Whoever was at the wheel was driving her hard into every twist of the lane and she was lurching and bumping into every pothole and puddle.

I'd already thrown on jeans, sweatshirt and a pair of trainers, so I was more or less ready to meet the world and, not wanting MacPhail or his pal in my house, I decided that this was an encounter that should take place in the great outdoors.

Carole appeared at the bathroom door as I passed, looking concerned. I told her that we definitely had unwelcome visitors and that she should stay put and out of sight. I suggested she call the police.

'What are you going to do?' she said.

'Get them away from here and you – if I can,' I said. 'I'm hoping they're just after me. I can outpace them until the police come. I think.'

'Be careful,' she said as I ran down the stairs.

I smiled grimly at the thought that it was more than a week late for being careful.

I emerged from the storm porch at a steady jog just as they threw all the doors open and jumped out of the car, Billy and Oscar, looking very hung over, from the rear, Nugent, who had been driving, and Martin more slowly from the front. I paused and looked at them.

Nugent straightened, gazed briefly up at the grey sky and then stared bleakly at me. He reached into his overcoat pocket and pulled out what was unmistakably a gun. So, it didn't look as if he was proposing to spend too much time talking, or attempting to persuade me, today.

I was aware of a sudden pounding in my temples and

I took several deep breaths to control my increased pulse rate. And then I was running, behind the house, reasoning that he couldn't shoot me through it, and off into the meadow that led to the dun.

I heard Nugent shout after me that I should stop, that he wanted to talk to me, that he wasn't going to do anything to me. But, somehow, I wasn't convinced and I increased my pace, determined to put as much distance between me and that gun as I could.

I must have been a hundred yards away when I heard the first crack of the weapon, closely followed by a second.

I kept running and had no idea where the bullets went. They certainly didn't whine past my ear or thud into any adjacent shrubbery. I was scared, but I reckoned that he'd either have to be a first-rate shot or unbelievably lucky – probably both – to hit a moving target with a handgun at that distance. It appeared that he was neither.

I slowed down to a steadier pace, carefully placing my feet on the boggy sheep pasture. I was breathing heavily. I've never been a sprinter and those first three hundred yards had really taken a lot out of me.

I heard some more shouting and then the sound of the Rover being overrevved. I couldn't believe that they were planning to chase me in the car but it sounded like it. I decided to risk a breather and take a look.

They were indeed driving the car behind the house and into the field. I rested my hands on my thighs, breathed deeply and watched. They didn't get any further than the first hollow where the cattle, when they are pastured here, tend to congregate and churn the grass to mud. The cattle hadn't been around for a month or so, but the mud remained.

I sighed as the Rover stuck fast.

Whoever was driving – I assumed it was Nugent again – did all the wrong things, savagely accelerating and wrenching the steering wheel viciously from side to side. Within seconds, the car was covered in a spray of fine, dark mud and the front wheels, far from finding any purchase, had dug an even deeper rut.

After about forty-five seconds, the driver realized that the car was not going anywhere and stopped the frantic revving. He left the engine running but all four doors opened at once. Simultaneously, four pairs of legs emerged and hung hesitantly over the pool of mud. Then they all gingerly stepped out and trod as delicately as horses, but they still slipped and slid and sank up to the ankles in the thick, black goo.

Nugent had been driving and Martin Crawford had been in the front passenger seat. Even from where I was standing, I could see that Nugent was unhappy and seriously pissed off. If I'd had any doubts that I was misreading his body language, the way he kicked savagely at the front wing of poor old Rover would have dispelled them. The slump of Martin's shoulders and the sluggish, reluctant way he slowly inched his way from the car towards the firmer grass at the edge of the bog suggested that he too was unhappy, but that his unhappiness had different origins. Maybe he'd wanted to drive and Nugent wouldn't let him and he figured he would have made a better fist of it.

Billy MacPhail and the brute Oscar tumbled out of the back of the car and both of them looked towards me. Oscar's great meaty hand reached into the pocket of his scuffed leather jacket, presumably for his brass knuckles. Then he lumbered around the side of the car, stepping more carefully than I would have imagined possible. Billy MacPhail came around the other side. He lost his footing a couple of times and I could hear his curses as clearly as if I'd been standing at his side.

I knew that I wouldn't be able to take them both on at the same time, but I felt sure that I could outdistance them comfortably and would stand some kind of chance after a long chase, if they became separated. I turned and started to run again.

At least Carole had, so far, followed my advice and remained inside. I hoped she'd called the police as well.

I also hoped she wouldn't choose that moment to make her presence known. With any luck, they'd forgotten all about her. The Golf was safely tucked away in the depths of the garage and not immediately visible. Maybe they'd assume that she'd left. If she'd been hesitating about calling the police, I imagined that the sound of shots would have concentrated her mind wonderfully. Maybe I could get away with this. Maybe . . .

After my short break, I was breathing more easily and I was running fluidly. I didn't look back. The dun loomed in front of me, dark and impassive.

By the time I started up the steep incline to the dun, I was sweating profusely, my heart was pounding and my breathing was more laboured than I would have liked, but I felt sure that I was in better shape than either Oscar or Billy and that I'd have sufficient time to recover and come up with some way of dealing with them.

Martin had never been particularly athletic, although I seemed to remember that he had played a little tennis in the past. I had no idea just how fit Nugent was and ran just a touch harder at the thought of him.

For some absurd reason I kept grimly repeating the opening line of Leopardi's great poem 'L'infinito' over and over again, like some bizarre mantra: 'Sempre caro mi fu quest' ermo colle, sempre caro mi fu quest' ermo colle, sempre caro mi fu quest' ermo colle, sempre caro mi fu quest' ermo colle . . .'

I ran to the majestic rhythm.

It was, of course, literally true: this solitary hill always had been dear to me, and the thought that its secret places were about to help me avoid capture made it infinitely dearer.

It suddenly occurred to me that Robert Bly, he of the brightly coloured braces on his trousers (or suspenders on his pants) and hairy-arsed male encounters in the woods, had translated that *ermo*, which just means solitary, as 'hermit's', when hermit is *eremita*. I wasn't sure why he'd done that. But then I wasn't sure why he'd written *Iron John* or started the male movement either. A minor mistranslation seemed a small misdemeanour in that context.

The greasy surface of the path was treacherous underfoot and the tread on my trainers was not gripping as well as I would have liked. I slipped a couple of times and decided to slow right down. I risked a quick look back and was relieved to see that Oscar and Billy were making very poor progress across the boggy sheep pasture. They were four or five minutes behind me and falling back all the time.

I was even more relieved to see that Martin and Nugent were watching the pursuit from the edge of the field, arms folded aggressively across their chests, flinty-eyed, I imagined, with jaws clenched, their suits, already mud-spattered, too expensive to ruin in a cross-country run. But that relief was short-lived. I started to worry that, if they decided to go back to the house and mooch around, they'd discover Carole. I hoped she'd keep out of the way.

I turned and trudged on, up the steep incline, the smug feeling that I was easily outpacing Billy and Oscar fatally compromised by my fears about Carole encountering Nugent and Martin. I thought she'd probably be OK. After all, they hadn't done anything to her the previous night. Although that had been before she'd thrown her lot in with me and helped in the Great Escape. But she was Martin's sister and I assumed that he'd make certain she'd be all right. But I wasn't completely confident.

I walked on.

I supposed that Bly had been trying to maintain something of the original sound pattern in his version of the poem. And that made sense, even if it did make for a slightly suspect translation. I'd have to think further about that.

I climbed the last few yards up the hill and started to clamber over the thick stone wall that surrounded the dun itself. I was on home territory. Magical things happened here. I'd be safe.

My immediate plan had been to go to ground in the – when I thought about it – not so secret passage and leave the rest to chance and time.

But, on reflection, that didn't seem like such a good idea. If, for some reason, Carole hadn't called the police, or they were inordinately delayed, Oscar and Billy could just wait me out. Billy would probably have a vague notion of where I was, assuming that he'd ever struggled up the dun before. If he didn't, then Martin certainly would. If they knew where I was hiding, then it followed that any advantage I'd gained would be completely lost.

I also hated the very idea of such passivity, and the thought of my confinement in that narrow and claustrophobic space, just waiting for discovery, wasn't at all appealing.

I sat on a large rock just below the summit and thought.

I wasn't feeling too bad at all. The few runs I'd taken in the last weeks and the lacklustre workouts with the heavy bag and the weights had served me better than I deserved. The legs were fine and the breathing regular.

Dawn still hadn't broken properly, and it looked as if it was the kind of day when it never would. It was still dark, overcast and brooding, with just a touch of rain in the chilly air.

I looked back down the hill, searching for my two pursuers, but there was no sign of them. That meant that they had made it to the foot of the hill, and were struggling up the steep incline, probably very slowly. Worryingly, there was no sign of Martin or Nugent either, which meant that they'd gone back to the house.

I tried to put them out of my mind and concentrated on Billy and Oscar.

I could wait for them, go down to meet them, hide, or outflank them.

Suddenly, it was obvious.

The path up to the dun was about eight feet wide for the

first hundred yards or so and closed in on both sides by a few hawthorn trees, some slender silver birches, a thick growth of young beech and the half-dozen or so mature Douglas firs that had been left by the authorities that tidied up Scottish historical monuments every once in a while. In the spring, a dense growth of tall, bright-green bracken and tangled bramble bushes with serpentine tendrils as thick as a finger, studded with thorns as sharp as a tack, suddenly erupted into unruly life. Now, of course, the ferns were just a sodden brown pulp and the brambles were bare and afforded little cover. But the scattered clumps of trees that made up a scruffy, silent and very small copse would do.

A narrow sheep track skirted the dun about fifteen feet from the top and I followed this until I was standing on the enclosed field where the ancient Scots would have herded their animals when under attack. This was a grassy area to the side of the fort, protected by the dun itself on one side and by walls that were still just visible as grass-covered humps on the other. There was no chance of Billy or Oscar spotting me with the dun between us.

From there, I plunged off into the undergrowth. This high up I wouldn't have to worry too much about getting bogged down in mud but, further down, I would have to watch my step. I wished that I'd been wearing something more substantial and suitable than old trainers, but then I wished that I wasn't in that situation at all. The trainers would do.

I kept losing my footing, though, on the old, slimy bracken, and I was making far too much noise, breaking branches underfoot. If they were close enough to hear me, I could only hope that Billy MacPhail and Oscar would assume a deer was thrashing its way through.

It didn't take long to descend about half the distance back down and find myself in among the thin cover afforded by the trees, and I managed it without major mishap, although my trainers, socks and the bottoms of my jeans were soaked and muddy. And I was cold, wet, and very uncomfortable.

This little wood, like so many others, was eerily quiet. There was the sound of running water, dripping and trickling, whispering over stony ground, gurgling into underground channels, echoing around, but nothing else. I didn't think that Oscar and Billy could be far away and I settled in to wait.

Then, suddenly, I heard coughing and spluttering as the two of them laboured up the path. I even heard the occasional vicious curse, but the noises were non-directional and I wasn't sure where they were, although I thought it unlikely that we'd passed each other and that they were above me. The only thing that concerned me was that they appeared to be keeping together and I'd been hoping they'd separate.

I carefully eased my way closer to the path itself, found a sturdy hawthorn, secreted myself behind the mass of tangled branches and kept my gaze firmly fixed on the path.

The men's movement was unlikely to find the wilds of Argyll to its taste, I thought: too wet for most of the year, and far too midgy in the summer. It wouldn't be much fun having your hairy arse covered in painful, itching red blotches after an overcast, windless, sullen summer's day spent finding your atavistic maleness. In any case, if Billy MacPhail was anything to go by, there was no pressing need for a men's movement in the west of Scotland, the land that feminism more or less forgot. They don't come much more primitive, male and atavistic than Billy MacPhail.

When they appeared, neither of them looked good. They were making very slow progress indeed and they hadn't reached the really steep part of the path. They were both slumped over and wheezing badly. Clearly, a diet of beer, Martin Crawford's good whisky, chocolate, cigarettes, French fries and Big Macs is not the best way to train for the great outdoors. They were too breathless even to swear by this time, and they stopped every few steps, bent double or racked by bouts of coughing. It seemed that they were in even worse shape than I could have hoped for.

My hiding place was only about ten yards from the path but there was a deep drainage ditch, which channelled the excess rain from the top of the hill down to the bottom, separating the two. Sometimes, in May or September, if those months have been exceptionally fine, the ditch ran dry. After October's torrential rains and the dreich days of November, water ran freely, soaking the area all around.

I waited until they were almost abreast of me and then stepped back a few paces and called out to them.

'Yous scunners looking for me?'

They both stopped and turned in my direction immediately, looking incredulous.

Oscar was the first to move. Finding some unanticipated reserves of energy, which must have astonished even him, with an inarticulate cry somewhere between rage and triumph, he plunged down the steep, three-foot drop into the drainage ditch and stopped abruptly, up to his ankles in very cold water, bellowing his unhappiness.

Billy followed him a little more circumspectly and stepped fastidiously, on surprisingly dainty feet, over the little stream to the boggy edge of the copse. When he was safely on firm ground, he reached back and offered the paralysed Oscar a grubby hand, helping to haul him across.

I paused long enough for them to start blundering through the bramble bushes, the infuriated Oscar leading the way, slipping and sliding on the greasy ferns, before I turned and led them further into the wood.

My plan had been to draw them on and take them one at a time as they became separated. A bonus would have been if one of them had turned an ankle, or even had a heart attack, which didn't seem such an impossibility judging by the state of them.

In the event, the words of one of my least favourite poets, something about best laid schemes (discuss in what sense, if indeed in any, mice scheme), should have warned me to tread very carefully through the brash. For a few minutes, I danced happily ahead of the pair of them – I couldn't even hear them. Then it all went wrong.

Oddly, I didn't feel the muscle in my right calf go when I found myself reaching out too far for footing and an apparently solid piece of ground mysteriously turned into a rotting-branch-strewn black bog. But I certainly knew that I'd done it serious damage when I took my next step. The pain shrieked from the torn muscle, the leg simply refused to take my weight and buckled under me.

I lay in the mud, hands desperately clutching and massaging the calf, cursing my luck, listening for the sounds of Oscar and Billy thrashing through the undergrowth.

I knew that I couldn't afford to let them catch me on the ground so, putting all my weight on to my left leg, with great difficulty I struggled up and limped off very slowly, dragging the injured leg, hoping to find somewhere to hide.

But there was nowhere suitable and, suddenly, there was no time either as Oscar bulled his way through a bramble bush that did its best to tear at his arms and stood only ten yards away from me, breathing hard.

There was a sturdy tree only three feet away and I managed the stride without too much obvious distress and nonchalantly leaned against it, staring at Oscar.

His blotched red face, bloodshot eyes and desperate panting suggested that my plan hadn't been such a bad one: intensive care beckoned to Oscar. Ordinarily, I'd have fancied my chances of taking him in that state. But I didn't dare even limp over and take a swing. First, he'd have seen that I was damaged and would probably have taken encouragement from that and, second, I would have had a great deal of difficulty in remaining upright after hitting him and so would have been a sitting, or even lying, duck when Billy MacPhail finally turned up.

We faced each other in silence, waiting for the errant MacPhail. It was difficult not to see that this had a funny side. He was far too knackered to risk an attack on his own, and I could barely walk.

'So,' I said amiably, 'what happens now?'

He stared at me in some confusion.

'What happens noo?' he said, shaking his head. 'What happens noo? What the fuck do you think happens noo?'

I shrugged.

'I don't know,' I said. 'We kiss and make up?'

He lowered his head and charged straight at me. I didn't have time to think about it, just hit him hard on the nose with a short left before he smashed me into the trunk of the tree. I slid slowly and painfully down the rough bark on to the wet earth, the breath knocked out of me, Oscar sprawled across my legs.

My hand felt numb from the impact and I realized that he'd run straight on to the fist, and had hit himself far harder than I could ever have managed to hit him. He was very groggy and his nose was pouring blood. He sat up with a vacant look in his eye and swayed from side to side.

It seemed that the mad charge had been Oscar's last hurrah. He was definitely out of it for the foreseeable future, but I just couldn't drag myself out from under him. Then, right on cue, Billy MacPhail burst past a bush that ripped at his disreputable anorak. He stopped still when he saw me and then glanced at the sitting, swaying Oscar, who was holding a hand across his face. A crafty look crossed Billy's ugly face and narrowed his mean little eyes even further. He was panting like an exhausted hound, his shoulders rising and falling with every agonized breath, and his forehead was gleaming with perspiration, emphasizing the blue veins that wormed their way down his temples.

'You shouldn't have done that to Oscar,' he said. 'He'll be madder than hell.'

'Then I'll hit him again,' I said, trying to pull myself out from under the dead weight of Oscar, who showed no sign of wanting to get up. I was at least getting feeling in the hand again but it was hurting so much I was sure that I must have cracked a bone or two.

Billy held his hands up, palms facing me, and walked towards us, always keeping his gaze on me. He stopped a couple of feet away, reached into his pocket, pulled out a large, grubby handkerchief and thrust it into Oscar's bloody mitt. But he never stopped looking at me.

'You gonna hit me noo?' he said. Strangely, there was no hint of whining in his tone. It was a simple enquiry, with just a hint of challenge and macho aggression about it. I guessed that Billy MacPhail had taken his share of lumps, as well as handing them out.

'Not if you don't make me,' I said. 'This isn't really your fight, Billy. All you have to do is walk away. And take the big yin with you.'

He nodded.

'Oscar,' he said, 'you'd better get up.'

Oscar didn't respond beyond clamping the handkerchief to his face. It was quickly stained a deep, dark red.

'How could anyone call that Oscar?' I said.

'It's no his given name,' Billy said. 'More of a nickname, on account of his other name.' He paused, then seemed to understand that I was none the wiser and added, 'Wilde.'

'Oh, aye, of course,' I said, feeling particularly obtuse.

Suddenly, Oscar burst into life and grabbed furiously at my legs. I couldn't kick him or knee him in the face, so I leaned forward and clubbed him on the side of the head with my right fist, which subdued him again. But I lost my balance in the process and Billy was on me immediately, wrapping his strong arms around mine, pinning them to my sides, and trying to nut me. I would have thought that he was all fat but his barrel chest was solid and firm. I tried to pull away from him but he caught me a terrible blow with his forehead just above my left ear and I was out of it for a second or two, seeing the traditional bright lights circling around and hearing only the sound of my own pulse.

With one of them lying across my legs and the other shrinkwrapped around my upper body, there didn't seem much point in struggling when I was able to focus properly again. We lay there for a while, steaming gently in the chill of the morning, and smelling about as rank as a long-dead rodent. It wasn't particularly painful sitting there, just very uncomfortable. And Billy did smell particularly foul.

I was aware that the weight on my legs was moving and saw that Oscar was sitting up and leaning away from us. I waited for him to attack me again but, instead, he started to retch violently.

I felt oddly sympathetic, remembering the aftermath of a competitive eight hundred metres I'd once run at uni without training for it properly. I'd thrown up for half an hour immediately afterwards and then slept in the changing room, utterly exhausted. And I hadn't even been placed. I wondered if Oscar might sleep for a while.

Billy MacPhail slowly relaxed his grip on me and then stood up. He whacked me across the back of the head almost affectionately.

'You're no going anywhere, pal, right?' he said.

'Right,' I said.

'Gie us the phone, Oscar,' he said, holding out his hand.

Oscar lifted his head wearily and very carefully reached into the pocket of his battered leather jacket and produced a mobile phone. Then he went back to the important business of retching.

MacPhail studied the face of the phone for a few seconds, then pressed some keys and held the instrument to his ear.

'Aye, Mr Nugent, it's me,' he said. 'Billy.'

I marvelled that he'd managed to get a signal and that Nugent was receiving one. Then I remembered that Dougie had received at least one call when he'd been around.

'No, he's no going anywhere . . .' Billy continued. 'Aye, but Oscar's no in such good shape either . . . No, it'd be better if you came up . . . OK, we're off to the side of the path, about halfway up. On the right. We'll all be here.'

He studied the phone again, pressed another key, then put it back in its case, hunkered down next to me and waited.

Chapter Nineteen

Mud-spattered and breathless, Archie Nugent, Martin Crawford and Carole arrived about twenty-five minutes later, which made me wonder where the police were. Even by their usual response time, they were overdue. I couldn't help thinking that when they did show up and found an empty house, they might have trouble finding us in time. At least the shipwrecked and abandoned Rover was there to point them in the right direction.

Nugent and Martin looked grim and pissed off. Martin was particularly uneasy. The twitch under his eye was very pronounced.

Carole was pale and wary. She knelt beside me and put her hand on my shoulder.

'You all right, Iain?' she said.

'I'll survive,' I said, looking across at Nugent. 'I hope.'

'Your man there,' she said, nodding her head at Nugent, 'was talking about torching the house, so I thought I'd better get out.'

'Jesus!' I said. 'He didn't, did he?'

'No,' she said. 'When he saw me his eyes glittered in a knowing sort of way and he calmed down. I'm guessing that he figured it might be easier to flush you out, if he had to, by using me than by burning the house down. Though I had the distinct impression that he might have done it anyway, just out of badness.'

Then she shaped some words without speaking aloud which I took to mean that she either had or hadn't called the police. Ever the optimist, I opted for the former and smiled.

Nugent very ostentatiously took the handgun he had been using earlier out of his overcoat pocket. It was an elderly Luger. Even I recognized the distinctive shape. He looked at it with distaste. It occurred to me that Archie Nugent could have been an Olympic sharpshooter and, with a worn and battered antique like that, he would still have missed me from more than ten yards.

Martin Crawford looked at the gun.

'Where did you get that, Archie?' he said.

'It's not very difficult to get a gun in the city, if you know the right pubs and you've a spare few hundred quid,' he said. 'But it's not so easy to get a decent one at short notice. Still . . .' He paused and looked over at the comatose figure not far from me. 'Oscar did his best and he assures me it will do the trick. At short range at any rate. And any more shooting is definitely going to be done at very short range indeed.'

He waved the gun vaguely in my direction. I looked away from him.

Martin's grim expression had altered subtly when the weapon appeared. His mouth had tightened a little and his eyes had briefly widened slightly before resuming their constant blinking. He seemed fascinated by the weapon. He started to rub at his left eye and the tic.

Like me, Carole had looked away. Billy MacPhail's face was about as expressive as a side of bacon.

Nugent took a step towards me and glowered down.

'You know,' he said, 'I used to think it was funny the way you wound poor old Colm Kelly up. I thought he needed to calm down, take a more relaxed approach to life. But now I'm beginning to have a lot more sympathy for him. You've managed to really piss me off. Do you know how difficult it is going to be to get those tyres replaced around here on a Sunday?'

'I've a fair idea,' I said.

398

'I just bet you have,' he said. 'Jesus, why are you always in the wrong place at the wrong time?'

'Just natural talent, I guess,' I said.

'There you go again,' he said, 'trying to wind me up now. And after I've been nice to you.' He looked up at the grey overcast sky for a moment. Almost as if he willed it, the first raindrops started to fall. He waved the gun at me. 'I don't want to use this,' he said, 'but, believe me, I will if I have to.' He paused again, looking thoughtful. 'I thought you understood what I was telling you on Friday. But it seems that you didn't. Now you have to disappear, one way or another. It's your choice.'

There was now a constant drizzle. It wasn't hard but it was seeping through our clothes and chilling us even more.

'About what you told me the other day,' I said. 'That wasn't to tell me you had nothing to do with Danny's murder, and that Colm Kelly is not a nice man and that his colleagues are not nice men, was it?'

He looked back up at the sky.

'I wasn't there,' he finally said. 'If I had been it wouldn't have happened. But I do like to protect my business interests, and one of the ways I do that is by keeping myself very well informed. I'd heard that Colm Kelly was up to something that had nothing to do with what we had planned, and I sent Oscar here to keep an eye on him. Oscar called in on his old cell-mate, Billy. And Billy made the connection between something he'd seen you hide on Friday night and the non-payout on Saturday. Never underestimate the native cunning of such as Billy.'

Billy MacPhail sat up straighter at the mention of his name, preening a little.

'I don't believe that,' I said. 'Oh, I believe that you weren't there. But I don't believe that you weren't part of the action. Where were the girls from? Eastern Europe, I suppose. Doubly exploited. Paying for their passage and then sold when they get here.'

'What girls?' Carole said sharply.

'The girls Kelly was planning to smuggle in using

Crawford's trucks as camouflaged transportation,' I said. 'It must have seemed like a good idea. Regular runs into remote parts of the west coast, with legitimate business interests to cover himself. He might even have got away with it once or twice, but he was wrong if he thought no one would notice. Danny noticed. Which is why he's dead.'

I started to shiver as the damp seeped through my clothes and chilled me to the bone. Carole put her arm around my shoulders. The tiny beads of clear water that had glistened in her hair had long since coalesced, darkening the gold to brown, and then had run in delicate streams down her forehead, flattening her hair to her head.

She had been as still as the rest of us until now, but I had been aware of a slight tightening of her mouth, and her grip on my hand strengthening uncomfortably. I was relieved when it had relaxed and she'd lifted her arm to my shoulders.

She stood up abruptly, shaking her head, shedding water in a fine spray, like a dog.

Nugent looked at her but then his eyes turned back to me.

'Are you clear,' he said, 'about what happens now, and why?'

He seemed to be his old self again, in control, of himself and events. He was calmer, almost reflective. There was still real ruthlessness there but he didn't seem to be angry or impulsive. I wondered if he would just blow me away without any warning.

I took a deep breath and cleared my throat. The Luger dangling nonchalantly from Nugent's right hand was a constant reminder that I should take care in my reply.

'I don't know,' I said. 'You implied earlier that I have a choice. Of course, it's not really a choice. I'm not going to choose to be shot.'

I heard Martin mutter an exasperated, 'For Christ's sake,' under his breath but Nugent just nodded at me to continue.

'Albeit inadvertently, I seem to have played some small part in hindering a scheme to land illegal immigrants in this country.'

He laughed but I didn't have the impression that I had amused him much. It may just have been the formal, rather pompous way that I'd couched it.

'You could say that,' he said. 'Certainly, it was inadvertent. You could just as easily say that you were inadvertently responsible for Danny McGovern's death.'

I ignored that, but he was right, of course. It had occurred to me before that I had been part of a long chain of events that had led to Danny being killed. But I hadn't killed him, nor commissioned his death. That was someone else's decision, someone else's action. And I hadn't set things in motion. I had only responded, inadequately and wrongly it was true, to what had been done to me. I'd been through all the arguments and I'd concluded that I couldn't be held responsible for Danny's death. But I wasn't going to be drawn by Nugent into even discussing it.

'And I am the thread that could connect you and Alan Baird to Colm Kelly,' I continued. 'Which means that you'd rather like me out of the way.'

'Well, you're not, of course, the only thread,' Nugent said and waved the old Luger around to encompass everyone gathered in the little wood, 'but you're the most likely one to set the police thinking. You, and your friend Dougie, already have, which is why it's important that you are discouraged from talking to them again. And talking to you as though you are a rational man clearly doesn't work. Therefore, yes, it would be better all round if you were out of the picture. Given the unpleasant nature of Colm Kelly's friends, should they seek retribution, it would even be better for you.'

I nodded in an understanding way.

'What happened to the girls?' I asked.

He looked puzzled.

'The girls on the boat?'

He shrugged. 'Who knows? Landed somewhere else in Europe, perhaps?'

I wiped my face with my hand.

'Don't you care?' I said.

He was silent for a long ten seconds and he appeared to be thinking about the question.

'No,' he finally said, 'I'm sorry but I don't. Not really. You'd better get up.'

'I'll need a hand,' I said.

'Why? Have they damaged you?' He looked at Oscar and Billy, who tried to appear both innocent and hurt at the suggestion. They merely succeeded in looking shifty.

'No,' I said, tenderly feeling the swelling on my head and wondering about the pain in my left hand. 'Well, not that much, anyway. But I pulled a muscle in my leg. I can scarcely move. If I hadn't, they'd never have caught me.'

'Well,' he said, 'it's an ill wind and a' that. Now, I take it that you would like to disappear of your own volition, rather than be disappeared.' He waved the gun around in an offhand fashion.

'Hold on,' Carole suddenly said. 'I've got a few questions I'd like some answers to.'

Martin and Nugent looked uneasily at each other.

'There are some things that are not clear to me,' she said.

She was staring at Martin, who had turned away from her, his hands thrust deep into the pockets of his green overcoat, his head bowed.

'If these were illegal immigrants who had paid to be landed in this country, what did Iain mean about them being sold when they got here?'

There was a long pause. It suddenly dawned on me that it hadn't been spoken aloud. When it was clear that no one else was going to answer her implied question, I cleared my throat.

'Carole,' I said, 'they were all girls, probably quite young girls. They were destined for the red light district somewhere, a life of prostitution.'

'Yes,' she said, 'that's what I understood. I just wanted

someone to say it. And it leads me to another thought. What, exactly, Martin, did you and Duncan know about this?'

Martin shuffled a couple of feet away from her and Nugent started to answer. But Carole cut across him.

'No, Archie,' she said, holding up her hand in an imperious way. 'I'd rather like to hear what Martin has to say.'

Martin turned back towards her, his face flushed. He pulled a hand out of a pocket and ran it through the wayward lock of hair that flopped over his forehead. He looked decidedly awkward.

'I didn't know anything about it,' he said. 'And nor, I'm sure, did Duncan.' He didn't sound convincing.

'Is that so?' Carole said. 'So, how did Kelly's men come to have access to one of our vehicles?'

'You'd have to ask the transportation staff about that,' he said. 'I really don't know.'

'I think you're lying through your back teeth, Martin,' she said. 'And if you say you didn't know about it, Archie, then I'd have to say that you are lying too. The pair of you knew all about this. Good God, it may even have been your idea. Come up to some remote spot, Colm, sink some money into an ailing company, then you do anything you want. You can land women and drugs and transport them to any part of the country using the company's lorries. Minimal risk of being discovered. I can hear the spiel now. You orchestrated the whole thing.'

Archie Nugent took a couple of steps towards Carole.

'Come on, Carole,' he said, 'there's no point in jumping to conclusions. None of us knew what Colm Kelly was up to and that's the truth.'

She stared at him fiercely.

'Right,' she said, 'that would explain why you're carrying that gun. Because you're just a hard-working businessman, trying to turn an honest buck.'

'Always that, Carole,' he said, 'always that and only that.'

Carole was pale, and the lines that ran from the sides

of her nose to the corners of her mouth looked as if they'd been scored in charcoal. She was tense and trembling with anger.

I suddenly remembered that she'd buried her mother a little over a week before and had seen her husband shot a few nights since. She was tired, grieving and probably still shocked. She cut a very dramatic figure, like something out of the *Oresteia*. She certainly had everyone's attention.

I looked at the dreary little wood, dripping with moisture, and through the trees at the rain-soaked dun. I was still sitting against the beech that Oscar had smacked me into when he'd charged into me, but I was some yards from the action.

Martin kept wandering a foot or two away from Carole but she followed him relentlessly. Nugent moved after them. They were edging further away from me. Billy and Oscar weren't part of the shuffling ballet, but they were avid spectators.

Neither of them had recovered from their earlier exertions and both appeared to be in a pretty sorry state but, for all that, they were probably more mobile than I was. The leg wasn't about to recover in anything less than two or three weeks and I wasn't certain that I could trust it to bear any weight. In fact, I doubted it could manage any, but I felt I might have to make a move soon. Carole was rapidly talking Nugent into using that gun. Although, when I thought about it, there never had been much doubt about it.

Carole suddenly stopped moving and stood completely still.

'Oh, my God,' she said. 'Now I understand. This is what Mum knew, isn't it? She must have worked out that something was going on. Maybe Baird even hinted at it.' She strode over to Martin and pulled at him. 'Look at me,' she said, hauling him round. 'Tell me just what Mum knew.'

'I don't know,' he said sullenly. 'I don't know. It's possible Baird said something to her but I don't know what he could have known.' He paused and looked across suspiciously to Nugent, then he looked back imploringly at Carole. 'Come on, Sis, we needed the money that Kelly was pumping into the company. You know that. We were practically bust when he came along. When Archie brought him along. Of course I, we, leapt at the prospect of an influx of cash. It had all been heading out up until then. We didn't really consider the origins of the money. Archie vouched for Kelly. And, well, we thought we could handle him. We thought he'd keep his nose clean up here. We thought he intended to stay legit.' Martin looked petulant and unhappy. I had the feeling that he wanted to be anywhere but in that little wet copse being interrogated by his sister.

'We?' she said. 'Who's "we" here?'

'Duncan, me, Archie,' he said.

'Is that true, Archie? Did you really think that he'd stay within the law?'

'It was my fervent hope,' Nugent said. 'As it was that you and your mother wouldn't find out just what kind of a businessman Kelly really is. But, since you have, as she did, we'll have to look to avoid any further fall-out.'

He was looking dangerously tense, his grip tightening on the thick, scored butt of the gun.

Martin had been edging away from Carole but she took one long stride towards him.

'You did kill her,' she said. 'You know that? You killed her. She found out somehow what you and Duncan had turned the company into.' She gave out a great sigh. 'How could I have been so foolish? Why did I not see that we were laundering money for gangsters? The company was just a front for drug smugglers and pimps.' She paused again and then closed her eyes before shouting, 'You killed her. Do you understand? You killed her.' She beat her hands ineffectually against his chest and started to sob.

'No, Carole,' he said, grasping her wrists, 'no, I wouldn't have done anything to hurt Mum. You know that.'

'But you killed her,' she yelled at him. 'Just as surely as you killed Dad. You stupid, stupid boy.'

'I didn't,' he said, 'that was a false memory.'

'No, it wasn't,' she said grimly. 'You shot him and Mum covered it up.'

Martin looked angrily across at me and stabbed a finger in my direction. 'Did he tell you that? Did he?'

'No,' she said, 'he didn't because he didn't know.'

'Then who did?'

'Mum did. More or less. In the letter she left for me. But it was Baird who spelt it out.'

Martin's hands covered his face and then slowly slid down to his side. Even from where I was sitting, I could see the tears in his eyes.

'She wrote to me too,' he said. 'She told me that she loved me and always had, whatever I'd done in the past, but that she couldn't bear to see what I was doing now. That she wouldn't watch me go to jail.' He paused and when he spoke again his voice was no more than a whisper and I could only just make out the words. 'I did kill her, didn't I?'

He stared into the distance and Carole walked slowly over to him. She reached into her bag, took out a tissue and gently wiped the tears from his eyes.

Suddenly, the two of them were embracing fiercely.

Nugent was only about ten yards from me. No distance at all to cover in the normal scheme of things, but it seemed like a nautical mile with only one working leg. There was aggression in the way he leaned in the direction of Carole and Martin, and there was tension in the way that he kept running his tongue over his lips and working his jaw. He was getting angry again and I expected him to use that gun at any moment.

I sat up straighter, trying not to attract any attention, and gently lifted myself into a kneeling position. Then I shifted all my weight to my left leg and prepared to thrust myself at Nugent.

As I changed position, I heard the unmistakable sound of a car changing down a couple of gears as it pulled off the road and into my driveway. I hoped that it was the cavalry arriving, even if they were more than a little tardy, far too far away and far too few. So, Carole *had* managed to get through to the police before Nugent and Martin found her. No one else seemed to attach any significance to the sound, although Martin did look up.

After a few seconds, Carole's phone started to ring and I guessed that it must be the police trying to locate her. I think that Nugent guessed that too as he peremptorily ordered her not to answer it.

As he did so, and was momentarily distracted, I pushed off with my left leg and scrabbled across the scrubby ground, smacking into Nugent's legs before the pain in my right leg screamed at me to stop. He tumbled over and rolled away from me, lashing out with his feet, and the sharp edge of the sole of one elegant leather shoe sliced the back of my right hand, drawing blood.

I was seeing only the red mist by this stage and lifted myself up to leap at him again but the pain in my right leg forced me to sit back down, and when Nugent regained his feet and stood up, the ugly Luger was still in his hand and it was pointed straight at me. We were only a few feet apart when he shot and I didn't see how he could miss.

But he did, more or less.

The crack of the shot and the searing hurt as the bullet shredded my right earlobe were simultaneous. I clutched at my ear, feeling real pain, and a great gout of blood washed down my neck. Billy MacPhail and Oscar, and Carole and Martin were all watching in shock as Nugent covered the two strides between us. He was shaking his head.

'Jesus,' he said. 'Iain, why are people all so stupid? That idiot Baird cashes a cheque that drops him right in the shit. What was he doing shaking down wee Carole here for peanuts anyway? And why did that clown Kelly have to leave that briefcase at your house? If he wanted to leave it anywhere, there was Baird's house, all quiet and secluded, only yards from the shore, and empty. In short, the ideal location.' He shook his head again. 'But drunken Duncan had to have his little joke and Kelly went right along with it. Unbelievable.' He paused. 'What an unbelievably stupid way to louse up. And now you. First of all, heading to the police when I'd specifically told you not to, and now going in for stupid heroics when I was about to suggest a long holiday.'

He stared down at me and I looked up into that thin, tanned, hard face. The scar fascinated me. It seemed to dominate his face, define it. A slender, white arid line incised precisely by a bright blade. I wondered again how he'd come by it, who had had the temerity to slash Archie Nugent.

'You probably don't believe this,' he said, 'but I rather like you. You fight your corner and I admire that. I'm sorry to have to do this. In fact, I really don't want to.' He hesitated long enough for me to gain a little hope.

I thought that I ought to say something, that I hadn't gone to the police, persuade him that he didn't have to shoot me, that I wasn't going to cause any trouble for him, but an image of my father's gentle, handsome face floated into my mind and I knew that he would never have lied or pleaded to save his life and I said nothing.

He aligned the gun with my head. I looked along the line that the weapon made with his arm. There was no sign of any tremor, the thin barrel didn't shake at all. I heard Carole gasp and I understood that Nugent really was going to shoot me.

He was right. It was all very stupid. At least, I couldn't regret all those unwritten poems. There weren't any. I'd written all the verse I was going to. Pity about not finishing the Caravaggio story, though.

Nugent blinked, dropped his gun arm and rubbed at his eye. Beyond him, in his tailored overcoat, and the thin, bony trees, the grey sky loured. It seemed endless. I thought of Leopardi again, his thoughts drowning in the immensity of it all.

Nugent stepped even closer to me, cleared his throat and pointed the gun again.

Then Martin broke away from Carole's embrace and strode decisively over to stand in front of Nugent.

'No,' he said, 'no, Archie.'

'What do you mean "no"?' Nugent said. 'It's got to be done.'

Martin still stood between us and there was a long silence. I was conscious that something unspoken passed between them.

'Get out of the way,' Nugent said. 'It has to be done. Everything's come apart. You and I'll be in it up to our necks if he says any more.'

'I'm in it up to my neck anyway,' Martin said. 'Give me the gun. I'll do it.'

'What?' Nugent said.

'Give me the gun. I'll do it. I knew what I was signing up for.' He held out his hand for the gun.

Nugent looked puzzled.

'Come on,' Martin said. 'You don't want to do it. Give me the gun.'

Nugent hesitated for a moment longer, then he shrugged and handed over the gun. Martin looked down at it and then turned to face me.

'No, Martin,' I heard Carole whisper.

I wondered if she'd be next, and I wondered if Nugent and Martin realized that the police were at my house and that they couldn't get away with it. But I didn't say anything.

For a long moment, Martin and I just stared at each other. There was anguish in his face and real despair. But he didn't seem to be seeing me, his gaze went beyond me, towards something in the past. The tic under his eye wasn't as constant as it had been.

'I did kill her, Iain,' he said very quietly. 'I didn't mean to, and I didn't stuff the pills down her throat, but I might as well have done.'

'You knew all about it, didn't you?' I said. 'You knew where the money being pumped into the company was coming from; you knew what the plans were, and you knew that Nugent was behind it all.'

He nodded.

'Carole's next,' I said.

His eyes came into focus and he gave me a puzzled look. 'What?' he said.

'After you've killed me, you'll have to kill Carole. She's next.'

'I know that,' he said wearily. 'You think I don't know that?'

'Well,' I said, 'I guess that'll make it a clean sweep. The entire family: father, mother and sister. Well done, Martin. Bravo.' I brought my hands together in mocking applause.

'Don't forget about the brother,' he said and, straightening his arm, he levelled the Luger at me. Then he pivoted on his right heel and spun swiftly around, turning to Nugent.

He fired once. Nugent's hands went to his chest and then he just folded in on himself and slumped, very slowly, to his knees, his head swaying, before finally keeling over without making a sound.

Martin looked at Carole.

'Sorry, for everything,' he whispered, put the gun under his chin and pulled the trigger.

The sound of the shot was muffled, but I saw the top of his head spray out in a fountain of blood and splinters of bone. He fell backwards, sprawled out in front of me. His left leg jerked spasmodically and then he was still.

I heard Oscar and Billy breathing heavily as they splashed their way back to the path, fleeing the scene, and I saw Carole fall to her knees and begin to sob silently.

Then I looked up the hill, towards the impassive dun, half-hidden by the trembling trees, bare and ruined.

Chapter Twenty

Life goes on, I thought, as I stood behind Danny McGovern's coffin, still favouring my right leg, and read some Robert Burns to the scattered congregation.

The low winter sun poured through the dirty windows of the kirk in dusty shafts, forcing the few who were present to squint awkwardly.

Dougie was sitting in the first wooden pew, resplendent in dark suit, white shirt and sombre tie, his neatly folded overcoat next to him. He'd shaved off his moustache and he looked younger, more innocent, vaguely angelic in the golden light that fell on him.

Carole was sitting with two of the policemen, who she'd come to know quite well in the last weeks, at the back. Her head was lowered and, unlike Dougie, who was beaming at me, she avoided my gaze.

In between the two of them, I counted only twelve people. The Lord's Prayer had been a muted affair and the rendering of 'Dear Lord and Father of Mankind' had not exactly made the rafters ring.

'"The rank is but the guinea stamp,"' I read; '"The man's the gowd for a' that . . . The honest man, tho' e'er sae poor, / Is king o' men for a' that . . . A prince can mak / A belted knight, a marquis, duke and a' that; / But an honest man's aboon his might . . ."'

The muffled coughs and the sound of shuffling feet suggested that I wasn't holding their attention too well, but I didn't care much and pressed on, finishing with

Burns's dream: '"That man to man the warld o'er / Shall brothers be for a' that."'

I thought of Danny's innate decency, the straightforward compassion that had cost him his life, and the stark contrast it made with the behaviour of those who, compared to him, had everything and who wanted even more, whatever the human cost.

And I tried not to think of Martin Crawford's shattered skull or of Archie Nugent's final moment, before he toppled on to the sodden brash of a Scottish hillside.

Carole had still been on her knees, still sobbing silently, when Sergeant Darling and the young constable with him had found us.

Billy MacPhail and Oscar had run smack into them. They hadn't, Darling informed us, been in any condition to put up a fight and he had left them handcuffed, one to the front bumper and one to the rear bumper of the police car, while he had, rather bravely I thought, given that he had heard three shots and was himself unarmed, come to look for us before his back-up arrived. He may have got part of the story out of Billy and Oscar and known there was no longer too much danger, but even so he could have waited, and probably would have done if he'd gone by the book.

By the time I heard the sergeant calling, I had dragged myself across to Carole and we were draped around each other, cold, wet, pale and shocked. My ear had more or less stopped bleeding by then but the right side of my sweatshirt was drenched in dark blood – all of it mine. Oddly the cut on my hand hurt more than my torn ear. I must have looked terrible because even Darling acted as if he were sympathetic.

There was silence in the church after I finished and I self-consciously limped back to sit with Dougie.

The minister, the same one who had officiated at the service for Margaret Crawford, stood up, coughed politely into his hand and then asked us to bow our heads in a silent prayer. I stared straight ahead and Carole was doing the same. We were both probably seeing the same awful scene.

Then the coffin was shouldered by the undertaker's men – I had cried off being a bearer because of my damaged leg and no one else had volunteered to carry Danny to his last resting place – and they swayed off down the central aisle. In due course, we all followed, out into the clear, cold day.

Dougie and I were slumped on high stools at the bar in the hotel. He had a pint of Guinness in front of him and I a large Ardbeg. Neither of us was drinking. We were just staring into the glasses, ruminating.

'What's with the Burns, by the way? I thought you didn't rate him,' he said.

'I'm a new convert,' I said. 'It seemed appropriate.'

'I saw Carole, briefly, outside the kirk before going in. And she was sure you'd read your poem about Danny,' he said.

'My version of Wordsworth's "Resolution and Independence"?' I said. 'Well, I confess that I did think about it, but it didn't seem right. The truth is, it's not very good. None of my stuff is.'

'That's not what the critics thought.'

'What do they know?'

'There's no pleasing you artistic types, is there? You're either fulminating against critics because they hate you, or dismissing them because they like what you do.' He shook his head sadly.

'It's always for the same reason, Dougie,' I said.

'And what is that?'

'Because they don't understand us.'

'Och, you sound like an errant husband. The truth is you're just depressed,' he said.

'Aye, well, I've had a bad couple of weeks,' I said.

He nodded sympathetically.

'I didn't say that depression wasn't an entirely appropriate response to your circumstances,' he said. 'I was just making the observation that your mood may be colouring your judgement.'

413

We lapsed into silence again.

I'd been shivering violently and feeling very weak when I'd limped slowly and painfully down the hill and back to my house. But I'd held Carole very tightly against me the entire way, and she'd supported me. We'd continued to hold each other after I'd changed into clean, dry clothes. Then I was whisked away to the hospital to have my ear dressed, my hand X-rayed and my leg prodded, and she was taken off to the police station to make an initial statement.

I'd been interviewed endlessly over the next few days but I had no clear memory of what had been said. I could remember sitting listlessly in waiting rooms, limping along corridors and drearily answering dreary questions. The police were far from unsympathetic and it seemed that the stories Carole and I told were consistent with each other and were corroborated by whatever the interviewers managed to prise out of Billy MacPhail and Malcolm Wilde (Oscar's real name) and the forensic investigations. Eventually, but probably only temporarily, I was left in peace.

Carole wasn't. The investigation into Crawford's began immediately and was likely to drag on for months.

She had accompanied the police back to the company's offices straight after Danny's funeral, which was why Dougie and I were drinking alone. At least, that's what I told myself.

'What's the word on Crawford's?' I asked.

'Aren't you getting that straight from the horse's mouth?' he said.

'No, I haven't seen Carole much, not since . . . She's been tied up with the police and, anyway, she's put herself into something like purdah again.'

'Oh,' he said and took a long swallow from his glass to cover any embarrassment he felt.

'So,' I said, 'what do you know about Crawford's?'

'Oh,' he said, putting his glass down and wiping his mouth with the back of his hand. 'Not that much. The investigation has barely started, really. Duncan's talking up a storm – mainly along the lines of "nuffin' to do wiv me, guv" – but he could be looking at some serious charges. There's no way someone in the company didn't know where the money was coming from. And, while Duncan is maintaining that that someone was Martin, others feel that he knew too. Whether they knew what Kelly was up to is another question. Again, Duncan is blaming that all on Martin. He may get away with it. The company's pretty much a busted flush, though. You can't launder drug money these days and expect to keep the proceeds.'

'And Carole?' I said, thinking as much of all the others in the village who would lose their jobs as of her.

Dougie shrugged. 'No one's seriously suggesting that she knew anything. And she's cooperating fully with the investigation. She should be all right.'

We both stared into our drinks again.

'Let's eat,' Dougie suddenly said.

'It's not six thirty yet, Dougie,' I said.

'So, let's eat early and long,' he said. 'You're about as convivial as a John Knox sermon and I need something to cheer me up. Champagne and smoked salmon, followed by haunch of venison and a robust red, I think. And then some cheese. I didn't know Danny but he should be sent on his way with a hearty meal. We owe him that.'

He stood up and swallowed down his pint. I left my Scotch on the bar untouched and slowly followed him, limping noticeably.

'I don't suppose Danny had a hearty meal in his entire life,' I muttered, as we climbed the stairs to the empty dining room.

'Och, I'll bet he enjoyed the odd fish supper,' Dougie said. 'And he wouldn't begrudge us this.'

'No,' I said, feeling surprisingly cheered at the thought, 'I don't suppose he would.'

I looked out of the big window at the dark harbour. The Christmas tree lights still danced, incongruously cheerful, on the placid water. It was too early for stars but the sky would be ablaze later with a breathtaking display. It was cold and clear. A perfect night. Venus was just visible, a steady point of light low in the black sky.

Mary Elgin had called me the day before, keen to get to work on her opera. She wasn't convinced by Henryson's *The Testament of Cresseid*, which, somehow, I'd remembered to mail to her, but she really was keen to work with me. Something original, she thought, something modern. I hadn't been very forthcoming.

I turned back into the room. Dougie was sitting at a table, talking expansively to the young waitress, who was smiling pleasantly at his nonsense. I walked over to join him.

'You know,' Dougie said as I sat down, the waitress standing expectantly by his side, her pen poised over her pad, 'I've been talked into the parsnip soup instead of the smoked salmon, and the rack of lamb instead of the venison. And I'm assured that the Rioja is so robust you can chew it. What about you? The same?'

I nodded meekly.

The waitress scuttled off to the kitchen and, as I looked over my shoulder at her departing back, I glimpsed out of the window the three-quarter moon, like a healing wound scarring the night sky, hanging over the harbour.

I decided to call Mary Elgin the next day. And I'd definitely call Carole when I got in. Or, better, pop around to see her. For a nightcap. Life, after all, goes on.